THE KNOWING

THE KNOWING

The Knowing Saga Book One

NINIE HAMMON

For our struggle is not against flesh and blood, but against the rulers, against the authorities, against the powers of this dark world and against the spiritual forces of evil in the heavenly realms.

The Bible, Ephesians 6:12

Chapter One

Theresa Washington stood in the middle of the crosswalk, holding up a "Don't Walk" sign to a group of giggling little girls so eager to cross the street for the last day of school they were hopping up and down like the whole lot of them needed to go to the bathroom.

The indulgent smile that started at the corners of Theresa's mouth froze, though, and a flower of uneasiness began to spread its petals inside her chest. That's when she heard it, an eerie, high-pitched wailing, otherworldly and utterly desolate, a sound like the shriek of ravaged souls writhing in agony, or the keening cry of lost children wandering alone in the dark. Her knees suddenly felt like bags of water.

The sound seemed to ride the warm breeze that ruffled Theresa's hair, but she knew it wasn't carried on no summer air 'cause it wasn't a sound you heard with your ears. The wailing bored relentlessly into the marrow of her soul with the power and pain of a dentist's drill.

The old black woman told herself she didn't know

what was coming next, tried to close up all her senses, crawl down into the middle of herself where she couldn't hear or see or smell or feel nothing. But it filled her nostrils anyway, like she knew it would. The stink of dead bodies mouldering in the grave, rotting flesh falling away from bones as maggots, beetles, and worms made dinner out of someone who maybe just last week was smiling and laughing and thinking they was gonna live forever.

A little girl with her red hair in pigtails tied with blue ribbons called out to her, lisping through the missing teeth in front. "Mith Theretha, can we cross now? The bellth gonna ring and we're all gonna be late!"

Theresa ignored her and turned toward the school yard, frantically scanning the throng of children, searching for—there he was! A chubby man wearing a baggy sweatshirt and a Cincinnati Reds baseball cap was making his way through the crush of children toward the back entrance of the building. As she watched, he dug into his pockets and brought out something—gum or candy, probably—and handed it out along with pats on the head as he moved along.

The man looked like somebody's dad who had come to the school to drop off the big leather case he carried, with a pink and blue My Little Pony sticker on the side. A saxophone or maybe a French horn that his daughter had run right out the door and left sitting on the kitchen table when she heard the school bus honk out front.

From where she stood, Theresa couldn't make out his features, but she didn't have to see his face to know he wasn't nobody's daddy!

Theresa Washington knew.

"Mith Te-re-tha," the little red-haired girl said again. "Pleeeease!"

Theresa stood mute on the yellow stripes in the middle

of the street, an unseeing, thousand-mile stare in her walnut-brown eyes. Her heart hammered a hole in her chest under her heaving bosom. The crossing guard sign hung limp in her hand.

Clearly a strong-willed child, the little girl on the curb took matters into her own hands.

"Nobody's coming," she said to the other children, looking both right and left, up and down the street a couple of times. "Leth go."

The child stepped out into the crosswalk and the lemmings behind her quickly fell in line. Another group of children on the sidewalk approached the curb behind them and slowed but didn't stop.

"Can we go, too?" called out a big, sandy-haired boy fully two feet taller than the other children.

Theresa looked at him, focused, heard and saw him. Then she shook her head to clear it, turned and searched the dwindling crowd of children in the school yard. The man carrying the My Little Pony case was already in the building.

"No!" Theresa cried. "No, you can't go."

She snapped up the "Don't Walk" sign in the face of the little red-haired girl and her friends who were only a few feet away. "You children get back up there on that curb 'fore I snatch every last one of you bald-headed."

Surprised and alarmed, they turned and hurried back to the curb as Theresa called out to the children still on the sidewalk. "Stay right where you are. Don't move!"

What should she do? What could she do? Not a car in sight anywhere on the street. Her cell phone was in her purse in the teacher's lounge where she'd put on the orange crossing guard smock, and the school's strictly-enforced no-cell-phones rule made it unlikely any of these children were packing. Theresa was too old and too fat to —she pointed to the big kid, a tree among saplings.

"You!"

He tapped his own chest and looked around to see who else she might be talking to.

"Yes, you! I want you to run to that house over there." She pointed to the nearest dwelling, a house with a big willow tree beside the porch. It was about seventy-five yards or so down the street that ran alongside the school. "You bang on the door and you tell whoever answers to call 911 and say there's a Code Red at Carlisle Elementary School. Can you remember that? Code Red."

~

Emily Burke pulled her blue CRV to a stop beside the "Drop Off Here" sign at the front entrance of Carlisle Elementary School, on the opposite side of the building from where Theresa Washington saw the man who wasn't anybody's father carrying a My Little Pony case toward the school.

As soon as the vehicle stopped moving, she picked up her phone and continued to type on the text she'd been composing at every stop sign and traffic light between her home and the school. She wouldn't text and drive, of course. Besides being dangerous and setting a bad example, she didn't want to tempt fate—not this morning.

Her daughter was chattering away in the seat beside her, a backpack with "Miranda Burke" stenciled in red balanced on her knees. "Miranda"—what a dreadful name, totally Dan's idea. Emily'd shortened it to Andi before the baby left the hospital nursery.

The gregarious ten-year-old had her mother's arresting pale blue eyes. Her hair, the same chestnut brown as her father's, hung in loose curls on her shoulders. She was what Emily's grandmother would have called a "babbler." The child could talk non-stop about anything, everything and nothing, and all you had to do was nod occasionally, give her a "hmmm…" or a "really?" and she'd hold up both ends of the conversation all by herself. The little girl's chatter was the pleasant white noise of Emily's existence, and in truth, Emily hardly ever really listened to anything Andi said.

"Well, can I?" Andi asked. When Emily didn't respond, the child said, louder, "Danger, danger, danger, Will Robinson!"

Emily held up a "wait!" finger, typed two more letters, hit send, then looked over and smiled absently. Though Andi wasn't a trekkie like her father, he had introduced her to other vintage television shows like Lost in Space that she watched in what seemed like a continuous loop, 24/7. Still, Emily supposed it was better than being mad, screaming in love with Justin Bieber. In fact, the Minnie Mouse t-shirt Andi wore was distinctly "little girl" —as were her deep-dish dimples in round chipmunk cheeks and the freckles Emily thought looked like she'd been dusted with cinnamon. Emily reminded herself to treasure Andi's childhood. Before long, that golden time would be gone forever.

"What hon? You need to shoo out or you'll be late."

The child would have bailed out of the car like there was a bomb under the hood if her friend Miss Theresa had been directing children at the crosswalk. She'd loved that old woman dearly ever since second grade. But the crossing guard in front of the school was a short, stout Asian woman who looked like a traffic cone in her orange vest.

"Earth to Mom, can I go to Lindsay's birthday party Saturday? You're supposed to SRVP—"

"RSVP," Emily corrected.

"Whatever. You're supposed to tell her today whether you're coming or not. Can I go?"

"May I go?

"Mom!"

"I suppose so. What time is—?" The phone in her hand chimed with an incoming message. She read it, smiled broadly and began to type a reply. Andi slipped her arms into her backpack and opened the car door.

"Bye, Mom."

Emily did not reply.

"I love you!"

Emily gave her another distracted smile and mumbled, "Hmm, me too, honey."

Andi rolled her eyes and closed the car door and headed into the building. Emily sat where she was, typing, until a horn sounded behind her. She turned and scowled at the honking driver, pulled up far enough to be out of the lane of traffic dropping off children, then stopped and continued to type.

"…just the beginning. You'll be begging for marcy…" The phone auto-corrected "marcy" to "mercury," and before she could change that to "mercy," the phone in her hand rang. The name of the caller shown on the screen.

Dan.

Only Emily called him Dan. No one else in his life had ever called him anything but Daniel. Emily stared at the name, felt an emotional response to the sight of it, but couldn't grab hold of what it was before it dissolved, a wisp of smoke from a sputtering candle. Guilt/fear/shame/remorse? No, none of those. Then she identified the feeling and decided that it was probably worse than any of them.

What was it they said—the opposite of love isn't hate, it's indifference.

For a moment, Emily had a flash of memory, a snippet. Emily and Dan, jammed with her huge wedding dress into a tiny motel bathroom, splashing water everywhere and giggling uncontrollably as they frantically soaped Emily's left hand in an effort to remove the wedding ring—which Dan had bought a size too small and then forced on her finger during the ceremony.

Her phone stopped ringing, Dan's name disappeared and a moment later the phone chimed with an incoming text message. She'd selected the chime for messages because she loved the sound—a single clear note, like the tolling of a church bell high in the mountains on a cold winter morning.

The message contained a single word: "HURRY!"

She smiled a radiant smile, put the car in gear and drove away.

When the first morning bell at Carlisle Elementary School rang, Bishop Washington near jumped out of his skin. That thing always startled him. You'd think after all these years as a school custodian, his body'd get accustomed to it, but it never did. Then he chuckled. The scurry of them little footsteps trying to get into they rooms before that bell always put Bishop in mind of creek water tumbling over rocks, singing its song. A creek'd talk to you if you had ears to hear, sing to you, too. Lullabies to lull you to sleep, carried on the night breeze with the smell of black mud and dead crawdads and the privy in the back yard.

Bishop opened the door of the storage room in the north hallway and eased his six-foot, seven-inch, three-hundred-fifty pound bulk down on one knee to fasten the wide dust mop head to the long pole. Had to get the hallway cleaned while children were in class and the hall was empty.

The school was shaped like the letter U, with north and south hallways connected on the east end by the administration wing, with the office of the principal, Mrs. Maxwell, and the lounges, secretaries' offices and such.

He heard adult footsteps behind him and was about to turn around and ask Mr. Masterson if—

Just a glimpse of the shadow, and the familiar terror stabbed into Bishop's belly. He stayed right where he was, bent over with his back turned until it passed. Bishop didn't have to see it to know what it looked like. A thick cloud, dark as tar, all around somebody's head, with tangled tendrils of black dangling from it all the way to the ground, like seaweed rotting on the beach, or the tentacles of some monstrous space alien.

Cold hit Bishop all at once when the thing was right behind him, felt like it did when he sneaked into the kitchen in the middle of the night, looking to snatch a bowl of ice cream when Theresa wasn't there to grouse at him about his cholesterol. But colder than standing in front of the open freezer door, painful cold, cold that hurt your skin when it touched, so cold it burned.

The cold paralyzed him and he stayed down on one knee, gasping, his breath frosting in front of him, unable to think.

One heartbeat. Two. Then Bishop drew a breath and inhaled the strong odor of Pine Sol and dust and chalk. He shook his head fiercely to clear it and looked after the figure striding down the center of the hallway. Through the black fog that surrounded the man, Bishop could see that he was chubby, wearing a sweatshirt and ball cap, carrying a big leather case with a My Little Pony sticker on the side—an instrument case, maybe.

Bishop looked down the hallway to the back door where the man had come in. The door would only open from the inside, so how'd the guy—Bishop froze again, this time in horror. The doors wouldn't open from the inside or the outside now. Chains and a padlock fastened the bars on the doors securely closed.

The man in the sweatshirt stopped at the intersection of the north hallway and the administration hallway, set the case on the floor and opened it. Bishop didn't wait to see what was inside. He had to get to a classroom. Any classroom.

With only a glance at the man, who appeared to be strapping some kind of belt around his waist, Bishop stood and began to push his mop slowly down the hallway toward the back door. Even with the hair on the back of his neck prickling and his heart clacking away in his chest, he managed to whistle.

Oh, Suzanna, don't you cry for me...

Involuntarily cringing away from a bullet he feared any minute would rip into his back, Bishop casually leaned the mop handle against the wall and opened the door to Erika Lund's fifth-grade classroom.

The teacher's aide, Mary Waznuski, smiled pleasantly when he stepped into the classroom. A short, sturdy woman, she radiated grandmother-ness. The teacher, Miss Lund looked up inquisitively, obviously annoyed. It was only her second year teaching, so she'd adopted a stern, no-nonsense exterior to cover her lack of confidence and experience—and the fact that she looked too young to be anybody's teacher.

"Hi, Mr. Washington," said Andi Burke. She peeked at him out of the storage closet behind the door where she stood holding an unopened packet of No. 2 lead pencils. "I didn't see Miss Theresa out front this morning. She's not sick is—?"

"Miranda, you didn't raise your hand for permission to speak. You know—"

Bishop crossed the distance between him and the young teacher in two strides, leaned close and whispered two harsh words. "Code Red!"

The color drained out of Miss Lund's face so quickly and completely that the veins in her temples suddenly appeared like streaks of blue Magic Marker. Her pale gray eyes pleaded with Bishop to tell her it wasn't so.

"Lock the door," he said, then turned to the inter-class-room intercom on the wall behind the desk, reached out and held down the button. "Code Red!" he shouted into it. "I repeat, Code R—"

Gunshots rattled in the hallway outside, like microwave popcorn with the volume turned all the way up, and there was a crashing sound of breaking glass accompanied by high-pitched, maniacal laughter.

The trophy cases.

Go on ahead, shoot them trophies, kill every last one of them and give us a few more seconds to lock these children in here safe.

~

Daniel Burke didn't even know how to think about the

words he saw on the screen in front of him. He stared at his wife's iPad and the letters in the open email blurred, went in and out of focus like he needed glasses.

He hadn't meant to…it wasn't like he'd been spying on Emily. He just didn't know how to operate this dang thing! Dinka tribesmen in the rain forests of Sudan probably knew more about computers and iPhones, iPads, iPods and iWhatever-Else's than he did.

When he'd finally come around to the belief that standing in the pulpit with an iPad in his hand made a statement the young Pastor Daniel Burke definitely wanted to make, he'd done what any other technically-challenged adult would have done. He'd gone to his ten-year-old daughter for help. Andi was teaching him the rudiments of operating his wife's iPad and he practiced with it whenever Emily was out of the house.

He stared at the words swimming around in—what? Tears? Was he crying?—and thought semi-hysterically: Where's a 10-year-old when you need one? He had no idea how he'd gotten to this screen, what buttons he'd pushed to transport him here.

I'll wear the black lacy one you got me. I want you to see me in it for a few seconds at least before you rip it off.

Daniel's knees gave way under him and he sat heavily on the deck chair, the morning sun flashing on the iPad screen. He'd brought his coffee out on the deck to work on her iPad while Emily was at her dentist appointment.

But Emily wasn't at her dentist's office. She was… somewhere…with— He scrolled down—he knew how to do that much—to the email below it, the one Emily had responded to.

We'll have the whole morning. If Daniel doesn't expect you back until noon, I plan to see how many different ways I can make you groan in ecstasy in three hours.

Daniel felt the coffee rise up in the back of his throat and was barely able to turn aside before acid vomit spewed out his mouth and nose onto the redwood decking at his feet. When he stopped reflexively gagging, he looked at the screen again, scanning down, searching for a name.

Jeff. He scratched around in his head, thumbing through the list of all the possible Jeffs who—

Jeff Kendrick. The dashing big-shot lawyer who was the chairman of the board of the Cincinnati Center for the Arts. Emily'd been asked to serve on the board last summer. Daniel had met the guy at the center's Christmas party. Kendrick had danced with Emily that night. Held her too close.

Daniel had never in his life felt an emotion like the one that swelled up in his chest then, as suddenly as inflating a Navy dinghy. It had no name, he was sure, or he'd have heard it sometime in his years of counseling married couples.

The emotion that shall not be named, he thought and barked a laugh, only it came out as a strangled sob.

He should pray.

He sat numb, waiting for words. None came.

Then he reached into his pocket and took out his cell phone. His hands were shaking so violently he almost dropped it. It took him two tries to punch "Favorites," and then "Emily."

He listened to it ring. Over and over again. Daniel thought that was the loneliest sound he had ever heard. Emily didn't answer.

❧

The tall blond boy stood staring at Theresa for a moment. "Sure, I can remember that. Code Red," he said, then took a tentative step out into the street.

"I said run, son. Drop them books and run like the devil hisself is after you."

The boy let the books slide out of his hand and took out at a gangly lope toward the house.

"Run!" Theresa cried after him.

He broke into a full-out sprint then, side-stepping the bushes and mailboxes in his way like a receiver dodging tackles as he heads for the end zone.

Theresa watched him. That was it. She'd done all she could do. Now it was her job to take care of her own, mind the little ones that was in her care.

"You all run, too," she said to the children standing stunned on the curb. "That way!" She gestured back up the sidewalk leading away from the school. "Go on now, git!"

She shuffled along as fast as she could behind the retreating children.

Lord, you see what we up against and ain't nobody but you can protect them little ones from it. Please…

And Bishop! He was in there, too. He'd understand instantly. Like Theresa—even more profoundly than Theresa—Bishop knew.

The blond kid was half way to the house, running dead out. Theresa watched him, knowing in her heart she'd sent him on a fool's errand. He wouldn't make it in time. It was too late, had been too late the moment she spotted the fat man in the ball cap in the school yard.

She'd taken only two more steps when an ugly rat-tat-tat-tat-tat ripped open the early summer morning with a sound like fireworks. The children in front of her knew it wasn't fireworks, though! With shocked terror on their faces, they ran screaming up the street.

She paused, turned back to the school, saw a sinister black fog billowing around it, a fog couldn't nobody see but those who knew.

Chapter Two

Police Sergeant Jack Carpenter was running long before he had time to will his legs to pick him up out of the chair behind his desk. So were all the other officers. The squad room of the Harrelton, Ohio, Metro Police Station emptied in less than thirty seconds. Every officer rolled on pure instinct when the hot call came over the radio, the six words every police officer prays he will never hear: "Active Shooter at Carlisle Elementary School."

The chief, the captain, the major, all the patrol officers responded—so would officers from other agencies, other nearby jurisdictions, but when they got to the scene, rank wouldn't matter, Jack would be in charge. He was the point man on the department's SWAT team and the tactical training officer for the whole state of Ohio. He was also the only man in the department other than the major who'd ever been shot at.

Jack squalled out of the police department parking lot in front of the others—Code Three, lights and siren. The wail of sirens rose in a symphony that curdled the crisp, jasmine-scented air. The school was only a couple of miles away. Half a block out from it, Jack careened his cruiser around the final corner and flipped the catch on his seat belt. As he pulled into the school parking lot, he hit the trunk release. It wouldn't open until the car was in park, but flipping the catch now was a second saved. Seconds mattered. He whipped the car so that it slid sideways toward the curb like a slalom skier stopping at the bottom of a hill—passenger side toward the building. He slammed the car into park with one hand and unclipped his M4 patrol rifle from the ceiling rack with the other and was out of the car in a crouch, scrambling toward the trunk in less than three seconds. It opened as he got there, and he snatched out his tactical vest. That had been a judgment call. He could have shaved off another couple of seconds by leaving it, but roll into the building without it and he had twenty-eight rounds of ammo. There were a hundred and fifty rounds in the vest.

Other officers were arriving now. He pointed to two from his department, "Paco" Ramirez and Sam Peterson, and a gray-uniformed Ohio State Police Trooper.

"You, you, you—with me, contact team."

They didn't have to be told what that meant. Cross-training of officers from all jurisdictions ensured that everybody was playing from the same sheet of music. First four officers on the scene—no matter who they were— formed the contact team. Their job was to follow the sound of gunfire and make contact with the shooter. If that meant they had to step over the bodies of bleeding and dying children in that single-minded pursuit, they had to be prepared to do just that. The next four officers would be dispatched as a search and rescue team—unless shots were still being fired, in which case they'd form a second contact team. Contact teams would continue to form until the gunfire ceased.

The role of every contact team was the same. Jack Carpenter had only one job: find the shooter; take him out.

~

Emily was careful not to speed, drove five miles per hour under the limit, came to a full stop at every sign, signaled before she turned. Oh, not because it would be difficult to explain to Dan why she'd gotten a traffic ticket on Donner Road when her dentist appointment was on the other side of Cincinnati in Mason. Though that would take some creative lying on her part, it wasn't her chief concern. What mattered most to Emily was time and not wasting a single second of it. A traffic ticket would steal precious minutes she could be spending with Jeff.

She reached up and hit the button on the sunroof and felt the warm summer breeze wash over her, setting her honey-colored curls dancing. Stylishly highlighted both dark and light, it resembled autumn leaves blowing across the ground.

Jeff wouldn't care that her hair was tousled. And even if it were perfectly styled, it would become a passion-tangled mess as soon as she saw him. When she turned off Freeman Avenue onto the Sixth Street Expressway, she glanced up into the mirror, a spot check of her makeup, which she had applied with special care this morning while Dan gave out Andi's spelling words.

As if summoned by the mention of his name in her mind, the phone rang and "Dan" appeared on the screen. She shook off the unease the call caused. He already had called three times, but left no messages. That wasn't like him. He should be at the church by now getting ready for the afternoon's deacons meeting. With the phone crying out on the seat beside her, it was hard to calm her jaded nerves. He wanted her to pick up his shirts at the cleaners, that was all, or stop by the store for— Finally, she couldn't stand the ringing any longer and reached over and punched the mute button. Of course, now she wouldn't hear the chime of a Jeff message either, but she was close. Whatever he had to say, he could say to her in person in a few minutes.

That thought caused a visceral reaction that flooded her body with warmth all the way to her toes. She'd be with Jeff soon, hold him, touch him, smell the delicious maleness of him. She inhaled the flower-scented breeze that wafted the aroma of honeysuckle and daisies into the car and thought that she'd never wanted anything in her life as much as she wanted Jeff Kendrick.

The secluded inn where they always met was an oasis in the middle of a collection of apartment houses between two strip malls upstream on the Ohio River from Harrelton. Though it wasn't the smallest of Cincinnati's suburbs —Harrelton boasted a population of about 100,000—it was still small enough that running into someone you knew in the grocery store or the movie theatre wasn't all that uncommon. Jeff had taken great care to secure their privacy by selecting The River's Bend, which was nestled at the base of a hill in a thick grove of trees, so even the driveway was secluded. Discreet, yet convenient, private, yet close enough that neither of them had to waste precious time getting there. It was so like Jeff to think of everything.

She turned off the street onto the winding driveway and around to the back—where her car would be safe from prying eyes. She pulled into the space in front of Room

No. 7, switched off the ignition and sat for a moment, listening to her heart thunder wildly in her chest. Another quick makeup check in the mirror, then she paused briefly to study the face beneath the makeup. She was a beautiful woman and she knew it, knew how to make the most of her perfect china-doll features and light blue eyes to produce an effect that was even better than beautiful. Emily Burke was striking.

She stepped out of the car into the warm summer sunshine. Slender and petite, barely five feet two, she stood snug in tight jeans.

The only women who look good in skinny jeans are women who have skinny genes.

Dan. Why did Dan keep popping into her mind?

She didn't want an answer to the question, and crossed the sidewalk to the No. 7 door quickly. It swung open before she had a chance to knock. The sight of Jeff took her breath away and she stood, staring.

In the distance she heard a sound, the wailing of sirens. Lots of sirens. Must be a wreck on Interstate 71. Then she stepped into Jeff's arms.

Bishop was proud of Erika Lund. The fragile little blonde girl—woman, she was a woman—musta had a stainless steel rod 'tatched to her backbone. She leapt to the door, rotated the knob that slid the deadbolt into place and grabbed the piece of green construction paper conveniently stabbed to the cork board beside the door. The paper was pinned next to a piece of red paper and both already had pieces of tape stuck to them, sticky-side out.

She whirled and taped the green paper over the small window in the door.

The piece of construction paper wasn't there by accident. Neither was the one on the window sill that Mrs. Waznuski hurriedly leaned against the glass. Every classroom was required to have both colors accessible near doors and windows at all times. Green paper would later tell police clearing the building that there were no casualties in the room. Red indicated injuries.

Lord, please keep that paper green.

The paper in place, Miss Lund turned to the children who had gone completely postal at the sound of the gunfire.

"Did I give any of you permission to scream?" she roared, like that sergeant who'd had to whip a bunch of Kentucky farm boys into soldiers before they shipped out to Vietnam. "Stop it right now!"

There was such an unaccustomed edge of menace in her voice, the children were shocked into momentary silence. While she had their attention, she continued, not comforting or soothing, merely matter-of-fact.

"We're safe. The door's locked and I…" she stepped to the desk, reached behind it and picked up her purse off the floor. The children held their breaths as she rummaged around in it until she found what she was looking for. "…I have the only key." Which technically wasn't true, of course, but it would do for now.

She held up a big gold door key on her key ring like it was a light saber from one of them Star Wars movies. Bishop could see that her hands were shaking, but the kids didn't seem to notice.

"Is he gonna shoot us?" cried a chubby girl whose

cheeks were slathered with tears. "I seen on TV where a man went into a school and shot the children. I don't wanna die."

Hysteria threatened to wash over the classroom again.

"Ain't none of you kids gone do no dying in this here room today," Bishop said. He had a deep, rumbling voice to match his huge stature but he always spoke quietly to children, as gentle as a fairytale teddy bear. He let the kids hear the steel in his voice now, though. His skin was as black as a crow's feather, but the hair that encircled his head, leaving a perfectly bare spot on top, wasn't cottony white. It had somehow got a touch of yellow in it. Theresa said it looked like popcorn.

There was another volley of gunfire outside in the hallway, and the sound of more glass breaking, and more crazy laughter. The children squeaked and whimpered in fear, but nobody screamed this time.

The crazy fool was taking out the trophy cases and the pictures of former principals and teachers that lined the walls. Then there was a pause between volleys, and Bishop heard it.

"You all hear that?" he asked. The warbling wail of a whole herd of sirens grew louder by the second. "In a couple of minutes, this place gone be plum broke out with policemen."

They just had to stay alive until help arrived.

"Here's what we gone do," he said, and glanced at Miss Lund to be sure she approved. She was holding it together real well but she didn't appear to be in any condition to execute any safety strategies. Mrs. Waznuski, a small woman with hair the color of snow-laden clouds, only worked half days, three days a week. Bishop hardly knew her, but it was clear she was as frightened as the children. "We're all gonna huddle together in that corner over there." It was against the wall, as far as possible from the door. "And we're gone turn over these desks and stack 'em up in front of us, make a fort like."

Bishop had no idea if that was the right thing to do or not. Maybe they should try to get the children out a window instead. But this was an old building with windows that opened wide at the top and about a foot or so at the bottom. To get the children out them, he'd have to break the glass—if he could locate something to break it out with—and then there'd be jagged glass everywhere. More important, Bishop figured it was safest not to call attention to themselves, which breaking out windows certainly would.

Besides, Bishop had seen only the one man, but that didn't mean there weren't others—outside maybe. Bishop's money was on staying in this hidey hole until the police showed up to blast what was out there in the hallway all the way back to hell. The safest place was right here where they had a locked door between them and the crazy man in the hall.

The children instinctively understood the need to be as quiet as possible as they hauled desks to the back of the room, picked them up—two kids to a desk—instead of dragging them. The sound of gunfire outside covered the sounds they did make as they piled the desks in a heap on top of each other. Then the children crawled in among the desks, burrowing themselves to safety.

It grew silent. The rat-tat-tat of automatic gunfire outside had ceased. Maybe the guy had left. Maybe—

In the hallway outside the classroom next door—the one that was locked up because they'd done touch-up painting in there before school this morning—he heard a cannon roar. That boom wasn't no automatic rifle. That was a shotgun.

Then another boom roared.

On one knee in front of the pile of desks, Bishop felt the pit of his stomach drop into his shoes, and turned as if in slow motion to look at the heavy wooden door. At the lock on the door. He held his breath. Time froze. Then there was another boom right outside in the hall and the wood around the lock on the door shattered and splintered. The children huddled together in the tangle of desks in the corner began to shriek and there was no calming them this time. One more boom and a hole showed in the door where the lock had been, leaving shards of wood and sawdust floating in the air. A hand reached in through the splintered hole, grasped the door, shoved it inward and the man in a sweatshirt and baseball cap picked his way almost daintily over the rubble of shattered wood in the doorway and stepped into the room.

Chapter Three

Jack led his team at a dead run from the parking lot to the school. He knew the general layout of the building. All the officers did. They were required to tour every school in their jurisdiction. Beyond the front door was an entry hall with offices on both sides. The entry hall opened into the main hallway, where the north and south wings of the school opened out at either end.

When he got to the set of double doors—both open—Jack crouched low, moved from one bit of cover to the next and the other officers followed suit.

Behind the column separating the double doors. To the wall on the right side of the entry hall, hunkered down beside a trash can. The trooper mirrored his action on the left wall, crouching down behind a display table of fire-fighting equipment from the local fire department—hats, hoses, boots. Jack's eyes swept the main hallway as far as he could see around the corner in front of the trooper, back and forth, taking in every detail. The trooper did the same for the hallway behind Jack.

The adrenaline rush had summoned flash images of

Somalia. Always did. They popped up and down in Jack's mind like targets in a cheap video game.

The skinny who'd come running at him, right out in the open, screaming wildly and brandishing a machete. They called the Somali militia fighters "skinnies" because they were emaciated, their teeth blackened from chewing khat, an amphetamine-like plant that kept them jacked up and juiced out of their minds all the time. Jack shot him, watched the blood spurt out the hole in his chest, but as the man fell he managed to throw the machete. Jack had a three-inch scar on his calf where the weapon had sliced through his pant leg. Had suffered through a massive infection, too, because the blade had been smeared with feces. But it could have been worse. Skinnies rubbed their own blood on their blades sometimes because eighty percent of the population was HIV positive.

Jack held up a closed fist, and the officers behind him froze in place. Then he stood, flattened himself against the wall, and edged to the entryway corner. He was broad-shouldered and tall, six-feet four-inches, with skin more coffee-colored than black, and he moved with athletic grace. Through the windows into the office behind him, he could see secretaries and teachers crouched behind the front counter and he heard them crying.

He peered cautiously around the corner into the main hallway. It was empty except for a lone gym shoe that had fallen out of the partially-closed locker above it.

The distinctive rat-tat-tat of an automatic weapon, along with the crash of shattering glass and a high, keening laughter sounded in the hallway that opened off the main hallway to the right. More gunfire, more breaking glass and laughter.

"Active shooter, north hallway," Jack said in a quiet

voice into the microphone clipped to the shoulder of his uniform.

"Copy that. North hallway," came back instantly.

There were big windows in every classroom. A sniper positioned across from the north hall might get lucky if the shooter were in one of the classrooms on that side of the building. Jack knew the captain would get one in place there as soon as he could. Corporal Roberts was the best shot in their department, but he was working the east end of the county today. With the gridlock of the instant traffic jam that by now had surely formed outside the perimeter officers were setting up around the school, he wouldn't be able to get within a mile of it. Maybe there was a sheriff's deputy, highway patrolman or state trooper on site who was a qualified sniper.

Not likely, though. Jack and his team were on the hook for this one.

There was a sudden boom from the north hallway. Shotgun.

Jack made eye contact with the trooper—his silver nametag said Purvis—and nodded. The trooper nodded back, lifted his M4 and aimed at the intersection of the north and main hallways. Then Jack raced across the main hallway to the far side, running Groucho Marx style, so named for its forward crouch. He flattened his back against the wall and began to work his way to the north hallway opening.

He heard another boom some distance down the hallway, and a third before he got to the corner. Then he peeked down the hall, his cheek against the cool brownish tile that lined the walls up to five feet or so—easy to wash. The hallway looked like a fifty-millimeter mortar shell had detonated there. The big trophy case on the left side of the hallway, probably fifteen feet wide, was a pile of rubble on the floor. Pieces of trophies, ribbons, and huge shards of glass lay in front of it. Obviously the shooter had repeatedly strafed it with automatic gunfire. It had sounded like an AK 47. Though the acoustics in an empty hallway couldn't be trusted, the size of the bullet holes in the walls could. The shooter was obviously firing 7.62 X 39 mm rounds. Equally obvious was that he had chosen to take out every past principal of the school, dating back to 1955. Pictures of each one had hung in glass-front frames between the classrooms on both sides of the hallway. Now they lay in shattered ruins on the floor.

A kind of haze hung in the air—dust, sawdust—but the hallway was empty. The shooter was in one of the classrooms.

Jack saw something else, too, and spoke softly into his microphone. "North hall exit doors chained shut."

"Copy that. Chained shut."

~

Cold flowed into the classroom, along with the man in the Cincinnati Reds hat who entered, an automatic rifle of some kind slung over his shoulder on a strap and a shotgun with a sawed-off barrel in his hands. Felt like the door'd been opened to an Arctic breeze that only Bishop could feel. The man himself looked as harmless as the driver of one of them ice cream trucks that played music so loud the kids could hear it coming a couple of blocks away and had time to pester their mamas for a dollar. Or would have, if not for his eyes, open so wide no eye lids showed at all, wild, crazed eyes. He had wispy blond hair sticking out from under the cap, fat cheeks—rosy cheeks—and a puckery little mouth where the top lip came to an owl's beak point and the pendulous bottom lip stuck out and down, like he was pouting.

The lip. A memory elbowed its way past Bishop's fear and stood defiant in the forefront of his mind. Bishop Washington never forgot a face.

The scrawny kid who'd played second base on the Little League All Star team Bishop coached years ago had had a lip like that. What was his name? Jake. Jacob. Jacob Dumas. Bishop stared into the placid face of the shooter, looking for the little boy he might once have been. Like the reverse of age-enhanced pictures of kidnapped children on milk cartons, the little boy's face appeared as an overlay on the man's. It was Jacob Dumas all right.

And that meant… No, Bishop shoved the thought away before he even had a chance to think it. No! It couldn't possibly be…

Dumas was smiling. The thing that materialized on his shoulders was not. As Bishop watched in revulsion, the black fog around the man's head transformed into a swarm of yellow-jacket wasps with elongated stingers like syringes. He could hear the hum of them, the sound of thousands of black flies with green bellies, the fat kind that made a big splat mark on the wall when you swatted them. The buzzing put him in mind of the time when he was eight that he'd come accidental upon the carcass of a recently dead deer in the woods and the stench'd made him chuck up his breakfast.

Then the swarm of wasps began to morph into a shape crouched on the man's shoulders. The shape became more and more solid until a thing emerged from the black swirling mass of wasps, a hideous creature with skin as alive as squirming maggots. It was roughly the shape of a deformed rat, with a long, spiked tail that hung halfway down the man's back—twitching restlessly back and forth—and claws as sharp as filleting knives. Jagged fangs that looked like shards of broken glass protruded from the maw at the bottom of a nose-less face. They dripped sticky strands of green drool down the side of Dumas's cap, where it clotted into a single stream that began to ooze down his cheek. The mouth at the bottom of the writhing-wasp face had too many teeth, blackened spikes curved inward so if it bit you, there'd be no hope of ever pulling free. It had eyes, too, pale yellow, the color of pus, with bright red centers.

Recognition slammed into Bishop's chest with the force of a wrecking ball. He'd seen those eyes before, too.

The eyes slowly surveyed the room until they landed on Bishop and locked there. The creature studied him, leaning its head to the side as it confirmed his identity. When it spoke, the voice was the sound of old, rusty chains dragged over a metal floor.

"The three who stood with the light," the voice growled, "I want them." The motion of speaking disturbed some of the wasps that formed its shape and for a moment the top of its hoary head disintegrated. Then, just as quickly, it reformed. "You know who they are. Where's Becca?"

Understanding dropped with the weight of a bowling ball deep into the pit of Bishop's belly.

It's come back. After all these years, it's got loose somehow and come back!

Bishop would have sworn it was impossible to be any more afraid than he already was. But now that he knew what the creature was, why it had come, what it wanted, a new terror clamped his heart in a vise. Then the monster laughed, the single, most horrible sound Bishop had ever heard. Like the roar of an avalanche that tapered off into the high-pitched wail of a hyena.

"Tell me, or the children die," the creature said through its laughter. "One by one, they all die."

"You there, old man," Dumas said to Bishop, "pull down the shades. Don't want peeping Toms prying into our business."

Bishop had recognized Dumas, but apparently the shooter hadn't recognized Bishop, though that crazy fool didn't look like he could recognize his own mother right now. Bishop did as he was told, got up from where he was kneeling and went from one window to the next, lowering the shades. He moved the piece of green construction paper out of the way, knew that the lowered shades and no colored paper would tell police the folks inside were in real trouble.

"So kiddies," said the man, his voice cheery, "who wants to be the first one to die? Any volunteers?"

Some of the children were crying softly, but most were merely whimpering, far too frightened to cry.

"Come on out of there, all of you." He reached out with his free hand and picked up one of the overturned desks and pitched it over his shoulder as effortlessly as tossing away an apple peel. It banged heavily against the wall beneath the windows.

"Bunch up here in front of me."

He spoke in a matter-of-fact voice, not threatening, more like the basketball coach telling the kids to line up so he could pick out who had to do laps around the gym.

"I won't shoot all of you, Scouts' honor. I want some of you to live the rest of your lives remembering our special day together." He made the high-pitched sound he'd made out in the hallway, a sound too corrupted to be called laughter.

Then he casually swung the barrel of the shotgun around toward Erika Lund, who was trying unsuccessfully to position herself between him and the children as they crawled out of the tumble of desks in the back corner. He wiggled his finger at her. She looked quizzical. He wiggled it again and she tentatively approached him.

"On your knees," he said. She hesitated for a beat, then straightened her back and dropped to her knees on his left, between him and the back of the room. He held out the rifle an inch in front of her nose.

The creature on Dumas's shoulders fixed its swarming eyes on Bishop.

"Tell me where to find the one who stood with The Light!" the creature rumbled.

"'Fraid I can't do that." Bishop's voice didn't have no volume, was so soft maybe only the creature heard. He had to suck in another breath to continue, to tell the creature he didn't have no idea where Becca was. He didn't have a chance to say nothing, though, before the creature on the gunman's shoulder lifted a paw where a vicious claw longer than the others extended from the middle finger. In a slow, lazy motion, it began to shove the claw downward into Jacob Dumas's skull.

Bishop watched Dumas tense. The creature paused, looked a question at Bishop without speaking. The young, blonde teacher who had signed on the loan for her first house only two days ago, who had a mother with Alzheimer's in Omaha, papers to grade in her desk, and the only key to this room safe and snug in her purse was seconds away from instant death.

But Bishop didn't know where Becca was. What could he do if he didn't know?

The impact of the shotgun blast propelled Erika Lund backward and she hit the floor with a thunk and slid a few feet, leaving a bloody snail trail behind until her limp body was still.

The children shrieked in total hysteria, Bishop fell backward against the window sill in shock, his eyes riveted on the now unrecognizable young woman crumpled on the floor on the other side of the room. Mrs. Waznuski grabbed a little girl who hadn't wormed her way into the pile yet and hugged her fiercely, turning her head away from the sight.

"Like I promised, kiddies," the gunman said, his voice still pleasant, "not everybody in this room is going to die today, but some of you definitely are. Correction, most of you are.

Chapter Four

Daniel wasn't even aware at first that he was pacing, didn't realize it until he passed the door leading to the deck and the smell of his own vomit coming through the screen gagged him. He reached out, pulled the sliding door shut and kept walking. Fit and trim, an even six feet tall, his stride was long as he passed through the family room to the kitchen, out the archway to the dining room and through the second arch to the living room. Emily'd re-covered the couch, love seat and overstuffed chairs there with bright floral fabric—yellows and greens that made the room cheery and bright. She'd done it herself, made her fingers raw and sore, stapling the heavy fabric—

Then he was crying, sitting in the overstuffed chair and sobbing. He couldn't seem to stop, to pull himself together. He ought to call someone to come over and—

And what? You called someone to come sit with you when you got sudden bad news, like a death in the family.

Hi Joe, this is Pastor Burke. If you're not too busy right now, could you come by my house. My wife's having an affair.

Who could he tell? How could he tell anybody? The wife of the senior pastor of a mega-church did not do such things. And he'd worked nights and weekends for years to be prepared when a big break like this church came along.

…nights and weekends for years …

Was that it? Was that why?

But she never said anything, never complained, never seemed to mind that he was gone.

He shoved his hand into his pocket, drew out his phone, and hit redial. He'd told himself he wouldn't call her again because the sound of the phone ringing over and over was a terrible, desolate, hopeless sound. And because when she didn't pick up, his mind pictured why she didn't pick up. What she was doing that she couldn't answer the phone.

Her voice mail came on. He didn't leave a message. Merely put the phone back in his pocket, got up from the chair and continued pacing. He had to keep moving, the emotion that shall not be named threatened to kill him if he was still.

Somewhere in the distance, he heard the sound of sirens—police, ambulance, fire truck? He couldn't tell. And didn't care.

~

Jack considered a moment, then took the team down the middle of the North Hall in the standard diamond-shaped formation, crouched low, rifles ready. The North Hall was lined on both sides with student lockers, eight to a bank, four upper and four lower. The locker banks were about fifteen feet apart, stuck out from the wall about eighteen inches, and each locker was probably two feet wide, with shelves on one side of a partition and hooks for jackets or book bags on the other. There were two sets of locker units between each classroom. Between the sets of locker units were four-inch-thick cinderblock partitions that stuck out about two feet, forming alcoves at the end of each unit.

Bent at the waist, Jack scuttled across the hallway to the alcove on the east side to the first bank of lockers and flattened himself against the wall there. Then he opened the bottom locker door and crouched behind it, shielded by the lockers and the open door. The locker door only shielded him from sight, of course. A bullet would go right through it. He made a hand motion and Ramirez did the same along the west wall. After that, they alternated, each ran from one bank of lockers to the next, while the others provided cover, passing closed and Jack was sure locked classrooms on the way. The windows in all the doors they passed were covered with green construction paper.

He and his men were less than a quarter of the way down the hallway when Jack heard the shotgun boom a fifth time in a classroom on the west side between him and the chained-shut outside entrance. The shot was followed by the screams of hysterical children. He did not respond in any way to the sounds except for a tightening around his mouth. One shooter located. There could be more than one.

"Active shooter, fourth classroom, west side," he said into his mic.

"Copy that."

Then Jack and Trooper Purvis continued in a shuffling crouch from cover to cover down the east side of the hallway; the two officers from his department mirrored them on the west until Jack lifted his fist and the others froze in place. He was now across the hall from the classroom where the shot had been fired and from his position crouched by the locker unit, could see that the door was standing about a third of the way open, the knob and lock shattered by a shotgun blast. It appeared that the door on the next classroom down from it was shattered and ajar, too. A second shooter could be in that room, though no sound came from it. The door across from Jack opened inward, so he could see into the room, but could see nothing but the teacher's desk. Neither the shooter nor any children was visible.

Jack concentrated, drew a diagram of the room in his head. It was shoe-box shaped. The door was at the front of the room. To the right of the door was a wall with bulletin boards and blackboards. The teacher's desk sat on the far wall by the windows. To the left of the door, storage units and supply closets lined the hallway-side wall; a sink unit and bookshelves formed the back wall of the room. Desks ran in rows, four, maybe six across, facing the blackboards. On the window wall, Jack could see that the shades had been lowered.

There was activity in the room. Besides the cries of the children, he could hear the sounds of desks scooting across the floor, or falling on it. He tried to picture what was going on inside, but the sounds didn't produce an image. Why were they moving desks? To shove them in front of the door, barricade it shut? If that happened, the tactical approach would change. Absent gunfire, it would become a hostage situation, and the hostage negotiation specialists would be called.

But Jack's gut told him the shooter didn't intend to take the children hostage. He intended to kill them.

~

As the children began to appear out of the tangle of desks in the back corner of the room, they obediently lined up in terrified rows in front of the man in the baseball cap, who grinned at them amicably. Bishop stood and moved toward the front of the room along the wall of windows. A plan was forming in his head, not a particularly good one, but the only one he had. He hoped to get slightly behind the shooter, who stood next to the hall side wall with his back to the partially opened door. Soon as the man glanced the other way, Bishop would jump him.

You old fool. You can't move fast enough to get out of the way of a golf cart. You think you can cross the whole width of this room and land on that man before he turns and shoots you?'

No, Bishop didn't have much hope that he could. But he had to do something, wouldn't stand by and do nothing while the creature of wasps massacred these children. And make no mistake about it, the creature was calling the shots. Oh, Dumas wasn't totally a puppet. If he exerted enough force of will—or was crazy enough—he could act on his own. But the black cloud/mist/wasp creature settled around the outside of his head was the mirror image of a creature on the inside, and wasn't no easy thing a'tall to defy what that cloud wanted you to do.

"Now, who wants to be the first one with a bullet in the brain?" the man beneath the swarm of wasps asked in an exaggerated stage whisper. His face remained pleasant, but a small stream of drool now escaped from the right side of his mouth and edged down his chin.

The terrified children whimpered and stared at him. The little blond boy on the far end—Dr. Hamilton, the dentist's little boy—wet himself, but didn't know it. If the children had been younger, there'd have been no controlling them; they'd have run screaming in every direction no matter what anybody said. Maybe the creature of wasps would have tried to mow them all down, but some of them might have escaped. Not these children. At age ten, they were old enough and well-behaved enough to do as they were told. They were sheep being led to the slaughter.

"You need to tell me now," the creature rumbled at Bishop, and Bishop thought he heard something like concern in its voice.

"You there, fatso," Dumas said to the chubby little girl who had told Bishop she didn't want to die, "how about you show the others how to hold your breath —permanently."

"Mommy," the child cried. "I want my mommy."

Bishop took another step backward. He had now backed up almost to Miss Lund's desk—oh, that precious girl—and tensed his old muscles to lunge.

"Next time your mommy sees you, you're going to be zipped up in a body bag." The man laughed, an ugly, shrill sound like the cry of a seagull.

Something outside the shattered door caught Bishop's attention. He cut his eyes in that direction, didn't turn his whole head. Crouched there behind an open locker door on the other side of the hallway was a police officer.

Chapter Five

He saw me!

Jack was certain the old man—must be a janitor—had spotted him. Would he give away Jack's position? The locker unit on the east side stood directly across from the classroom door, so Jack wasn't crouched behind a locker unit and an open door—only the open locker door, which offered zero real protection. If the shooter stepped to the doorway and started firing, Jack would literally be a sitting duck.

But shooters were notoriously bad shots. Contrary to the myth created by cop shows and cowboy movies, it was seriously difficult to deliver a mortal wound to a moving target, and Jack would definitely be moving. Jack would have a chance and that's all he asked. Because if the shooter showed himself, Jack would shoot, too. And Jack wouldn't miss.

Nothing about the janitor's countenance changed. Either he hadn't actually seen Jack, or he'd had the presence of mind not to let the shooter know Jack was there. Then the old man spoke. He had a booming, James Earl

Jones voice and he had the volume turned up loud; Jack had no trouble hearing him above the crying children.

"You children hush now and do what the man says," the janitor said. "Mrs. Waznuski, get them bunched up right here in the middle of the room. Close together nice and tight."

He gestured as he spoke and Jack realized the old man was getting all the children in one spot and telling Jack where they were! Letting him know they were all in a tight group in the area where the desks were located. Apparently, the desks had been moved.

Then the janitor turned toward the wall that backed on the hallway, angled his body to face a spot a little way past the partially open door and spoke again in the same loud voice.

"That where you want 'em, boss?" the old man asked.

The shooter was standing against the wall behind the door.

~

It seemed to Bishop that the man in the cap turned toward him in slow motion.

"I don't recall asking for any help," the shooter said. There was a razor edge of restrained rage in the words and he swung the rifle back in Bishop's direction. At that moment, Bishop understood that the number of heartbeats he had left was not a two-digit number. Apparently, the wasp creature had come to the same conclusion, because it instantly came apart, lost the form it had assumed and merely swarmed in a whirling cyclone around the man's head, shrieking with a thousand voices at once, "No!"

"My mama always did say my big mouth was gonna get me in trouble one of these days." Though his insides were trembling like Jell-o hit with a fork and his heart was thumping so hard his vision pulsed, Bishop's voice was firm, didn't shake. He was glad of that. A man had ought to die with as much dignity as the circumstances allowed.

Did that cop get what he was trying to tell him? Does he know where that monster's standin'?

Bishop knew he'd never find out the answer to either question, and watched in fascinated horror as the wasps swirled around the man's head so fast they were a blur of motion that totally obscured his features.

The man in the Reds ball cap lifted his rifle, pointed it at Bishop's chest.

"Looks like you ain't gone find out what you come here to find out," Bishop said to the creature.

"No!" the monster shrieked in the man's face. "You fool, don't shoo—!"

That was the last sound Bishop Washington ever heard.

If this had been a training exercise, Tactical Training Officer Jack Carpenter could have spent an entire afternoon going over in great detail how everything he was about to do was wrong.

After all, he was only guessing where the shooter was. Guessing where the children were. Guessing none of them would be in the line of fire.

"Guessing will get you killed," he'd said at least a thousand times.

And he'd be exposing himself to close-range, lethal fire. He'd be so near the shooter the man wouldn't even have to aim—just point the shotgun in his direction and pull the trigger. You didn't have to be a crack shot to hit a man with a shotgun blast from ten feet away. If he was wrong about where the shooter was standing, didn't drop him with the first shot, there'd be no second chance.

All of that passed through Jack's mind between one eye blink and the next, and none of it mattered. He had three, maybe four seconds and then kids were going to start dying.

Even before the old man's body crashed into the teacher's desk, Jack was moving. He shoved the locker door out of his way, exploded out of a crouch, launched himself across the hallway, and dived through the partially open door into the room, turning his body in the air, lifting his rifle as he flew. Jack's eyes were fixed on the hallway side wall of the classroom before his body ever cleared the doorway. His rifle was already aimed at that spot even before the man in the baseball cap came into view.

The janitor had given his life to draw Jack a picture, and the reality was exactly as he'd painted it. Shooter in front of the supply closets on the hallway side wall. Check. Children bunched together in the center of the room, out of the line of fire. Check. Jack pulled the trigger three times. Fired three rounds so close together it almost sounded like one shot. Two rounds in the chest, the biggest target, then one shot to the head.

The first round caught the man dead center of the chest and likely plowed a hole right through him and out the other side. Obviously, the man wasn't wearing body armor. The second was lower, left side. The third planted a red splotch in his forehead above his right eye. He'd been swinging his rifle back toward the children after shooting the janitor, and reflexively pulled the trigger. The round blasted a hole in the floor less than a foot in front of a little girl in pigtails who probably didn't even realize she was sucking her thumb.

Jack's body hit the floor and slid toward the dead janitor. He hadn't even stopped sliding when Purvis appeared in the doorway half a step behind him, back to the shattered door, then spun around it, rifle pointed where Jack had fired. When he saw the gunman on the floor, he rushed to him, rifle aimed at the crumpled figure, and kicked away the shotgun the man had dropped as he fell.

"One shooter down. Repeat, one shooter down," Jack gasped into his mic as he sat up. "Still checking for additional shooters."

"Copy, one shooter down."

He knew Ramirez and Peterson had moved on to the classroom down the hall where the lock had also been blown out of the door.

Paco appeared in the doorway and gave him a thumbs-up. "Clear," he said. "Classroom's empty." He held up a hand with a pale blue streak across the palm. "Fresh paint."

While Peterson covered the door—this building was hours away from being declared "safe," Ramirez grabbed the cloth off a table under the window and covered the body of a blonde woman whose face had been blown away. The teacher. There was nothing left in the room to cover the dead janitor.

Jack set his rifle on the floor and rose. Though Purvis kept his own rifle trained on the body, he stepped away from the man on the floor. Until a paramedic or the coroner said so, you never assumed a suspect was dead—even one missing most of the right side of his brain. Jack had shot the man, and black-humor law enforcement etiquette was clear. You bag it, you pack it. So it would be Jack's job to turn the body over, cuff the shooter's hands behind his back and secure the weapons and ammo belts.

Jack stepped to the shooter, stood for a moment looking down at him. A distinct unwashed-body/dirty clothes stink, mixed with the copper smell of blood, wafted up from the body. Then Jack turned to examine the children.

They were clustered together, white from terror, some crying, some catatonic, all with a look on their faces he'd seen before, a look of vacant, hollow-eyed shock occasioned by horror way beyond a child's capacity to process. He'd seen it on children's faces in Kosovo and Somalia and Rwanda. An older woman who must have been the teacher's aide stood in the center of them like Mother Goose and they clung to her skirt for comfort. She gazed at Jack with such profound wonder and gratitude, he was suddenly embarrassed.

He turned aside and keyed the mic on his shoulder.

"No children injured," he said into it.

Despite the dispatcher's professional control, Jack could hear the joy and relief in the woman's response.

"Copy that, no children injured."

What happened next always replayed in Jack's memory in a series of snapshots, black and white with harsh relief and dark puddles of shadows.

Click-click.

The look of surprise on Purvis's face when they both heard a sound behind Jack, behind the shooter lying on the floor.

Click-click.

The room blurred from the speed of Jack drawing his handgun from its holster, turning and pointing it with both hands in the direction of the noise—all in one motion.

Click-click.

A little girl with long, chestnut-colored curls standing in the now open door of the storage closet behind the shooter, a red smudge of blood blossoming in the middle of the Minnie Mouse face of her tee shirt.

Click-click.

Her huge pale blue eyes locked on Jack's with a look that wasn't fear. Surprise, maybe even…compassion?

Then Miranda Burke's eyes closed and she collapsed in a heap on top of the body of the shooter on the floor in front of her.

Chapter Six

He had heard the knocking for some time—a few minutes? A few days?—but ignored it. Daniel Burke had stopped pacing. Now, he sat quietly on the couch in the family room, his phone in his hand. He set the timer on it for five minutes. Every time the buzzer sounded, he called Emily. He heard the ring, ring, ring echoing off damp rock walls of dark chambers deep in his soul. She didn't pick up; he left no messages. When her voicemail kicked in, he listened to the carefree sound of her voice. Then he hung up, started the timer again and stared into a vast nothingness that had opened up on the floor in front of him.

The banging on the door got louder. Someone was standing on the porch, calling his name.

"Pastor Burke, open the door!"

It was Clarice Shutterbaum from next door. He might even have ignored her knock on a normal day, a day in which everything he believed was true hadn't come loose and floated out to sea.

"Pastor Burke!"

He looked up, startled. Clarice had obviously gone

around to the deck, to the door beside the puddle of vomit he'd spewed out. When she found it unlocked, she walked right in. He was so surprised by such audacious rudeness he merely stared at her in wonder.

"I know I shouldn't have come in here like this, but you wouldn't answer the door and I could see your car in the driveway, so I knew you were home."

He felt rage rising in him, flickering the pure blue of a gas flame. It wasn't anger at Clarice, but she was a convenient target. He got to his feet and glared down at her. Though he had an open, friendly face and warm brown eyes, at six feet tall he was almost a foot taller than his chubby neighbor, and the sudden tension in her as she looked up at him was satisfying. She even took a tentative step back.

"If I'd wanted to talk to you, Clarice, chances are I'd have answered the door. A reasonable person would take that to mean they weren't wanted and should go away!"

He took her elbow and started to give her a bum's rush to the front door.

"Pastor, wait." She shook off his grasp and kept at him, determined as a rat terrier.

"Your little girl, Andi—she goes to Carlisle doesn't she?" All the air whooshed out of Daniel so fast he was surprised there was no accompanying wind sound.

"What about Andi?"

"Didn't you hear the sirens?"

He had heard sirens, but he'd ignored them.

"What do the sirens have to do with Andi?"

"Pastor, there's been a shooting at her school. It's all over the news. They're saying thirty or forty kids have been shot, dead kids and teachers laying everywhere."

Daniel let go of her elbow and rushed past her to the door, without ever forming a clear intent to do anything.

"They're telling parents to stay away, not to go congregating down at the school."

He left the front door standing open and burst into a run toward his car.

"You can't do anything. You'll only get in the way."

He slammed the car door, dragged the keys out of his pocket and started the engine.

"Last I heard there was still shooting! You shouldn't go down there, Pastor. You—"

He didn't hear the rest. He slammed the transmission into reverse, tore out of the driveway and peeled rubber as he squalled down the street.

~

She couldn't hear no gunfire, a block away and tucked in behind a hedge like she and the children were. Bishop had been pestering her for years, saying she'd ought to get hearing aids. But the children could hear gunshots. Or said they could.

Then they all jumped at the same time, so they must have been able to hear something.

"That's a shotgun," said a freckle-faced boy of about eleven, awe tingeing his speech. "The other one was an automatic, but that's a shotgun."

"Are there two of them, then?" a scrawny black boy asked.

Theresa knew how many there were. She'd seen it. They was only one.

"How do you know ith a shotgun?" asked the strong-willed little redhead. "Maybe ith a bomb."

"It's a shotgun," the boy persisted. "My daddy uses one

to kill the gophers on my grampa's farm. I can tell by the sound."

All that gunfire and her Bishop right there in the middle of it! He'd have known there was a demon, of course, just like she did. Only he would have seen it. Maybe when he did, he run off and hid.

But she knew Bishop wouldn't run away from no demon. He'd stand his ground.

All them kids is the priority to them po-lice officers—I know that, Lord. But they's a ornery old man in that building, too, and I know you care as much about him as—"

There was another shotgun blast, and this time Theresa heard it. She wasn't sure she heard it with her ears, though. And she felt cold after that, cold and scared.

The children jumped at gunshots she didn't hear one more time, and then she watched the gray miasma around the school dissipate, vanish like creek fog hit by the morning sun. Theresa knew it was safe, now. The menace was gone, but she was in no hurry to get back to the school. No hurry at all. There was a knot in her stomach, a fear like she hadn't felt in a long, long time. And she absolutely, positively, one hundred percent did not want to know what was causing it.

~

Jeff was at the minibar, making Emily a drink as she lay on her back with the sheet pulled demurely up to her neck. Jeff liked "the reveal" when he pulled it slowly off her body.

She was smiling an enigmatic smile, but truthfully couldn't seem to keep her mind in the game, as her football coach father would have said. The wailing sirens that went on and on had set her teeth on edge. Whatever had happened was big. Though a suburb of greater Cincinnati, Harrelton had its own city council, fire, police and EMS departments and from the sound of it, every one of them had been called out to something. Maybe it was something dangerous, like a propane tanker turned over on the interstate, or a derailment of hazardous chemicals somewhere along the lone train track that meandered through the city.

Yes, city. Technically. But in reality, it had the feel of the small town in Iowa where she grew up, with parks, playgrounds, lots of "green space," and some of the best schools in the state. Great place to raise a family, or so Dan had said after he preached the first time at Voice of Hope Community Church. The church had been teetering on the brink of explosive growth and the young, passionate pastor from Chicago with his lovely wife and precious daughter had been just the fire to light the fuse.

Now, officially a mega-church, it was poised for greatness. What was it Dan always said, "Positioned to do some serious damage for the Kingdom."

"Sure you don't want anything but wine?" Jeff asked and when her attention turned back to him she realized he'd been staring at her with a look of such feeling—longing? Love?—on his face she felt like her bones had turned to butter.

He was strikingly handsome. She thought he looked like Pierce Brosnan, with hair as dark and shiny as black agate and a cleft in his chin that added an extra touch of rakish sexiness. He was a junior partner with the biggest and most influential law firm in the state—the newspapers called them "king-makers," and they had big plans for Jeff

Kendrick. She'd felt a spark, something electric between them, the first time she'd sat across from him at an Arts Center board meeting. The fire got hotter with every meeting, until eventually she'd started orchestrating chance encounters. She found out later he had been doing the same thing.

"Wine is fine." She patted the bed beside her. "Hurry. I'm getting cold."

The sound of a low-flying helicopter filled the room as one zoomed by overhead, sounded like the wheels must have clipped the elm trees outside.

What was going on? Had Cincinnati been invaded by aliens?

Jeff caught her concern. He was so astute and attentive nothing escaped his notice.

Note to self: add that to the list of reasons why you love this man.

Love? She'd never used that word before, purposefully did not think in those terms. Did she…love him?

Emily literally gave her head a shake to fling the thought out of her mind. Now was not the time to be asking herself questions for which she had no answers.

"Would you like to turn on the television and find out—?"

"No!" Then softer, "no." That would let the world into their private space, their magical time together and she wouldn't have that. "I'm not that curious. Whatever it is, it's not my problem."

~

Jack was never sure if his memories of what happened

after that were accurate, colored as they were by what he'd long ago dubbed "adrenaline-rush psychosis." The adrenaline dump into the bloodstream during a life-and-death struggle narrowed a man's field of vision so he saw the world like looking through a pipe. It made senses keener— you could hear better, see clearer. It could also cause your mind to play the same reality over and over. That was called "getting in a loop." He'd seen an officer once shoot a man, then stand over the dead body and continue to yell at him to drop his weapon.

Jack didn't do that, but he did stand lifeless for a time, as unmoving as a clay pot, without any clear thought of any kind in his mind. There was a hum in his ears, the sound of an old refrigerator kicking on in the night. Something inside him, something always taut, had snapped, leaving him momentarily flaccid and limp.

Some parts of the next few minutes played in his mind like the scenes flashing by when you fast-forwarded through a commercial. Other parts elongated and it seemed to take a thousand years between forming the intent to do something and actually taking action.

It seemed to take a millennium to lower and holster his pistol, a geologic epoch for Purvis to bark out a clipped, "One child down, repeat one child down!" into his shoulder mic.

But the sequence where Paco came to him, said something soothing that contained the words "through-and-through" and "not your fault" in it, and the subsequent evacuation of the injured child and the other children, played out like some manic video game.

When the hatchet of realization—I shot a child!— hacked into his chest, Jack went numb and Purvis stepped up and took control of the situation, seamlessly easing Jack out of a decision-making role and into a go-here, stand-there, do-this capacity, which he knew was all Jack was capable of.

The state trooper directed Peterson to administer first aid to the child, conferred briefly with the command post over the radio, then told Paco to move the children to the back of the room.

"Use your break-and-rake on that window," he told Jack, and Jack robotically pulled his nightstick from its holster and shattered the window next to the teacher's desk.

As Jack raked away the shards of broken glass from the frame, he saw a cordon of officers with riot shields form up on the grass outside and a stretcher with accompanying paramedics wheel down through it.

The injured child didn't have time to wait for search-and-rescue teams to clear the building. It would be hours before the structure was declared safe—there could be other shooters hiding in any one of the other locked rooms. Every square inch of the structure would be systematically, meticulously searched—from the rafters to the floor tiles.

Randomly-firing synapses posed unanswerable questions

I wonder which shot it was that passed through the shooter and hit the little girl?

Peterson had rolled the little girl onto her back. Paco had grabbed a full roll of paper towels and Peterson had jammed it into her wound. Purvis turned to Jack.

"You take her out," the trooper said.

He gets it. He knows I need…

Confirmed—Jack did, indeed, like this guy.

Jack lifted the child tenderly into his arms with Peterson in front, still maintaining pressure on what was rapidly becoming a blood-soaked roll of paper towels. The two marched together toward the window, lifted her up and over the sill into the waiting arms of the paramedics, who had her strapped onto the stretcher and rolling back through the cordon of officers in seconds.

Jack did remember that part clearly. The child's limp body against his chest, her head hanging loose on her neck, chestnut curls dangling like the fringe on a table cloth.

He didn't remember much else—evacuating the children down the cordon as he watched the Med-Evac helicopter set down in the middle of the baseball diamond beside the school. He saw someone break free from the cordoned off crowd of horrified onlookers and race to the paramedics shoving the stretcher. Officers caught him and started to drag him away, then let him go and he got into the chopper with the child.

His little girl. Jack had shot that man's little girl.

Then he was standing beside a big gray police van in the school parking lot, a spectator as Peterson, Ramirez and Purvis gave brief, animated statements to the captain and major.

And in the space between one breath and the next, the world righted itself. The fuzziness lifted, the slo-mo/fast-forward reality vanished, the world was in crisp focus, no tunnel. Jack was back. When the captain gestured for him, his step was sure.

A trim, silver-haired man, the captain carried himself like the Senior Senator from Somewhere, but every officer knew he was all hat and no cattle. A blowhard posturing in front of a mirror, the man's staunch, resolute facade disguised a limitless capacity for spinelessness. Jack met his gaze with his own eyes clear.

"They said a through-and-through," the captain said.

"The shooter was firing a shotgun," Jack said. "The little girl's wasn't a shotgun wound. Had to be"-he hesi-

tated a beat, but when he continued his voice was firm.-
"one of the three rounds I fired. That's the only explanation."

"Ramirez said the teacher's aide didn't even know the little girl was hiding in that closet."

"No," Jack said. "I guess nobody knew."

The words sounded hollow, like they'd come up into the world from some deep, dark well.

Standing beside the captain, Major Charles Crocker said nothing, merely offered Jack the scraps of a smile. Crocker, "Crock" to fellow officers, was a round man without a hair on his head and legs bowed out so far you could drive a Buick between his knees. He was also sharp, tough and fair—one of the finest officers Jack had ever served with. He placed a hand briefly on Jack's shoulder.

"I'm sorry, Jack," Crocker said.

Jack understood the two-fold message in those three words.

The major was sorry it had happened—to the little girl and to Jack, too.

The major was also sorry that he was about to relieve Jack of duty, take his gun and his shield and plant him in a chair, riding a desk until a board of inquiry ruled that the use of deadly force had been necessary—or not. Standard operating procedure for every officer-involved shooting. Jack had been there, done that. But this time was different. He hadn't just capped the shooter—he'd shot a little girl! Guilt would stitch this moment into his memory forever.

"Carpenter, consider yourself relieved of duty and placed on administrative leave..."—the major took a breath—"...as soon as you get back from securing the shooter's house. Lieutenant Harrison only lives a couple of miles from there and I just dispatched him, but he's asked for backup."

Perhaps there was an accomplice. Not likely, but not a rock you dared leave unturned, either. More weapons, explosives? That was likely. Someone had to make sure the shooter's place was locked up tight for the forensics guys. The Harrelton Police Department was small and right now it was stretched to the limits.

"Isn't Harrison still out on medical?"

"Cleared for duty tomorrow morning…so I'm stretching it. With both of you. Meet him at the Sunoco Station at the corner of Lanyard and Gupton." The major looked at a clipboard. "Drivers license says the shooter's name is Jacob"—he paused and spelled the last name—"D.U.M.A.S." He paused again for a beat. "And you can pronounce that any way you want." He glanced at the clip board again. "He lives at 3747 Hurst Lane, out there in the Oakwood Subdivision."

Jack nodded, grateful to have a task to do, a service to perform, glad he was still on the team, on the case, even if it was from a distance.

"Yes, sir," he said and headed toward his cruiser.

Chapter Seven

The frenetic activity around Daniel had a frenzied, insectile quality. Movement—Hurry! Hurry!—voices, racing steps, the thump and clatter of metal somethings, the beeps and hums of machines.

Everything and everybody whirled in a maelstrom, but he was in the eye of the hurricane. He alone was still, rooted to the spot where he'd been parked outside the treatment room when the paramedics rushed Andi at a dead run out of the Med-Evac helicopter and into the emergency room of Jefferson Memorial Hospital.

Waiting.

Waiting for somebody to push through the treatment room doors and tell him his little girl was going to be all right. Only a flesh wound, the doctor would say, and he'd pull off that stupid scrub mask and smile at Daniel. Nothing to worry about. She'll be back playing soccer in no time, might even make Saturday's game.

But those words were a distant sound he heard from somewhere deep and dark in his soul, a place where he could only barely make out a shaft of bright light high above where Daniel stood in the waiting room. Someone in that light was telling Daniel Andi'd be fine, just fine. But she wouldn't be fine in the dark shadowed place where he was. Here, in this place where no light reached, children didn't get better. They died and you stood next to a tiny casket and said comforting words to a devastated father— then looked into his face and discovered he was you.

Pain and loss were here in the dark place. He'd been here before—you didn't do ministry for almost fifteen years without seeing it all—death, disease, heartbreak. But from the other side, the comforting side, the God's-ways-are-not-our-ways side where you left the accident scene or the ICU waiting room or the graveside and went home to a house that smelled of pot roast and cherry pie and rang with the laughter of a healthy child.

Terror was here, too. Bigger and uglier even than what he'd felt during the wild drive to the school, leaping out of the car with the door left open, like he'd left the front door of the house, sprinting across someone's lawn, leaping somebody's begonia garden like he was running hurdles in high school.

He'd been amazed he could run at all, because he couldn't get his breath, hadn't been able to breathe all the way in since Clarice Shutterbaum said someone was shooting…shooting!

He'd elbowed his way through the crowd—ignoring the cries of "Pastor Burke!" and "Daniel!"—making his way to the front. Maybe the cop cut him some slack because of the clerical collar, didn't realize he was a frantic parent just like the rest of them, thought he'd come to minister to the terrified teachers and children huddled under a maple tree beside the baseball diamond.

He'd escorted Daniel there as the big med-evac helicopter dropped out of the sky like a dragonfly on a pond.

EMS personnel were shoving a stretcher from the school through a corridor of officers in riot gear, making for the chopper.

There was a small form on the stretcher, a child.

Andi.

It couldn't be. Couldn't possibly be. He was in total denial even as he fought the officer to run to her side. The paramedic on the chopper was Ben Avery! Daniel had performed his wedding ceremony not six months ago. He motioned and the officer let Daniel go.

Andi! Andi!

He'd called her name but there was no response. Blood, so much blood it dripped off the side of the stretcher and dropped in dollops on his shoe. Her eyes were closed and he could see the little blue veins in them. He didn't ask Ben about her condition. Didn't want to bother him. Distract him. But knew he'd smile and say—

Up there in the light, Ben would smile. Down here in the dark, he'd give Daniel the look Daniel'd pretended not to see on the paramedic's face as he leapt out of the helicopter and shoved the stretcher into the emergency room. The look that was as dark and ugly as the place deep in his mind where he read it clearly. She's not going to make it.

A nurse rushed out of the double doors and blew by Daniel as if he weren't there. He'd reached out to take her arm but didn't. Didn't want to bother her.

No, didn't want her to give him the same look Ben had.

Andi had been so cold. Her little hand when he took it was like ice, with the pink nail polish on the fingernails that had some kind of stickers on them—too small on her blunt, chewed-off nails.

She'd been so pale, too! White. Her freckles stuck out on her face like the chocolate sprinkles on the cupcakes Emily made her—

Emily.

A hole opened up beneath Daniel. Just her name threatened to knock him over the edge into a place as dark as the other cavern in his mind, only this was not a place of frightened darkness. It bubbled and boiled with ugly, raging blackness veined with white-hot betrayal. In some real-world place, his wife was...while her daughter, their little girl lay on a hospital bed fighting for her life, Emily was in bed, too. A different kind.

He lifted the cell phone in his hand and hit redial. Again. How many times? He could see the layers of fingerprint smudges on the shiny face of the phone, one on top of the other.

The sound again, as lonely as a cold, polar ocean. The hollow ring...ring...

"Hi, Dan." Emily's voice. "Turned my phone on and I see you've been calling me—something's wrong with the counter, though. It says fifty-four times." She sounded irritated. "What's up?"

~

Jack used his flashing lights and an occasional whoop of his siren to part the sea of humanity that stretched out for blocks in every direction around the school. Terrified parents. Eager rubber-neckers. Carrion-gorging media vans with satellite dishes on the top and bold Chanel 11 News First emblazoned with an NBC or CBS or CNN logos on the side.

He made it out of the throng. Made it through neighborhood streets where the sun shone so bright the world looked overexposed. Made it all the way to the on ramp of Interstate 71. But then he had to pull over.

Jack flung open the door of the cruiser and leaned out in time not to spew his breakfast all over the side panel. With a sound like a bad driver grinding a manual transmission, he splattered it on the gravel, instead. Then he leaned his head on his forearm on the door and let reflexive heaving take him, felt the hot tears—from the nausea? No, he didn't think so—stream down his face. It seemed to take a long time for the retching to stop, but Jack knew it was a time trick again, that he probably hadn't been there three minutes before he leaned back in his seat and slammed his door shut, instantly better once he couldn't smell the vomit.

But he didn't drive on right away. He sat with his breathing ragged and shuddery, tears still spilling down his cheeks—no, it hadn't been the nausea—and let the memory form in his head he was sure would haunt his every waking moment for the rest of his life.

His trained observation skills had been on autopilot at the time. Now they reported to him the information they'd collected. The little girl had been standing on something, a box of paper, perhaps, must have climbed up there to look out through a slit at the top of the metal door of the storage unit cabinet. She'd seen it all.

If she'd been on the floor, the upward trajectory of his shots might have missed her altogether. Or hit her in the head instead of the chest.

It was the first shot that got her. He was sure of it. He'd adjusted his aim left automatically when the force of the first bullet knocked the man sideways. It was the shot that took the shooter out, stopped the madman from butchering a roomful of children—that had passed through him into the child.

His mind's eye followed the path of the bullet, slow motion. He watched it leave the barrel of his rifle, fly like a leisurely bee toward the shooter, plow through the shooter's chest and continue through his body, out the other side and leisurely bee-fly through the air, through the door, into the little girl.

The pain of a headache he only now noticed cored into his left temple like an electric drill. He glanced at his watch and was stunned. It wasn't even noon yet! The ground felt different under his feet, the world had shifted, would never again revolve the same way around the sun—a change like that ought to take more than a couple of hours.

He wiped his eyes with his shirt sleeve and glanced into the side mirror on his cruiser to make sure his cheeks were dry. The man who looked back at him had a serious—no, stern—face, not much accustomed to smiles, and angular features he could bring to bear in a flinty stare so razor-edged it would cause internal bleeding. He had the flash of a childhood memory, then, a snippet. A white boy, Dano, had asked him once if black people got pale or sunburned.

He was pale now. He shook his head, took a deep breath and let it out slowly. Then he put the cruiser in gear and eased into the flow of traffic north on Interstate 71.

Harrison was already at the Sunoco, leaning against his car, smoking a cigarette, when Jack pulled up. He was a likeable guy who talked way too much, a big man who carried all his weight in a ponderous belly that hung out over his belt. Nobody'd been surprised when he took a medical leave for hernia surgery, and Jack couldn't imagine how he'd ever pass a physical to go back on active duty. But then, he'd been passing physicals somehow for going on twenty years.

When he got into the cruiser, Jack actually felt the vehicle tilt slightly in his direction.

"Good to see you, Jack. Told the major I'd be glad to help if he'd send a uniform. Not quite up to chasing a bad guy yet."

Jack merely nodded and turned the cruiser onto Lanyard Street.

"Hear you popped the shooter this morning," Harrison said, disappointment that he'd missed all the action evident in his voice. "Talked to the major a minute ago. Far as they can tell, there was only one and you took him out."

Jack caught the emphasis.

"Press got hold of the teacher's aide and she's saying you showed up like the Second Coming. You're a hero."

"The little girl, is she…?"

"I asked. Sorry, Jack. No news yet on her condition."

Jack changed the subject.

"You know an Ohio State Trooper named Purvis? Never met the man before this morning but I'd have him watch my back any day."

"Purvis? Yeah, I heard he…"

And Harrison was off to the races. Jack tuned him out, knew the big man would dribble the conversational ball the rest of the way down the court all by himself. When they rounded the curve onto Hurst Lane, both men shifted gears.

All the houses on the street were keep-up-with-the-Joneses huge, ensconced in wide, manicured lawns. But even in that setting, the dwelling at 3747 stood out. Gigantic bronze lions sat sentinel on either side of the driveway and the yard was littered with bird-baths, concrete gnomes, ponds, even a faux Venus de Milo statue beside a pool of goldfish and koi. Ostentatious on steroids.

Jack turned in the curved drive, pulled up to the porch,

and got out of the car, then stood behind the opened door as he studied the house. Harrison did the same. Jack checked the curtained windows for movement. All was still.

Drawing his pistol, he gripped it in both hands, pointed it toward the ground and did a quick Groucho walk from the car to a large azalea bush. From there he rushed the house, leapt up the porch steps and flattened himself against the front wall beside the door. Harrison hung back, watchful. Without moving in front of the door, Jack reached over and knocked on it.

"This is the police. Open the door."

A well-dressed, older woman flung the door wide— almost as if she'd been standing just inside waiting for his knock—and instantly began to babble, oblivious to Jack's drawn weapon and stance.

"You're here about Jacob, aren't you? I knew it. I told Mildred, I said 'Mildred, that boy's going to get himself in some kind of trouble.' And he has, hasn't he?"

Jack holstered his gun and Harrison joined him on the porch.

"He's…not right, you know," she continued. "Never has been. We found out when he was a teenager that he was bipolar. They didn't call it that then, but…he's harmless, wouldn't swat a fly…but different. At least he used to be."

She took a deep, trembling breath, and looked over her shoulder as if she expected the Bogey Man to jump out of a closet and grab her. "Then he changed, overnight he changed and became…mean, secretive, somebody I didn't even know." She leaned close and whispered urgently, "I'm sure he murdered Bentley."

Harrison stiffened. "Who's Bentley?"

"My precious Pomeranian. He was in the back yard

barking at Jacob's cat—Jacob adores his cat—and then suddenly he was quiet. I went to check on him and…"

Her hands began to tremble and so did her voice.

"Sweet Bentley was lying on the patio by the back door. And his…the vet said his neck was broken."

A picture formed in Jack's mind. A little girl with blonde hair was holding the bloody body of a dog. She was crying. Then the image vanished—poof!—and was gone.

"So Jacob doesn't live with you here?" Harrison asked.

"Oh, heavens no. After he…after what happened to Bentley, I changed all the locks on the house and he doesn't have a key. About a week ago, I was cleaning the attic and found a box of his stuff—Mama's keepsakes—old report cards, crayon drawings, things like that, and I was so afraid of him, I left it on his porch. The box is still sitting right where I left it. If he weren't my baby brother, I…he lives in an apartment below his…office…in the carriage house out back." She paused. "You know, the same thing happened when he was a boy. He suddenly became mean and ugly. For one whole summer, he—"

"Thank you for your time, Ma'am," Harrison corked the flow of her stream of words. "Other officers will come by later and they'll have more questions for you, but right now—"

"What's he done? The look in his eyes sometimes… what's he done?"

"You can discuss that with the other officers. I'm sure they'll be here soon to talk to you. If you'll excuse us, we want to see your brother's place."

"He's not home. I heard him drive away early this morning. He keeps the place all locked up, the curtains drawn. I guess because"—she looked embarrassed— "when you see it, you'll understand what I mean…that he's not right."

Something was definitely wrong with Emily's phone. As soon as she turned it on, it showed more than four dozen incoming calls—in only a couple of hours. All from Dan. But only one message, which she didn't listen to.

The last thing she wanted as she pulled reluctantly out of the parking lot of The River's Bend was to hear Dan's voice. She wanted to hold onto the moments for a little while longer. The fantasy-perfection of their time together was a silver light shining all around her. Not on her, from her. It was light Jeff had ignited in her that no other man ever had.

She didn't want the light to fade, and fade it would, as soon as she returned to the real world with traffic and shirts at the cleaners and Andi's orthodontist appointment. She wanted to hold onto the magic a little longer so she didn't pull out of the driveway of the inn right away. Sat for a few moments, feeling the touch of his hands on her skin, of his lips on hers. Feeling the fiery eruption of passion she'd never dreamed was within her.

She imagined she could smell his cologne, the scent of —his cologne! That sobered her. Surely, she was imagining it. She couldn't really smell it—could she? That's all she needed, to show up back home from her dentist appointment reeking of a man's cologne—not a brand that boring Dan would ever wear.

Had he actually been that boring, that predictable, that maddeningly colorless when they got married? If he had, why in the name of common sense had she gone through with the ceremony?

But she knew the answer to that. She hadn't been running to Dan, she'd been running from—

Bam! The sound of that door slamming shut in her mind seemed so loud she wondered if it had actually made an audible sound.

At the time, Dan hadn't seemed boring. He'd seemed safe. He was a minister, but not just any minister. He was young and bright, and maybe he'd even been fun at the time. Emily couldn't remember anymore. He was a star, he was…what was it they called him—he was "the package." Charming, charismatic, a dynamite preacher. He'd moved quickly up the ranks, hopped from one church to another, like crossing a creek on the stones until he'd finally grabbed the brass ring.

Voice of Hope Community Church, the biggest church in its denomination in the whole country. Teetering on the brink of mega-church-dom. And she liked being the preacher's wife associated with that. Liked the social standing, the respect and the deference—and the money and the big house.

Oh, Emily saw behind the curtain, all right. She knew the Great Oz was only pulling levers and pushing buttons and making lots of steam. She wasn't entirely convinced Dan saw it, though. Did he recognize the game he was playing?

Maybe. Maybe not. What did it matter?

She sighed. She should probably listen to Dan's message.

No, better to talk to him. She picked up her phone but before she had a chance to dial, it rang in her hand.

"Hi, Dan." She tried to sound cheery but didn't think she pulled it off well. "Turned my phone on and I see you've been calling me—something's wrong with the counter, though. It says fifty-four times. What's up?"

When he answered, the phone started acting up again, garbling his words. It sounded like he said Andi'd been shot.

"Dan, slow down. There's something wrong with my phone and you're breaking up. What did—?"

"I said Andi's been shot!" he screamed at her.

Emily couldn't catch her breath. A mistake. A joke. It had—

"There was a man with a gun at her school. Didn't you hear the sirens?"

She'd heard, but—

"And Andi was shot. Am I getting through to you, Emily? Do you understand what I'm saying? She's at Jefferson Memorial Hospital. Your daughter has been shot."

Emily didn't want to listen for fear of believing him, didn't want to hear the rest of what he was saying.

She cried out something, some word, made some noise, but the shrill sound of her own voice terrified her. A cold rock formed where her stomach had been a moment before and began to pull all her organs downward, twisting them, stretching them out of shape, filling them with hard cold and sharp edges.

She could hear someone screaming, a woman's voice, making a sound like an animal caught in a trap. She had no idea who it could be, who it could possibly be.

Chapter Eight

Jack and the detective made their way around to the back of the house to the two-story building in the corner of the yard snuggled up to a big oak tree behind a kidney-shaped swimming pool. Jack approached the building, gun drawn, as he had the main house. He scooted the cardboard box the woman had mentioned out of the way with his toe so he could flatten himself against the wall beside the door. No one answered his knock.

Then the men heard a sound from inside, a thump, and somebody, or something cried out. Jack instantly responded. That was probable cause to kick the door in.

Only in TV cop shows did officers slam their bodies into a door to break it down. Good way to dislocate a shoulder. Jack leaned back on one foot and smashed his other into the door beside the knob, and the jamb wood shattered. When the door flew inward, a cat leapt gracefully between Jack's legs, streaked across the back yard and was gone.

They stepped inside, both with guns drawn. It was

quickly clear the woman had not imposed her ponderous bad taste on her brother's living space. It was as austere as a monk's chamber. The few furnishings were modern—all chrome and glass and asymmetrical sharp angles. The art consisted of bare canvasses with splattered-paint designs that reminded Jack uncomfortably of the breakfast he'd left on the roadside this morning.

The officers systematically searched the downstairs of the building, room by room, every closet, under the bed, inside every cabinet. Nothing out of the ordinary. The bedroom smelled like an old sneaker, but that wasn't surprising. Jack had noticed the guy had a serious hygiene problem. Still, there was no hint that the man who lived here had gotten up this morning—didn't shower or shave, the shower was dry—then loaded his car with guns and chains and went to an elementary school to shoot children.

They mounted the stairs to the second floor. The door at the top of the steps opened into a single large room darkened by drawn drapes. Jack felt along the wall until he found the light switch. When he flipped it, the room was bathed in flickering florescent yellow from a lone tube bulb hanging by wires from the ceiling. It provided the kind of light that gave everything a sickly tint, made your face in a mirror look like you were dying of pancreatic cancer.

When Jack and Harrison surveyed the single room, they understood what Dumas's sister had meant by "not right." There was not a centimeter of wall space from the floor to the ceiling that wasn't covered with something, stuck to the bare wood with stickpins, layers and layers. Newspaper pages, mostly, though there were magazine pages, too, roadmaps, calendars from 2006 and 2009, nautical maps, floor plans, three-foot squares of yellowed butcher paper with diagrams and geometric shapes drawn on them, napkins, pages torn out of books, ribbons, catalogue pages showing guns and ammunition.

There were assembly instructions for God only knew what, spiral notebook pages ripped out so they still dangled tails of ragged holes, yard sale signs, black-and-white photos of things like park benches and lamp posts—not artsy shots with cool shadows and shading. Just a park bench, dead on. And every scrap of paper was dotted with red spots. Sets of two dots and three. Dots forming squares and triangles—looked like from a Sharpie, so many dots the walls looked like they had diaper rash.

There were strange symbols in blue Sharpie, too, shapes that looked to Jack like a lame attempt at hieroglyphics.

"Reckon that's Japanese? Chinese, maybe?" Harrison said, nodding toward the symbols.

"Don't think it's either," Jack said. Jack could read basic Japanese, courtesy of a short-lived fling with a Japanese girl in college during which he'd taken several language courses so he could write her love letters.

There were numbers and math problems, arrows connecting one unintelligible collection of gibberish to another. The layers of paper were an inch thick—maybe two in some places—looked like they'd feel spongy to the touch, though Jack knew better than to touch anything.

Pieces of cut-up newspapers, like streamers, hung from the ceiling and swayed gently in the breeze from the doorway. They, too, were marked with strange symbols in red and blue Sharpie ink.

Harrison whistled softly. "If I was one of the forensics boys, I'd take early retirement before I'd tackle this!"

As soon as Jack reported in what he and Detective Harrison had found—no other suspects and no firearms of any kind—he set about the task of securing the scene for the forensics team. They liked to be called CSI but Jack blew that off, wouldn't grant them the vanity of being the stars of their own TV show. While Harrison draped yellow-and-black Don't-Cross-This-Line tape from the oak tree to a bush on the other side of the house, Jack sealed the front door with a strip down the door and across the jamb so you could tell if it'd been tampered with, and a big X from the top of the door frame to the opposite corner on the porch floor, securely sealing in the fruits of Jacob Dumas's bull moose crazy.

As he knelt to stick the last piece of tape firmly to the bottom of the jamb, he glanced into the cardboard box Dumas's sister had set on the porch beside the door. It held an old Ohio State University yearbook, yellowed report cards bound together with a rubber band, a team picture, a cup emblazoned with a Cincinnati Reds logo, pens, pencils, a small rebel flag and other miscellaneous keepsakes.

Jack gave it all a cursory glance, started to stand, and then his eyes snapped back to one of the items in the box with the force of a man yanked upward by a fully-extended bungee cord. He stared at it in rapt attention, unaware that he was shaking his head slowly in surprise and wonder.

"Well, attention K-Mart shoppers..." he muttered softly.

He felt his arms pebble with gooseflesh and found that for a few moments he could only draw quick shallow breaths. Except for the sudden jarring of his pounding heart, he sat as frozen as Mount Rushmore. Just staring at it. He didn't touch it, of course. This was evidence. But he did slip his cell phone out of his pocket and take a picture of it.

Harrison was standing in the shade of the oak tree, smoking a cigarette and talking on his cell phone, and Jack went back to his cruiser to sit. That would be his job for the next—who knows how long?—until the forensics guys showed up or someone was dispatched to relieve him. Somebody had to make sure no one set foot in that house, and that nothing that could be evidence was tampered with. He was that somebody.

He scooted the seat back and leaned his head on the headrest, and as soon as he stopped moving, post-adrenaline-high exhaustion washed over him. The public attributed the brevity of most hostage situations to the skill of the negotiation team, and those guys were top notch. But they had human anatomy working for them, too. The body was not designed to remain in intense fight-or-flight mode for more than a few minutes. Adrenaline fatigue—not lack of sleep or exertion—was what hammered soldiers in combat.

He reached into his pocket and pulled out his cell phone, clicked on the last picture taken and sat looking at it, shaking his head in wonder.

~

Emily raced into the emergency room, her eyes wild, then saw Daniel and fell sobbing into his arms. When she did, a door somewhere in his soul slammed shut.

He couldn't hold onto both images of his wife at the same time, two different realities.

Emily—his best friend, his wife, his lover and Andi's mother.

And Emily committing adultery with Jeff Kendrick.

The two were mutually exclusive, and if he tried to embrace both of them at once, it would rip him apart at his core. So he put the unthinkable into a solid wood box, set it on a mental shelf in an empty room in his mind, then walked away and left it there, slammed the door behind him. Oh, sure, the corrosive evil inside that box would eat through the walls eventually. He knew that. One day, the reeking corruption would ooze out from under the door and begin to eat away at the rest of his mind. He'd deal with that when the time came.

Right now, he cradled his hysterical wife in his arms, smoothed her hair back out of her face and whispered, "shhh, Honey, shhh" as the two of them rocked back and forth.

She pulled back out of his arms and some part of him noted that her makeup hadn't smeared. How could she cry like that and still look so beautiful?

"Where is she, Dan? I want to see her." Her voice was garbled by her hiccupping sobs.

"You can't. They—"

"I'm her mother and I want to see my little girl!" Emily's eyes were wild, darting around like a frightened rabbit looking for some place to run. She was only barely holding onto her emotions enough to speak.

"You can't—"

"You make them let me see my baby! Dan, please, only for a minute, a few seconds, I—"

"She's in surgery, Em."

Emily sagged, like she might fall, but didn't.

"How long?"

"They didn't say. We have to wait."

Emily fell back into his arms, her sobbing less intense,

more mournful. Then she pulled away to look at him as if a thought had just occurred to her.

"Did you see her? Before they took her into surgery, did you—?"

"I was at the school and Ben, you know the Ben who… he's a paramedic and he let me ride in the helicopter—"

"How was she? Did you talk to her? What did she say?"

So much blood. He didn't look down but he knew if he did he would see it there—Andi's blood, maybe even still wet on his shoe.

"She was unconscious, but they only kept her in a treatment room for a little while, then wheeled her right into surgery, didn't…whatever's injured, they got to it quick." He knew that was lame, but it was all he could think to say.

He could feel Emily trembling—so small, petite and fragile, her whole body was vibrating beneath his hands. They were standing together in the doorway of the surgery waiting room. He could hear voices, a crowd, in the emergency room waiting area down the hall, see hospital security staff standing at the door between it and the hallway, keeping people inside.

His congregation, of course. In a church of almost twenty-five thousand, hundreds of people would come running as soon as they heard. He knew they were jammed together in that waiting room. He could picture them standing in small groups, holding hands and praying.

Daniel hadn't prayed. Hadn't even occurred to him to pray. An errant synapse fired a thought about a sermon he'd preached once on how prayer should be a first response, not a last resort.

Yes. He needed to pray. He should do that.

Emily was crying more softly now and he held her tighter. His mind was jammed with a thousand thoughts and as empty as a dusty sarcophagus. Then the double doors, the doors, the ones Andi had disappeared into—how long ago?—pushed outward and a man stepped through them. His mask dangled on his chest by the strings tied behind his neck. He spotted them immediately and crossed the hallway to them.

"Mr. and Mrs—" He spotted Daniel's clerical collar. "Reverend and Mrs. Burke? Miranda Burke's parents?"

Daniel didn't like the way he said that, something about the way he said that.

"Yes," Emily cried. "I'm her mother. How is she? When can we see her?"

"She's in the recovery room and I'll let you go back to see her in a few minutes..."

Daniel sensed a horrible, unthinkable but coming and the doors to a thousand fears flew open in his mind.

"But her condition...she's stable right now, though her injuries were extensive." Then he launched into unintelligible doctor-speak, using terms Daniel didn't understand, syllables strung together that somehow managed to sound like crackling flames.

"Speak English," Daniel cried. "Just tell us she's going to be all right."

"I'm afraid I can't do that, Reverend Burke. There was no way to repair the damage the bullet did. We did the best we could to stop the internal bleeding...temporarily. But your daughter's organs will start to fail soon—a few hours, maybe. She's in a coma and I don't expect she'll regain consciousness."

Someone said "...a few hours...?" Maybe it was Daniel.

"She won't live through the night. I'm sorry."

Emily stopped crying so abruptly it was like the sound

had suddenly been switched off a noisy television set. She gasped, or maybe Daniel did. He couldn't tell which. His knees felt boneless and rubbery.

"I'll take you back now so you can see her. We'll keep everyone away, give you some privacy…to tell your little girl goodbye."

Chapter Nine

Didn't nobody have to tell her. The knowing of it had been coming on her slowly and powerfully for a right smart while before Theresa saw Mary Waznuski's face and soon's she did, she knew for sure.

From her position behind the school, she and the children had listened to gunfire as crowds grew around them. The police had blocked off traffic somehow, but folks on foot was streaming down the street, far as they could go before officers forced them back. They was all kind of people, some merely folks driving by the barricades got out to see what was going on, folks lived near the school, frantic parents, grandparents, relatives. News travels fast in a town the size of Harrelton.

There was this one lady in particular, only a gawker, you could tell, and she was going on and on about how she'd heard they was a hundred kids dead, bodies laying everywhere, and was about to expound on what all them bodies looked like before Theresa elbowed her in the ribs.

"You'll want to hush up about all that stuff now," she said, using her chin to point out the wide-eyed tribe of children she'd gathered up at the crossing. "No need you scarin' them kids more'n they already is."

But there was nothing to be done about the sincere parents, terrified and hysterical. They was gone do whatever they was gone do and wasn't no good trying to keep them from upsetting the small tribe of children bunched up around her.

When the tall blond boy come back, he climbed a tree next to them and provided a blow-by-blow of the flurry of activity outside the third window from the end in the north hallway—that'd be Miss Lund's room, but Theresa didn't tell the children that for fear they knew somebody personal who was in that class.

The mama of the little red-haired girl who'd tried to lead an insurrection against the crossing guard an hour— a lifetime?—ago come running, looking wild-eyed and crazy, didn't even see the youngster 'til she yelled, "Mommy!"

Then that poor woman fell all over the child, hugging her and kissing her, then holding her out so she could look in her face 'fore she crushed her back against her chest again. Didn't none of Theresa's tribe of children get unmanageable upset 'til then. Seein' that put them in mind of their own parents, probably somewhere in the crowds encircling the school, looking for them, scared as this lady. And suddenly they realized how much they wanted they mommies and daddies, too, to hug them like this little girl's mother and be tearfully grateful they wasn't lying shot in the school.

They become a handful then, all wantin' to go find their parents, the shock beginning to wear off so the scared could start leaking out of they little bodies in tears and hysterics. She held onto them all, though, 'til they started letting the other children out of the school building. Then she drew herself up tall in her crossing guard uniform and made her way through the crowd so she could set these younguns free with the others.

Police let her bring the children to the ever-growing crowd of escapees from the school and hand them off to teachers and officers who could match them up with their parents waiting wild-eyed in the crowd.

That's when Theresa seen Mary Waznuski, the teacher's aide from Miss Lund's room. They was trying to rush her off to an ambulance, but the reporters were on her like sticky on taffy, shoving microphones in her face. She stood her ground then, make them quit shoving her toward the ambulance so's she could tell the press what a hero that police officer was who come diving into the room and killed that monster right as he was about to start shooting children.

"He wasn't the only hero, though," she said. "If it hadn't been—"

Then she seen Theresa and stopped. Didn't say nothing else, merely looked at her. Seemed like she was about to cry, but Theresa couldn't tell for sure with the world suddenly swimming in her own tears.

Theresa turned and walked away through the frantic/relieved/sobbing crowd, wasn't going anywhere in particular 'cause there wasn't nowhere to go. Found herself sitting on the merry-go-round, kind of swayin' it back and forth.

He was gone then. Bishop was dead. He'd been in one of the two black bags they'd hauled out of the building on stretchers. She didn't have to hear Mary Waznuski say it to know he'd died for them kids, give his life for 'em. And that was good, real good.

'Cept her Bishop was gone.

She put her face in her hands and tried to cry, like you want to throw up when you's nauseated cause even though that's awful, it feels better for a little while after. Gives you some relief. But Theresa's hurt was too big right now to 'low her solace as simple and freeing as tears.

Some folks found her there later, the principal, Mrs. Maxwell, and a real kind policeman named Crocker. But she'd done crawled down inside herself by then, like a old, sick dog goes to find somewhere warm and quiet all by hisself to get well. Or to die.

~

Jack wasn't at all sure what he was doing here. Maybe he shouldn't have come. No, strike that, he definitely shouldn't have come. He ought to go home.

He sat for a few more moments where he'd parked his cruiser in the lot of Jefferson Memorial Hospital. Then resolutely got out and walked toward the emergency entrance.

Fifty or sixty people were milling around, talking quietly among themselves outside the emergency room door and he soon realized that was because they couldn't get into the building. The hallway beyond the door was packed, and so, presumably, was the emergency room waiting area which would be as far as any of these people would be allowed to go.

The little girl's father was a minister. That's what the captain had told him when Jack returned to the station after he handed off the shooter's carriage-house residence to the forensics team. Said he was the pastor of that huge church on Market Street, the Hopeful Voice Church, or something like that. From the street, the building looked more like a sports arena than a church.

Most of his fellow officers were still at the school, probably would be for the rest of the night, keeping it cordoned off while the guys from the Bureau of Alcohol, Tobacco and Firearms went over it with magnifying glasses and tweezers. Jack was glad of that, didn't want to make a scene putting his shield and gun on the major's desk. He tried to get out of the building as fast as he could, but it wasn't fast enough to avoid the sympathetic looks of the two secretaries, or the dispatcher's murmured, "Sorry, Jack. It wasn't your fault." Of course, it was his fault. He pulled the trigger. He shot a kid!

Neither of the secretaries knew the child's condition, said it hadn't been released yet.

And he also wasn't fast enough to avoid some huge, white news van that looked like a sperm whale in a fish tank sitting in the small parking lot beside the station. They were on him the second he stepped outside and was recognized, but he plowed through them, tossing out, "you need to direct that question to the captain," and "I'm not allowed to talk about that now," and "I can't comment on an ongoing investigation," like scattering feed to chickens as he made his way to his cruiser.

Mary Waznuski had made him a hero. He wouldn't be one long, though, when the press found out that it was he —not the wild-eyed lunatic—who had shot the little girl. You shoot a civilian, let alone a child, and the press ate you alive. Cost of doing business. But the captain had not released that tidbit of information in his brief statement, and wouldn't until ballistics confirmed that the bullet in the little girl had come from Jack's gun.

The crowd in the hospital corridor parted for Jack like he was Moses with a staff as he made his way toward the emergency room door. He heard murmured "That's him," and "he's the one who shot the guy," but these people were too polite to fawn on him. He was sure nobody noticed he wore no badge on his uniform and carried no weapon. He made his way down the hallway the same way, with the sea of people parting in front of him.

When he reached the hospital security guards, they assumed he was there on official business and let him through wordlessly. He approached the nurse's desk and had already decided he'd throw his official weight around if he had to in order to find out what he wanted to know.

"I'm Harrelton Police Sergeant Jack Carpenter and I'm here to check on the condition of Miranda Burke, the child who—"

"I'm sorry, but I'm not allowed to give out that information."

Jack drew himself up to his full six feet four inches and spoke in a quiet, controlled voice. "Ma'am. That wasn't a request. I'm investigating a school shooting. I'd like to speak to your supervisor."

That rattled her.

"There's another nurse's station in the surgery wing where they operated on her," she said, and pointed down the hallway to the left. "I'm not sure what they can tell you either, but..."

...but she was happy to pass the buck off to somebody else.

Jack went down the hallway the direction she pointed, then turned down another hall. And another. In minutes, he was hopelessly lost in the rabbit warren of hospital corridors. Personnel, doctors, orderlies hurried past him. Given directions by an orderly that sent him to the boiler room and a candy striper that sent him to the cafeteria, he reached out and grabbed the next person who passed, a lab technician obviously late for something vitally important, like everybody else in the hall seemed to be.

"I'm here about Miranda Burke, the little girl who was shot," he said, "and I need you to take me to someone who can tell me her condition."

"Your best bet'd be somebody in surgery." The young man pointed to double doors that opened off the end of the hallway below a sign: Recovery Room. "If anybody can tell you anything, it'd be them."

Jack pushed on one of the double doors and stepped into a quiet hallway. Unlike the busy thoroughfare behind him, it was deserted, but he could hear voices from a room on the right. There was no door on the room, only a separating curtain, and it was pulled back. He walked quietly to the doorway and saw a couple inside, talking to a child, a little girl lying on a bed, hooked up to monitors and IV lines. Then he saw the man's clerical collar. These were the Burkes. And Miranda.

He knew then he had to say something. He had to tell them he was sorry.

~

Daniel stood on one side of the bed holding Andi's left hand, Emily on the other side held her right. His eyes gobbled the child whole, looked at her with such intensity the very force of his gaze alone would keep her here, would not let her slip away from them. But he could hear the monitors, the beeps slower and slower.

NO!

Emily was singing her a lullaby, stroking her hair back out of her face, kissing her cheek every few words, but Daniel couldn't force a sound out his parched throat. Images of the child flew through his mind in a whirlwind, too fast to really see any of them, like trying to examine the details of a single bird when a whole flock of them suddenly takes flight. In her pink newborn cap. Her hands buried up to the elbows in her first birthday cake. Snow angels. The warmth of her in his arms when he read her a bedtime story. The smell of her shampooed hair. The soft wetness of her kisses.

This was NOT happening. It couldn't be happening.

God, where are you? You stop this! Stop it right now. Fix it! Please, oh God, please don't let her die.

The prayer hit the ceiling above his head with a poof sound, and disintegrated like a snowball hitting a wall.

He stifled a sob, lifted his head to get a breath, and saw a police officer standing in the doorway. The image barely registered on his consciousness and he looked back down at Andi.

"Excuse me, Reverend Burke," the officer said. "I didn't mean to intrude, I didn't know you were…"

Emily had her back to him and didn't even lift her head when she heard his voice.

"Go away and leave us alone," she said. It was only a whisper, though, and Daniel knew she couldn't find any breath either. It was like there was a huge hole below his chest and his whole midsection was gone. The wind blowing through it wailed mournfully.

The officer instantly began to back out of the room.

"I only wanted to say," he said as his back hit the door. "I didn't mean to…if I'd known she was in the line of fire, I never would have pulled the trigger. I'm…I'm sorry."

Daniel felt like he'd been hit by a freight train. The officer came in and out of focus with the pounding of his heart.

"You…?" Daniel's voice sounded strange to his own ears. "Are you saying you…?"

The officer froze, his eyes huge.

"You didn't…?" he began.

Emily lifted her head and turned then. Daniel had never seen a look like that on her face. He'd never looked at his wife that he didn't think she was beautiful, but at that moment her face was as contorted and ugly as a witch.

"You killed my baby?" Her voice was only a whisper, but so intense it bounced off the walls like a shriek in a cathedral.

The officer seemed to be having trouble forming words, too.

"I didn't know Miranda was—"

Emily snapped then, the dam holding back her hysteria let go, and the flood of raw emotion washed out all the stops. She dropped Andi's hand and rushed at the officer, grabbed his arm, and began dragging him across the room.

"No," she screamed, and there was volume to it this time. "No, she is NOT Miranda." She shoved him in front of her toward the bed. "That's not who my little girl is, do you hear me? She's Andi. Andi!" She forced him to lean over the bedside toward the little girl lying there so still. "Say it. Say her name!"

In the breathless stillness that followed, Daniel could hear the monitor that had been beeping slower and slower. It beeped…it beeped…then the beep became a single, long buzzing sound. Daniel looked at the monitor and saw not mountains and valleys anymore but a single, flat green line.

Emily sucked in a horrified gasp. Daniel could not breathe at all as the buzzing sound cored into his soul.

The police officer spoke into the silence, his voice soft, gentle, a whisper on a breath. A single word: "Andi."

The monitor began to beep again. Not the languid, turgid ever-slowing rhythm from before, but crisply, briskly. Beep. Beep. Beep. Beep.

Daniel shot a glance at the black screen above the bed and saw the flat green line begin to form a jagged mountain range. Then a valley. Then more mountains. Up and down, uniformly in rhythm with the steady, beep, beep, beep sound.

He looked at Andi. She'd been so white. Now, color was returning to her face. Her icy hand seemed warmer. This was crazy. This couldn't be happening. Had he passed out? Had he died?

Then he saw movement in the little face. Andi's eyelids fluttered once, twice, and she opened her eyes. The beautiful bright blue eyes were clear and alert.

She looked up into the face of the police officer who was still bent over her bed, and she smiled.

"Mr. Jack!" she said.

Suddenly, the room was full of doctors and nurses. They merely appeared, like they had sprouted out of the floor, summoned, he was sure, by what they must have seen on their monitors, too.

A doctor shoved Emily and the police officer roughly out of his way and leaned over Andi, his stethoscope hopping from one spot to another on her chest.

A nurse spoke authoritatively, "I'm sorry, but you'll all have to leave now." And she began shooing the three adults out of the room.

"But..." was all Emily was able to sputter before the tank of a nurse shoved her away from the bed.

"You must go. You don't want to get in the way, do you? You have to leave and let us do our jobs."

Another nurse took Daniel's arm and the snowplow effect of both nurses began to shove them to the door.

Above the sudden hubbub, Daniel could hear Andi's voice—clear and firm.

"I heard you, Mr. Jack. I heard you call me."

Then they were out in the hallway, the three of them together and the doors swung shut behind them.

Chapter Ten

Jack, the minister, and his wife stood motionless where they were, like action figures some child had set in place, facing the closed double doors. There were sounds of activity on the other side of the doors. Voices. The swish of hurrying feet. But the sounds didn't seem frantic or desperate.

Jack took a step back, his heart knocking in his chest like the fist of a lunatic on a padded door. He drew in a deep breath, then another, trying to knit back together the raveled fabric of his composure.

"What just happened?" he asked, surprised his voice was level.

The others turned to look at him. The minister wore the dazed expression of one who has watched an avalanche thunder past, sweeping away the people right in front of him.

But there was something else, something about the man's face… An image—summertime, a baseball game— flashed into Jack's mind. But it was gone so quickly he barely caught sight of it before it vanished.

"It was a miracle," said the minister's wife.

Jack's mind backed up from that thought so completely he had a momentary feeling of overbalance, like he was running backward and had lost his footing. It was clear both the minister and his wife were in shock because the minister mumbled, "There's no such thing as miracles."

"Well, something happened," Jack said.

Yep, something that couldn't possibly have happened. But it did. Jack didn't have anywhere in his mind to put a thing like that. Oh, he didn't believe the universe operated with the precision of a pocket watch. You could sentence yourself to a long-term stay in the Funny Farm by insisting everything in life made logical, rational sense, that it followed a this-because-that logic. Occasionally, you had to accept the unexplainable. And Jack was down with that. But this was so far the other side of unexplainable you couldn't have found it on Google Earth.

How could that child possibly have known his name?

He shook his head, literally tried to shake the fragmented pieces of the past five minutes into some essential, fundamental order. Obviously, the little girl had just—spectacularly—regained consciousness after her surgery. That's what had happened—right?

The woman turned to her husband, joy and wonder on her face. "She's alive, Dan. Andi's alive!"

She was crying as she said it, though she probably didn't know she was. The minister reached out and took her into his arms, patted her back and Jack suddenly felt like he was an intruder on an intimate moment and wished he could disappear. But there were things he had to know, had to understand.

"So…she just now woke up?" he asked tentatively. "After her surgery, the anesthesia wore off and…"

The minister said no, she wasn't coming to, she was dying, had been given only hours to live. He said the monitors had shown her heart rate sinking and sinking…and then it stopped.

Jack felt himself beginning to unravel again.

"The doctor said to 'go tell your little girl goodbye,'" he said, "that her wound was…"

Wound. That sobered all three of them.

"What did you mean in there?" The woman's voice was tear-clotted. "When you said she was in the line of fire? Did you mean—?"

"I fired on the shooter, killed him. And we thought none of the children had been hurt. Nobody knew Mir… Andi had hidden in the supply closet when the shooting started. It was behind the shooter. One of my rounds passed through his body and the closet door and hit your little girl."

"Then it wasn't your fault," she said.

Jack was getting real tired of hearing it wasn't his fault! He felt more strands loosen in the fabric of his composure.

"It was my fault. I shot your little girl. I could have killed her."

"You didn't kill her; you saved her," she said.

Jack had come to believe a long time ago that the only two absolute necessities to sustain life were air and illusions. Obviously, this woman needed to believe—

How did the child know my name?

—that something happened in there…

Something did happen in there. What?

"Ma'am, I—" Jack began.

"Emily. Officer"—she read his name off the nameplate on his uniform— "Carpenter, I'm Emily. And this is my husband, Dan."

This was surreal, shaking hands all around like they'd just met at a dinner party or a wedding reception. Jack started to speak again, but before he had a chance, the door to the room they'd been thrown out of opened and one of the doctors appeared. Jack was certain the look on his own face mirrored the one on the doctor's.

In the room behind the doctor, Jack could hear the little girl's voice, chattering and giggling.

That was it. Jack was done.

"I'm sorry, I'm on duty," he said. "I have to go."

He turned as precisely as a Marine in a dress parade and headed down the hallway, wishing he'd left a trail of breadcrumbs to lead him through the labyrinth of corridors and out to his cruiser. Eventually, he found an exit. He was about to put the key in the ignition of his cruiser when it hit him.

Dan Burke. Daniel. Daniel Burke! No, it couldn't possibly be…

Like a man in a trance, he reached into his pocket and pulled out his cell phone. He touched the icon that looked like a camera and the last picture he had taken filled the screen. He studied it for a moment, then felt his breathing constrict, like his Kevlar vest was suddenly two sizes too small. He wasn't much of a drinker, but at that moment he didn't just want a drink, he needed a drink. A drink strong enough to dissolve the swizzle stick.

~

As Theresa crossed the parking lot, the first fat drops of rain splattered on the asphalt beside her. Daylight was fading. Distant thunder rumbled with the sound of heavy work boots on carpeted stairs. Soon the coming storm would wash darkness down the day.

Theresa's steps were slow and ponderous. Carrying a

heavy weight like she was, wouldn't have been surprising if she couldn't move at all. The sky mirrored her pain, gray and brooding. But out west, the storm clouds was the purple of a day-old bruise—this was gonna be a gully-washer for sure, and her without an umbrella. Didn't think of it what with everybody fluttering around her like a flock of twittering birds, bringing enough food to the house to feed every blond man in the Norwegian army, and all Theresa wanted was to be left alone. 'Cept she didn't want to be alone, neither. Soon's everybody finally left last night, she'd wandered from one room in their small house to another, and the presence of Bishop's absence was everywhere she looked.

Probably wasn't no lonelier act in all life's journeys than picking out a casket.

Well, maybe not picking out a casket—because you didn't have no body to bury—maybe that was worse. But that time Bishop'd been there to hold her as she gave herself up to grief. Not this time. They was gonna put Bishop in the ground tomorrow, gonna shovel dirt in so it made that awful crunching sound when it hit the top of that metal box and slid down the sides, down in a dark hole in the ground where wasn't never no light or sun or birdsongs.

Theresa bowed her head.

Thank you, Jesus that he ain't gone be in that dark hole tomorrow, that right now they's more sunlight and sweet smells and birds singing than all his old senses can take in at once.

She let out a sigh with a half sob tangled on the end of it.

But Lord, I'm still here, and the hurt in my heart is near more'n I can bear.

First thing in the morning, all their friends and relatives was gonna get in them black cars with they little purple "Funeral" flags on the radio antennas and drive behind that hearse the long road back to the little cemetery in the woods so's Bishop could be buried beside his parents. There was space there for her, too, one day. And space where there'd ought to be another grave, but wasn't, an empty expanse of dirt—but maybe not. Maybe. These last few years, though, the flame of hope for Isaac had burned down lower every year 'til it wasn't no brighter than a birthday candle.

Most every minute since that police officer came up to her sitting on the merry-go-round on the school playground and confirmed what her heart had already told her hours before, she'd felt so close to tears she hardly breathed, didn't dare try to talk because making any sound at all would set the pain free, and some part of her feared if she did that, if she let go of all the pain inside her, the power of the grief would overwhelm her and she'd cry and cry and cry until she couldn't breathe at all. That she'd grieve herself to death.

'Course, another part of her was sure it was holdin' onto the grief that was gonna kill her, that it would get bigger and bigger, swell all up inside her 'til she popped like an over-inflated balloon.

She didn't say none of that to the folks hovering over her, friends and church folks, because a lot of them was real "holy," thought you hadn't ought to mourn 'cause he was "in a better place." Shoot, she wasn't grieving for the place Bishop was; she was grieving for the place he wasn't. He would have understood. Bishop understood everything.

Miss Minnie and Mr. Gerald got that part. Old and frail as they was, they figured to go out of this world side by side. They'd been married seventy-three years, and she'd looked after them for ten of them years—five as a hired caretaker, and the next five just 'cause she loved those old folks and they children had up and abandoned them. When they'd showed up with a pineapple upside-down cake still warm from the oven last night, Miss Minnie'd took Theresa's hand and squeezed it hard, them rheumy blue eyes of hers all brimmed up with tears. She understood. Theresa was certain that soon's either one of the two of them stopped breathing, the other one would, too. Why wouldn't God let it be like that for her and Bishop, too?

Theresa'd took it long as she could, but she finally had to run off from them people. But getting away from good, caring people was a sight easier than dodging the self-serving ones. She'd no sooner set foot outside her house than this reporter shoved a microphone in her face and asked her how she felt about her husband giving his life for those children. And she wanted to tell him, "What you think it feels like, fool? It feels like he's a good man who's brave and sacrificing, and also dead."

Only place she could think to go, only place she wanted to go, was to see her sweet Andi. Even as bad as she felt, a small smile warmed Theresa's face at the thought of the child. She'd always been special, that one had. Theresa'd mentioned it to Bishop once, trying to puzzle out what it was about the little girl that had set her apart from all the other seven-year-olds the year Theresa'd been a teacher's aide in her second grade class. He'd said if they was people in the world who was naturally bad—not possessed, just bad human beings—then the reverse was true, too, and Andi was one of them.

Folks was saying there'd been a miracle, that Andi had come back just as she stepped over into Glory. Theresa wondered what an experience like that would do to a little girl.

And besides, it was probably time. She and Bishop had talked about it on and off ever since the first Sunday they seen the Reverend Daniel Burke preaching on television, standing tall behind a see-through pulpit in the sanctuary of that enormous Voice of Hope Community Church on Market Street. That boy was using language so beautiful it'd take your breath away, but wasn't no power at all in anything come out of his mouth.

And him so puffed up he even brought his own church bell with him from Chicago. They said his church there had burned, wasn't nothing left of it but the bell. Still, to bring the thing all the way to Ohio—and it didn't even fit! They'd took off the top of the belfry, lifted the bell as big as a Volkswagen up with a crane—folks stopped they cars on the side of the road to watch. And then they'd realized the bell was too big! You'd think somebody'd have took the time to measure, Bishop had said when they'd watched clips of it on the local news. Guess they was too proud to admit they'd screwed up, though, because they put the thing in anyway. You couldn't tell it was too big until it rang. Then the bell stuck out five feet beyond the belfry— first on one side, then the other—bong, bong, bong. Bishop got a big kick out of that.

But mostly they didn't smile about Daniel and his new church. They talked about what they ought to tell him. And not tell him. But they hadn't made no decision. Now, Bishop was gone and she was going to have to do it alone —the first of all the hard things for the rest of her life she would have to do without him.

She stopped in the hospital gift shop and bought an overpriced stuffed monkey and rode up in the elevator with a young man who was so covered up with tattoos he didn't have no unmarked skin to speak of on any body part she could see. She wondered how much he was gonna like them tattoos in fifty years when you couldn't see no design a'tall on his wrinkled skin. But kids was gone do whatever they was gone do.

Bishop had got hisself a tattoo after he come home from Vietnam. On the top of his hand—so it was right there in front of him all the time: 1 John 4:4. Whenever he'd get that haunted look in his eye, remembering the awful thing that happened to him over there, she'd hear him mumbling the words under his breath, probably didn't even know he was talking out loud: He who is in me is greater than he who is in the world. Over and over again. Even old as he was, she could still see that tattoo clear when he'd reach up at night and turn off the bedside lamp. His voice would come out of the darkness then, saying the same thing he'd said ever night of their sixty-year marriage. "You need anything in the middle of the night, elbow me in the ribs and say, 'Hey, bub, wake up.'"

He hadn't been there to elbow last night; wouldn't never be there again.

Wasn't hard to tell which room was Andi's, all broke out with balloons and streamers like it was. The door was standing open and Theresa walked in, saw there wasn't nobody in the bed, but there was so many stuffed animals and toys on it wasn't no way a little girl could fit in there, anyway. Theresa should have kept her twenty dollars and left that stupid monkey in the gift shop. The room was empty except for the Reverend Burke, sitting in a chair by the window. When he saw her, he got to his feet and came to take her hand, all solicitous like.

"Theresa, isn't it? Theresa Washington? Andi's downstairs getting another X-ray, to confirm the one they took this morning, but she and Emily'll be back up here soon. Please, sit down."

As she sat, he said, "We met once when I came to pick up Andi from school, practically had to pry her out of your lap."

He had a good smile, showed lots of teeth and they was all straight. Voice was…modulated. Yes sir, he was smooth, slick as Teflon.

She could almost hear Bishop clear his throat the way he always done as a warning like, that maybe she'd ought to think about what she was about to say 'stead of just blurtin' it out. And maybe there wasn't no need to go where she was about to go. But for the life of her she couldn't think of any reason not to, either.

"You probably don't remember me, but—"

"Oh, I remember you for a fact," Theresa said. "A right smart better than you remember me. I remember when you didn't have your collar turned around backwards, 'fore you was a big, important man of God."

The old black woman had appeared during the first break in the non-stop parade of visitors who'd been streaming through Andi's room all morning—mostly elders, deacons and church staff. There'd have been a hundred times as many people if Daniel hadn't sent out an appeal—in an email blast and posts on the church's website and Facebook page—asking the twenty-five-thousand member congregation not to visit, to "give my family some time and space to heal."

He didn't know what to make of the old woman. What did she mean she knew him better than he knew her?

Chocolate-chip cookies.

The aroma of hot cookies was suddenly so strong he was momentarily disoriented—was he actually smelling them, or merely remembering what they smelled like? He imagined he felt a blast of heat on his face, and the scent of the cookies on the cookie sheet coming out of the oven made his mouth water.

The memory was so powerful, so real—and then it was gone. Poof. And all he could smell was the cloying aroma of the bouquets of flowers in vases all over the room. Why in the world had he thought about…?

He shook it off and concentrated on the old woman. She was a big woman, had been pretty once, maybe even beautiful. Now, her face was a delicate meshwork of lines and wrinkles, like she'd been made out of black tissue paper that'd been crumpled, then carefully smoothed out again. There was something in her manner that gave him an uneasy feeling, though, as if she were…what? Reproachful.

He reached out and took her hand and said as kindly as he knew how.

"I've been praying for you, Mrs. Washington. Your husband's in a better place now."

She didn't let go of his hand, just gave him a look that felt like a slap.

"No, you haven't," she said as matter-of-fact as "pass the salt." "And you don't believe a word you just said."

The intensity in her black eyes was sharp enough to peel an onion layer by layer all the way to the pearl.

Daniel was so surprised he was speechless.

"When was the last time you prayed?"

The challenge in those words sent Daniel's mind

reeling back to the agony of dialing and redialing and redialing Emily's phone—he'd prayed then. And when Andi was—he'd prayed then!

He had, hadn't he?

"You ain't been praying for me, or for yourself, or your wife, or your little girl. Or for that big congregation of yours shows up every Sunday for you to impress with your fancy words—and you don't b'lieve none of what you're telling them. You don't b'lieve my Bishop's in a better place, neither. He is, but you don't believe that."

"I beg your pardon…"

"You need to be begging God's pardon, son, not mine. You done traded in real faith for 'religion' from the Dollar General Store—the kind that don't cost nothing and ain't worth nothin'. You's just skatin' around on the shiny outside of believing, gliding along, barely even touching the surface."

Daniel stared at her. It was even possible his jaw had dropped open.

"You wasn't always that way, though." she continued and her tone softened. "It was real once." She sighed. "But now you've whittled out an image of yourself for everybody to look at that ain't who you are at all, sticks out phony as a dog in a duck parade. You think God don't know that? "

Daniel had no idea how to respond. Gratefully, he was spared having to by Andi's squeal.

"Miss Theresa!"

To the great dismay of the nurse pushing her wheelchair, Andi hopped out of it and started toward Theresa. The nurse put a restraining hand on Andi's shoulder, but nobody could resist Andi's dimpled pleeeease smile, and as soon as the nurse relented, Andi raced to the big woman and threw herself into her arms.

"How you doin', Sugar?" The old woman's face was wreathed in a smile as tender as a new mother seeing her baby for the first time. "You lookin' fine, sweet thing, mighty fine."

"I didn't see you at school, and after what happened I was afraid…" Andi's voice trailed off.

Daniel definitely wasn't going to allow the conversation to go there.

"Up into the bed you go, sweetheart," Daniel peeled Andi out of Theresa's arms and set her on the bed.

"I don't want to go to bed," she said. "I'm not sick. I don't have a fever. I want—"

She was looking over Daniel's shoulder. Her eyes widened and a smile planted the deep-dish dimples back in her cheeks.

"Mr. Jack!" she cried. "Look, Daddy, Mr. Jack's here."

Chapter Eleven

As soon as Jack stepped through the hospital room doorway, he noticed an old woman sitting at the foot of the bed, holding a stuffed monkey just like the one he'd bought in the gift shop downstairs before he came up. When she turned toward him, she must have noticed his monkey, too, because she looked startled, and her eyes widened in surprise.

A sudden flash of memory blew through his mind so intense it took over reality, became reality. Not an image this time, though. Music. The Blue Danube Waltz, played in the hinky-tinky notes of a music box. It flooded his brain, filled his whole head up until there was room for nothing else. Then it was gone. It didn't fade away; it vanished as if somebody had switched off a radio.

Jack felt like he'd collided with an invisible wall—no, had been swatted by an invisible fly swatter. It took him a moment to refocus on the world outside his mind and when he did, he noticed that apparently he and the old woman weren't the only ones who'd decided it'd be a plan to buy the little girl a stuffed animal. There was barely room for the child in the bed piled high with all manner of fluffy creatures, a herd of teddy bears, several ducks, rabbits—even a large black-and-white something that was either Shamu the Whale or a stuffed maître d'.

Andi sat in the middle of them, beaming at him.

The little girl was fine. You didn't need a medical degree to see that. But, of course she couldn't be. He had felt her warm blood soaking into his shirt when he carried her to the window, had seen her pasty-pale face on the bed in the recovery room, had heard the heart monitor stop beeping, watched the green line flatten.

Now, the child appeared to be in better physical condition than he was. He hoped he didn't look as bad as he felt —courtesy of a lost night of sleep and hours of pacing, his feet following his mind as it chased thoughts down wandering rabbit trails, meandering tunnels that started nowhere, ended nowhere and went nowhere in between.

He'd found no answers in those dark holes, or in the daylight hours since, and had finally been compelled to come here looking for them. Oh, he'd been able to come up with a plausible explanation to solve one mystery, a lone straw, but he clung to it with the fierceness of a man who'd spent hours grasping at them. It wasn't something "supernatural" that the little girl knew his name. Unconscious people often heard things nobody knew they heard—didn't they? Somebody—Purvis maybe, yeah, had to have been Purvis—had said Jack's name, or perhaps one of the officers had when she'd been wheeled through the cordon of them to the waiting helicopter. She'd heard it somewhere and remembered.

Even that felt hollow, though. And the rest of it—the buzzing sound of the flat, green line—had echoed in his head all night long. Still echoed there now, a serpent of sound with its fangs buried so deep in his skull he feared he would hear that sound every waking moment for the rest of his life.

He'd come here seeking answers, but now he stood in the door as awkward as a hippo on a hamster wheel.

Thunder rumbled in the distance. Gusts of wind quarreled with the treetops he could see out the window. A storm was coming.

"Come in, Jack, and have a seat," Daniel said. Daniel Burke. Yes, indeed, a storm was definitely coming.

He stepped into the room before the moment could draw out, went to the old woman and lifted from her lap the soon-to-be-sold-out gift-shop monkey that matched the one he carried. He held the two of them out to Andi.

"Twins separated at birth," he said. "Frick and Frack. Put one on each shoulder when you go to sleep at night and they'll whisper bedtime stories into your ears."

Andi giggled. Her dimples were so deep you could eat pudding out of them. "Thank you Mr. Jack and Miss Theresa," she said, and gathered the monkeys to her chest in a tight hug. "These are my very favorite stuffed animals ever."

Jack was certain the child had said the same thing about each of the animals in the menagerie on her bed. And had meant it every time she said it. He liked her for that.

"How you doin', Jack?" the old woman said, in the familiar way of old friends who haven't seen each other in years.

Suddenly, he smelled chocolate chip cookies. The smell was so strong he actually looked around, as if he expected to see a piping hot plate of them sitting on the bedside table. He noticed Daniel was looking around, too, but he had his head cocked the way you do when you're trying to determine the direction of a sound.

The smell was gone as quickly as it had come, but its departure left Jack shaken.

What was up with the 3-D memory blasts?

"I'm sorry, but do we know each other?" he asked.

"This is Theresa Washington," Emily said. "Her husband—"

"Mrs. Washington, I am so sorry for your loss," Jack said. "Your husband was a brave man."

"Braver than you know. The rest of you didn't know what you's fighting. He understood what he was up against."

Jack had no idea what she meant by that, but he wanted her to understand her husband hadn't been a random victim, that he had given his life to save the children.

"He spotted me in the hallway and had the presence of mind to gather all the children in one place, out of the line of fire." He couldn't help darting a glance at Andi, who was happily playing with the twin monkeys. "He showed me where the shooter was."

"Mary Waznuski told me about that. She come over last night, said she didn't think to tell the police about the desk, though, how that man tossed one across the room with one hand like it didn't weigh nothing at all."

"The shooter threw a desk?"

"Right before he shot Miss Lund. Bishop started talking real loud after that and Mary said she didn't figure out until after you come running into the room why that was."

"I heard him clearly. He said…" Jack's voice trailed off. He hadn't thought about it until this moment, the last thing he'd heard the janitor say to the shooter.

"Said what?" Theresa asked. Her eyes narrowed. "He

was talking to that bad man and he said something didn't make no sense to you a'tall, didn't he?"

Jack was so surprised he blurted it out.

"He said, 'you're not going to find out what you came here to find out,'" Jack said.

The old woman looked startled and something like— no it was—frightened. "Said that, did he?" she said softly, more to herself than to anybody else in the room.

"Why did that bad man want to shoot us?" Andi asked. It had been all over the news that Dumas had been a wack-job, but apparently nobody had told Andi the guy'd been crazy.

Big raindrops splattered against the windows, rattled like a timpani drum, and then cried silently down the panes.

"Honey, there is a mental illness called paranoid schizo—" Daniel began.

"Bishop always said 'sometimes evil comes from the pit of hell and sometimes evil comes from the hearts of men, and most times you can't tell which is which,'" Theresa said. "Not this time, though. This time it's plain it was both."

"I watched," Andi said, her voice soft. "There was a slit in the door and I climbed up and looked out before"—she looked down at the front of her hospital gown—"my chest hurt and then I couldn't get to the door knob. It took a long time to open the door."

Emily Burke was standing on the far side of the bed, between it and the window. She leaned close to Andi and put her arm around the child.

"Shhhh now, Sweetheart. Try not to think about what happened."

"But I didn't see all of it through the slit, not then. Now though, when I think about it, it's not so dim as before. Everything used to be dim, but I didn't know it was dim until it got bright. Sometimes it's so bright now it hurts my eyes."

Jack saw Emily and Daniel exchange a concerned look.

"You're tired, Honey, maybe you need to—" Emily began.

"What's the bright look like, Sugar?" the old woman asked. She heaved herself out of the chair, went to the bed and took the child's hand, then she looked deep into Andi's eyes. "Tell me about it."

A look of concentration stapled itself between the little girl's eyebrows.

"It's hard to explain. It's like the world was smoky, like it's always been smoky, kinda, or foggy and then somebody turned on a lamp and I can see. Only the bright's on the inside, in my head, not on the outside. And it lights up… other things in my mind."

"What things? Theresa asked.

"Like Mr. Bishop's breath frosted," she said. "It was so cold you could see him breathe."

"Cold?" Daniel said.

"Uh huh." Andi wrapped her arms around herself as if she could still feel a chill. "The man brought the cold into the room with him, the bad man with the thing…"

Andi shuddered, but not from cold. Jack shivered, too. He had a sudden sense of such profound foreboding it took an effort not to leap up and run out of the room. He absolutely did not want to hear what the little girl perched on the edge of the hospital bed was about to say.

"The thing…made out of wasps that was sitting on his shoulders."

Daniel looked like he'd just had a stroke. He stared at the child, too shocked to speak for a moment, then he took over.

"You've had too much excitement," he said, his voice father-firm. He moved a teddy bear and a rabbit off the pillow so she could lie back. "You need some rest, maybe take a nap and—"

"She don't need rest," the old woman snapped at him. "She needs to talk. And you need to listen to what she's got to say."

Tension sparked between them, but before Daniel could form a response Jack stepped in.

"If Andi saw something when she was hiding in that storage closet, I need to hear what it was," he said, trying to sound dispassionate and as official as it was possible to sound with neither a badge on his chest nor a gun in his holster—though he suspected nobody in the room had noticed either was missing. And it was true, maybe the child had seen something important, but that's not why he wanted to keep her father from shutting her up

He wasn't interested in some fanciful swarm of insects. He wanted to find out how she knew him. Oh, not just his name. He'd pacified himself last night about that part— that she'd heard it while she was unconscious. That explanation sounded as hollow now as an empty oil drum. Andi Burke hadn't just known his name. She had opened her eyes and recognized him.

I heard you, Mr. Jack. I heard you call me.

He spoke more gently, tried to soothe the worried father. "Besides, she needs to get it all out in the open, Dano. It's better she doesn't bottle it up. Let her talk."

Daniel's attention snapped from Andi to Jack. He opened his mouth to say something, then closed it.

"What thing made out of wasps, Sugar?" Theresa asked.

A haunted look came over the child's face and she spoke in a whisper.

"It was sitting on the shoulder of the man with the gun. There were so many wasps they were solid, shaped like a rat." Andi began to tremble. With her arms wrapped tight around herself, she started to rock back and forth on the bed, staring out in front of her. With a look of terror and revulsion on her face, she described a creature that had tusks and claws and pus-yellow eyes with red centers—formed out of a swarm of wasps.

Emily sucked in a gasp; Daniel's face turned ashen.

"Its voice was"—Andi shuddered again—"awful when it talked to Mr. Bishop."

"What'd it say?" Theresa asked.

"It said something about three standing by a light and asked Mr. Bishop where to find Becky."

Theresa's spine went rigid; her gasp was audible. "Becca?" she whispered.

"That's right, Becca. But Mr. Bishop didn't answer, and then it stuck a claw down into the man's head and the man…shot Miss Lund."

Jack wanted to ask a dozen questions, though he doubted he'd have been able to wrap words around any of them even if he had the chance—which he didn't. Something had shifted in the room. An unnatural stillness had come over it. And it was quiet—absolutely silent—as if a giant had dropped a bell jar down on it. None of the hospital clatter, obvious only a moment before, penetrated the silence. Neither did the rain against the window. He could see the drops pelting the glass, but they made no sound. And the source of all that quiet and stillness was the old black woman and the little girl with bright blue eyes sitting in a puddle of stuffed animals on the bed. Their connectedness had stopped the world in its tracks. He knew he should not speak and break the invisible strand running from one to the other. He was also pretty sure he wouldn't have been able to make a sound even if he'd tried.

"The wasp thing didn't want the man to shoot Mr. Bishop," Andi said, her small voice a barely audible whisper. "It told the man 'nooooo,' but the man shot him anyway."

Nobody said anything then. Lightning flashed, shattered like bright icicles against the window and fell away in shiny fragments. Thunder clapped instantly, the rumble ripping open the quiet stillness of the room, dragging the hospital sounds in on its coattails. The light through the tracks of rain on the windows projected squiggly gray images onto the white sheets where Andi sat clutching twin monkeys, creating images of transparent worms inching across the bed.

Theresa took a deep, shuddery breath, released Andi's hand and stood up straight, shaking her head slowly.

"She knows," she said, her voice almost as quiet as Andi's had been.

"Knows what?" Daniel asked.

"Knows!" She paused, then spoke in the cadence of often-repeated words. "For our struggle is not against flesh and blood, but against the rulers, against the authorities, against the powers of this dark world and against the spiritual forces of evil in the heavenly realms."

"Ephesians 6:12," said Daniel.

"You believe that?" she asked him.

"It's Scripture. Of course, I believe it."

"No, you don't. Christians all say they do, but most don't, not really."

The old woman turned to Jack. "You believe we live in a supernatural world, Jack?"

Jack's head was spinning, Bishop's voice echoing in a dark, hollow cavern. *Looks like you ain't gone find out* what you come here to find out, the words painted on a canvas of sound, a relentless flat-line buzz.

"I believe there ought to be a reasonable, rational explanation for everything…but sometimes there isn't. A lot of times there isn't. If that's what you mean by supernatural, then yeah, I believe we live in a supernatural world. But if what you mean by supernatural is angels and gremlins and demons and fairies, then—"

"Both of you"—she looked pointedly at Jack, then at Daniel—"used to believe it, used to know the truth in here." She patted her chest above her heart.

Jack felt the kind of unease you feel when you know you've forgotten something important—that a suddenly violent drunk had been packing a switchblade the last time you busted him, maybe, or that the familiar face of that bus boy had been on a wanted poster.

Did Jack know this woman? She certainly acted like she knew him.

"For centuries, everybody believed it, understood there's a spiritual battle going on around us all the time." She sighed. "The smartest thing Satan ever done was to get folks to believe he don't exist." She turned toward Andi. "But they's those who do see the battle, folks who know. My Bishop knew. Looks like Andi does, too, now."

"Are you saying Andi can see…what? Demons?" Emily was incredulous.

"Not only demons. Appears she's been give eyes to see it all. What's dark for the rest of us, she's been give the light to see."

Jack couldn't hold onto the question any longer.

"How did you know me?" he asked the little girl, tried to keep his voice casual, but failed.

Andi looked thoughtful. "I'm not sure," she said. "There are things I just…know. I don't know how, but I do.

When you called me, I knew who you were and that you needed me. So I came back." A wistful look skittered across her features. "It was so bright there. I brought some of the brightness back with me. Not much, but enough to light up what's around me and what's in my head."

Andi smiled, and Jack would have sworn the shadows in the room drew back into the corners when she did. "I know you saved my life"—he started to protest, but she didn't let him—"and I know I don't ever have to be afraid, Uncle Jack, because you'll always keep me safe."

Uncle Jack? He merely stared at her, afraid to say anything because of the real possibility that if he opened his mouth he would burst into tears.

Chapter Twelve

The two men left the building together—Jack to go home and pace some more, Daniel to go home and pack a small suitcase for Emily so she could stay the night in Andi's room. The doctor wanted to keep the child one more night "for observation."

The rain had stopped, leaving the empty parking lot an eerie swamp where tendrils of mist rose off the hot asphalt. Jack shivered though the breeze that tickled his neck was warm.

When they were about to step off the curb to go their separate ways to their cars, Daniel spoke, "What Theresa said in there, and Andi…what do you think—?"

"I don't think." Jack didn't look at him, merely stared into the parking lot where gauzy mist drained cars and bushes and trees of color, faded them, softened their shapes and made the ordinary alien. "I can't right now, system overload. My circuits were already fried before"— he made a sort of all-encompassing gesture at the hospital behind them—"whatever that was. I'm so far out of my comfort zone UPS doesn't even deliver here."

He turned and looked at Daniel. Peered into his face, but saw nothing, no recognition. It was certainly understandable. Less than twenty-four hours ago the man had been told his little girl was going to die. Not surprising his mind wasn't keeping all the plates spinning right now. Jack let it go.

"Did what she said shock you?" Jack asked. "Didn't you already believe that stuff?"

"I don't know what I believe," Daniel said, his voice flat. That surprised Jack, surprised him even more that Daniel was honest enough to admit it. No, actually it didn't surprise Jack at all. "So many thoughts are chasing each other around in my head I can't manage to catch one and hold on long enough to think it."

"Copy that," Jack said.

"Why did you call me Dano in there?"

"What?"

"Dano. You called me Dano."

"I did?"

"Yeah, you did." Daniel paused. "That was my nickname when I was a kid."

Jack's heart kicked into a gallop. He didn't say anything, but Daniel must have seen something on his face.

"What?" Daniel asked.

Far-away thunder rumbled, the storm grumbling its retreat.

Ok, it was time. He was pretty sure Daniel would figure part of it out on his own soon anyway. And the "good reverend" was, after all, involved—whatever that meant. Daniel should know—all of it. Besides, if Jack didn't share this with somebody, he was going to go as crazy as a nuclear waste dump rat.

"I want to show you something, Daniel. Do you have time to come with me? It's not far. It won't take long."

"Sure," Daniel said. "What is it?"

"You'll see when we get there."

Daniel told Jack he'd never ridden in a police cruiser before; Jack allowed that if he'd spent less time in church as a kid and more time drinking and carousing, he could have earned any number of all-expenses-paid trips in the backseat of one. Their banter was easy and relaxed, a level of companionship not commensurate with the amount of time they had spent together. Jack found that both odd and normal at the same time.

They kept the conversation light by mutual unspoken agreement. There had been enough "heavy" already, and Jack was about to pull a dump truck up to Daniel's mind and pour in another full load. Jack stopped the cruiser in front of a big, ornate house. All the windows were dark.

When Daniel spoke, his voice had lost the bantering tone. "You ever hear of a thing called an earwick?"

"I think it's earwig, and yeah, used to have nightmares about them when I was in Panama. I'd imagine one of the teeming hordes of bugs that were crawling on me was going to slither into my ear and lay eggs in there and when they hatched they'd eat my brain."

"I thought about earwigs when Theresa was talking. Something that gets in your head and..." Daniel didn't finish.

Jack felt a small tree of sweat begin to form between his shoulder blades that had nothing to do with the fact that he was about to break the law.

"If you're still interested in taking a ride in the backseat of a police cruiser, I'm about to give you a shot at it. Come on."

He got out and led Daniel across the lawn toward a house, then veered around it to the back yard. They circled a kidney-shaped swimming pool toward a building in the far corner. Fat raindrops splatted on Jack's shirt from the leaves of the big oak tree Detective Harrison had tied a piece of yellow-and-black police tape to the day before. He leaned under the tape and Daniel followed him to the porch of the carriage house. Jack paused in front of the door.

"This is where the shooter lived," Jack said. "His name was Jacob Dumas."

Daniel's eyes grew large.

"I secured it the day of the shooting. And I saw something here I wanted you to take a look at." Jack paused. "It was in a box on the porch, but forensics must have taken the box into the house."

Jack stood for a moment, considering, then began to loosen the police tape sealing the door. He'd broken the lock when he kicked it open, so the police tape was the only thing holding the door shut.

"Uh…in case you're interested, the name of the crime we're about to commit is 'breaking and entering,' a fifth degree felony punishable by six months in jail and a fine of $2,500."

"Well, that's good to know," Daniel said. "I hate it when I commit a crime and don't even know its name."

When Jack had removed enough of the tape to push the door open, he turned to Daniel.

"Forensics has already scrubbed this place with a toothbrush, but still, don't touch anything."

When Jack switched on his flashlight, black smudges were visible where CSI had lifted fingerprints all over the door, the door frame, and what had been pristine chrome and glass furnishings. They stepped inside, Jack pulled the door shut behind them and swung the flashlight beam in a wide arc, looking for the box. Among the austere furnishings it would be easy to spot. He quickly checked the other downstairs rooms, then focused the flashlight beam on the floor so he wouldn't trip as he led Daniel to the stairs.

On the second floor landing, he opened the door to Dumas's "office" and swept his light around the room, revealing the inch-thick layers of paper attached to the walls, decorated with red dots and blue squiggly lines.

Daniel whistled softly. "And I thought Andi's room was a mess." He looked around. "This is what you wanted to show me? Why?"

The cardboard box of keepsakes was sitting on the floor in the middle of the room.

"What I want you to see is in here."

Jack led Daniel to the box and they both knelt beside it. When he shone the light into the box, he could see forensics had riffled through it—but had taken no fingerprints there and the object he was looking for was still on the top. Jack pointed at it.

"Look close," Jack said, but didn't need to. Daniel tensed moments after he saw it, so Jack knew the picture had had the same effect on him it'd had on Jack.

It was an old, yellowed, eight-by-ten photograph, tattered and worn, of a Little League baseball team, identified in black letters on the top as the Bradford's Ridge Rangers, 1985. A big piece of the upper left hand corner was missing, so all that was visible of the coach was his hand on a boy's shoulder.

Daniel peered closer.

At the bottom of the picture, the boys' names were listed, left to right, many of them unreadable and many of the faces were too faded to make out the boys' features. But the ones that mattered were clear.

Jack heard Daniel suck in his breath.

"That's me," Daniel said. He pointed to his name beneath the picture, then searched for the corresponding face in the crowd. "The kid in the middle of the second row, that's me. Why would…?"

"Because Jacob Dumas was on the team, too. Third row, second from the left."

"You mean I was on a Little League team with the lunatic who tried to massacre a room full of kids?"

"You're not the only one."

"Huh?"

"Keep looking."

Daniel turned back to the photograph in the beam of Jack's flashlight and continued to study it. When he spotted the second name, Jack saved him the trouble of locating the boy.

"Right there," he said, "the big kid on the front row. Jackson Randal Carpenter. I was on that team, too."

~

Theresa pulled the house key out of her big purse and unlocked her front door.

It was quiet inside, but the silence was crowded with smells—fried chicken and pot roast and apple pie and… every possible dish you could think of. All cooked with tender care and given in love. But grateful as Theresa was for the good intentions, she didn't have no desire to taste a single bite.

It had been all she could do to convince her sister Margaret to get all them well-meanin' folks to go home so she could be by herself tonight. She'd called on the way back from the hospital and Maggie'd argued she'd ought not to be alone, grieving like she was, the night before they put her man in the ground. But Theresa'd insisted.

Now, as she closed the door behind her, stepped into the parlor and switched on the lights, she wondered if maybe Maggie'd been right. The vacant emptiness of the house curled its fingers into a fist and punched her in the belly, knocked the breath out of her.

"You hadn't ought to a'took him, Lord," she said aloud into the stillness. Then she looked up at the ceiling and shouted, "You listenin' to me, God? You supposed to be near to those who's grieving, but I can't find you nowhere."

The outburst took what little remained of her energy and she sank down on the couch opposite the big chair where Bishop would never sit again.

She put her face in her hands and tried to cry, but couldn't. Her shoulders shook for a little while, but the tears didn't come. Felt like having the dry heaves. Her eyes were so scratchy from not crying it was like somebody'd taken a piece of sandpaper to the insides of her eyelids.

Bishop had spoke to that monster right before it killed him. The last words her Bishop had said before he crossed over was to a demon! Jack had heard him.

Jack Carpenter.

Can you imagine that! The good Lord's ways was mysterious, all right. She and Bishop had known where Daniel was—couldn't miss him preaching every Sunday on television—not bad sermons, just empty ones, saying what the itchin' ears of the bums in the pews wanted to hear. But until he showed up in Andi's hospital room tonight, Theresa didn't know Jack was anywhere around, hadn't laid eyes on that boy since the days he'd sit with Daniel on the lumpy old couch in the parlor of their little house in Bradford's Ridge, eating her fresh chocolate chip cookies, all fired up, ready to take on the whole pack of them boys as was mistreatin' Becca.

And Becca sittin' there between him and Daniel like a

life-sized china doll, paying no mind to them boys pounding on they chests, her eyes sparkling as she watched the little silver ballerina go around and around on Theresa's old music box.

Becca.

That monster was looking for that girl, and Theresa couldn't think of but one reason a demon would be trying to find her. A sick dread settled deep into the pit of her stomach, snuggled up close to the fear that had already taken up residence there. Yeah, she was scared. Ok, admit it—soon's Andi said what the demon'd wanted, that horror, that awful otherworldly terror had seized her guts and made it so she could hardly get her breath.

She shivered, then got up heavily, went into the kitchen to look at the only pictures she had of Becca. When each of the two photographs had come in the mail years ago, Theresa had stuck them with magnets to her refrigerator door.

Theresa flipped on the kitchen light switch, and then stopped and stared at the shiny silver door. The two photographs were gone. She went to the refrigerator and moved other stuck-with-magnets things around, trying to find them. A church bulletin with a phone number on it was affixed to the door with a "Maid of the Mists" magnet they'd brought home from Niagara Falls years ago. Coupons were stuck to the door with a "Visit Myrtle Beach" magnet and a black bear magnet from the Smoky Mountains. A handful of crayoned drawings from the kids at Vacation Bible School were there…but the pictures were gone.

Theresa had no recollection of when she'd last seen the pictures there, but knew they couldn't have been missing for long or she'd have noticed. One of the dozen or so ladies from her church who'd been fussing around in her kitchen must have moved them. Theresa still hadn't located where they put her pepper mill and the ice tea glasses was all in the wrong cabinets.

Then she noticed a post-it note near the top, stuck there with a smiley-face magnet. She took it down and read it. "Pick up shoes Friday before 5." Bishop's handwriting. She held the note tenderly, wondering if she had the heart to go into the repair shop her own self and pick up shoes for a man who wasn't never going to wear them, a man who was…

Killed by a demon.

And Jack sent that monster screaming back down into the bowels of hell where it belonged. She wondered if Bishop had recognized Jack when he spotted him crouched out in the hallway that morning. Reckon Bishop knew it was Jack gonna kill that bad man and save them children? She hoped so and she smiled a little at the thought. 'Course Jack didn't recognize Bishop. He didn't recognize her either, and neither did Daniel. But they would—soon. It was coming back to them. It wasn't no accident they was thrown together like this. There was a plan at work, one she had better sense than to try to figure out.

But apparently, that plan didn't include Bishop.

She started up the stairs to the silent bedroom where she'd finally given herself up to tears last night, alone in that empty bed, cryin' for the man she needed to be there, sobbing so hard she finally exhausted herself and she fell asleep.

She set her purse on the bedroom dresser and wondered what Bishop would think of the man Jack Carpenter'd growed up to be. She didn't feel the same… disillusionment with him she did with Daniel. Didn't seem quite so bad to lose your faith altogether as it did to exchange it for a plastic imitation.

"Should I a'told them?" she asked out loud, not sure whether she was asking God or Bishop. "Should I have tried to prepare them for what's out there sniffin' around for 'em?"

She sat down on the side of the bed and began to take her shoes off, straining with the effort. Her size had sneaked up on her, getting a little bit bigger ever year. But she was feeling it now. Whatever was coming for them, she'd have to stand her ground and fight it head on because she was too fat anymore to run.

"I didn't tell them 'cause I'm not sure, I mean maybe it's not…it could be—" She stopped. Who'd she think she was fooling? "I didn't tell them because I didn't think they's ready to hear it. They still can't even say the word demon 'thout getting the willies. If I's to tell them now what else they's facing…"

She got her right shoe off and her left one loose enough that she could kick it off. It banged against the dresser and fell to the floor and she sat staring at it, physically, emotionally and spiritually exhausted.

"I got to tell them soon, though," she said under her breath.

Pretending a demon didn't exist wouldn't make it go away. Ignoring one was dangerous business, particularly one as big and powerful as this one.

"Maybe we'd ought to—" she caught herself talking to Bishop like he was right there and was gonna help her through this awful time. But Bishop was gone. Tomorrow they was going to put him in the ground and say nice things about him…and then walk away and leave him there.

She put her face in her hands then and the tears came.

Chapter Thirteen

An awed hush bloomed after Jack pointed out to Daniel the big kid in the front row of the picture of the Little League team. It grew, swelled up too big for the room, was jammed so tight within the walls Jack felt pressure on his ears. But to open the door and let it out into the night was to condemn the whole world to silence.

Jack reached out and picked up the picture carefully, a tiny piece of the top right corner pinched between his fingertips. The two men got to their feet and stood together, looking at it in the glow of Jack's flashlight.

"Let me see if I'm tracking here," Daniel said. His voice sounded breathless, but it was steady and firm. "You and I and Jacob Dumas were on the same Little League team in 1985—right?"

"Pictures don't lie." Jack paused, then continued in a tone he hoped didn't sound as eager—as desperate as he felt. "What can you tell me about that team? What kind of kid was Dumas…was I?"

Daniel turned from the picture toward Jack, his face all harsh lines and shadows in the glow of the flashlight.

"I have absolutely no idea," he said. "I don't remember."

Jack felt the bottom fall out of his stomach. "Neither do I," he said.

They both took a moment or two to absorb that.

"You grew up in Bradford's Ridge?" Daniel asked. Jack nodded. "I don't remember you."

"I think you and I were friends," Jack eased the words out into the space between them. "Not just friends, good friends, best friends. But I'm not sure."

"We moved to Nashville right before school started in the fall," Daniel said, "probably not long after this picture was taken. I graduated from high school there."

"My father got drunk and drove his truck into a tree that summer—was in the hospital for months and I went to live with my grandmother in New York. Then he died; I never went back to Bradford's Ridge."

Silence pooled around them again. No matter how soft his voice, Jack's words seemed over-loud in his own ears in the stillness. "All my childhood memories are…blurry, the images are vague, like I lived my whole life before I turned thirteen in a fog."

Daniel shook his head. "You've pulled up to the wrong pump if you want to fill your tank with childhood recollections. Mine are lousy. People talk about what they did when they were kids and I can't…I don't…it's like you described—a fog."

Both men stood quiet for a moment before Jack laid his final card on the table.

"Daniel, I spent most of the day today creating a fuzzy, hazy timeline of growing up. I could come up with blurred scenes from my first day of kindergarten, the time I broke my arm when I was seven, making snow angels when I was nine with—I think it was you—and a little blonde girl. But no matter how hard I concentrated, I couldn't…there was something odd about the summer of 1985—the summer this picture was taken. The memories aren't just fuzzy, Daniel. They're gone. I don't remember you, the other guys, the team, the uniforms, practice, games—not one thing between the end of school in June, and when I visited my father in the hospital the last time before I left for New York in August. Not a normal just-can't-remember void. It's a big, blank, empty space, a nothing. Like it'd been…erased."

Daniel looked deeply shaken. No, Daniel looked afraid.

"If you're holding your breath for me to produce a list of my activities from the summer of 1985, you may proceed with your regularly scheduled respirations." Daniel was obviously straining for levity but couldn't pull it off. "A couple of years ago, we took Andi to the twelfth birthday party of a neighbor kid and Andi asked what I did the summer I was twelve. I couldn't tell her a thing, not one thing. That freaked me out, so I got serious—looked up world events that happened that summer, songs that were popular, movies—anything to spark my memories. Nothing. It's this weird, empty spot. Like I'm walking down a foggy road and it just ends. The bridge that's supposed to be there in front of me has washed out. I can see the rest of the road, but there's nothing but air between me and the other side."

~

Emily went to the window in Andi's hospital room to lower the blinds so the streetlight outside wouldn't glare on the television screen.

Andi pointed to the cord in her mother's hand and teased, "Ride the rope back up, Mommy."

One of Andi's favorite activities at church when she was younger was to "ride the bell rope." A two-inch thick rope extended from the oversized bell in the church's belfry to a small room off the sanctuary. Andi would stand on a chair beside the rope, waiting while Dan shook it free from the clasp high above. Then she'd leap out, grab the rope and her weight would pull it down until her feet were only inches off the floor. Then she'd ride the rope high into the air when the bell swung back. Back and forth like a seesaw. Andi would have rung the church's bell for hours if Dan had let her.

When Emily turned on the television, set high on the wall opposite Andi's bed, the first image that appeared on the screen was the Dread Pirate Roberts hopping from one rock to another, in a sword fight with Inigo Montoya, who was looking for the six-fingered man to tell him "you keeled my father. Prepare to die."

Andi literally squealed with delight. The Princess Bride was her all-time, forever-favorite movie. She had seen it so many times she could quote the dialogue along with the characters, but she never tired of it, begged to see it again and again.

Emily studied her daughter's rapt face, lit by the flickering images on the screen, and felt that horrible tightness grip her chest, the terror she'd felt when the doctor said...

No! If she went there, if she let her mind travel down that dark road, she might start screaming and never stop. She tucked Andi's brown curls behind her ears and asked if she wanted some juice. But neither her presence, nor her question ever got to the higher centers of her daughter's brain. The child sat enchanted, mouthing the words along with the characters on the screen.

Then Emily's phone chimed. It was an ordinary chime, not a special ring tone. But as soon as she heard the sound, she knew it was Jeff.

Her heart began to hammer in her chest. She turned from Andi to her purse on the bedside table, took out her phone and walked to the window with her back to Andi. Her hands were trembling when she touched the message icon and his words blinked alive on the screen.

"Em, are you all right? I've been so worried about you. I wanted to call, to come to the hospital, but—" The sentence ended there. Auto-correct must have eaten the final words. "Tell me how I can help you. Anything! It breaks my heart to know how much pain you're in and I'm not there to hold you. What can I do?"

The words were suddenly blurry, swimming in the tears that had pooled in her eyes. Jeff! She had not given him a moment's thought since…

She started to write a response, hesitated, then stood reading the words over and over. So worried about you… breaks my heart…there to hold you.

"Mommy, are you crying?"

And Emily realized she was. She wasn't making a sound, but her shoulders were shaking so hard Andi could tell even from behind her. Emily punched the "off" button on her phone and put it in her purse, then drew in a deep breath and faced the child, a big smile draped across her face between tear-slathered cheeks.

"No, Honey, I was laughing—just trying to be quiet about it so I didn't disturb your movie. Did you ever do that—laugh so hard it looked like crying?"

"Uh huh—when Donkey told Shrek, 'I've got a dragon and I'm not afraid to use it,'" Andi said and giggled. "What was so funny?"

"You're not old enough to understand." Emily crossed

the room and planted a kiss on her daughter's forehead. Then she hugged her, held on fiercely for a moment. "Just a joke, Sweetheart, that's all." She drew in a shaky breath. "And the joke's on Mommy."

~

Daniel stared at the picture, tried to look through the blurred images to the reality captured there with dark and light, shadows and shade. No memory formed. Nothing. His mind turned, instead, to the first—actually the last— memory he had from his growing up years.

When Daniel slides into the front seat beside his father, he's grateful for the rush of cold in the air-conditioned interior of the big sedan. He slams the door and shakes his head, tries to get his bearings. He feels…dopey. Kind of like he's wrapped in cotton. Sounds seem to come from a long way off. There's a gentle roaring in his ears, the way he feels when he has a fever.

But Daniel doesn't realize something is wrong, seriously wrong, until his father asks the question.

"What'd you and Jack do today?"

Jack! He and Jack! There it was. A memory from his childhood that had Jack in it! But the boy who'd been asked the question couldn't answer it.

Daniel doesn't know what he and Jack had done! He doesn't remember.

But that's crazy. How could he possibly not remember what he did five minutes ago?

His heart begins to thump in his chest, pounding so

hard he thinks you might be able to see the movement of his shirt. What's wrong with him? His fear grows, balloons. Fear of this…not knowing…and fear of something else, too. Something…He doesn't remember what!

His father isn't looking at Daniel, but back over his left shoulder, checking for traffic before he pulls out onto the road in front of Jack's house, so Daniel has a moment to compose himself.

"Oh, you know, the usual stuff," Daniel says. He can hear a tremor in his voice, but apparently his father is too preoccupied to notice. Big surprise there.

"We shouldn't be gone long," his father continues, as if Daniel hasn't said a word. "An hour and a half—two tops."

His father babbles on about Daniel's babysitting job at their rustic cabin high in the hills above Blue Ridge Lake, what a big deal it is that his parents trust him to take care of precious Marianne there all by himself while his father conducts an outdoor wedding on a houseboat in the marina below. Daniel barely hears him. He is concentrating, focusing his every mental faculty on remembering today—anything about today. Getting out of bed. Brushing his teeth. What did he eat? Anything!

But there is nothing in his head where the memories should be but…fog. Or smoke billowing off a campfire, thick and gray. Impenetrable. Worse, it seems to be spreading. It's like it's flowing out into his memory banks, blurring and obscuring everything it touches. Yesterday is…what did he do yesterday? And Monday? Marianne was playing in the sprinkler on Monday. He remembers unscrewing the hose from the sprinkler head and he sees himself putting his thumb over the nozzle and spraying the water into the air to fall on her like rain. Then he watches in horror as the fog rolls in, blotting out the back yard, Marianne's shrieks of delight, flowing over him. Then all he sees is the fog. The memory—he had remembered something—but the memory is gone now.

Is he having a stroke? Does he have a brain tumor?

"Dad!" he cries, terrified. "I can't remember…"

"Can't remember what, son?"

"Sunday," is all Daniel can force out through his lips.

"Sunday? Oh, I preached on the ten lepers that Jesus healed but only one came back to thank him. I said…"

Daniel scrambles backward in his mind, looking for something, anything—Christmas morning! Yes. The smell of the spruce tree. The sound of Marianne's giggles as she rips off wrapping paper. His mother, taking pictures of Marianne from every possible angle, one after another. He remembers it all, crisp and clear—no fog! He grabs the memory and holds on with the fierceness of desperation, clasping it to him as if his life depends on it. Which, of course, it does.

"I grabbed hold of Christmas and held on," Daniel said.

"What?"

"My father came to pick me up—at your house—when the memory of that summer…left, was wiped out—whatever. I was afraid I was losing all my memories—my whole mind!—so I concentrated on remembering Christmas."

Jack made a humph sound in his throat. "At least you remember that much. I don't even remember forgetting. Did it happen all at once? Do you remember anything else that happened that day?"

Daniel went rigid. Sudden horror stabbed a frozen ice pick into his belly. When he spoke, his voice sounded as hollow as the void of that summer in both their minds.

"I don't want to talk about that day!"

Jack backed off. Neither man spoke again. Jack put the

picture back in the box where he'd found it, then they turned without speaking and left the carriage house. Jack stuck the police tape back in place, and they walked in silence to the car. When they got in, Jack didn't start the engine, merely stared sightlessly out over the steering wheel.

"Something's all wrong here." Jack's voice was quiet.

"'Industrial strength' wrong?" Daniel asked. He knew, but didn't know how he knew, that that was something Jack used to say when they were kids. Apparently Jack remembered, too, because a small smile skittered across his lips.

"Yeah. Wrong on steroids. I don't know what it is." Jack turned to face Daniel, a determined set to his jaw. "But I will find out. Trust me, I will find out."

Chapter Fourteen

"Give me a call if you find out anything else," Jack said to the man on the other end of the line. Then he sat holding the receiver in his hand for a long time, staring. If he was thinking anything at all, he couldn't have said what it was.

The hits just keep on comin'!

He slowly replaced the handset in the cradle and struggled to find some place to put what he'd just found out. But his mind had recently become the passport of a world traveler—so many stamps from so many different places, there was not a single empty spot to put anything new. Needed to order a new passport with additional blank pages and until it arrived, Jack would just have to stay home—get up in the morning, brush his teeth, burn his breakfast toast, pick up his laundry, go to a movie—Ok, so he never went to movies—get a little drunk—do life!

Shoot, even the crazy media attention for the last week was easier to take than this. Cameras snapping his picture, a microphone shoved in front of him every time he stepped out of the station. He'd suffered through dozens of inane questions with remarkable patience, he thought. All except the ones that contained the word "hero."

"You want to meet a hero? I can introduce you to dozens of them—some of them are missing arms and legs, and all of them carry battle scars you can't see. Combat soldiers are heroes. I was only doing my job."

He hated how corny that last part sounded, and took considerable razzing about it from fellow officers. But he had been just doing his job—a job he knew and understood and that made sense. The rest of this…what? Insanity? No, it wasn't insane. He could deal with crazy. But how do you deal with a fuzzy childhood that had in the past week started molting, losing its fur covering in bits and hunks? He supposed eventually there'd be nothing left but the bare dog underneath, and he was certain that it was one ugly mutt.

Only a week ago, he'd gone running into a school, armed and focused on cold, hard reality—and had raced through the looking glass and into Wonderland. Something fundamental had shifted in the universe, or in Jack's ability to perceive the true nature of the universe, he didn't know which. Now, he felt vulnerable and exposed, no longer the man with a gun who was in charge, but the dude with a clipboard on the sidelines trying to figure out the rules of the game the big boys were playing.

Major Crocker plopped a file of papers on the table in front of him.

"I'm trying to wrap this all up and put this case to bed," he said. "You wouldn't be making stuff up just to give an old man indigestion, now would you?"

Crock picked up a mug inscribed with a picture of two dinosaurs looking out over the water at a retreating ark. Beneath were the words, "Oh crap, was that today?" He poured coffee into it, took a big gulp, made a face and set the mug beside Jack's Snoopy mug of half-drunk, cold coffee on the squad room table.

"Tastes like yak pee," Crock grumbled.

"Drunk a lot of yak pee, have you?"

"So you're saying you were on a Little League team in 1985 with the shooter," Crocker said. "Not just you, but the father of the little girl you shot. And the shooter had a picture of that team"—Crocker fished inside a folder in his other hand, came out with a photocopy of the picture and dropped it on top of the report—"and he walked right past it as he left the house that morning packing guns, chains and a padlock on his way to off a classroom full of ten-year-olds—that right?"

"It's all there in the report."

Jack had an office, but he rarely used it, only when he needed to close the door so he could ream out some patrolman for sloppy paperwork or careless procedure. He joined the men who reported to him in loathing the former, but was a tyrant when it came to officer safety. Sloppiness could get you yelled at; carelessness could get you killed. He preferred to do his own paperwork at the table that held the ancient coffee pot, mugs and a ragtag assortment of condiments in a Spiderman cup in the back of the squad room. He liked to be in the center of what was going on, not holed up in some windowless cave. He had a distinct aversion to closed-in spaces. Translate that: he was full-bore claustrophobic, avoided elevators when-ever he could, hated to fly, even disliked revolving doors, though you could see through the walls.

Jack drew in a deep breath.

"Actually, it's not all in the report. I just found out a couple of other interesting tidbits." Crocker lifted an eyebrow as his signal for Jack to go on. "I got curious, got to wondering what happened to all the other boys on that team. So I spent all last week digging. Of the eighteen pictured here, five are dead now."

"Doesn't say much for the health benefits of playing Little League baseball." Crocker observed.

"One manages a car dealership. One's in a Texas nuthouse. One drives a taxi. One's a fisherman and one has a Roto-Rooter franchise—little worker minions, living worker minion lives—at least the ones with names that weren't too blurred to read, or that I haven't heard back on yet."

"But you did find out something interesting about somebody."

"Two somebodies." Jack picked up the photo copy of the team picture and pointed to a boy on the second row, third from the left. "This is Walter Stephenson. He's a long-haul trucker based in Little Falls, Minnesota, and this"—he indicated a boy on the far end of the front row—"is Roger Willingham, who owns a shoe store in Bakersfield, California."

"Sound like guys right off a terrorist watch list to me. What have they done to lift themselves up out of minion-dom?"

Jack found that his chest was tight, making it hard to talk without sounding breathy.

"Stephenson parked his eighteen-wheeler on the street in front of his house, spent twelve hours building a bomb in his basement, and then climbed back into his rig and drove it—loaded with wilting lettuce he never delivered—to Savannah, Georgia, where he decided to celebrate the Fourth of July by blowing up a multi-plex movie theatre."

Crocker pulled out a chair and sat at the table opposite Jack. The other officers in the room stopped their chatter to listen.

"And Willingham flipped the sign from open to closed

on the front door of his store, got into his car and drove straight through for twenty-three hours to Saint Louis so he could set fire to a daycare center."

"Ok, you got my attention," Crocker said. "What's the rest of it?"

"The rest of it is that these fine gentlemen both committed their 'random acts of madness' in the fourteen days since the Carlisle shooting."

Crocker didn't have a comeback for that one.

"What was the body count?"

"Just two—Stephenson and Willingham. They were both amateurs and total idiots. Stephenson apparently made himself a dynamite vest—they still don't know what kind of detonator he was using, but security camera footage shows he didn't get far. He yelled he was wired, everybody scattered, he took two steps into the theatre lobby and boom! Accidental detonation."

"Ouch," Ramirez said. "That'll leave a mark."

"They identified him from his truck in the parking lot —but nobody else had serious injuries."

"And the shoe salesman?"

"Willingham was after some kid. He showed up at a day care and took the place hostage, splashed gasoline everywhere, and said if they didn't produce the little girl, he'd strike a match."

"His kid?"

"Probably, but they're still checking. Can't ask Willing-ham, though. He walked in front of a window and a police sniper capped him."

Crocker ran his hand over his head as if there were hair on it. Jack had always thought the major bore a striking resemblance to Elmer Fudd, and often had to quash the refrain that played in his head—kill da waaaab-bit...kill da waaaabbit.

"What are the odds of all this being a coincidence?" the major said.

"That must have been one kick-ass Little League team —a preacher, three mass murderer wannabes and Carpenter," said Patrolman Peterson. He leaned back in his chair and sailed a paper clip across the room at Ramirez. "The good, the bad and the ugly."

Images suddenly formed in Jack's mind as crisp and real as the faces of the men sitting near him, the smell of coffee burning in the bottom of the glass pot and the sound of Peterson's honking laugh. It was a flashback. He'd had them before. But this one wasn't Somalia.

It's hot, sticky, but not Africa hot. Kentucky-summer hot. There's shade nearby beneath a gigantic oak tree, but he's not standing in it. Neither is the white boy beside him —Daniel Burke!—or the little girl named Becca. The three of them are squinting in the sunshine, surrounded by— encircled by a group of boys. One of them, a redheaded kid bigger than all the others, starts the chant. He pokes his finger into Daniel's chest.

"The good…"

He turns to Jack and jabs him in the chest.

"…the bad…"

Then he turns to the little girl. He doesn't poke her in the chest, though, actually seems reluctant to touch her. He wags his finger in her face instead.

"…and the ugly!"

The other boys in the circle laugh.

Jack launches himself at the redheaded kid, plows into his chest and knocks him to the ground. He is able to punch the boy in the face once, a good, solid hit, smashes his lip and makes it bleed, before the boy roars in maniacal rage, a sound more feral than human.

Jack looks into the boy's eyes and time pauses. In that frozen moment, Jack doesn't see the anger he expects to see in the pale blue eyes. He sees fear. But it's not fear of Jack. It is an abject terror unlike anything Jack has ever seen in the eyes of another human being, a terror unlike any fear Jack has ever imagined. Only for a second, though. Then it vanishes and the eyes change, narrow to slits that look like the eyes of some savage beast, an animal from another time or place—eyes that don't even look human. The total foreignness of the eyes stabs a chill into Jack's heart, an irrational, bogeyman fear. It's as if he's looked through a crack into the deep dark lair of some unthinkable evil.

Jack suddenly feels himself flying through the air. The redheaded boy has flung him off like a ragdoll. From flat on his back on the ground, the boy has launched Jack into the air above him, knocked him twenty feet backward, where he slams into the trunk of a tree with the force of being hit by a truck.

Jack slides down the tree to the ground with a grunt, all the air knocked out of his lungs. The other boys are on him then. They yank him to his feet, their own eyes mirroring the primal hatred he sees in the redheaded kid— Cole Stuart.

The fingers of the boys gripping him dig into his flesh like the talons of eagles, the strength of their grip cutting off the circulation in both arms.

They don't drag Jack, they lift him off the ground as if he were made of paper mache. Cole gets to his feet and the other boys hurl Jack across the space separating them, where he lands with a plop in the dirt in front of the redheaded boy. Cole reaches down, grabs Jack by the hair with one hand, and lifts him up into the air like a mouse by the tail, holds him out so they are at eye level.

Those eyes, those horrible eyes, all beast, no humanity anywhere!

Cole slams his fist into Jack's belly. The pain is excruciating. Jack tries to lift his arms to swing at Cole, but he has no strength and no breath. Cole holds him there, dangling, hits him in the belly again, like a prizefighter punching a bag.

Jack sees black spots in front of his eyes, hears Daniel as if from a great distance, cry, "Leave him alone!"

The redheaded kid lets go his grip on Jack, and he drops in a heap on the ground, still unable to move or breathe. Then Cole turns on Daniel.

"You want some of this?" he growls.

Daniel is a big kid, though soft, not tough like Jack. But he stands his ground.

"If you think you can take me, yeah," Daniel says.

The redheaded kid snarls and swings at Daniel, who is surprisingly nimble, and ducks away so Cole only lands a glancing blow on his cheek. But even that is staggering, and Daniel falls back—into the waiting arms of other boys who have circled behind him. Each boy takes an arm and they suspend Daniel between them as Cole hones in on him.

Jack has enough of his breath back to stagger to his feet and dive at Cole. Without even looking, the redheaded kid backhands him, a casual blow that smashes Jack's mouth, bloodies his nose and loosens his front teeth as it knocks him flat on his back on the ground. The boys not holding Daniel descend on him, kicking him and he rolls into a ball in the dirt, trying to protect his head.

"Stop it!" the little girl cries. "That's enough."

Then her voice changes, or seems to. When she speaks again, there is such power and authority in her words everyone freezes. "Stop! Now. Leave, all of you. Go!"

Jack squints up at her from the ground, the sun in his eyes, and thinks as he has thought a thousand times before that Becca Hawkins is the most beautiful creature who ever walked the earth.

Her hair is the pale blonde of that movie star who's trying to hold her skirt down as air blows up under it on a calendar picture he'd seen once in Richardson's Garage. It hangs down her back, silk from an ear of corn, all the way to her waist. Her face is delicate, her features so fragile they look like they were carved out of blown glass. Wide sea-green eyes, with lashes that lay like fans on her cheeks, pale skin so fair it's almost transparent. And now, with the sun at her back, a halo encircles her head that lights her face in a fierce brilliance.

The attacking boys falter. They stop hitting and kicking to stand looking at her, their faces unreadable.

"And if we don't?" snarls the redheaded kid. But the threat is meaningless and even he seems to know it.

She says nothing, merely looks at them all. Jack rolls over, staggers to his feet, blood pouring down his chin and dripping on his shirt. He reaches over and helps Daniel up, noting as he does that the preacher's son will be packing a glowing shiner in church in the morning.

"Let's go," says the redheaded kid. "Gotta be careful. Can't hurt anybody. Can't leave a mark."

All the others turn to leave, except the blond kid, whose lip is stuck out as if he's pouting. Jacob Dumas spits in the dirt and takes a step toward Jack, his eyes open way too wide.

"Uh uh. I'm gonna get me some dark meat."

The redheaded kid is on him in a second, grabs his arm and spins him around. "You're not—!"

And instantly they are at each other, biting and hitting and kicking like animals. The others join in the fray, either trying to drag them apart, or getting in their own licks. The savageness and brutality is stunning, as is the ferocity and strength of the combatants. Blood and hunks of hair fly. Dumas bites off a piece of someone's ear. A boy is launched six feet into the air—amid grunts and sounds like growls.

Jack, Daniel and Becca back away from them in shock, forgotten in the spontaneous combustion that set the group of boys against each other.

"Losers," Daniel says, but his voice is shaky. Jack and Daniel have never spoken of it aloud, even to each other. But their thoughts don't need words. What twelve-year-old can hit like Cole Stuart?

When Daniel turns to Becca, Jack sees on his face the same adoration that must be painted on his own.

Jack dusts his hands on his pants and looks at the two of them.

No, there are three of them.

The Jack sitting in the squad room smelling burned coffee, who stood as a spectator to the vivid flashback, could see what the boys—and maybe the girl, too—could not. There was a figure standing beside Becca. A figure made of such bright light it was impossible to look at it straight on, a form that glowed with a brilliance that set Becca's pale hair sparkling.

And then it was all gone, the whole scene a puff of frosted breath on a cold morning that instantly disappeared.

Chapter Fifteen

"Is there something in the water in Bradford's Ridge, Kentucky?" Ramirez asked as he ducked the flying paperclip Peterson had launched at him. "Mass murderers and politicians." He paused for a beat. "Which are pretty much the same thing, come to think of it."

Jack felt momentarily disoriented, like he'd felt in those first months after he'd returned from Somalia, when reality tended to blink on and off like a Joe's Beer Joint sign. This had been different, though. This had been a memory-on-steroids, not a true flashback—a memory more vivid than any he'd ever had, with a visceral texture that was chillingly real. He'd been able to smell the hot grass, and the sweating boys, feel the heat on his neck and the pain of the punches in the gut.

Of course, it wasn't simply a memory, because he'd distorted parts of it, made it into a fantasy—no, nightmare. It couldn't have happened the way this scene had played out in his head, with a kid knocking him twenty feet across the grass into a tree, and holding him up by the hair with one hand.

So why had his mind gone to the trouble of changing those parts, stretching, elongating and exaggerating the incident? And why was the "memory" unlike a real memory or flashback in viewpoint? Jack had been both a participant and an observer, he'd been inside the drama and on the sidelines, too, watching his younger self from the perspective of adulthood.

From that perspective he saw what the boy did not. He saw the creature of light beside Becca, a vision stranger than anything he'd ever seen in his life.

At least he thought it was stranger than anything he'd ever seen. He had, after all, completely lost the whole summer when he was twelve years old. This was the first memory he'd ever had of it. He didn't know how he knew the scene he'd watched had taken place that summer, but he was certain nonetheless. It was the most vivid memory of any event from his whole fuzzy, foggy childhood. That it had erupted out of his head the way it had was shocking. And that's how it'd felt, like it had been catapulted out of his unconscious mind into the mental world where he was awake and aware. Expelled, almost. Flung out into the light from some dark depth.

Why?

As simple as making a connection between the two good-bad-and-ugly remarks? He didn't think so.

When he tuned back into the conversation, he groaned audibly. The memory/flashback had taken long enough for the discussion to go where it invariably did. Any time Bradford's Ridge, Kentucky, was mentioned, the conversation progressed in one of two directions, both subjects Jack never wanted to talk about. The first was the fire at Twin Oaks, the deadliest nursing home fire in U.S. history. The second was Bradford's Ridge native son Chapman Whitworth—which, essentially, was the same conversation.

"Yeah, but you gotta admit Whitworth had some stones even as a kid, hauling those old people out of there with his hair on fire!" Peterson said.

Ramirez imitated a commanding voice, "You'll have to go through me!"

Jack rolled his eyes. Even at the time it'd sounded canned, rehearsed and phony, a Clint Eastwood make-my-day line. And even with the video as proof, Jack had remained steadfastly unimpressed—who said that kind of macho crap in real life, facing real danger? Apparently, the answer to that question was Chapman Whitworth, the man who, shortly after saying the words—and certainly because he'd said them—was elected to the United States Senate.

Whitworth was older than Jack, and Jack had no memory of him—not surprising, given that he had no memories of anybody else, either. Whitworth's heroism during the nightmare fire had cost him much of the right side of his face, though the scar gave the man a singularly commanding presence. It had also secured for him an appointment to West Point where he graduated at the top of his class. That was something else Jack had against him. Jack had been an Army Ranger, one of the youngest ever, and rangers held West Point desk soldiers in particular contempt.

Whitworth had been deployed during the Gulf War. Later press releases about him said that he had "served with distinction" there, whatever that meant.

Still, Whitworth would likely have slid quietly into obscurity afterward had he not been seated in the front row of First Class on US Air Flight 734 from Cincinnati to Los Angeles on March 4, 2003.

It was never determined what exactly the knife-wielding lunatic on the flight actually wanted—much less how he'd gotten the knife through security, which was, admittedly, sketchy at the time. But it was clear he intended to use the weapon on the pilot and co-pilot in the cockpit, and would have done so had it not been for Chapman Whitworth.

Not a particularly big man, he had seemed larger than life that day. Leaping from his seat to block the door leading to the cockpit, Whitworth had stood, arms crossed and glared at the lunatic.

"Get out of the way," the crazy man had shouted, "I'm going in there."

"You'll have to go through me," Whitworth had said calmly.

The man had attempted to do just that. And Whitworth had killed him.

That part stuck in Jack's craw as well. A trained soldier, Whitworth could have—and in Jack's view should have—merely disarmed the man. Instead, he'd wrestled the weapon away and it had subsequently ended up in the lunatic's chest.

That part hadn't been captured by the passenger who'd been filming her grandson's reaction to his first airplane ride when the crazy man leapt into the aisle. She'd turned her camcorder on the drama and filmed it in glowing detail. Once the media got hold of the video, it was shown —Jack believed ad nauseam—around the world.

So soon after 9/11, with every airplane passenger hinky about terrorists on board, the mood of the country was such that nobody seemed inclined to question whether or not Whitworth had used excessive force.

Instant hero—add water and stir. Whitworth was nominated and elected by a landslide to the U.S. Senate from Kentucky less than a year later. His cheesy campaign slogan became as iconic as "Let's Roll."

You want to mess with America, you'll have to go through me.

Jack had seen a picture in the Louisville Courier-Journal on a newsstand in Cincinnati when a garish monstrosity of a sign had been erected in his hometown. It featured a picture of Chapman Whitworth's head, thirty feet tall sticking out of the top, his mouth open as if the shot had been taken as he'd spoken the words printed in the little speech bubble next to it: "You'll have to go through me." Beneath the head was the inscription: "Bradford's Ridge, Kentucky, home of U.S. Senator Chapman Whitworth." He'd only served one term as senator before securing an appointment as a federal judge in Cincinnati, but Jack would bet his running shorts the sign in Bradford's Ridge remained.

Crocker was either not paying attention to the Whitworth conversation, or didn't hear it. The major had weird hearing issues. Sometimes, he missed a whole conversation and sometimes he could pick up a whisper across a crowded room. There was a crease of concentration across his brow that was the only mark of any kind on his head from his eyebrows to the tag on his shirt collar. Jack recognized it as his "I'm going to get to the bottom of this" look.

"I don't believe in coincidences," Crocker said. "Until the board of inquiry puts your batteries back in, you're as useless around here as bumps on a pickle. Why don't you do some more digging, see if you can come up with a bone that ties all this together. Unofficially, of course."

"I'll see what I can find out."

No prob, Crock. I'll just ask the eye-witnesses in Savannah and Saint Louis, "Say, any of you good folks see a swarm of bugs with fangs perched on the perps' shoulders?"

~

Opthalmologist, Dr. Paul Fredricks, at Addison Gilbert Hospital in Gloucester, Massachusetts, was scrubbing for the emergency surgery that had called him off the golf course this morning before he'd even had time to tee off. He'd played every Monday with the same foursome for going on ten years now and they had razzing-rights about his abandoning them.

"I have an agreement wiz my patients," said Sergei Afanaseyez, the obstetrician, in his melodious Russian accent. "If I 'em not dere when the bebe showszup, they go ahead and hiv it widout me."

In truth, Dr. Fredricks didn't often miss a game for an emergency, but a seaman with a horrendous injury had been airlifted from a commercial fishing vessel seventy-five miles off shore last night and flown in on a Coast Guard chopper.

As an intern more years ago than he liked to admit, Dr. Fredricks had always hated the emergency room rotation. Oh sure, if you asked him, he'd maintain there was no such thing as a squeamish doctor. Nobody got through four years of medical school, two years of internship and another four of residency without developing a profound tolerance for all things bloody, oozy, wet and squishy. But he was honest enough to admit to himself that one of the reasons he had selected opthalmology was that it afforded him minimum exposure to the maimed and mauled. And the older he got, the more grateful he was that while others were called to bind up the wounds of the world, he got paid to help the humanity in his little part of it see the world better.

He'd flinched inwardly when he'd been briefed on the

patient coming in on the chopper. Occupations all had their hazards, but he had never heard of a fishing injury like this seaman had sustained. He wasn't looking forward to this surgery.

Rachel Zaremba, the nurse he'd worked with for so long she handed him instruments before he asked for them, stepped into the room. He turned so she could help him glove up, but her mask was pulled down off her face.

"He's gone," she said. Her voice had a peculiar quality he'd never heard in it before.

"Who's gone?" Dr. Fredricks asked.

"The patient."

Dr. Fredericks stopped scrubbing.

"Gone where?"

"Just…gone. He's not in there. The floor nurse went to get him, found the lines unhooked and the bed empty. His gown was on the floor and his clothes weren't in the closet."

What she said was confusing, but far more disturbing was the look on her face. Rachel Zaremba was a rock, calm and unflappable. You wanted her in the trench beside you when it hit the fan. Now, she seemed about to cry, breathing in short little gasps like she was in shock.

"A man with that kind of injury…" Dr. Fredricks couldn't process it. "You're telling me he got up and walked out of the hospital with a fish hook in his eye?"

"No, that's not what I'm telling you," she said, with a little squeak that sounded like incipient hysteria. "He didn't walk out with a fish hook in his eye."

Dr. Fredricks noticed the instrument tray in her hand for the first time when she held it out to him.

"He left his eye behind."

Lying in a small puddle of blood and fluid was a human eye, trailing broken blood vessels and ligaments where it had been ripped from its socket. The orb looked like a ball of white bait. A three-inch hook had been stabbed into one side of the eyeball and the gory prong end protruded out the other. Centered perfectly.

The eye stared sightlessly up at Dr. Fredricks. It was a startling pale blue.

~

Growing in Daniel's chest like a festering boil, it got bigger and uglier every day. He'd been waiting for the right time to talk to Emily about it, had planned out what to say. But he had underestimated the force of the building pressure. One day it burst and the stinking, vile infection squirted out all over him, and all over Emily, too.

Andi was asleep. He had brought the book downstairs with him to ensure she didn't pull out a flashlight and read it under the covers after he left.

He'd sat on the edge of her bed earlier, reading it to her and having with her the same discussion they'd had so many times before.

"The movie," Andi had pronounced firmly. "I love the book, Daddy, but the movie's waaay better."

"Maybe you have a fever," Daniel had said, and reached to put his hand on her forehead, but she'd batted it away. "All the good lines in the movie came right out of the book, Sweetheart."

"But Billy Crystal as Miracle Max," she crinkled up her nose and did a pretty fair imitation, "'Have fun stormin' the castle, boys.' That was epic, Daddy. And how beautiful Princess Buttercup looked when she floated down out of the window onto that horse."

"That's exactly how you float down when we play Catch Me," he teased. That was a game Andi'd started when she was maybe three years old—just hopped up onto the back of the couch one day, put her arms out to her sides, closed her eyes, called out, "Catch me!" then dropped straight backward. Daniel had had to leap halfway across the room that first time to keep her from landing splat on the floor.

Andi rolled her eyes, "Riiiight."

Back and forth they went. Eventually, they'd declared the perpetual Princess Bride argument a draw, as they always did.

He'd been smiling to himself about the book, hadn't even been thinking about the dark, rotting hole in his heart. Then Emily had breezed into the room, looking radiant, and had casually brushed a kiss off the top of his head when she passed where he was sitting in his recliner. Something about the offhandedness of the gesture, the superficial, perfunctory nature of it stabbed into his chest, an ice pick that punctured the swollen boil within.

"I know," he said quietly.

She had been crossing the room toward the kitchen, but the tone of his voice stopped her and she turned to face him. Several looks washed over her face at once. Uncertainty. Surprise. He saw apprehension there, too— no, fear.

"Know what?" she said, and was almost able to carry it off as an innocent question. But not quite.

He hadn't meant to say it, but once the words were out there in the room, he not only couldn't call them back, but couldn't stem the tsunami of tangled emotions that had propelled them out of his chest.

He took a slow, deep breath, and rage/love/hurt/indignation and all the other feelings solidified and settled around him in a blanket of icy calm.

"No games," he said. "At least show enough respect for me not to pretend you don't know what I'm talking about."

Emily had the most amazing ability to charge a room with electricity, with a kind of "game-day" excitement just by her presence and her dazzling smile. As she stood expressionless, studying him, he could feel the "charge" go out of her. She diminished before him, some of her power taken from her.

"How did you find out?"

"What difference does it make how? I know. I know that…"

He paused for only a moment in real time, but in soul time, the earth stopped, ceased spinning and revolving around the sun. On the other side of what he was about to say was a world he did not know, a reality he'd never even considered. And a door would slam shut behind him as soon as he spoke the new world into existence and he would never be able to return to the old one, the world of innocent trust and security and commitment. How did two people, two married people, relate in the world he was entering, where all the rules had been broken, the trust shattered, the vows abandoned? How did they make a place there, and make a place they must, because the world of innocence would be forever lost to them as soon as he spoke.

"…you were shacked up somewhere rolling around in the sheets with Jeff Kendrick when Andi was shot, when your little girl was bleeding—dying."

The sudden rage that catapulted him into the new world was all-consuming and almost overwhelming. He hadn't expected it at that moment or wanted it, but was grateful for the strength it gave him. Righteous indignation did, indeed, bestow great power and authority.

Emily looked like he'd slapped her. She sank down onto the arm of the chair she stood beside, her face white. She didn't look at him, merely stared at a spot on the floor in the middle of the room. When she finally spoke, her voice was barely audible, clotted with unshed tears.

"I love my baby. When I thought we might lose her, I…" She stopped, took a deep breath, then another. Slowly she raised her eyes to meet his and there was such unexpected steel in her gaze that if he'd been standing, he would have taken a step back. "I will be forever sorry I wasn't available to my daughter every second that she needed me…but I am not sorry for where I was and what I was doing, so don't expect me to fall at your feet and beg your forgiveness."

"Emily, how could you?" He realized how trite and pathetic that sounded but it just popped out. "Why?"

"Why? Oh, let's see…maybe it's that there hasn't been any passion in our marriage since…I don't know…since Bill Clinton 'did not sleep with that woman.' Or maybe that you look at me and talk at me, but you haven't really seen or spoken to me in years. Or that—"

"So it's my fault? You commit adultery and it's my fault?"

"Adultery? Oh, please. Adultery is one of those church words you love to throw around that don't mean a thing to you."

This was wrong, all wrong. How had he gotten on the defensive?

"So you're not committing adultery?"

"If it makes you feel morally superior to paint me with a scarlet letter, be my guest. Certainly, that word's your get-out-of-jail-free card. Plop that baby out there and 'poor pastor Daniel' will instantly become a hyphenated word. Poor-Pastor-Daniel's wife committed adultery and that gives Poor-Pastor-Daniel Biblical grounds to get a divorce."

They both were shocked into silence by the noxious sound of the word. It hung there between them, stinking like a dead fish on a stick. Emily recovered first.

"Is that what you want—out? A divorce?"

Daniel's head was spinning. In all the times he'd pictured this scene, all the times he'd imagined what would be said, he had never pictured Emily unrepentant. No, not just unrepentant—defiant. How did he…what was he supposed to do with that? He'd prepared himself for contrition, tears, pleading for forgiveness. He'd searched his heart for compassion to give to her. He had prayed for…

No, he hadn't.

The words of the old black woman, Theresa Washington, rang in his ears.

"When was the last time you prayed? You ain't been praying for me. Or for yourself or your wife or your little girl."

He hadn't prayed for anything.

"You didn't answer my question, Dan. Is that what you want? A divorce?"

"Is that what you want?"

Emily wavered, didn't seem prepared for the question. He got the sense that the conversation had gotten out of hand for her, too, that perhaps it had gone places she didn't expect or intend for it to go. She looked down, not meeting his eyes for a time, but none of what she might be thinking showed on her face. Finally, she sighed and looked up at him.

"This is the truth, Dan. As much of the truth as I know. It will probably surprise you, but I like my life. It works. I like this house. I like being…" She made quotation marks in the air with her fingers, "'Pastor Burke's wife.' Maybe my life's dull, uninspiring, but it's safe. I don't know how I would survive alone."

"Alone? You mean you wouldn't dash into Jeff Kendrick's waiting arms?"

"Leave Jeff out of this."

"Leave him out of this? He's the reason for this."

"No, he's not. He's not the cause, he's the effect. You're the cause." She paused, then added grudgingly, "we're the cause."

She got to her feet.

"If you're asking me if I'm willing to pick up the phone right now and call Jeff and tell him I never want to see him again, the answer is no. Whatever you have to do about that, you'll just have to do. But if you're asking if I want a divorce, the answer to that is no, too."

She looked at him, vulnerable for a moment, and he could see that the strength and resolve were not as sturdy as she would have him believe, as she herself wanted to believe. He saw confusion, uncertainty and—no, he wasn't deluding himself—he saw affection there, too. Love? That he couldn't say. But she cared about him, that was certain. She still cared.

"I'm not ready to give up, not yet…" she finished softly, "on…us."

She seemed to catch herself, then, to realize she'd let her guard down and the door to her soul slammed shut in his face.

"Besides…there's Andi."

By mutual unspoken agreement, they had not talked about that strange afternoon when Theresa Washington had said their little girl could see demons. And the longer they didn't talk about it, the more comfortable they became with the illusion that it'd never happened, that the strange old woman was addled by her grief and Andi... They couldn't go there, explain how Andi had come back from...how she had seen...so they simply didn't talk about it.

"Andi is fragile right now. I don't know what's going on with her..."

Emily's voice trailed off. Daniel had nothing to say, to add.

A creature made of wasps?

The heart monitor's sudden beep, beep, beep.

But right now was absolutely not the time to go there.

"I don't know what it means that she...what any of it means about her, or about...God." Emily's voice had the same wonder in it Daniel was sure he'd hear in his own if he tried to talk about it. "But I do know that there's enough turmoil in that child's life and we can't add to it. Right now is not the time for her parents to decide to go their separate ways. She needs us, Daniel. She needs both of us."

The words echoed like they were bouncing off the walls of an ancient church.

She needs both of us!

But the second time he heard them, it wasn't Emily who spoke them. It was Jack Carpenter.

Daniel's mind was suddenly filled with a scene so tangible that it shoved reality out of the way and took its place.

Chapter Sixteen

"She needs both of us," Jack says.

Daniel shakes Jack's restraining hand off his arm, his own hands balled into fists of rage, and turns toward the woods.

"We have to stick together. You go running off trying to be a hero, that leaves me here by myself. Just me"—he gestures toward the little girl sitting in the dirt a few feet away, covered in blood, sobbing uncontrollably—"and Becca."

Daniel sags.

"Ok, you're right," he says.

Daniel doesn't like it that Jack is right, doesn't like admitting that he is not big enough or strong enough to inflict revenge for Becca's loss all by himself. He wants to be, but knows he isn't. And he understands that it's more important to be with Becca right now than to score points with her by making Jacob Dumas and Victor Alexander pay for what they've done.

Still, the sound of Becca sobbing hurts Daniel's heart in a way he's never felt before. He wants to fix it, to make it right. But he can't. He looks at Becca's face, a mask of grief as she cradles the dead animal—most of it anyway— to her chest and rocks back and forth.

"Vic's probably watching us right now," Jack says, softly. "Sent Jake to get the others." Jack scans the nearby bushes. "We need to get her home before the rest of them show up."

Daniel glances uneasily over his shoulder. The three of them are in the woods, in a clearing beside a big sycamore tree. He can hear a nearby stream laughing its way over small stones, and birds chirping in the trees. That's good, the chirping birds. Means nobody's coming. Yet.

Jack gestures with his chin toward the round, bloody object lying in the dirt a few feet from where Becca is sobbing. Daniel shoots a questioning look at Jack, who continues to communicate with looks rather than words. Jack looks at the round thing lying in a puddle of blood that's already attracted a couple of flies, then back at Becca.

Jack's right again. Daniel walks slowly to it, bends over and picks it up, trying not to look at it, trying not to get blood all over his hands. But there is no way to keep from doing either.

The sightless eyes are glazed over with a film and look like dirty marbles, the mouth is open, the tongue hangs out and blood is still dripping from the gory hole in its brown fur where the head had been attached to the dog's body.

He kneels beside Becca, not knowing what to do, what to say, holding the dog head awkwardly—how do you not hold the still-warm head of a butchered animal awkwardly?

She sits in the dirt clutching the rest of the dog's bloody body to her chest, tears streaming down her face from eyes squeezed shut tight.

"Becca, we need to go now," he tells her as tenderly as he can. "I'll—we'll—carry McDougal for you. Jack and I will dig a grave and we'll bury him."

"I shouldn't have let him off the leash," Becca says, the words interspersed between wracking sobs, her wet face turned up to the sky. "But he loves to run in the woods and I never thought…"

She opens her eyes then, looks at the bloody body she has pulled into her lap, and then at the dog's head that Daniel's holding. She bursts into hysterical sobbing again, hugging the limp dog in her arms and shaking her head.

"Dougie," she cries. "Precious DD."

The truth is, they never should have come out in the woods today at all. Things between them and The Bad Kids had been getting worse every day. Becca's father was the biggest, meanest dope grower in the state and nobody messed with him or his little girl, but these guys didn't seem to care. Nothing frightened them. Their animosity toward Becca was as vicious as it was unexplainable. And she couldn't stay holed up in her house all the time.

That's why Jack and Daniel had let Becca talk them into hiking up to Red Rock, which was only a little over a mile from her house. She'd taken McDougal, the beloved mutt she'd adopted from the animal shelter, used the leash as they walked beside the road because McDougal—AKA McDo, McD, Dougie, Dougal Dog and DD—was an unrepentant car chaser. When they turned up the logging road and then into the woods, she'd unclipped the leash and slipped it into her pocket.

It was a hot, sticky day as are most summer days in Kentucky. They'd taken off their shoes and waded upstream in the creek. McDo plopped down in the cool water, rolled over in it until he was soaked, then stood and performed his amazing full-body shake that sprayed water on them all. They paused often for Jack and Daniel to try to wrestle each other into the creek. Becca and Jack had been laughing at Daniel, who'd eluded Jack's attempts all afternoon to dunk him, then slipped and fell flat on his backside in the water, when they noticed that McDougal was missing.

"Dougle Dog," Becca called. "Here, D.D."

One call was always sufficient to bring the dog charging out of the undergrowth, tail wagging. But McDougal didn't respond. He'd been running out ahead of them, sniffing every leaf, stump, rock and tree limb he came to, but now they couldn't see him anywhere.

"Dougie," Becca called again. They were slightly below the crest of a hill and climbed up to the top of it, sure they'd see the dog there, or at least be high enough he'd hear Becca when she called.

But the dog wasn't all they found when they got to the crest of the hill.

Daniel was ahead and saw them first. About thirty feet away beside a big rock were Jacob and Victor. Victor had McDougal clutched tight to his chest with his fingers around the dog's snout to keep his mouth closed so he couldn't bark.

As soon as Becca saw them, she cried out, "McDo!" and started toward them.

"I'd stay right where I was if I's you," said Jake. "Wouldn't want anything bad to happen to your worthless mutt."

Becca froze. "Don't hurt DD. He never did anything to you."

"Give Becca back her dog," Jack said and began advancing on them.

"Say please," Victor said.

Daniel could actually hear Jack's teeth grind together.

"Please," Jack said.

"Ok, since you asked so nice—sure, we'll give him back to her."

Then Victor lifted the dog up, holding him in one hand by the neck. McDougal was a good-sized dog, weighed at least sixty pounds, and he was wiggling frantically, squirming and whimpering, trying to break free.

"Here, you go," he shouted. "You can have him."

Vic reached up and took the dog's head in both hands, then twirled the dog's body around it, the way you wring a chicken's neck.

It had all happened so fast, Jack and Daniel had no time to react. Around and around the body went—once, twice—then Jacob snapped his wrist like popping a whip, and the dog's body flew out into the air and plopped down a few feet away, blood gushing from the hole above its shoulders where its head had been.

Becca let out a horrified, anguished shriek. Victor tossed the dog's head on the ground, turned and fled with Jacob into the woods.

Now Becca rocks the dog's body and sobs, strangling out anguished words, "It's my fault. I shouldn't have let him out of my sight. All those other dogs, you know Jacob and Victor killed them, too."

Jack and Daniel had suspected as much, and this proved it. What other explanation was there for the sudden reign of terror that had descended in a freight-train rush on animals in Bradford's Ridge? Seven small dogs had been killed in less than a week, their mutilated bodies left on their masters' porches. Other small pets—rabbits and cats—had been set on fire.

Four big dogs—two German shepherds, a pit bull and a Rottweiler had been found with their throats slit. The whole town was in a full bore, raging panic about it, eager to form a lynch mob if they could find somebody to string up, and unwilling to let their pets out of their sight.

It wasn't only pets, though. Suddenly, snakes had started turning up everywhere. Two middle-aged women were digging through the bin of "on sale" accessories in Franklin's Department Store, and one pulled out what she thought was a leather belt. It turned out to be a three-foot-long black snake. Mr. Franklin closed the store for the rest of the week, found four other snakes in the building—two in shoe boxes, one in the coat pocket of a man's suit, and one wrapped like a necklace around the neck of a mannequin in the storeroom.

A tangle of half a dozen garter snakes were found in the trash can in the girls' bathroom at Harper's Drive-In. The manager couldn't even lure teenage girls back into the building with free milkshakes.

When Mrs. Milligan almost stepped on a hog snake on the steps of Daniel's father's church last Sunday, she'd had a heart attack and was still in the hospital in intensive care.

Obscenities and swastikas and yellow stars-of-David had been randomly spray-painted on downtown store fronts, sewage dumped into the swimming pool at the park and the fountain in front of City Hall.

And that's only what Daniel and Jack knew about. There were other things—obviously worse things—that grownups stopped talking about when they got near.

Jack puts his hands on Becca's shoulders. "We have to go," he says.

She nods. She eases the dog's body off her lap onto the ground. Jack helps her to her feet

"We'll go to the sheriff now, the three of us, we have proof." Daniel says, but knows as soon as the words leave his mouth that no one will believe a twelve-year-old boy could kill a sixty-pound dog that way.

Jack elbows him and gestures with his chin. Standing at the base of the small hill they'd climbed are Jacob and Victor and a handful of other boys. The boys stand looking up at them for a moment, then start up the hill. Jack leans toward Becca.

"Dano and I are going to take them," he says softly. "When we jump them, you run, run as fast as you can all the way home, don't look back until you get there."

"No," she says.

Then she calls out to the boys climbing the hill. "I see you and I'm not afraid of you. You don't have any power over me."

Jack and Daniel look at each other, uncomprehending.

The gang of boys stop, their faces so expressionless they look like robots.

"Really?" Jacob says. He is carrying a gunny sack. He reaches down, pulls open the drawstrings, then flings the sack at them so that whatever is in it comes out in the air. "Not afraid of this?"

The snake lands in the dirt not three feet in front of Becca.

"A rattlesnake?" Victor roars at Jacob, grabs a handful of his shirt front and yells in his face. "You stupid—"

The diamondback is huge, probably five feet long, and it curls instantly into a striking position, its head in the middle of the coil, its tail sounding a rattling alarm. Jack and Daniel freeze.

The other boys don't freeze, though. In fact, they'd started backing up even before the snake came out of the sack.

Then the snake begins to lift off the ground. Daniel gapes at it, slack-jawed, watches as it is flung at the retreating boys as if by an invisible hand.

"Dan," Emily said his name in the tone of voice you use when this isn't the first time you've said it.

The image Daniel saw so clearly in front of him faded. But before it blinked out altogether, Daniel saw something he hadn't seen when he was in the scene, living it with Jack and Becca. He saw a light beside Becca so fiercely bright the sight would stick pins in his head through his eyes if he looked directly at it.

A light like Andi described, so bright you can't look at it straight on.

Then it was gone.

"Dan!" Emily said. "Are you ignoring me?"

"No, I … I saw something, Emily. Something strange."

"Not you, too." There was real apprehension in her voice.

"No, not like that," he said. "Just a memory, a vivid memory from the summer when I was twelve years—"

They both heard it at the same time, the sound of Andi crying. But not from her room upstairs. They turned together and saw her, sitting on the stairs halfway up with her head in her hands sobbing. Daniel felt the sudden weak, boneless sensation he'd felt that day they'd been playing Catch Me, and he'd tripped and almost missed her.

Had she been sitting there when…had she overheard?

Chapter Seventeen

Ossy hopped up onto the bed with Andi. The big calico circled around twice before curling snug up against Andi's side. Ossy was short for Curiosity—but not because curiosity killed the cat. Ossy was a curiosity because he was a male Calico and Daddy said only about one in every three thousand calicos were boys.

And he was an even bigger curiosity because only one in every thousand boy Calico cats can be a daddy, but Ossy was the father of the kittens the purebred Persian cat next door had last spring—which made Mrs. Shutterbaum mad, but Andi thought they were adorable. No matter how special the cat was, though, he still wasn't supposed to sleep with Andi, but he did almost every night.

Andi waited until she was sure her father was all the way downstairs, until she could hear the hum of voices which meant he and Mommy were talking, before she reached into the top drawer of her bedside table and took out her mother's iPad. She tapped the screen a couple of times, then settled back on her pillows with a sigh to take up where she'd left off last night.

Ossy began to purr.

"Who are you?" Prince Humperdink asks Westley who is pretending he is totally fine but really he can't move.

"No one of consequence." Westley says.

"I must know," the prince says.

"Get used to disappointment," Westley says.

Andi giggled. She always giggled at that part. It was one of her favorite Princess Bride lines, but not as funny as when Westley tells Princess Buttercup about the time he spent on the pirate ship, how the Dread Pirate Roberts said to him every night before he went to bed, "Good work, Westley. Sleep well. I'll most likely kill you in the morning."

Suddenly, Andi heard a sound that she had no name for, a sound like singing, only there were no words, and like music, except there was no instrument she had ever heard that could create such a melody. The sound was also color, which made no sense, but it was, a rich golden glow, soft and sometimes so bright you couldn't look at it. It was smell, too, the air after a spring rain, and the sound felt smooth against her cheek, like satin or velvet, or the touch of the blond curls that tickled her nose when she held the Kirby's baby.

She knew instantly where the sound/sight/smell/touch came from. She had only heard it one other time in her life, but she would never forget it. Mommy and Daddy had been standing beside her as she lay on the bed in a hospital. She knew they were there, but she couldn't open her eyes to see them and she could hear her mother's voice but she couldn't make out what she was saying.

Then the light had come, the light and sound. This light and sound.

But this time the light was not nearly so bright, not piercing. It pooled at the foot of her bed and standing in the middle of the pool was Princess Buttercup.

Ossy lifted his head, turned and looked at the figure at the foot of the bed. He let out a soft "meow," then put his head back on his paws and went back to sleep.

Maybe Andi ought to be afraid. After all, somebody had appeared out of nowhere in her bedroom, even if it was Princess Buttercup—no, Princess Buttercup lit from the inside like a nightlight. But Andi wasn't afraid at all.

"Who are you?" Andi asked, though she was almost sure she already knew. "You're not really...?"

Princess Buttercup walked around the bed and sat on the edge of it next to Andi. Ossy had to scoot over a little to make a place for her but he didn't even wake up.

"Do you know the one thing that's said in the Bible more often than anything else—more than three hundred and fifty times?"

Andi shook her head.

Princess Buttercup smiled. "'Do not be afraid,'" she said. She made a gesture toward herself. "Princess Buttercup isn't scary, though, is she?"

Andi shook her head again. Normally, she'd have been babbling and chattering and asking questions. Now, she merely stared in awe and wonder—couldn't think of a thing to say.

"I want to show you something, Andi," Princess Buttercup said. "I need you to watch carefully."

Andi's room vanished. It was replaced by a darkness that was not scary because there seemed to be light on the edges of it, like a blanket thrown over a lampshade so the light shone through.

Then images began to appear in the blackness. It was almost like the movie she'd been watching on the iPad, only the images didn't speak, and they were huge, way bigger than could possibly have fit inside her little bedroom. But they did fit, because there were no walls or ceiling or floor in her bedroom now, only the black all around with light behind it and the images.

Though it was similar to watching a movie, it wasn't like a movie. No special effects she'd ever seen could possibly have looked like this. And there was no talking, no people to talk, only images, huge and bright, colored with the shades of logs burning in the fireplace, tumbling slowly over and over in front of her. And there was no plot either, just the images in the air, huge and scary-looking, only she wasn't afraid. She couldn't feel afraid as long as the music-sound that wasn't actually music played in her ear and Princess Buttercup was sitting right there beside her.

She saw the same scene three times. Exactly the same, like she'd hit rewind on a video and played it again. The images made no sense, but by the time she had seen them for the third time, she could have identified them anywhere and they were impressed in her memory so vividly that she could see every detail of each one.

As suddenly as her room had vanished, it reappeared. The blackness was there and then it wasn't. The sound was there and then gone, taking with it the pleasant smell of early rain and the soft touch of a baby's curls.

She was in her bed in her room as she had been before everything vanished. Princess Buttercup was gone. Andi reached over and felt the sheets next to where Ossy was sleeping. They were cold, not warm like somebody'd been sitting there. In fact, there was not even a break in the movie playing on the iPad in her hand. It was like the scene in the air had shown up in a space between time, between one second and the next, so the world didn't even know it'd been there, didn't miss the time it took to see it.

Andi pushed "pause" on the movie and turned the iPad off, plunging the room into darkness since the only light in the room had come from the iPad screen. Then she sat holding the iPad in her lap, staring into the space at the foot of her bed where it was plain old dark now, like she'd seen every night of her life.

Whatever it was she'd seen, Andi was certain it was important. Princess Buttercup had told her to watch carefully. It had come from the place where she'd been when Uncle Jack had called out to her, and she had been shown the same thing three times for a reason.

She needed to tell Mommy and Daddy about it right now.

Andi hopped out of bed, leaving Ossy asleep behind her, slipped her feet into her house shoes, padded down the hall and then down the stairs, not intending to sneak up on anybody, just quiet because it was hard to make noise when you were wearing house shoes on carpet.

When she got half way down the stairs, she heard her mother's voice.

'There's enough turmoil in that child's life and we can't add to it. Right now is not the time for her parents to decide to get a divorce and go their separate ways."

Divorce?

Andi knew what that word meant. Sara Henry's parents had gotten one and now Sara only saw her daddy on weekends and her mother was sad and cried all the time and Sara had to drop out of piano lessons because her mother couldn't afford to pay for them anymore.

Could…would her parents get a divorce?

Andi sat down hard on the carpeted stairs because she couldn't stand up anymore, and besides she was afraid she was about to be sick. Why would they do a thing like that —get a divorce? Sara had said her parents stopped loving each other and that's why they did it. Had Mommy and Daddy stopped loving each other? And if they had, had they stopped loving her, too?

She was suddenly as frightened as she had been in the school that day, looking through the crack as the bad man shot Miss Lund and Mr. Bishop. Tears sprang into her eyes, she put her head in her hands and started to cry.

~

Emily ran across the room and up the few steps to where Andi sat, her heart in her throat.

Had she heard? Did she actually listen to her parents discuss getting a divorce?

"Honey, what's wrong?" she asked and gathered the sobbing child into her arms. But Andi said nothing, merely cried harder.

What had she done? The hole in Emily's belly was so deep and painful it felt like the whole bottom portion of her body had fallen away. Not Andi. What she and Jeff were doing was never supposed to hurt her precious child.

And Andi was precious to Emily, had come at great cost and sacrifice.

Hers had been more than a difficult pregnancy. It had been high risk from the beginning, when her blood pressure shot through the roof at three months and refused to budge downwards. By six months, she was hospitalized in full bore pre-eclampsia, with her doctors—and Dan!—weighing every day the risk to mother and baby that allowing the pregnancy to continue presented. Every day she carried Andi, she put her own life in lethal danger. And every additional day Andi stayed in Emily's womb increased the chances that she would survive.

The nightmare of Andi's birth began when the infant monitors suddenly showed a baby in distress. Not beeps getting slower and slower as the other monitor—she couldn't even think about that—but racing, the heartbeat getting faster and faster, like the frantic heartbeat of some fettered bird. An emergency Caesarian section followed, along with hemorrhaging the doctors only barely controlled.

Andi was Emily's miracle, and she had blocked out of her mind any possibility that her relationship with Jeff might hurt the child.

Had she heard?

Please, God, no.

The words brought Emily up short. It was a prayer, and she hadn't prayed since…she hadn't even prayed when the doctor told them to tell Andi goodbye. She had been in such terror and shock then she couldn't have formulated words if she'd tried.

But she was praying now. Please, God, don't let her have heard.

"Honey, what's wrong?" she pleaded with the sobbing child. "Tell Mommy."

"Did you have a bad dream?" Dan asked her.

The child looked up into his face, then turned to her mother, the tears a smear down both cheeks. For a moment, an odd, unreadable look skittered across her features.

"Uh huh…I had a bad dream."

She was trying hard to get herself under control.

"Tell me about it, Honey," Dan said. He sat beside Emily and lifted Andi out of her arms into his lap and cradled her tenderly there. It struck Emily that it had been a long time since she'd realized what a good father Dan was.

"I don't want to talk about it," Andi said. "Can I go back to bed now?"

"Not until you tell us what frightened you," he said.

Again, Andi turned to look into Emily's face, then back at her father. She sighed, then, appeared to make a decision.

"I wasn't crying because I had a bad dream," she said.

"Then why were you crying?" Emily asked.

She reached up and tried to dry her cheeks and Dan magically produced a clean handkerchief for her to use. When she spoke again, she was calmer, seemed to be trying hard to concentrate.

"It wasn't a dream and it didn't scare me. It was…" She paused. "First, the room went away. It was dark, but light showed through the dark. And it smelled and sounded and felt like it did the day I went into the light and then came back when Uncle Jack called me."

Emily felt her stomach heave. No, not this. Please…

"And then I saw the same thing three times."

"Saw what?" Dan asked. His voice sounded as insubstantial as a reflection on a windowpane.

"Splashes of color—first red, then purple, then green, then blue—like paint splatters, only made out of light. And after the color came the shapes."

Andi closed her eyes, visualizing the images as she described them.

"There were shapes—eight of them. They tumbled over and over. Right side up, then upside down, doing summersaults. A square, two circles, a triangle, two capital T's, the little one in front of the big one—kinda like a telephone pole. Then a bell, a cross that was pointed at the top and a line—is that a shape?—just straight up and down."

She opened her eyes.

"The square and the T's were beside each other. They were black and the square had little feet, kinda. The two circles were silver, the triangle was red and the line was brown."

She stopped and smiled tentatively, as if she was proud that she remembered it all and described it correctly.

"And the sky was on fire, too, sort of. Sparks were flying everywhere around where the fire was, a big fire with black smoke.

Then Andi began to cry again, not hard this time, not a frightened cry. Emily recognized the sound, a sad cry. Andi must be remembering the teacher and the old black man she had loved, who'd been gunned down before her eyes. That's why she was sad. It was, wasn't it?

She put her arms around Andi and Dan, held both of them close.

"It's Ok, now baby. You're here, safe with us. Mommy and Daddy are here and we won't let any bad things get you, ever."

"Both of you?" she asked.

Why would she ask that unless she'd heard? Emily didn't drop a beat.

"Of course, both of us. We'll be here together to protect you."

Chapter Eighteen

Jack's investigation was definitely off the grid, skating on ice so thin he could see down through it, could see images there he didn't want to look at. But Crock had told him to nose around, so he'd been doing his job when he'd asked to meet with Daniel and Theresa Washington to see if the three-heads-are-better-than-one rule applied. Daniel had invited the other two to his home, said Emily and Andi would be attending the Mother-Daughter banquet at the church all evening and they'd have privacy to talk.

Jack looked up over the coffee Daniel had poured for him into a cup way too dainty for his big hands, and thought that Daniel didn't look well at all.

"Daniel, you don't look good," Theresa said. A big Calico cat rubbed against Theresa's leg and she reached down and petted it. "Sit yourself down and stop making nice. I want more coffee, I can get it my own self."

Jack smiled at that. The more time Jack spent with Theresa Washington, the better he liked her.

He took a breath, might as well get to it. He'd heard a phrase once—couldn't recall where—that had become one of the guiding principles in his life: If you have to eat a frog, don't look at it too long. And if you have to eat two frogs, eat the big one first.

"Like I said on the phone, I've been assigned the unenviable task of explaining the phenomena of the 1985 Bradford's Ridge Little League team and its sterling membership." He held up his hand and began to tick them off his fingers. "Which included a school shooter, a police officer, a minister and…" He'd been holding up three fingers. Then he paused for a beat before gulping down the big frog. Slowly, he opened his hand, palm out. "Two mass murderers."

"Mass-murderers!" Theresa cried.

"Wannabe mass murders," Jack amended. "Two guys, Walter Stephenson and Roger Willingham tried, but they didn't manage to kill anybody but themselves." He smiled a half smile. "Struck out, so to speak. Needed better coaching."

Theresa, who was still rattled by what Jack had said, merely mumbled, "He done the best he could."

"Who did?" Jack asked.

"Bishop."

She smiled a little then at what must have been twin looks of confusion on his and Daniel's faces. "Uh, huh. My Bishop was the coach of yore Little League team."

"You're from Bradford's Ridge, too?" Daniel was incredulous.

For Jack, the first tumbler in a big combination lock clicked into place. "That's how you know us." Jack put his head in his hands. "Am I the only one here who hears the theme song from the Twilight Zone?"

Theresa made a humph sound in her throat. "Twilight Zone's made-up magic stuff and what's happening here's real. That demon Andi and Bishop seen was real. It come to the school so's it could threaten them kids to get Bishop to tell it what it wanted to know."

Daniel sighed out the words. "Which was the location of 'the three who stood with the light' and Becca. That's what Andi heard the demon say." Daniel ran his hands through his hair. "I can't believe I just said that, talked about what my little girl heard a demon say as casually as 'I got tickets to the Reds game Saturday—wanna go?'"

"Actually that thing wasn't looking for the three," Theresa corrected. "Just Becca."

Daniel got to his feet and began to pace, and the way he fell so easily into the rhythm of it gave Jack the impression pacing was a regular activity.

"I don't know what to do with a thing like that—seeing demons."

"What you do with it is the same thing the disciples done with it when Jesus sent them demons packing out of that man wandering around naked in the cemetery."

"And that is…?" Daniel said.

"What they didn't do was say there wasn't no such thing as demons 'cause they couldn't see them with they own eyes. They knew they was demons working because they could see what the demons was doin'. You don't have to see the wind to know it's blowin' when it knocks your house down around your head."

She paused.

"And they believed what Jesus said about demons, just like you got to b'lieve what Andi says 'cause she knows."

"So what's the connection between a…" it took a physical effort for Jack to force the next word past his lips, "demon looking for Becca, the wack-job he rode in on, 'three who stood with the light' and your husband…your late husband? And where do those lines intersect with the shooter's and his crazy chums on a Little League Team with Daniel and me twenty-five years ago?"

"That's easy," Theresa said. "You and Daniel is the three. Well, two of them anyway."

If there had ever, in all of human history, been a conversation stopper, that was it.

Jack heard a great roaring sound in his head, Niagara Falls released between his ears. But even that sound couldn't smother the omnipresent heart-monitor buzz. He opened his mouth to speak, but words flat out refused to walk out onto the end of his tongue and jump.

"Jack and I are…the demon was looking for us?"

Daniel's words were barely audible through the rumble in Jack's head. It took a huge command of will to silence the noise—at least turn down the volume enough for Jack to spit words out into the room. "What for? What'd we do to piss off a demon?"

Theresa started to respond, but the wires suddenly connected in Daniel's head, and with a blink the pinball machine turned on.

"Jack and I are two, and the third was—"

"Becca," Jack said.

"She had long blonde hair that hung all the way down her back to her waist," Daniel said, and you could hear the wonder in his voice. "And a white light beside her you couldn't look at."

A light. The three who stood with the light!

"She had a dog, a mixed-breed mutt named—" Daniel began.

"McDougal," Jack would have sworn he said the word a second before he thought it. "McDo, Dougal Dog."

"The skinny kid named Victor wrung her dog's neck that day in the woods," Daniel said.

"They called us 'the good, the bad, and the ugly.' Why would they say that? She was beautiful," Jack said.

"You had a crush on her," Daniel said.

"So did you." Jack paused, breathless. "Why would a demon be looking for the three of us?" Jack heard the words come out of his mouth and checked back out again.

Jack Carpenter was a simple, garden-variety man. He drank a little too much sometimes, needed to get out more, liked to watch old black-and-white movies, eat Ethiopian food, cheer for the Cincinnati Reds, and he had started training to do the Iron Man competition in Oahu, Hawaii in the fall. The only thing that set him apart from the masses was that he was probably the only human being on the planet who had never seen a Star Wars movie—any of them—and had believed for years a light saber was a sword that wasn't heavy.

People like Jack Carpenter didn't see demons, didn't talk about demons. This was lunacy. Things like this only happened in the movies.

Grab the popcorn, folks, show starts in five minutes.

People like Jack didn't have demons trying to find them to…to what? Yeah, to what? Probably not to sell him Girl Scout cookies.

"What does it want us for?" Jack asked.

"It ain't looking for the two of you 'cause it already knows where you is, and apparently it don't know where Becca is," Theresa responded. "As for what it wants…I can't say what that'd be."

Yes, you can.

You didn't get to be a police sergeant without learning how to tell when somebody was tippy-toeing around the truth, and Theresa Washington wasn't exactly an accomplished liar. But he didn't press it. He turned his attention to Daniel. "I thought your whole childhood was a fog—now you say you remember Becca?"

Daniel told him, then Jack shared his memory—an edited version. He didn't include the parts he'd obviously made up. When both men said they'd felt like the memories had been catapulted out of their minds by force, Theresa shook her head.

"Appears to me they's somebody bigger than demons working real hard to get you men to remember something."

"Bigger than a demon…like what?" Jack felt that whirling sensation again, like he was about to fall off a high place into a dark hole that had no bottom. Theresa must have read the look because she smiled.

"If they's demons fighting a war, Sugar, who you think they's fighting against—Sponge Bob Square Pants?"

"Ok, so what does this…" He couldn't do it. He wouldn't do it, wouldn't say the word "angel" out loud. "What is it we're supposed to remember?"

Theresa looked uncomfortable. "Can't answer that, neither," she said,

No, won't answer that.

Theresa picked up the Calico that had taken a fancy to her, set it in her lap and smoothed its mottled fur.

"It's about that summer when we were twelve," Daniel said, his voice soft. "The summer that's just gone, when we played on that team, you knew us then, didn't you, Theresa?"

"I knew the two boys who grew up to be you two. But I don't know you 'cause you ain't the men I 'spected those boys to grow into."

Jack decided he didn't want to know what she meant by that.

"And this Becca. You knew her, too, right?"

"You and Daniel moved away from Bradford's Ridge before school started in 1985. One day you's there and the next you's gone. Just like that." She paused and looked tenderly at Daniel. "After what happened to your little sister, didn't surprise nobody that your daddy took you and your mama and left."

Jack saw Daniel flinch. He seemed to curl into himself, wouldn't look at Jack or Theresa.

Theresa turned from Daniel to Jack. "I didn't know your grandmother'd come and got you 'til you's already gone." You could hear the hurt in her voice when she continued softly, "Didn't neither one of you come over to say goodbye."

Then she shook it off. "But Becca stayed. She had to. Didn't have nowhere to run to. And if any of the three of you needed to run, it was Becca." She shook her head. "Poor thing, lost her two best friends and her stuck here all alone. Soon's she graduated from high school, she was gone, too."

"And you never heard from her again?"

"Not to speak of. I don't know anybody who did. She sent us a couple of pictures, early on. They was custom printed so they said 'Becca Hawkins' in white script on the front. But there wasn't no letter or nothing—just a few sentences scribbled on the back."

Theresa stopped then, an odd look on her face.

"What?"

"Nothing…just thinking 'bout them pictures. I stuck 'em up on the refrigerator and…nothing."

"So Becca was with us…no, we were with her and a light when something happened that summer," Jack said.

He seized the lead, the only one he had. "Sounds like this Becca and I need to have a little chat." A thought returned to his mind that had been half-forming there.

"And somebody needs to warn her. If a wack-job who tried to shoot a room full of children had been looking for me at the time, I'd want to know about it."

"We need to find her," Daniel interrupted. "You're playing with my chips here, too, you know. I want to help."

He shot a glance at Theresa but didn't look at her as he spoke. "I've taken a leave of absence from the pulpit. One of our teaching pastors has taken over for me until I...get some things sorted out."

He stopped again and dragged the conversation back to Becca. "I'm not sure it's a lead pipe cinch Becca knows any more about all this than we do. It's not natural that we don't remember. Something happened that... And maybe the same thing happened to her."

"She's got big holes in her memory," Theresa said. "Me and Bishop seen her—some, not like before—after you boys left. They's lots she don't remember, but it's not like everything's been erased the way it was with you two. Still..." Theresa stopped again. "The thing with Becca is —what she says she remembers might not be accurate. Becca wasn't never the same after that summer."

"Do you know how to get in touch with her family, somebody who might know how to find her?" Jack asked.

"She ain't got no kin a'tall, least none that I know of, 'cept her daddy."

"Does he still live in Bradford's Ridge?" Daniel asked.

"Nope. He's been gone from there a good long time."

She must have seen Daniel's face fall because she continued.

"He ain't hard to find, though. He's in the iron house. The Kentucky State Penitentiary, serving twenty years for growing dope." Her voice dropped in pitch, had a sharp shadowy edge to it. "That's what they got Billy Ray

Hawkins for, but I b'lieve he done worse than that, a whole lot worse than that."

~

Daniel and Emily hardly spoke when she got home from the banquet. Even Andi was subdued. Normally, the little chatterbox would have filled up every silent moment, giving Daniel a blow-by-blow account of the whole evening.

He wanted to believe she was just tired. After all, it had been barely two weeks since she got out of the hospital. She just needed time to get her strength back, that's all. Her withdrawal didn't, couldn't mean she'd heard her parents discussing divorce.

The night they found Andi crying on the stairs, Emily had slept on the daybed in Andi's room. You know, so she'd be right there if Andi had another dream.

He was sure she'd sleep there again tonight—and from now on until… Yeah, until what?

So Daniel undressed and went to bed because that's what you do. You perform the simple, mundane functions of life on autopilot when your conscious mind has been relieved of its command by fatigue, shock, fear, anger, grief —any of the above, all of the above.

Ever since…he couldn't even force himself to give a name, a label to that time. It was only images and sounds. A phone ringing and ringing. A little green ball on a monitor climbing each jagged hill slower than the last.

It had taken only one day.

Happy marriage. Loving wife. Rock-solid faith. Healthy child.

Badda boom, badda bing. Broken marriage. Adulterous wife. Everything he thought he believed shattered, and a little girl who died, but didn't—and now saw invisible creatures made out of bugs.

One. Day.

He was shocked at how easy it was to lose everything you thought you'd have forever.

The engine of energy, the life force, the persona of the Reverend Daniel Burke—the golden boy with a smooth, conversational style of preaching that was most of all comforting, and if there was anything folks needed in the uncertainty of today's world it was comfort—kept chugging along on autopilot while everything that was Daniel Burke had come unfastened from it and was slowly rolling to a halt on the track behind. Daniel watched it go, watched who he thought he was get more and more distant until he couldn't see it at all anymore.

It felt like he was taking off a mask. Only there wasn't a face behind the mask. There wasn't anything at all.

Daniel lay alone in the cold, silent bed where sleep was out of the question. Dozens of thoughts and images roared around his mind, witches on broomsticks, whirling and cavorting, each with a face from hell itself and all of them too fast for him to catch. He'd reach for a thought, grasp it, then it would turn to ash in his hand and blow away. Maybe he could sort things out if he could only hold on to any of his thoughts long enough to think it.

Theresa said he didn't believe a word he preached, and he suspected the old black woman wasn't wrong about much in life. He had believed once—really believed. He was certain he had, though he had not a single memory of that time. But then something had happened. Or maybe nothing had happened. All he knew was that right now he was operating on the cold dregs of faith, what was left in the bottom of a bucket with a hole in the bottom. And when he'd needed to drink from that bucket, needed the cool liquid to calm his heart and soothe his soul, the cup scraped across the bottom with a metal-on-metal sound he could feel deep in his soul.

Daniel looked up, watched the shadows of the ceiling fan march across the ceiling, elongated black shadows that looked like the legs of a spider.

And he remembered.

Chapter Nineteen

In the time it has taken to pick up his mother and sister, the armload of supplies to stock up the cabin and drive up into the hills, Daniel has lost the entire summer. It is as completely obscured by fog as a valley seen from a mountaintop on a cool autumn morning when the creek mist fills it like cream in a bowl.

But the summer is all that's completely gone. Daniel had watched in mute terror the relentless flow of the fog across his mind, but it came up short at the last day before school had let out this summer. Like that was some mental barrier, a dam of some kind, the thick gray-black fog stopped there, boiled and rolled behind it but went no further.

Mist did, though. A thin veil of mist the color of frost flowed right out past the barrier and into the rest of Daniel's memories. Obscuring. Making them soft and muted and fuzzy and out of focus.

He grasps frantically and latches hold of his memories of Christmas. And they are there, still intact. That soothes him a little. He is still frightened by what has happened, but the blind terror is beginning to recede. It didn't, after all, cloud up his entire mind and leave him a vegetable. He couldn't remember this summer. That was it—horrible as that was, it could conceivably have been a whole lot worse. Right?

And there might be some reasonable, rational explanation for the phenomenon. For all Daniel knew, it wasn't all that uncommon! As soon as he could get the attention of either of his parents long enough to talk to them about it, he might discover that what had happened to him was only temporary, that he'd wake up in the morning and all the memories would be back, and it would be like it had never happened at all.

Of course, he isn't likely to get the attention of either one of them now. There has been a horrible disaster, a fire at Twin Oaks Nursing Home, and his mother is almost hysterical about it. Though she doesn't know anyone personally who lived or worked there, in a town the size of Bradford's Ridge, she knows dozens of people whose mother/father/sister/brother/uncle/aunt/son/daughter or cousin did, and she has worked herself into a frenzy of sorrow and grief on their behalf. His father is in his own state of vicarious distress. He is, after all, a minister, and there are hundreds of hurting people in his congregation who need him right now, but he has obligated himself to perform this wedding and he must honor that obligation.

As Daniel's father cranks the cabin's generator into life to supply electricity, his mother fusses around Marianne like a fly buzzing around a piece of watermelon. Margaret Burke adjusts the clip in Marianne's hair, licks her own thumb, and uses it to wipe off an imagined smudge on the little girl's cheek. Marianne is blissfully unaware of her mother's doting and sits on the hard plank floor with her blocks, setting one carefully on top of another.

Daniel smiles. It would be impossible for anyone to begrudge the little girl the attention that is showered on her. Tiny and delicate in a size eighteen-months dress instead of a size three, she is in every possible way a little princess. Wide eyes a stunning shade of jade green, eyelashes so long they brush her cheeks like feather dusters, shiny hair the color of rust in a tangle of curls on her shoulders and a heart-shaped mouth that's spread in a perpetual smile, lighting her face from within like a candle.

"Build it, Dan-Dan," she says, and holds out a block that looks huge in her tiny hand. "Make it big as the sky."

Daniel's mother babbles all manner of instructions about how to care for Marianne, as if Daniel had never met the child. And what is there for Marianne to get into here? The cabin is as bare as that monk's chamber he'd seen once at Gethsemane Monastery. The meager essentials of furnishings—no drapes on the windows or rugs on the floor. No telephone. There is running water from a cistern out back and electricity—if the generator remains running.

"...and if that generator dies, you take Baby Girl outside on the deck and wait there for us to get home," his mother is saying, smoothing Marianne's curls behind her ears. "There's a big yellow moon tonight. That's plenty of light. I don't want you burning a candle with your little sister around."

Even Daniel's father rolls his eyes at that one, takes his wife's arm and guides her away.

The room is suddenly quiet, like a twister has blown through and out the front door. Daniel hears the car start and the crunch of tires on the gravel driveway leading to the dirt road. He looks out the front window and watches the car's headlights, visible until the car reaches the huge oak tree on the other side of the lake that towers above the cove where

Daniel's father likes to go fishing. It is a couple of miles away along the road that encircles the water and the marina where the wedding will be held is a mile or so beyond that.

When the car is out of sight, Daniel sits on the floor beside Marianne, slumps back against the wall and tension whooshes out of him in a long sigh. Relieved of the burden of pretending he is fine, Daniel allows himself the luxury of an emotional reaction to the fog/smoke/mist/brain tumor that has stolen his whole summer! He begins to tremble. It's unnerving so he puts his hands under his butt and sits on them.

Marianne notices nothing, of course. She sits beside his feet, stacking blocks, making that sound that isn't quite humming she makes when she is concentrating.

Daniel leans his head back against the wall, closes his eyes and tries to think.

"Look, Dan-Dan," Marianne squeals. "What I find!"

"That's good, Sweetheart," he says without opening his eyes. "Build me a castle."

She giggles.

"It comed out of the cuft in your pants,"she says. "It tickles."

The cuff of my pants?

"Lookit!"

Daniel opens his eyes.

Marianne is on her knees beside his feet, her hair shining copper and burgundy in the lamplight. Her face wreathed in a joyous smile, she holds out her chubby hand to him. In the center of her tiny palm is a gigantic black widow spider, so huge two legs dangle off the side.

Sometimes, when Daniel remembers the scene, the spider turns slowly around in her little hand to face him. But that isn't real, couldn't be real.

Time derails and crashes into a tree on the side of the track. His mind is at once racing with a thousand jumbled thoughts and so sluggish it can't form a simple coherent one.

But in reality there is no time to think anything at all, no time even to blink before Marianne suddenly screams and shakes the spider off onto the floor. The biggest black widow Daniel has ever seen, it moves with astonishing speed—scuttling across the hardwood floor slats back toward Marianne's leg.

Daniel leans forward and slaps it, knocks it away. Then he leaps to his feet and while the spider is still sliding sideways across the floor, he stomps it with his heavy boot, again and again, smashing it until it is nothing, a gooey black smear, no recognizable anything.

With his pulse a great rushing waterfall in his ears, he stands rigid for a moment before the sound of his sister's screams penetrates. Then he drops to his knees beside her and grabs her hand. Two small red holes are visible in the center of her little pink palm. The skin has turned an angry bright red in a circle around them, like a target.

Marianne shrieks, wails, tears slathering her cheeks, obviously in agony.

God, help me! What should I do?

The better question is what can he do? With no telephone, there is no way to summon help. There are no neighbors between the cabin and the marina three miles away. There is no first aid kit in the cabin, not that Daniel would know what to do with one if there were.

Ice!

When he sprained his ankle, his mother put an ice pack on it, said it would keep down the swelling. He leaps up and rushes to the refrigerator and yanks open the freezer door. But the electricity hasn't been on long enough and the ice trays are filled with water.

Marianne is now writhing on the floor.

"Dan-Dan," she screams, looks at him with desperate, pleading eyes. "Hand huuurts. Tummy hurts. Mommieee!"

She is crying so hard now she is having trouble catching her breath.

There is only one thing Daniel can do. He scoops the child up into his arms and runs to the door. He has trouble with the knob with Marianne wiggling, but finally pulls it open, dashes across the deck and down the gravel driveway to the road marked by a lone set of tire tracks visible in the moonlight. Then he races down the hill at a dead run under the cratered face of the blind moon.

Within half a mile Daniel is panting, gasping for breath. But his breathing is not as labored as Marianne's. She is thrashing so violently in his arms he has trouble holding onto her. Screaming, incoherent, her flailing left arm batters his face and her fist smashes his lip. Repeated blows eventually bloody his nose. Her right arm hangs limp at her side, though, swelling so huge he fears the skin will rip from the pressure.

Right before they reach the big oak tree, Marianne goes into convulsions. She stops screaming and her body goes suddenly rigid. Her eyes roll backward in her head, her teeth clench, her lips turn blue and saliva drips out the corners of her mouth. Then her back arches upward and her legs and arms begin to jerk.

Daniel pulls up short, struggling not to drop her as she jerks and spasms. It seems to go on for a long time, though it probably doesn't last more than a couple of minutes. Then, as suddenly as flipping a switch, she goes limp in his arms, and he feels a sudden warmth down the front of his shirt where she has wet herself.

Daniel begins to run again. The short stop allowed him to catch his breath and with her body quiet, she is easier to hold and he can go faster. He talks to her now in spurts between breaths.

"…be there soon, Sweetheart…

Gasp.

"…see Mommy and she'll…

Gasp.

"…fix it, make it…

Gasp.

"…all better."

The awareness of it comes on him slowly, steels over him like ice spreading out into his veins from a bottomless pit of cold, dark emptiness in his belly. He runs from it! Though already gasping for every breath, he bursts into a sprint. Running faster than his exhausted legs should be able to carry him. Flying through the air, his eyes blinded by tears.

Running and running and…

He staggers to a stop, can't run another step, drops to his knees and stares down at the precious little girl in his arms. Though he is panting, sucking in air in mighty, heaving gasps, Marianne is absolutely still, her body unmoving. She isn't breathing at all.

Sweat, tears and blood from his split lip mingle and drip off his chin in droplets on her flowered sundress. She is peaceful now. The moonlight caresses her beautiful face, as perfect and still as a hand-painted china doll. And he thinks he can see, imagines he can see a ghost of the sunny smile that always bathed her face in light.

He cradles her to his chest in a gentle hug, rocks back and forth. He hears a sound that is more than crying, a grunting, groaning noise that his mind has trouble connecting to the ripping ache in his own throat.

Back and forth, he rocks. Back and forth. He kisses her forehead and her cheek, wants to sing her a lullaby, but the only sound he can produce is the grunting sound of feeling his heart torn slowly out of his chest.

Minutes pass. An hour. A week.

Finally, he gets slowly to his feet and sets out down the dirt road. He cradles his precious baby sister tenderly in his arms, but all feeling has drained out of him. The nightmare of running with the road elongated in front of him and the end never in sight is now reversed. He takes a step, then two, time snaps back like a stretched rubber band and he is stepping up onto the plank walkway leading from the shore out to the brightly lit dock. He passes some people, a few. They stop and stare. A man speaks to him, a woman blurts out a little cry and covers her mouth with her hand. But he stops for nothing, moving relentlessly toward the big houseboat on the end, aglow with thousands of white Christmas lights and adorned with balloons and streamers. He can now see his father standing on a raised platform under an arbor on the back deck in front of a woman in a white dress and a man in a suit.

When he enters the group of people surrounding the boat on the dock, it parts before him like the Red Sea and he passes through amid muttering he ignores. He is floating now, cannot feel his legs move or his feet touch the planking. Word of him flows ahead through the crowd like wind through wheat. People turn to stare, men suck in their breath; women utter stifled cries. When the shock wave finally reaches the people on the deck of the boat, his father looks up over their heads. He is confused, looks around, wonders what—

Then he sees Daniel. There is no look on his face of any kind. It goes utterly blank. His arms go limp and he lets go of the Bible in his hands. It falls to the deck, the sound strangely noisy in the sudden hush. There is a beat or two before Daniel hears a scream, an agonized wail that he recognizes is his mother, though he cannot locate her. Then he spots her, knocking people out of her way, her face so distorted by emotion she is hardly recognizable.

She rushes toward him, limping and he sees that she has lost one of her high heels.

"Marianne," she wails and snatches the lifeless child out of his arms. "Annie, baby, talk to Mommy. What's wrong, honey? Talk to Mommy. Marianne!"

A man appears out of the crowd who is clearly a doctor and tells Margaret to put the child on the boards of the dock under one of the bright lights where he can examine her. Daniel stands watching, momentarily forgotten. His father appears beside his mother, who is babbling hysterically to the doctor, her voice rising in volume and pitch with every word.

"Wake her up, she's fine, she just needs to wake up, open your eyes, Sweetheart and give the doctor a big smile, Marianne, talk to Mommy now. You're scaring me—Marianne! Marianne!"

The doctor kneeling beside Marianne, rocks back on his heels, turns and scans the crowd until his eyes fall on Daniel. His look is compassionate, his voice kind.

"Snake or spider, son?"

"Black widow." Though the words come out in a harsh rasp, Daniel is surprised he is able to speak at all. "Huge." He makes a circle with his thumb and forefinger to indicate a shape three inches across. "In the cuff of my pants, she found—"

Daniel's mother lifts her head slowly to look at him, then. Her face twists in horror and rage. "You brought a spider into the house! You brought a poisonous spider... you let it bite your little sister!"

"I didn't…I—"

"I trusted you. She's only a little girl, a baby. Why didn't you protect her?"

His mother is screeching in a voice Daniel has never heard, her face a mask of undiluted hatred.

"I couldn't…it—"

"You brought a spider…? My precious little…you killed—" She stops as abruptly as if she has run into a steel beam. Her face is totally expressionless for an instant, then her features rearrange themselves into a pleasant concerned expression. "You're in big trouble, young man. You know that, don't you? It'll be a long time before I let you babysit again." She turns back to the dead child lying on the dock. "Marianne's little hand is going to be sore for days. I bet I have to sit up with her all night with an ice pack on it, poor little thing." She reaches over and pushes the child's curls behind her ear. "You sleep now, Sweetheart." She glances up at the stunned crowd of onlookers. "Shhh, don't wake her. That bug bite is going to sting when she wakes up."

Daniel glances at his father, realizing with surprising maturity that the man has lost his wife as well as his daughter. And that Daniel has lost all three of them.

Hot tears leaked out of the corners of Daniel's eyes. He thought about Marianne every day, every day of his life, but he hadn't cried for her in a long time. Or for his mother, who had remained in denial until the funeral, then had to be sedated. Within a week, his devastated father had packed up his shattered family and moved back to Margaret's hometown in Tennessee so her mother and sisters could help care for her, see her through her grief. Daniel's mother never spoke to him again, refused to look at him. On Christmas morning, Daniel found her hanging from a rafter in the garage.

Maybe Daniel was crying for her. Or maybe for Andi, who almost died but didn't, who came back from—somewhere!—profoundly changed.

Maybe he was crying for the wife who had betrayed him.

Or for Theresa, who had lost her beloved Bishop.

Or for Jack, who had a haunted look in his eyes, the pale shadow of some unspeakable tragedy.

Or maybe he was crying for himself.

He watched the fan shadows, sentries marching around and around the room, and felt his tears slide down his temples and soak into the pillow.

Chapter Twenty

The sky was robin's-egg blue without a cloud in sight when Jack and Daniel drove out of Cincinnati on Interstate 71, crossed the bridge over the Ohio River, and headed south toward the Kentucky State Penitentiary in Danforth. Jack was in something approaching a good mood. The sunshine had dispelled some of the gloom he'd been feeling. He was wearing an open-neck shirt and jeans, not a uniform, though as of nine o'clock this morning, his uniform was no longer "naked"—with no badge or gun. When he'd stopped in at the station to tell Crock where he was going, Crock had plopped both on his desk and given him the good news: the Board of Inquiry had ruled that the bullet Jack had put in Miranda Burke's chest was a "righteous shoot."

"Helps that you only winged the little girl," Crock had said, "that she wasn't hurt as bad as everybody thought at first."

Just winged her. Right. She died!

Jack faced resolutely forward, didn't look at Daniel when he spoke. "You haven't said anything—publicly, I mean—about Andi and…how she came back—or whatever it was. Why not?"

"I can't talk about what happened because I don't know what happened," Daniel said. "Do you?"

"No, but I'm not supposed to. You are."

"You want to know if what happened to Andi was a miracle? And if it was, what that means? Sorry, Charlie, but my answers are I don't know, and I don't know."

"You think God saved her…right?" Jack said.

"I didn't say that. But you don't think so, or you wouldn't have asked. Don't you believe in God?"

Jack snorted. "Of course, I believe in God. You'd have to be an idiot to believe all this"—he gestured at the beautiful summer day outside the car windows—"just happened. But did God save Andi?" He paused, then pressed resolutely forward. "See, I've got a history-of-the-world full of evidence that God's way more into letting horrible things happen to people than he is into 'saving' people from them."

Daniel said nothing and Jack continued. "But you can't say God's not 'good' because he gets to define what good is. So he always wins."

"And that's cheating."

"Which is one of the reasons I don't trust him. I don't like stacked decks."

Still Daniel said nothing. Maybe Jack had been expecting an argument, but he didn't get one. Instead, Daniel said, "You think we can trust Billy Ray, believe what he says?"

"Of course not. But he might give something away—if we're lucky."

"And you think that'd be lucky—to find Becca?"

"You don't?"

"I know we have to find her, but am I looking forward to it? No."

"Why not?"

"Theresa said she had…the knowing, or whatever it is, like Andi. I don't want to know what an adult Andi is like, what all this is doing to her." He paused for a beat. "And now Andi's having…visions." Jack glanced over at Daniel, whose face looked positively gray.

"Visions?"

"Vision. Singular, one." He described in detail what Andi had told him and Emily. Jack asked questions, but nothing about it seemed to make rational sense. Big surprise there.

"She saw it, the same thing, three times," Daniel said.

"Paint splatters, then shapes. A double-T, like the Texas Tech logo beside a square?"

Daniel nodded.

"A red triangle, two silver circles, a straight brown line, a bell and a pointed cross—that all?"

"That's enough. It's senseless."

"That's why I do want to talk to Becca. To her, or anybody else who can make some sense of all this." Jack suddenly pounded his fist on the steering wheel, surprised by the intensity of his own emotions. "I want to know what's going on! How, maybe even why, it involves me."

"And you think Becca knows."

"Maybe not all of it, but I think she knows more than I do."

They didn't talk after that. Jack thought about what he would say to Billy Ray Hawkins, who likely would have refused to see them—Theresa didn't seem to think he was a particularly sociable kind of guy—but he was due to be released on parole soon and likely wanted to at least appear cooperative.

The Kentucky State Penitentiary in Danforth was about twenty miles east of Lexington, Kentucky in a surprisingly scenic location, a collection of ugly gray buildings in a shallow valley, fenced only by forests and fields. The visitation room was as bare as an empty footlocker and smelled vaguely like one. A wooden table, straight-back wooden chairs, a bare light bulb—but the window offered a view of a meadow filled with wildflowers.

Jack and Daniel had only been seated at the table a couple of minutes when a guard brought Billy Ray to the room. No handcuffs, no leg irons. This was, after all, a minimum security facility.

He wasn't a big man, maybe five feet eight, had likely been called "small, but scrappy" as a child and "tough and sinewy" as a young man. Older now, he looked less tough than merely skinny, with boney elbows protruding from the sleeves of his orange jumpsuit, clavicles as sharp as axe blades and a face of craggy angles—high cheek bones, a prominent nose and a jutting chin that looked like the knob of a femur.

There was a tear-drop tattoo inked in blue below Billy Ray Hawkins's left eye, but Jack suspected the unmarked skin on the rest of his face was the only space left on his entire body that was. Full sleeves of tattoos—dragons, skulls, fanged-creatures—extended down both arms and crawling vines inched up the sides of his neck out of his collar. The top two buttons of his shirt were undone, revealing tattoos down his chest into the mat of hair that had once been black, but now was the color of ashes.

The hair on his head was thin and limp, his eyes a muddy, unreadable brown.

"We appreciate you agreeing to talk to us," Jack said and rose from where he'd been sitting at the table, "and we won't take up much of your time."

Billy Ray barked a laugh at that. "Like you think maybe I got plans? Social obligations? You're in luck 'cause my dance card happens to be bone empty at the moment."

Jack wasn't expecting the sound of Billy Ray's voice. It was startling, a deep raspy base, ragged, hoarse and gravelly—like you'd sound if you'd cheered too loud and long at a football game. The man had severely damaged his vocal chords somehow.

"I'm Jack Carpenter," Jack said, didn't bother to offer a perfunctory handshake. "This is Daniel Burke."

Daniel nodded. Billy Ray pulled out a chair, but didn't push it back up to the table when he sat in it. Jack returned to where he'd been sitting.

"Billy Ray Hawkins here. Ain't William Raymond, or nothing like that. Plain old Billy Ray. Friends call me Hawk." He paused for a beat, glaring at them, though his face remained impassive. "You boys can call me Mr. Hawkins." He leaned back in his chair and extended his long thin legs out in front of him. "And I don't need no introductions. I know who are."

"That so," Jack said.

"You're the cop, right?" He turned to Daniel. "And you're a preacher. Yore little girl got shot up Cincinnati, I hear. She doin' all right, now? Hate to think of a little one getting hurt like that."

He said it all with a crocodile smile and Jack knew then Billy Ray wasn't going to tell them anything. He was only playing with them, amusing himself because—well, like he said, it wasn't like he had anything else to do.

"How do you know about my daughter?"

Billy Ray barked out another laugh. "Ain't you never heard that 'Google is your friend?'"

"I didn't know you had—"

"Internet? You see any bars on these windows, any

locks on the doors, or razor wire fences? This here's a minimum security prison for those of us who ain't no threat to society no more." Billy Ray paused, then spoke with a look on his face Jack could not read. "I hear ole Bishop Washington bought the farm that day, too. I hated to hear that."

"You're scheduled for parole soon is what I hear," Jack said. "All rehabilitated and ready to go home. Looking forward to that, are you?"

Billy Ray caught Jack's meaning.

"I am for a fact. That's why I looked you fine gentlemen up before you got here, so I'd be prepared to help you out any way I can." He paused for a beat. "I didn't have to look you up, though. Took me a little while, but I finally recognized those names. You's friends with Becca when you's kids, wasn't you."

"That's why we're here," Jack seized the opportunity. "We're trying to locate her and we are hoping you can tell us where she is."

"Lost touch, didja, and now you want to catch up on old times. That how it is?"

"Something like that," Daniel said.

He turned to Jack. "Don't surprise me none, you looking for her." He looked full into Jack's face, then slathered his next words in loathing "I seen the way you used to look at her. Her all blonde and fair and you black as the ace of spades."

Daniel tensed, but Jack showed no reaction whatsoever.

"Tell us where she is and you'll be assisting in a police investigation," Jack said evenly. "I'll see the powers that be hear how you cooperated."

Though the look of hatred never left Billy Ray's eyes, he'd made his point, and now he slithered back behind his facade of conviviality. "I'm always glad to help out the police any way I can," he said, spreading out his hands in a gesture of compliance. "But I'm sorry to say I can't accommodate you boys in locating my daughter."

"Why not," Daniel demanded.

"'Cause I ain't got no idea where that kid is, that's why not. I ain't seen her since…she was in the courtroom the day I got sentenced. Didn't say nothing, but I seen her sitting in the back." He let out a long sigh. "And I ain't seen hide nor hair of her since. That was goin' on eighteen years ago. Not so much as a letter, a post card, a Christmas card—nothin.' You know what I think?" he leaned toward Jack and grinned. "I think she up and jumped off a bridge somewhere and ain't nobody ever found her body. She was like that—pouty and moody, depressed like. You ask me, I say she's dead."

Jack and Daniel walked out to the car together in silence. They got in and Daniel asked, "You believe him?"

"I wouldn't believe Billy Ray Hawkins if he told me pigeons crapped on statues," Jack said. "That is one seriously bad human being." He sighed. "But I don't think he knows where Becca is. Would you keep in touch with that Neanderthal? I'm sure she saw his imprisonment as her reprieve. She may have spent the past eighteen years becoming invisible so he'd never find her."

~

Whenever he could snare some weed, Hawk smoked it in the shed behind the storage buildings that held supplies for the kitchen. As one of the kitchen "trusties," Hawk had a key to the building, which would likely be bulldozed if the state come in next spring to do the renovation they'd been promising for the past seven years. Wasn't fit for much of anything now the way the roof leaked, and nothing was stored here except the riding lawnmower that hadn't worked for the past two summers, various broken garden tools, and in-need-of-repair lawn equipment.

'Course, Hawk didn't care one way or the other what the state might do next spring. He wouldn't be here then. He'd be free!

He took a deep drag on the joint, pulled the smoke as deep as he could into his lungs and let it out slowly, sighing the word out with it, "Freeee…"

Yep, ole Hawk'd be sleepin' in his own bed real soon, getting up in the morning to the smell of honeysuckle on the trellis by the back door and going to bed at night with the warmth of a woman by his side, maybe more'n one woman. He planned to have lots of them in the months to come, as many as he could stand up to—he burped out a bleat of laughter at the unintended pun and almost choked on the marijuana smoke.

He'd been dreaming of women every night for months, had allowed himself to think on 'em soon's he found out about his parole. Couldn't do that in the years before, or he'd have gone bug-crap crazy with wanting 'em. He'd seen men get like that—what they done because of it. But soon as he was free he was gonna spend a whole month in bed, doin' one after another. He could afford it. Could afford to pay for the services of a whole herd of women— and for them little pills that'd make it possible for him to pleasure ever one of 'em, too. Keeping his mouth shut about his dope money had cost him an extra ten years on his sentence, but it was worth it now. Now, he was set for life.

He took another long drag on the joint, leaned back against the wall to get comfortable, and thought about the nigger cop who'd sashayed in here high and mighty as you please, wanting to know where his Becca was. Like he'd a'told that black ape even if he'd known.

It'd been all he could do to sit there and make nice with that buck when what he wanted to do was jump up and plunge the shiv he carried in his sock into the man's chest, feel his blood run out over his hands. He smiled, remembering the first time he'd killed a nigger, how he'd actually been surprised their blood looked like a white man's blood. That's why he'd kept some of it, scooped it up off the boxcar floor and put it in that little vial with a stopper inside the amulet he wore round his neck—the one he'd stole out of the back of one of the campers where them carneys lived who come to town every summer with their rigged games and rickety old carnival rides.

No, that wasn't actually why he'd filled that vial up with nigger blood. He'd done it so's he could stand right up next to Bishop Washington with the blood of the big ape's son in a vial around his neck. Stand there and make nice with King Kong, tell him how sorry he was to hear the man's son had gone missing, and all the time that boy's blood was right there, dangling inches from the old man. It'd been all Billy Ray could do not to bust a gut over it.

He sighed out the breath he'd been holding, took another drag and held it again, thinking how much he wished he still had that vial of blood. He could have got a whole gallon if he'd wanted to, the way it splattered every-where. Chainsaws made a fine mess, for a fact.

And he'd be lookin' at the stain that blood had left on the slat floor in only three weeks and six days, in that boxcar everybody said was a myth!

"Wasn't no such thing as buried boxcars full of dope money," folks'd said, "that's crazy talk." And he'd nod his head and allow as how they was absolutely right, a made-up story was all, couldn't be the truth. And all the time he had the key to one hanging around his neck on the same chain as the vial of Isaac Washington's blood!

He laughed out loud then when he remembered how shocked that stupid boy had been when he saw that boxcar. Billy Ray had let him get a real good look around it before he killed him.

There was a sudden banging on the door of the shed where Billy Ray sat leaned against the back wall. The force of the blows released a cloud of dust lacing the strands of sunlight from the cracks in the ancient walls that striped the floor.

"Hawk! You in there, Hawk? It's me, Walker."

Billy Ray had leapt to his feet at the first blow on the door, looking around frantically for somewhere to ditch the joint, or to hide himself. The small shed offered no place to do either. He gasped out a sigh when he heard Walker's voice and started for the door.

"What do you want?" he called out. "Liked to scared me—"

"Get your butt out here, now!" Walker said. "A surprise count and you ain't where you's supposed to be. I covered the best I could, but—"

Billy Ray yanked open the door before Walker had a chance to finish. He knew he smelled like dope, but there was nothing he could do about it. He had stubbed the joint out on the floor of the shed and then swallowed the remains.

"Where they at now?" he asked.

"Admin wing. I said I thought I'd heard you say you needed to talk to the counselor, make sure all the I's was dotted and t's crossed 'bout your job when—"

"I owe you," Billy Ray said, "now git!"

Billy Ray took off at a leisurely walk down toward the

trees at the edge of the property. He stopped there and quickly unzipped his pants. Then he shoved the remainder of the small bag of dope into his mouth and chewed frantically. He knew what it'd do to him to eat marijuana; he'd done it before. But his body's response was exactly what he needed right now. He swallowed hard, then kept swallowing back reflexive heaving, breathing in little sips of air as his stomach tried desperately to revolt. As soon as he saw the guard in charge of his wing come out the admin building door, he pretended to be emerging from the trees, zipping his pants.

"You, Hawkins, where you been?" the guard called out to him.

Billy Ray leaned over and vomited noisily on the ground in front of him, gagging up the dope and his breakfast in one noxious heave. He retched a couple more times as the guard approached, then spoke breathlessly.

"I'm sick, man," he said. "The trots hit me so fast I barely made it to the trees 'fore I crapped my pants."

The guard wrinkled his nose at the smell of the vomit.

"Get over to the infirmary," he said and stepped away. "And don't breathe on me. I don't want whatever you got."

Billy Ray turned and walked in the slow, careful way of a sick man down the walkway and turned toward the infirmary. Didn't allow himself the luxury of a smile, but he was smilin' on the inside. He'd outfoxed them again, like he always done. Like he always would do. Think fast on your feet and you always ended up on top. He could have lost it all, blown through the parole and had to spend the remaining ten years of his sentence locked up, but he'd beat them.

Home in less than thirty days. Get him some cash. Have himself some women.

And then find Becca.

~

Ruby Walsh saw it all. Peeked out the door in the men's toilet in the recreation room and watched the whole thing.

Ok, not all of it.

She didn't see the part where the patient everybody called BB, for Blubber Butt, went and found Nurse Phillips. Ruby'd been hiding behind the urinals, hadn't yet got the nerve to crack the door open an inch so she could see what was happening.

But she did see the part where he dragged the nurse by the hair into the room—her screaming and crying—and threw her down on her knees in front of the nurse's station.

"You're sorry now, ain't ya," he yelled at her. His voice was strange, made an odd rumbling sound in his throat like Ruby hadn't ever heard anybody make. "Sorry you got me locked away in solitary, left me to rot in that dungeon, couldn't talk to nobody through them rock walls. Say you're sorry!"

She cried, said she was sorry, begged him not to hurt her, said she had little kids, went on and on. But the man in black didn't have any patience for her. He reached out, grabbed the nurse's head and twisted it on her shoulders— Ruby heard the crack sound—and the nurse went limp. He kept twisting, though, until her head was pointed back- wards, her face all purple and her eyes bugging out.

The one-eyed-man was an Eliminator, all right. He'd come for Ruby, but she'd outsmarted him—kept a metal bedpan on her head so he couldn't find her as she peeked out of the bathroom, watching.

She'd known The Force Supreme would send an Eliminator after she'd blocked its control beams with the foil lining in the cap she wore all day—nurses wouldn't let her sleep in it. Ruby had seen him in time to hide, though. She had sneaked out onto the roof to catch a smoke like she always did on Wednesdays after her sister visited the day before and slipped her a pack.

She was sitting on the roof tiles outside the glow of the lighted sign out front that said "East Texas Regional Psychiatric Hospital, Texarkana" when she saw the car.

A service road wound around to a gate in the back of the stone fence surrounding the facility and she watched a car drive down that road—with its headlights turned off. It parked in the mesquite grove under where she was sitting, just drove right into it. She heard the brush and dry limbs scrape down the side of the car with a sickening there-goes-the-paint-job sound.

The man who got out of the car was dressed in black, head to foot. Even had a black patch over one eye. He walked along the base of the wall until he found a place where overhanging tree limbs formed deep puddles of darkness. Then he jumped up to the top of the fifteen foot wall. In one leap! That's when Ruby knew for sure he was an Eliminator! She almost wet herself, crawled as fast as she could back in the top floor crafts room window, then raced down the stairs to the men's bathroom on the ground floor where the storage closet was full of metal bedpans.

Now, she sat trembling as BB and the one-eyed-man yelled at each other.

"You done now?" the Eliminator snarled. "We've got more important things to do than—"

"Ain't nothing more important than revenge. I'm gonna get me some payback!"

BB turned to walk away, the one-eyed-man grabbed his

arm and suddenly they were at each other like animals. Rolling around on the floor, knocking over tables and lamps and chairs, growling, hitting, kicking, biting—didn't stop until the double doors opened and in stepped Matthew Mitchell, the skinny little orderly, come to see what all the noise was about.

The fat man was as quick as a snake. Before Mitch even registered what was going on, BB jumped up and grabbed the front of Mitch's shirt and threw him across the room. All the way across the room! He slammed into the wall and fell away groaning. His face was smashed, his lip bloody.

BB went to where Mitch was lying stunned on the floor. "Warned you! Said you'd be sorry for taking away my TV privileges."

"No reason to get upset," Mitch said. He sounded stuffy, like his nose was stopped up. It must have been broken. "Look, we can work—"

BB reached down and lifted Mitch off the floor—grabbed his neck with one hand and a handful of his scrub pants in the other—and...broke Mitch in half over his knee, like you'd break a stick for firewood. Mitch shrieked and Ruby was afraid she was going to be sick, heard herself making little whimpering, retching sounds, couldn't stop even when she put her hands over her mouth so they wouldn't hear.

BB dropped Mitch's broken body on the floor, leaned over and took Mitch's watch off his arm.

"Always liked this watch," he said as he fitted it on his fat wrist. "I know you want me to have it since you won't be needing it anymore."

Mitch didn't say anything. He wasn't dead, but maybe he couldn't speak. He just looked up at BB, so pitiful, like a dog got run over on the road. Then the Eliminator got to his feet, took two steps, bent over Mitch, and casually twisted his head around on his neck like he'd done Nurse Phillips. Ruby didn't hear the snap, but she was glad Mitch wasn't suffering no more.

"We done now?" the man in black said. "It's a long drive. Come on!"

Ruby reached up and held the bedpan down on her head, gritted her teeth together to keep silent so tight her jaw hurt.

And that was it. They left, but Ruby didn't come out of the bathroom until the police arrived.

She tried to tell them about the Eliminator, why he'd come and what he could do. She got right up in that policeman's face, started crying just talking about it. No one believed her, though. But because she was close to hysterical, the nurse let her sleep the night with her foil-lined cap pulled snug over her ears.

Chapter Twenty-One

It was a modest brick house with a well-kept lawn—a small one because the rest of the yard was devoted to flowers. Big flower beds bordered the fence and the driveway, a riot of daisies, daffodils, asters and dahlias. The winding path to the front porch was lined with orange and yellow marigolds and sunflowers, their colors forming a lattice, and Jack had the impression of wandering toward the Emerald City down the Yellow Brick Road. But the most impressive flowers were set around the porch. Roses— white, pink, red and multicolored—grew on bushes that encircled the house, leaving only a narrow pathway up the front steps. Bordering the rose bushes were huge hydrangeas in shades of pink, blue and white.

An image flashed in his mind and was gone almost as soon as it formed. A smaller house, wood frame, not red brick, but with rosebushes lining the porch just like this one. There was a swing on the porch, the kind you knew would produce a melodious eek-eek with every movement back and forth. Above the front door of that house was a plaque made of dark wood with a swirling grain—stained oak, maybe—that had words burned into the surface. "As for me and my house, we will serve the Lord." Joshua 24:15.

The same plaque hung above the door of this house.

Jack stared at it as he pushed the doorbell, wondering if he'd only imagined the other house and the other plaque. No, correction: the other house and the same plaque, even down to the border of wood-burned morning glory vines laced around the edges.

Theresa opened the door while he was still staring at the plaque.

"Bishop made it," she said, "years ago. It's hung above the front door of every house we ever lived in." She eyed him carefully. "You recognize it, Jack?"

"No." He paused. "Yes." He shook his head, embarrassed. "It's like I 'almost' remember it, then the image is gone. I'm sorry, I know that doesn't make any sense."

"Makes perfect sense to me," Theresa said. "If you'd a'come to my house a month ago, you'd a'looked at that plaque and it wouldn't have rung no bells whatsoever." She studied him. "An 'pears to me if you come back a month from now, you gone remember the plaque and the door and maybe what happened years ago behind a door just like this one once it was shut tight behind us."

She stepped back.

"Ya'll come on in this house and make yourselves at home." As Jack and Daniel filed past her into the room, she asked, "What can I get you to drink? I got coke-cola, tea, water, coffee and fresh-squeezed orange juice. I recommend the orange juice, but I 'spect you fine gentlemen ain't the orange-juice-drinkin' kind."

The room wasn't what Jack expected. It was large, stretching across the whole front of the house, the walls painted a rich, amber brown. But it wasn't dark or confining. Half a dozen lamps of different shapes and sizes resting on antique end tables joined two antique floor lamps to bathe the room in a rich, warm glow through shades of gold and ivory. A large picture window looked out on the front yard and big windows on both ends of the room brought in abundant sunlight. The shiny hardwood floor was a different shade of the amber brown on the walls and it was covered with two oval rugs, the kind his grandmother called rag rugs. The furniture was all antiques, big and sturdy. Jack would have expected nothing less given the size and bulk of Bishop Washington.

"Sit yourselves down"—Theresa made a sweeping gesture that included the whole room—"while I fetch the drinks. What did you say you wanted?"

Jack knew better than to say he wasn't thirsty.

"I'll take coffee if you have it," he said. "Black."

"Double that," Daniel said.

Theresa returned shortly with two mugs of coffee—no tray, no saucers.

"This here's strong enough to trot a mouse across. You sure you don't want no cream?"

Both men shook their heads. Jack took a sip and found the coffee rich and strong, not the bitter antifreeze-tasting swill from his office. He saw Daniel wince after he swallowed a big gulp.

Theresa eased herself into the recliner that sat across a coffee table from the couch where the two men sat. Jack suspected it had been Bishop's favorite chair.

"Well?" she asked. "What'd that pole cat say?"

"Nothing helpful," Daniel said. "He said he doesn't know where Becca is, said he hadn't seen her in eighteen years." He sighed. "Unfortunately, I believe him. I don't think he has any idea where to find his daughter."

"Them locking Billy Ray in a cage unlocked Becca

from hers, and she likely flew far away as her wings'd carry her," Theresa said. "I woulda, if Hawk'd been my daddy. She never come home, not one time after she left. Far as I know she didn't talk to nobody."

"You said she sent pictures, though, right?" Jack asked.

Theresa nodded. "It was like she wanted us to see she was doin' all right, but she didn't want to establish contact or nothing like that. She didn't want nobody to come looking for her!

"On the back one of them pictures, she wrote, 'You could never find me, Theresa, but maybe you could, Bishop. Maybe you know where I am every minute.' That was nonsense, of course. Just 'cause they both could see demons didn't mean they had some special ability to see each other. But after awhile, Becca got where she didn't make no sense at all sometimes."

Theresa thought for a moment.

"On another one, she wrote how she was afraid that you boys—'the ones who stood with me'—could find her, that you could 'follow the strand that binds us together.' I think she was scared you'd both show up on her porch someday like you's trying to sell her Girl Scout cookies."

"Mind if I see the pictures?" Jack asked.

He could have asked to see them the other night when Theresa first mentioned Becca had sent them. But for all his protests to the contrary, he wasn't all that different from Daniel in his reluctance to actually connect with Becca. His reasons were different, though. Daniel didn't want to see an adult version of Andi. Jack harbored the admittedly irrational fear that with one look at Becca Hawkins's face the whole summer of 1985 would download into his mind like a file off the internet. He wasn't prepared for that. He was prepared for somebody to tell him about it, but not to relive that whole summer with the clarity and visceral reality of his only memory of it—particularly when he suspected his lone orphan memory was a pitter-pattering spring rain compared to the Hurricane Katrina of the whole load.

"Can't. They's gone. Kept them stuck with magnets to the refrigerator, and I went to look at them the other day and they's not there no more. 'Course my kitchen was full of all kinda people right after…women from the church bringing food and such. They was only trying to be helpful, but they moved stuff around, must have misplaced them."

Jack couldn't help a little sigh of relief that he had, at least temporarily, dodged that bullet.

"The pictures were only of Becca, nobody else in them with her?" he asked.

"Nope, her all by her lonesome, just standing out in front of buildings. We figured they was places she was working 'cause Becca always did like little kids and movies."

Jack felt the hair on the back of his neck stand up. He seemed to have trouble shoving the next words out between his teeth.

"Could you identify the buildings in the pictures, were there names on them?" he asked.

"One was the Carnival Multiplex Theatre, sign said 'Serving south Savannah since…' but Becca was blocking the date so I couldn't see how long. In the other, she was sitting on a bench holding a bunch of helium-filled balloons. Couldn't see the name on the building, but the balloons all had smiley-faces and said, 'Happy Toddlers Day Care Center.'"

"Do you know where that was located?" Jack heard himself ask, detached, a good investigator.

"It didn't say, but there was an arch in the logo that was either the Saint Louis Arch or McDonalds."

Jack saw that Daniel's face had gone pale. He started to say something to Jack, but didn't. Jack heard his own detached, official voice as if someone else were speaking. "I'd bet my last Tootsie Roll I can guess the name of the little girl Willingham was asking for in St. Louis."

Jack and Daniel spoke in the perfect unison of a Greek chorus: "Becca."

Theresa looked from one of the men to the other.

"What are you two talking about?" Jack could hear the apprehension in her voice.

"I told you about the two wannabe mass murderers. One tried to blow up a crowded theater—that theater in Savannah."

Theresa gasped and her hands flew to her mouth.

"And the other—"

"They was after Becca!" she whispered.

Daniel finally found his voice. "Now, let me get this straight," he said carefully, articulating every word individually. "You're saying that somebody broke in here and—"

"Wouldn't nobody have to break in. Most nights we didn't even lock the back door. Wouldn't have to do no snoopin' around, neither. Them pictures with her name on them was right there on the fridge beside the door."

"Somebody got their hands on those pictures." Daniel plowed doggedly ahead. "And then used them to go looking for—"

"Close, but no Kewpie doll," Jack said. He felt that familiar icy calm steady him, the kind that only settled over him when everything in his world was about to hit the fan. When he spoke, it was to Daniel, but he was looking at Theresa.

"It's not somebody who's trying to find Becca. It's something. All three of our former teammates went psycho because they were possessed," he said. And held his breath.

Theresa nodded but didn't speak.

"So the demon at the school was also in—?"

"Not exactly," Theresa interrupted. "Sorry, Jack, you ain't gone get no doll, neither."

Jack knew then. Maybe it'd been dancing around the outside edges of his consciousness for awhile, but now it kicked open the front door and stood hot and stinking right there in front of him.

"What exactly does not exactly—?" Daniel began.

"It means she's not saying that the bug-creature Andi saw at the school possessed all three men." Jack turned to face her. "You're saying there were three different demons."

~

Michael Rutherford lay back on the starched white pillowcase, gasping, then looked at the pretty little nurse with what passed for a gleam in eyes made rheumy with illness and medication.

"Got so depressed about all this"—he gestured at his room in Bradford's Ridge Regional Hospital, the IV poles, monitors, the plastic tube of oxygen that fit like a horse's bit in his nose—"I called the Suicide Hotline… and the automated attendant said to press one for English."

She patted his hand.

"You shouldn't try to talk, Mr. Rutherford," she said.

"…and when I did, they connected me to a call center in Pakistan." He had to pause to gulp in a gasp of air but he'd have paused there anyway, for effect. In comedy, timing was everything. "When I told the dude at the call center I wanted to kill myself, he asked if I could drive a truck."

The little nurse couldn't help a smile. Michael chuckled air-lessly.

"Tell me something," he whispered. "If four out of five people suffer from diarrhea, does that mean one of them enjoyed it?"

She giggled then and he struggled to stifle his own laughter and the resultant fit of coughing. But he didn't have the strength. She snatched a handful of tissue from the box on the bedside table and gave it to him as he hacked, then took the blood spattered tissues and deposited them in the trash when he fell back on the pillow, wheezing.

"Like I said, Mr. Rutherford, you need to stop talking and rest."

He wanted to tell her that Michael Rutherford never stopped talking, that he was a Talk-A-Holic, the original Talk-a-tron, Talk-errific Talk-A-Lator, that even when he was a kid, his machine-gun fire speech had awed his friends. Well, maybe not awed…

"Mikey, will you shut up, zip it, put a sock in it," Jack Carpenter says, then snaps a pitch into the center of Daniel Burke's glove as effortlessly as swatting a fly. "Don't you ever stop talking?"

Mikey isn't offended; he's pleased. He has carved out his place as the "fourth musketeer" with the inseparable threesome of Jack, Daniel Burke, and Becca Hawkins by being a clown, making them laugh. That's what fat kids did, right? They made other people laugh.

Mikey fires another line as pointedly and effortlessly as Jack had fired the pitch. "Ever wonder who was the first person to see a cow and think, 'I believe I'll squeeze those dangly things and drink whatever comes out?'"

Mikey always laughs at his own humor, a braying donkey laugh that is itself funny, and the sound of it finally brings a smile to the taciturn Jack. Daniel smiles, too, and Becca, who is standing beside Mikey, watching the other two play catch, actually giggles. Her giggles sound like the ringing of tiny bells and Mikey is afraid his throat will swell completely shut from the joy of hearing it.

"If you choke a Smurf, what color does it turn?" he asks, in an effort to keep those bells ringing.

Michael coughed again, but weak this time, not in a chain of irresistible barking that made black spots appear on the edges of his vision and ground like broken glass in his chest. The agony of it brought tears to his eyes. Even with the huge doses of whatever painkiller they were giving him, it hurt so bad he wanted to sob. But you had to have breath to cry and he didn't have any left. You had to have breath to laugh, too, and he couldn't do that anymore, either.

His thoughts went again to Jack, Daniel and Becca. Funny how the past seemed more real than the present sometimes. Maybe it was that way for everybody at the end. Is that what folks meant when they said they saw their lives pass before their eyes?

But in the past week, it had been more than memories that had made Michael's life pass before his eyes. He knew he ought to tell somebody about it, though he didn't know who. Or what he should say.

All that bad stuff that happened before—well, it's happening again—that's what he should say. But to whom? Who would understand? Who would care?

He was surprised by how badly it still scared him to

think about those days, that one summer, even today, more than a quarter of a century later. And he'd been on the sidelines, purposefully, intentionally on the sidelines, not right in the middle of it all like Becca, Jack and Daniel.

For years, he'd told himself he'd imagined most of it, that it couldn't have happened the way he recalled. But dying had a way of stripping away pretense. He knew now that it was real, it had all been real twenty-six years ago. And it was real today, too.

He shivered, a stab of that old terror running down his spine like ice water dripping down his collar. Even now, he still felt that out-of-proportion fear he'd felt then, that terror that didn't match the circumstances. What had happened was…impossible, the things he'd seen couldn't have happened, only they did.

But even the impossibility of what he saw couldn't account for the level of horror and terror he felt watching it. There was something more, something worse than his eyes could see, something darker and uglier than his mind could even imagine, some evil intent that turned his thoughts to images of mouldering corpses and his senses to the reek of decay.

He'd never been able to reconcile that fear, had merely run mindlessly away, blind flight that had left him panting and sweating, heedless of the spreading warm wetness that stained his pants.

Then it was gone. Over. As quickly and strangely as it had begun, the cloud of terror that hung over him, over the whole community, or so he'd imagined, was gone.

Now, it was back.

He glanced out the window at what he could see of the sky through the trees and imagined he saw a dark pall blotting the light.

Well, Michael McKinley Rutherford wasn't going to

have to live through those days again. He cocked his head and gave an imaginary salute to the Big C, the cancer that would spare him another summer like the one he'd lived through in 1985. Actually, it wouldn't be the out-of control cells chewing up his lungs that would spare him, though. This time at least, he would be the master of his own fate.

He fingered the big syringe with the needle that must have been three inches long—the one the cute little nurse with the turned-up nose had called a "garden hose needle." Bless her heart, she'd looked high and low for that thing after he'd snatched it off the metal tray when she wasn't looking. Now, he kept it hidden under his pillow, waiting. Screwing himself up to it, gathering his nerve.

It wouldn't be long now. The way his pain level was outrunning the meds they gave him to relieve it, before long it would take more courage to keep on breathing than to put the needle in the juncture of his IV and shove air into it. He'd read that it might take a lot of air—maybe the length of a whole IV line, to do any damage. Michael didn't care. He'd just keep pumping in air like he was blowing up a bicycle tire. Something would pop eventually.

But not yet. He had awhile yet. Another sunrise or two, maybe. He wanted to pet his dog again—they'd be bringing Charger day after tomorrow. He could hold out that long, wait long enough for the feel of the golden retriever's soft fur. He wanted to listen to the sound of the "Rolling Stones Greatest Hits" on his iPod again, too. And stay on the earth long enough for one more peek down the front of the uniform of the nurse whose top button was always undone.

He wrapped his fingers protectively around the syringe and slept.

When he awoke, it was dark. And he wasn't alone.

"Three of them?"

Daniel spoke with such wonder and horror and revulsion that his words hung out in the air between them like a curtain, separating each from the other, momentarily isolating them all.

"Why couldn't it have been only one——?" he asked.

"'Cause demons is wherever they is, just like people—can't be in two places at one time. When Jack shot that crazy fool who killed my Bishop, he sent that bug creature screaming back to hell where it belongs," Theresa said. "The demons that possessed them others—they's sent back to hell, too, when them men died."

"So now we're not trying to figure out what we did to piss off a single demon, we're trying to figure out what we did to piss off three of them." Daniel groaned.

"If it's all wrapped up in that missing summer, then the playing field's a little different, but the rules of engagement haven't changed," Jack said, trying desperately to sound reasonable and rational when he didn't feel either one. "We still have to find Becca—whether it's one demon that's willing to commit mass murder to find her— or a whole herd of them. She's the only one who knows why. And until we know——"

"No, not the only one." Daniel turned and looked at Theresa. "You were there that summer. You knew us and the other guys on the team. "You must have seen something going on. What was it?"

"They was lots of things going on that year, starting on…Valentine's Day," she said. "But I can't tell you much about nothin'. I might have been smack up there in the middle of it all…but for a year, maybe two after that Valentine's Day, I wasn't worth shooting."

"What happened on Valentine's Day?" Daniel asked, and as he did, his cell phone rang. He looked at the screen, saw it was the hotline volunteer, and sent the call to voicemail.

Chapter Twenty-Two

The big streetlight at the corner of the building usually filled Michael Rutherford's hospital room with so much light the nurses had to pull the shades so he could sleep. But tonight the light was inexplicably out. The room was dark except for light from the hallway that fell in a golden arrow through the slit of his partially open door, and the glow of monitors that painted the area around his bed a bilious green. He could hear sounds from out there in the hallway, the muffled whush, whush of nurses' shoes on the tile floor, the clatter of metal water pitchers and bedpans, the murmur of voices.

What he could hear in the room was breathing. Heavy breathing. Not labored breathing like his own, though— sick and clotted. Heavy like someone had been running. Or was excited.

"Who is it?" Michael asked the darkness. "Who's there?"

"Hello, Mi-key." The voice didn't sound familiar. But the childhood name, pronounced in two syllables, and the tone of contempt that colored the words planted a niggling itch in his memory. Where had he heard—?

"Got any jokes to tell, Fatty Cakes?"

Michael couldn't even gasp. Takes air to gasp. But he was afraid—oh, my, yes!—he was so stricken with mind-numbing terror his bladder let go and wet warmth flooded the bed.

The only person in his life who'd ever called him Fatty Cakes was Ronnie Martin. And he hadn't seen Ronald Martin since that long-ago summer when dark horror stalked every corner of his world.

Denial tried to leap to his defense. They were grownups now, after all. He should laugh and tell Ronnie to turn on the light, let Michael get a look at him, see how the years had treated him, maybe joke about a growing paunch or receding hairline.

He didn't laugh or joke, though, because he didn't have enough air, wouldn't have had enough air even if cancer hadn't chewed a hole through both his lungs. He wouldn't have been able to say a thing if he'd had the lungs of a young boy, a twelve-year-old boy, who couldn't speak then either.

"You were with them, Mikey," the darkness said. "Too fat and stupid to be one of the group, just the tail they wagged behind them. But you helped the three and the light. Now you're gonna help me."

The inky blackness formed words in a pitted throat full of rocks and pieces of broken glass. "Where's Becca?"

Becca Hawkins?

Michael hadn't seen Becca Hawkins since high school! She'd become invisible after that summer. Michael had tried to talk to her, engage her, make her laugh those little bells again. But it was almost like she didn't know who he was. Becca had melted into the background of the school and life until after graduation and then she vanished for real and no one ever heard from her again.

When Michael didn't answer the question—because he didn't know the answer and because he had no breath at all for speech—the thing that had spoken moved closer.

What Michael Rutherford experienced then could have been a trick of his failing eyesight, or an illusion occasioned by the massive doses of narcotics in his bloodstream. It was neither. Michael had a foot in both worlds. Teetering on the brink of living and dying, dangling between ultimate light and absolute darkness, had granted Michael a gift. Or a curse. Michael Rutherford knew.

A form appeared in the glow of light around his bed. It didn't step from the darkness, it was made of darkness—not only in this room, but all darkness everywhere, all bottomless pits, all deep holes filled with black water where horrible things had drowned and left behind their formless, mouldering corpses. Its shape was of some great winged creature with the hideous face of a deformed ape. One eye was lower than the other, both were red and looked out from under a brow ridge with no forehead above it. The top of the creature's head was lumpy, with horns protruding at odd angles, and incisors the size of daggers stuck up past pendulous black lips below a pig-snout nose —only half of it was missing.

Cold flowed out from it in a wave. It frosted the tiny stream of Michael's breath that leaked out his nose past the oxygen tube, then hung in a shiny white trail of lace in front of his upper lip.

Though the form had wings like a bat, it had the hairy legs of a spider wrapped tight around Ronnie Martin. The left side of Ronnie's face drooped, his left arm hung useless, but he held in his right hand a screwdriver that glowed in the green monitor light.

"We used one of these on Jack," Ronnie said and his breath glowed white in the frigid air. "Drilled it into his bones."

Michael knew what they'd done to Jack with the Phillips head. He'd watched them.

"I'm going to use this on you like we did on Jack unless you tell me what I want to know."

Michael looked pleadingly into eyes the gray of frozen ashes. He was unable to beg for mercy because he had no air for speech.

And for a moment, an instant, Michael saw a spark of humanity in Ronnie's eyes, so sunken they looked like twin holes in his face. For a heartbeat, those eyes locked with Michael's and he saw there a terror and desperation he had never seen in another human being.

Then the look vanished and one of such feral savagery took its place that Michael would have gasped if he could have.

Ronnie leaned over the bed, his face inches from Michael's. The creature on his back spoke, its voice as empty and cold as an Arctic wind blowing across a thousand miles of barren ice. "I want Becca!"

From Ronnie's throat came a sound unlike any Michael had ever heard. It was a human growl, the snarl of a mad dog.

Michael's panic exploded. He shrieked soundlessly with his poisoned, rotted lungs and struck out in a reflex to push him, to push it away. Ronnie let out a high-pitched squeal and a drip of warm liquid splashed on Michael's cheek. Then Ronnie grabbed Michael—or seemed to—but didn't hold on. The weight on Michael's chest slid instantly away and he felt a stinging pain as the IV needle in his arm yanked free. On the heels of the pain was a clattering sound and a thump. He sucked in air and began to cough and suddenly light flooded the room.

Voices. A nurse—the cute little one?—screamed.

The room was suddenly filled with people, stepping around something by his bed, but when Michael tried to see what it was, his view was blocked. He struggled to sit up, but nurses pushed him firmly back on the pillow. Then, for a moment, the crowd of people parted enough for Michael to catch a glimpse of what was on the floor. It was Ronnie Martin, lying face up. The three-inch, garden-hose needle that had been in Michael's hand when he fell asleep was buried up to the syringe in Ronnie's left temple.

Then Michael Rutherford let go. With what little air he had, he wailed a wordless cry of horror and revulsion, and gave himself up to mindless hysteria.

~

"What happened on Valentine's Day?" Theresa echoed Daniel's question. "Why, that was the day the world come crashing down around my head and I liked to never dug my way back out."

The knock on the door come so early it couldn't have been nothing but bad news. You don't get woke up at four o'clock in the morning to find out you won the lottery.

Bishop got up, put on his robe and started downstairs with Theresa right behind him. But he told her, "You wait here. I got this."

Translate that: "If it's something awful, I want to take the first staggering blow."

Theresa sat where she was on the top stair, apprehension such a heavy mantle she couldn't stand up under it.

Count your blessings, she told herself. It ain't Bishop. He's right here. It ain't Isaac, he asleep in his room.

But beyond that it could have been anybody—a lifetime of working with boys, mentoring them, growing them up into fine young men had populated Bishop and Theresa's world with dozens of possible victims for a catastrophe.

She heard Bishop's rumbling voice and another man's voice. Then Bishop appeared at the bottom of the stairs with the county sheriff behind him.

And in that pregnant moment before Bishop opened his mouth to speak, Theresa took the last pain-free breath she'd ever draw in.

"They say they found Isaac's car all smashed up at the base of Scott's Ridge," he said.

That was crazy. Isaac was—

"Musta got stole out of the driveway in the middle of the night," she said and her voice sounded high-pitched and squeaky.

Then Theresa couldn't get down the stairs fast enough. Shoving Bishop and the sheriff out of her way, she thundered down the hallway and flung open the door to Isaac's room. His bed was still made. He hadn't slept in it all night.

"My Isaac went missing on Valentine's Day," Theresa said, and tears sprang into her eyes. "Ain't nobody seen him since." She looked at Jack, "Shoot, for six months I wouldn't even admit he was gone, tole myself all kinda stories about where he'd run off to and how he'd come home all apologizing, saying he's sorry he made us worry."

She looked from Jack to Daniel. "Either one of you boys remember Isaac?"

Jack did. The image of a tall, broad-shouldered young man with Bishop's strength and Theresa's kind eyes. He could hear the sound of his laughter—rich and full, and recall how he could throw a pitch so fast it'd burn right through the leather of a catcher's mitt.

Jack remembered something else, too, and the pit of his stomach was suddenly hollow. Whatever it was that had happened to Isaac…it had been Jack's fault. He was absolutely certain.

Theresa must have seen the look that washed over Jack's face—gone as fast as it had come.

"You boys been remembering other things about that summer?"

After a fashion, yes. Jack was beginning to see holes in the blackout cloth that hid that summer from him, like a pair of worn jeans where the last frayed threads finally break and the fabric separates. Memories were surfacing that way. Oh, not big ones. He suspected if he recalled anything important it'd be flung out of his mind like a shot put. Smaller ones, though, were escaping through the frayed fabric.

He remembered trying to sneak a water gun into school for the last day of class and having to spend that glorious day of almost-freedom cooling his heels in the principal's office. He remembered a mishmash of other totally inconsequential things—the fruit aisle in the grocery store, making paper airplanes out of old church bulletins and sailing them out of the balcony of Daniel's father's church, and Daniel's little sister running around the sanctuary trying to catch them, squealing with delight. Something bad had happened to that little girl, but Jack couldn't remember what it was.

"I'm glad to tell you what I know about that time,"

Theresa said, "but it'll only be tatters and snips." She paused to focus. "I remember a lot of things about you boys, of course, but the others not so much. Being an all-star team, the players come from all three of the schools in the county—the two private schools and the public school where you three went. We didn't know none of them boys from the Catholic school or Brewster Academy, and you boys didn't know each other. So we had us a barbecue for the team in our back yard on the Friday before practice started on Monday so you could get acquainted. Them boys from Brewster Academy kinda stuck together and I seem to recall you and Daniel getting into an argument with them that first night."

"About what?" Jack asked.

"I don't think I knew even at the time. Some chests-out and shoving was all. Bishop broke it up. Seems like they's calling you two names—sissy, chicken, things like that. Do you boys remember?"

Both men shook their heads.

"You will 'cause they's a angel out there wants you to remember. Needs you to remember."

"I want to talk about that"—Jack swallowed hard—"angel."

Daniel silenced another call on his cell phone.

"Andi says there was a demon on Jacob Dumas. She saw it, but I didn't. So is there an angel around here somewhere, too, that I can't see?"

It took a great force of will to keep from peering into the shadows, as if he expected a being with a halo and wings to materialize. And he was struck, yet again, by the otherworldliness of the question. He was asking an old woman if there was an angel in the room, for crying out loud.

Theresa read his mind. Well, all right, his face.

"You remember what Scripture says happened to yore namesake?" she asked Daniel.

"Well, yes… what are you talking about in particular?"

"I'm talking about when the angel appeared to Daniel on the bank of the Tigris River and told him God had heard his prayer on the first day he'd prayed it—three weeks before. You remember that part?"

Daniel nodded. "And the angel said it had taken him twenty-one days to get there because…"

"…because 'The prince of the kingdom of Persia was withstanding me for twenty-one days,'" Theresa completed the Scripture.

Jack didn't like where this conversation appeared to be heading, but he hadn't liked the direction of most of the conversations he'd had lately.

"So you're saying a battle between an angel and a demon delayed the angel for three weeks?" Jack asked.

"It ain't what I'm sayin'," Theresa said. "It's what Scripture says. And they's a whole lot more references to angels fighting demons in other books like the Koran. "

She paused and looked deep into Jack's eyes. "You don't b'lieve that, do you?"

"Does it matter?"

"You think it don't matter what you b'lieve, that you can deny the truth and it'll go away and leave you alone?"

"I don't know what I believe," Jack said.

"Good!" Theresa said, and that surprised him. "That's a right fine place to be. Rather be there than all puffed up knowing 'xactly what you believe and it's all wrong."

She paused again, then quoted words she said came from the end of the tenth chapter of Daniel. "'The secret things belong to the Lord, our God, but the things revealed belong to us.' God don't let us know all of it by a long shot, but what he does let us know is ours to make use of, to help us live in this here supernatural world."

The room grew quiet. A rumble of distant thunder sent a chill down Jack's spine. A nameless dread, like a swarm of winged creatures, flew around and around in his stomach, fluttered in his bones.

Get a grip, Carpenter. It's a thunderstorm!

Daniel ran his fingers through his hair in frustration.

"This is certifiably crazy. What does this demon, or this herd of demons, want Jack and Becca and me for?"

"Ain't you figured that out yet?" Theresa said, cocked her head to the side and then shook it. "They always was boys quicker on the uptake than you was, Daniel Burke." She leaned closer to him and said softly, "Them demons don't want you for nothin', son. They want to know where the three of you is so they can kill you."

Into the profound silence that followed, Daniel's phone rang again. This time he answered the call.

Chapter Twenty-Three

The cute little nurse with the turned-up nose put the telephone receiver back on the hook and saw that her hand was trembling. Another nurse stopped at the nurses' station counter where she was seated, leaned over and asked quietly, "Well?"

"You think I did the right thing?" she asked, still holding the receiver, reluctant to let go.

"Couldn't do any harm," said the second nurse. She glanced down, noticed the top button on her uniform was undone, but didn't bother to fasten it, merely nodded toward the door of Room 109—where a heavily-sedated Michael Rutherford slept. The room where he had been for the past two weeks was still a beehive of activity. The coroner had only removed the body a few minutes ago. "You saw how he calmed down when I told him I knew that guy he was hollering about."

"You sure it's the right guy?"

"Has to be. My mother watches Rev. Daniel Burke preach on TV every week, even drove all the way to

Cincinnati one Sunday to see him—him being a local boy and all."

The cute nurse looked at the room where even from the nurses' station a puddle of blood was still visible on the floor. She'd have cleaned it up hours ago, but they wouldn't let her. Said it was a crime scene. She turned back as the other nurse continued. "If you hadn't promised you'd call the guy, Mr. Rutherford would probably still be hollering. What'd the preacher say?"

"At first, I talked to the church hotline volunteer, had to convince him this was a real emergency. He gave me the preacher's cell phone number, but I had to try three or four times to get him to pick up, and by the time he did I'd decided I wasn't going to tell him about..." she nodded toward the room where policemen talked in low voices. "I just said an old classmate of his was dying and was crying out his name. He sounded real concerned; said he'd be here first thing tomorrow."

As Jack and Daniel crossed the bridge over the Three Forks River into Caverna County, Kentucky, Jack felt like he was taking a ride through more than space, that he was traveling through time as well, back to another era and into a world that was profoundly different from the one where he had conducted his life since his grandmother took him home to live with her in New York right before the beginning of school in 1985.

He hadn't been back in Bradford's Ridge since then— not surprising since he couldn't remember any childhood friends and had no reason to go "home." But after what had happened lately, he suspected that even if he'd had a reason to return, he'd have avoided it. Something…bad had happened here, something he and Daniel and the mysterious Becca had been a part of—Theresa and Bishop too, apparently. And getting near that bad made him uneasy, the kind of gut feeling that'd make a police officer look over his shoulder and pat the Glock in his holster.

Jack glanced up at the gigantic sign beside the road, featuring a smiling Chapman Whitworth and his slogan, "You'll have to go through me," and grimaced. Daniel saw the reaction.

"Not a fan of our native son made good?" Daniel asked.

"Nope," Jack grunted.

"Me neither," Daniel said.

Jack raised his eyebrows in a question.

"No reason," Daniel continued. "Well, at least not a good one. My parents took me to see Indiana Jones and The Temple Of Doom in Louisville when it came out. After supper that night, my father—we're talking my father, here, who never had an unkind word to say about anybody—said the big ugly dude who stole the Shankara stone reminded him of Chandler Whitworth."

Daniel smiled. "You notice how I casually dropped that childhood memory into the conversation, like I was one of those people who actually have childhood memories."

"Things are coming out of the mist for me, too," Jack said. "Just not important things. My only retrievable memory of Chapman Whitworth's father is that my father was convinced he was rich. That little house on Peach Tree Lane that'd belonged to Granny Whitworth—my father thought it was full of all kinds of treasure. Called Whitworth 'an archeologist with sticky fingers and a deep pocket' who always came back from a dig with something for himself."

"Think your father was onto something?"

"He was never sober long enough to be onto anything. He and Chandler Whitworth would have been about the same age, though, maybe went to school together. But they weren't friends. White kids didn't have black friends, not in the fifties in Kentucky."

Something occurred to Jack. "You do remember that the Twin Oaks fire that killed Chandler Whitworth was the summer of 1985," he said.

Daniel looked like he'd had bad sushi for breakfast.

"I do now." He paused. "And I remember I wasn't there. We weren't there, none of the three of us. Everybody else in town watched it burn, but Becca and I… something. We went somewhere together, but it's 'lost in the mist.'"

They passed the Twin Oaks memorial—a granite monolith with a big plaque inscribed with the names of all who died. It was tasteful—surrounded by flower gardens and benches.

"I used to go with my father to Twin Oaks on Saturdays to serve communion to the old people," Daniel said, a note of wonder in his voice. "I just remembered that. And one Saturday, when I was filling the tray of communion cups in that little room off the kitchen, I spilled juice on the plank floor and it slid down through the cracks and was gone—like there was a hole there or something."

Daniel warmed to the story, describing a movie he'd never seen before that was now playing in his head.

"So I tried to pry up on one of the planks and it was a trap door. Most of it was covered by a rug, but as soon as Dad was busy on the second floor, I pulled the door up and crawled down through it."

"And you found a basement like the one under the opera house in Phantom of the Opera?"

"Nope. I was sorely disappointed. Nothing but an empty dirt basement where there must have been a furnace once because there was a coal chute."

The two men rode on in silence, Jack's GPS telling him to "turn right on Beckley Street" and to "bear left at the crossroads."

It seemed to be a prosperous community, with wide streets, big trees in the lawns of old, well-kept houses. Certainly, there was a poorer section of town than the one they were driving through. There was in every community. But what they saw bespoke old South and old money, not new subdivisions, but families that had been here for generations.

They didn't comment on what had changed, since neither could remember much of what it used to be like. The hospital was obviously a new addition, though. Its architecture was jarring—all glass and sharp angles—and didn't fit the old charm. A sign out front proclaimed "Bradford's Ridge Regional Hospital, a member of Midland Health Care's family of fine medical facilities." Big corporations never got it, or got it, but didn't care when their trendy modern architecture didn't suit the nature or the topography of the communities where they did business.

The look on the face of the woman at the reception desk when Daniel asked for Michael Rutherford's room number primed Jack's something's-going-on-here alarm. When they got to the third floor and stepped out of the elevator, the man in a brown sheriff's uniform who greeted them set the alarm off: clang, clang, clang.

"You're Reverend Daniel Burke, I take it," the officer said, his pleasant face neither smiling nor frowning. He extended a beefy hand to Daniel and then to Jack. "I'm Caverna County Sheriff Hezekiah Lincoln." The sheriff was a stocky man, squat, built like a fire hydrant with reddish brown hair in a semicircle around a bald dome usually hidden by a hat, and deep-set, intelligent eyes.

"Jack Carpenter," Jack said. Since he wasn't in uniform, he added. "Sergeant Carpenter, Harrelton, Ohio PD."

The man's eyes widened.

"You're the guy capped that school shooter," he said. Police officers always kept up with news about their own. Jack nodded. "Good job," the sheriff said, and meant it. "And you're here because…?"

Jack could have bobbed and weaved, but something about the sheriff struck a chord and he decided to shoot straight with him. "I don't have any idea why I'm here. Daniel's here because Michael Rutherford has been calling for him, but we both went to grade school with Michael and…let's just say there's been a lot going on lately with our former classmates."

The sheriff lifted his eyebrows, but said nothing. Jack played tit for tat. "And you're here because…?"

"Because a guy named Ronald Martin, who lives in Montana, but grew up here, tried to kill Mr. Rutherford last night."

Daniel gasped. Jack didn't blink.

"Apparently, he didn't succeed," Jack said.

"Nope, Rutherford offed him with a hypodermic needle."

Jack liked the sheriff. He often made snap judgments about fellow officers—like Trooper Purvis—and he was seldom wrong. "Sounds like quite a story," he said. "I'd love to hear it."

"And I'd like to hear about the shenanigans of your

other classmates, too," the sheriff said. "You got time for a cup of coffee in the cafeteria?"

Jack turned to Daniel.

"Why don't you go see Michael Rutherford," he said. "He might want to talk to you privately anyway. I'll be back in a little while."

Jack turned in place and punched the elevator call button.

"You probably didn't put the names together, but Daniel is the father of the little girl I"—he still couldn't say 'shot'—"who was hit by the through-and-through."

"That so?"

"And the school shooter, Jacob Dumas, was one of our classmates, too, went to elementary school here—with Daniel and me and Michael Rutherford," Jack said.

"I did not know that," the sheriff said thoughtfully. "No sir, I did not know that for a fact." He looked Jack up and down. "Would it interest you to know that, given what's gone on in Bradford's Ridge in the past few weeks, that does not surprise me?"

"It would, sir," Jack said as the elevator doors opened. "But you're going to tell me why that is, aren't you?"

"Indeed, I am."

Michael Rutherford opened his eyes a slit, barely wide enough to see the man standing at his bedside. He acted as if he were sleeping still, wanted to be sure it wasn't...who? Wasn't somebody trying to kill him, that's who!

His heart began to race again and he began to cough.

He opened his eyes—no use pretending to sleep when

you're hacking your head off—and felt the ground glass in his chest slice him open on the inside. Each coughing spasm was an agony that sent silent tears streaming down his face—and they had him so doped up the room looked like he was seeing it from inside an aquarium.

The man by his bedside—Daniel Burke, he was sure of it now—handed him a wad of tissues out of the box and Michael coughed and gasped into them until he was too weak to cough, even though the reflex still hitched in his chest.

"Can I get you anything?" Daniel asked. "A drink of water? Some juice?"

Michael shook his head, unable yet to speak. Daniel's voice was the same. Even as a kid, Daniel had sounded like a preacher. It was something about the way he pronounced words, or the rhythm of his speech. And his voice was deep. At twelve, it had already changed and he sounded like a man.

At twelve, Mikey Rutherford had sounded like one of those munchkins from The Wizard of Oz.

Daniel and Jack had both sounded like men, as a matter of fact. The others, the bad ones, weren't nearly as…mature and self-possessed. They were squeaky and wimpy and cowardly. Bullies. Mike believed, at least he had at the time, that Jack and Daniel could have stood them down—all of them—even outnumbered. Well, maybe not, but they'd have kicked some major butt in the effort.

As it was, they never had a chance to kick butt. Never had a chance, period. What the others could do, did do, no twelve-year-old on the planet could have stood up to that. At least, if that part had been real, had happened the way Michael remembered it. Of course, it couldn't possibly have happened the way he remembered it.

But it had.

"Stop it," Cole Stuart says. He reaches out a big hand and grabs a hank of Jacob Dumas's hair, yanks his head back. "You can't do that!"

Mikey is crouched behind an azalea bush, hidden from view by the big fronds of leaves and the pendulous clusters of pink blossoms. He'd wanted to run as soon as he heard Dumas's voice, edgy and menacing, but if the others were with him and spotted Mikey, he'd be sunk, fat as he was. So far, he'd managed to escape their wrath. Focused as they were on Becca, Jack and Daniel, they'd let him slide, contenting themselves with menacing glares that sent him scurrying away from their confrontations with the other three. Not all the way away, though. They didn't know he hung around, watched what they did. And he doesn't want them to find out.

There was a wooded area in the park next to the baseball fields and he'd been on his way through it to baseball practice—early so he could get all the equipment in order. He wasn't on the team, of course. He was the manager. Ronnie Martin called him the Fat Boy instead of the Bat Boy when Coach Washington was out of earshot.

He had come around the big rock that rested beside the shaggy bark hickory tree next to the footpath when he heard the voices and recognized them at once. Should have run then, should have turned tail and run fast as his fat legs would carry him.

But he'd crept closer instead, finally hiding in the azalea bush where he could watch Jacob Dumas torture Jack. And that's what he was doing. Other boys pinned Jack's arms behind his back while Jacob landed one blow after another in his belly. Then Jacob pulled out his pocket knife, flipped out the sharpest blade and held it up next to Jack's cheek.

"How'd you like to lose an ear, nigger?" he'd purred. Jack tried to turn his head away but Jacob grabbed his chin in a vice grip and held his head still. "Tell you what, I'll cut off both of them so you'll match. But you'll have to give up wearing sunglasses."

Jacob roared at his own humor, then began edging the knife toward Jack's ear.

"Hold still, nigger. I ain't planning on cutting off nothing but your ears, but if you keep on wiggling, you could lose a nose..."

That's when Cole Stuart showed up, grabbed Jacob by the hair and told him he couldn't hurt Jack.

"I ain't gonna kill him, just—" Jacob snarls, squirming free.

Cole grabs the front of Jacob's shirt and leans over until his nose is inches from Jacob's.

"You're as stupid as you are ugly." He snarls the words into Jacob's face. "Don't you get it? You hurt him, do something that leaves a mark—on any of them—and they can turn us in. Parents—police, maybe. We got a job to do." He holds Jacob out in front of him. "You wanna have to explain how you brought the law down on our heads because you cut a nigger?"

He lets go of Jacob's shirt and shoves him away, then turns to Jack, who stands with his arms still pinned behind him by the other boys.

"You owe me, nigger," he says. "I saved your black butt."

Jack spits in his face.

Cole instinctively draws back his fist in response, then stops. He wipes the spittle off his cheek as something resembling a smile pulls up the corners of his mouth.

"Grab his legs," he says to Jacob and the others. "Don't let him kick me."

Jacob drops to one knee and grabs Jack's left leg as another boy kneels and grabs the right. Jack struggles, but the boys are so strong it's as if he's in a vice.

Cole reaches into his hip pocket and pulls out something. Mikey can't see it well, some kind of tool. A screw driver, Phillips head.

"Won't leave much of a mark, just look like he banged into something," Cole says. Then he places the point of the screwdriver on Jack's shin halfway between his ankle and his knee and begins to gouge it into his flesh. Jack howls, but Cole continues.

"There," he says to the other boys. "I've hit bone." He grins. "Now we're gonna really screw you, nigger."

He begins to grind the screwdriver back and forth, digging it deeper and deeper into the shin bone of Jack's leg. Jack lets out a ferocious wail before Jacob clamps his free hand over his mouth and muffles his cries. Cole continues to grind, a maniacal grin distorting his face as Jack squirms and screams soundlessly, tears streaming down his cheeks.

Mikey has do to something! But what can he do? Before he has time to think about it and lose his nerve, he darts back up the trail about forty feet and begins to talk loud, his machine-gun babble, non-stop.

"Wow, Coach Washington, I didn't know you ever walked through the woods to the field. I thought you always drove your car. That's a great car, sir, a fine car. Wish I had me a car like that. If I had me a car like that, I'd …"

He hears scuffling sounds on the other side of the rock, thumping, then silence.

Continuing to talk, he slowly edges around the rock. The little clearing where the others were torturing Jack only a few moments before is empty. Where did they go? Where's Jack?

Then Mikey hears a sound, a groan above him. He looks up and sees Jack crumpled among the tree limbs twenty feet off the ground. How in the world…he didn't climb up there. The only possible way he could have gotten there was if somebody threw him.

Michael Rutherford gasped and reached out for Daniel Burke's hand.

"They jammed that screw driver into his leg," he said, clutching the hand as tight as he could. He had to explain, tell Daniel that what had happened before was happening all over again. That Ronnie Martin, who'd called him Fat Boy, had tried to do the same thing to him that Jacob Dumas had done to Jack in the woods that day. And that… an ape spider with wings had come into his room last night wrapped around Ronnie Martin and…

But the walls were spinning around him wildly, around and around. And the words in his head began to spin along with them.

Chapter Twenty-Four

Jack took a sip of his coffee and was grateful his years of drinking police department brew had toughened the walls of his stomach.

"Tastes like battery acid," he said, and sat the Styrofoam cup on the table in front of him.

"Sugar helps," the sheriff said, then proceeded to dump three little white packets of it into his cup. He stirred it with the red plastic swizzle stick, then sipped it. "I lied. It doesn't help." He set his cup next to Jack's in the center of the table.

Jack had selected a sweet roll and a banana from the cafeteria line. The sheriff had picked up a bagel and a tin of cream cheese. He began opening the tin as Jack spoke.

"So tell me about Ronnie Martin" Jack said.

"Don't know a whole lot yet. He lived in Great Falls, Montana, worked in a pool hall. Police there say he wasn't exactly Man of the Year material, but he wasn't a real bad-ass either. Had a rap sheet for petty crimes, floated checks, B & E amended down to criminal trespass. Worst thing he ever did was stab a guy in a bar fight about five years ago, but they didn't prosecute."

Jack lifted his eyebrows.

"Friends of the guy he stabbed beat the crap out of him before the police got there, put him in the hospital for months. Head injuries paralyzed him on his left side. He walked with a bad limp, couldn't use his left arm."

The sheriff picked up a plastic knife and smeared cheese on the bagel.

"Which is the good news for Michael Rutherford. The guy's dying of cancer—you knew that didn't you?"

"I do now."

"Weak as a drowned pup like he is, there's no way he could have fought off somebody who had use of both hands."

"Why'd Martin want to kill Mikey?" Jack remembered the childhood name only as he spoke it. He knew better than to hope there was a normal explanation for Martin's behavior, but he had to ask.

"You got me, pal, I couldn't tell you. Martin's boss says he was at work yesterday, left at the usual time. Then apparently, he got in his car, drove twenty-six hours, straight through—only stopped for gas—to Bradford's Ridge, sneaked into Rutherford's hospital room and tried to kill him."

Jack felt his own face harden and knew the sheriff picked up on it.

"What?" the sheriff asked.

"It's just not the first time I've heard that story," Jack said.

The sheriff said nothing as Jack told him about Stephenson and Willingham—and about the picture of the Little League team from 1985. He stuck to the facts, omitted the parts that would have made him sound like a raving lunatic—demons made out of flies, little girls coming back from the dead, his memory of three months of his life a blank slate. When he finished, he slowly peeled the banana as the sheriff sat opposite him, chewing his bagel in silence.

"I've tracked down as many of the team members as I could," Jack said. "A lot of the names were illegible, faces faded out, too. Some are dead, some I couldn't find—Martin was one of those. I'll mark him off my list. But the ones I did find—garden variety stuff. A plumber, a car salesman, one's a high school baseball coach—doctors, lawyers and Indian chiefs. Leading normal lives." He paused. "Of course, Willingham, Stephenson and Martin were leading normal lives, too, until they suddenly went inexplicably psycho and tried to kill people. Dumas was always a nutcase, sister said he was bi-polar, but he was a harmless nutcase until a few weeks ago."

Jack took a deep breath and let it out slowly. "So it's not outside the realm of possibility that anybody who was on that team could suddenly drop whatever he's doing and…"

The sheriff plastered another gob of cream cheese on his bagel and lifted it to his mouth.

"You said you wouldn't likely be surprised by what I told you 'given what's been going on here lately,'" Jack said. "Such as?"

The sheriff put the bagel back on the paper plate without taking a bite.

"Spiders."

"Spiders?"

"Dozens and dozens of 'em, seventy-five, a hundred—all kinds. The big old ugly brown wolf spiders and cobweb spiders and crab spiders and…you name it." The sheriff took a deep breath before he continued. "Crawlin' all over the little kids in Sunday School at First Baptist last Sunday!

Them little kids was so freaked out, was screaming and running around, trying to get em off." He paused to take a breath. "Horriblest thing I ever saw in my life," he said, and his face was pale.

"Where'd the spiders come—?"

"How would I know!"

Two old ladies seated at a table near the door looked up and the sheriff lowered his voice to a rasping whisper. "I don't have any idea and neither does anybody else. They were just…there. Somebody brought 'em and let 'em loose, of course, but how could anybody collect that many spiders, musta been near a hundred of them. And what would possess somebody to…?"

Possess. Jack pushed the thought out of his mind.

The sheriff cleared his throat and continued.

"There's more," he said.

Jack said nothing, merely listened.

"Far as I can tell, there ain't a single dog left in this whole town that weighs less than fifty pounds. Ever last one of 'em— Mrs. Pruit's Pomeranian, the Talbot's miniature poodles, Sarah Warren's Dachshund—every one of 'em was found laying in the yard or on the porch, or shoved through the doggie doors onto the kitchen floor! All of them dead and horribly mutilated."

Becca's precious mutt—McDougal. Daniel had described how he remembered Victor Alexander killing it and suddenly the memory flooded into Jack's mind, too, in full living color. Becca wailing, Victor swinging the dog around and around by its head until…

Jack was sure his face had registered the horror of it but the sheriff was so intent on his own gruesome tales he didn't even notice.

"And cats. Had four of 'em…burned up. Somebody put gasoline on 'em and…" He stopped, gathered himself.

"Folks started keeping their cats inside after that. Until a few weeks ago, people didn't even lock their doors in this town. Now, you can't buy a deadbolt anywhere for fifty miles in every direction."

"Any suspects?"

"Nobody reasonable. Several people have said they saw children around. I've talked to the kids, but they don't know anything. And where would a bunch of little kids come up with a hundred spiders? Besides, killing dogs and cats like that, them animals would have fought back! Little kids couldn't have done it."

"Don't bet the grocery money," Jack said.

The sheriff looked startled.

"Have you...?" Jack didn't know how to frame the question, but he had to ask it all the same. "Have there been stories...have little kids told stories about other little kids who can...?" The sheriff's eyes were boring into his. Jack shifted his gaze to his coffee cup. "Little kids who can do things that they couldn't possibly do, but..." His voice trailed off. He knew he wasn't making sense.

"Like?" the sheriff prodded, but Jack heard no skepticism in his voice.

"Like throwing a ninety-pound boy twenty feet up into a tree."

Jack waited for the grunt of disbelief. It didn't come.

"Or a little girl ripping up a garden full of rosebushes?" There was wonder in the sheriff's voice, and something like understanding.

Jack's head snapped up and he stared unbelieving into the sheriff's eyes.

"Who...?"

"My daughter...my Jenny, she's eight. She told me her friend Ariel Murphy had suddenly changed, was different, had gotten mean, but I told her it was only kid stuff, that

Ariel'd get over it. Four days ago, I got home and found Jenny sitting on the front porch crying. She said Ariel had destroyed her rose garden for no reason, went berserk and tore it up. I figured maybe the kid had…you know, tore off all the blooms, maybe even took a hatchet and…" He paused. "Went out in the back yard and every plant—seven of them—was laying on the ground, ripped out by the roots. You ever try to pull a rosebush out of the ground with your bare hands?"

Jack sat still.

"Do you know what's going on here, Sergeant Carpenter?" the sheriff asked. His voice sounded almost pleading.

"No," Jack said carefully. "But what you're describing…the same kinds of things happened here in 1985… the summer when I was twelve years old."

"Folks have told me that, claimed there's a "copycat assassin" on the loose in Bradford's Ridge. I've only been here eleven years. There were several police reports filed in 1985 about pets being killed, but nothing else in the jackets —it's been twenty-six years! Nothing to follow up on, no evidence, nobody was ever charged. And you gotta remember, that was the summer of the fire—folks were so traumatized by that it's hard to know what to believe."

Jack was feeling his way, not knowing what he thought until he heard the words come out of his mouth. "That summer, a lot of what happened, the mean-ness, was directed at specific people."

"Who?"

"Me, for one."

"Why you?"

"Some folks are partial to vanilla, don't much care for chocolate."

"You and who else?"

"Daniel. And a little girl named Becca Hawkins."

"She wouldn't be kin to—?"

"Billy Ray Hawkins? She's his daughter."

"And the people who singled you three out were children, other children?"

Jack nodded.

"I believe I'm going to have me another sit-down discussion with some kids, starting with Ariel Murphy," the sheriff said. Then he shifted uncomfortably. "But… spiders?" he asked. "Did the kids who were after you—?"

"No." Jack's voice was quiet. "Not spiders. Snakes."

Jack and Daniel rode together in silence down the tree-lined streets of Bradford's Ridge that now seemed sinister to Jack. It was a sensation deeper and stronger, though less tangible, than his cop's sixth sense. It was as if what he had seen as he'd driven into town only a couple of hours earlier, what the casual traveler saw out their car windows was air brushed reality. Reality with the ugly covered over. Now Jack saw shadows of the old hag…the old witch… beneath the pretty powder and red lips of the town facade.

When they passed beneath Chapman Whitworth's welcome sign, Jack spoke.

"What Michael Rutherford said to you, it's not privileged information is it, like what you say to a priest?"

Daniel continued to stare out the window, his face expressionless.

"Daniel!"

Daniel started, turned to Jack.

"What?"

"You know, sometimes talking to you is a lot like being

on hold with no music. It's hard to tell if you're actually connected."

"I'm sorry, I was…" He stopped. "Ever since we got here, I've been remembering things, but the images don't make any sense. They're random, like pictures dumped into a heap on the floor, out of sequence."

"And when you do get a clear look at an image," Jack continued Daniel's thought, "it's like….like there's a bell jar turned upside down on top of it. You can see it, but you can't get in there to feel it, like a real memory."

Daniel nodded agreement and seemed to relax. The ghost of a smile passed across his face. "Misery may love company," he said, "but lunacy truly thrives on companionship."

"Did you remember Rutherford after you saw him? Was he on the team with us?"

"Flashes, images of this little fat kid was all I got, but he said he wasn't on the team. He was the bat boy."

"What did he want with you, why did he want to see you?"

"I'm not sure I know. He was in terrible pain, stuffed so full of morphine most of what he said didn't make a whole lot of sense. I've been trying to piece it together. He talked a lot about this one time when he was with Becca and me at—he called it 'the crack in the rock,' said it was an awful, scary place."

"Where was he talking about?"

"I don't know. I tried to ask but I'm not even sure he heard me. He said he begged us not to go in, that the 'others'—he called them the Bad Kids—would kill us if we followed them. Then he went off about vines and moss that'd grow over our faces, and the screaming would drive us mad, stuff like that. He said we wouldn't listen, though, went in anyway. But he didn't. He was so scared he wet his pants and ran away."

Daniel stopped.

"At that point in the story, he came to, sort of. It was the only time I was certain he knew who he was and who I was, that he was in the present, understood what was going on. He grabbed my hand and said…let me get this right, he said, 'When you came out of there with Jack, your eyes were blank and you walked away separate, in different directions.' He said that after that, you and Becca and I weren't the Three Musketeers anymore, that it was like we didn't even know each other."

Jack could see storm clouds moving in from the west and knew they weren't going to make it back to Cincinnati before the rain hit. Sometimes he enjoyed the pummeling of a hard rain—watching it from the comfort of a warm room with a glowing fire, of course. But he distinctly disliked driving in the rain.

"Mikey said it was happening again, the stuff that happened when we were kids. Do you know what he's talking about? Do you remember it?"

"Some. And more is coming back all the time." Jack told Daniel about his conversation with the sheriff.

"Does it make any sense to you, Jack? Twenty-six years ago, a bunch of kids in Bradford's Ridge did horrible things to us—to get at Becca, I think."

He looked a question at Jack.

"Yeah, I think they were after Becca, only messed with us because we got in their way."

"And now those kids are adults and they're willing to kill people to find her, and meanwhile other little kids in Bradford's Ridge are doing the same kinds of bad things they did. It's crazy."

"What did Rutherford say about the Bad Kids?

Did he know who they were, specifically—names?" Jack swallowed hard. "It wasn't the whole team, was it?"

It was clear Daniel hadn't even considered the possibility that all of the boys in that picture—fifteen of them besides himself, Jack and Michael Rutherford—might go inexplicably nutso and start killing people.

"No, not the whole team," he said quickly. "He said there were six of them, Jacob Dumas, Walter Stephenson, Roger Willingham, Victor Alexander, Ronald Martin and Cole Stuart. Cole was the ringleader, the head bad-ass, I think."

Jack had relaxed perceptibly as soon as Daniel said there weren't fifteen potential assassins.

"And we know where four of them are," Daniel continued. "They're dead. So that leaves Victor Alexander and Cole Stuart." He looked earnestly at Jack. "Did you find those two when you were trying to locate the members of the team?"

Jack stared ahead as pudgy raindrops began to splat down onto the car and tried not to let his relief show.

"Yup, and neither one of them is going anywhere anytime soon so we've got a little breathing room before..." he didn't finish. "Victor Alexander is locked up in a mental hospital in Texas, in solitary in an old building with walls three feet thick. Cole Stuart is a deck hand on a commercial fishing boat that left port in Gloucester, Massachusetts, three weeks ago. Those boats stay out for two or three months at a time."

Daniel squinted and pinched the top of his nose, then rubbed his temples as if his head were throbbing. Dark half-moons showed under his eyes.

"Are you Ok?" Jack asked.

"Emily's having an affair."

Jack managed not to respond at all, merely stared ahead through the windshield.

"I said that out loud, didn't I?" Daniel asked, his voice soft.

"Yep."

"I'm sorry, I…"

"I handle all such disclosures like they were soap bubbles," Jack said. "Just let them float there in the air, don't touch them, because I know how fragile they are."

"I didn't mean to say anything, it just popped out. A thing like that… when you have a rotted tooth, your tongue goes to the hole all the time, even when touching it lights you up with pain."

Jack hadn't ever blown bubbles. Had never felt safe enough with anybody to be vulnerable about his private life.

"I was married once." The words felt strange in Jack's mouth. "My wife's name was…"

He pictured her often—daily!—and remembered her, but he never said her name, hadn't said it aloud since the night he'd wandered through their apartment calling out to her, crying out in disbelieving agony while the dust still hung in the air in the city. He wailed her name again and again until his voice grew weak, made an eerie rasp and rattle, a sound like wind-driven sleet against a window pane or the whispery, scratching sound of scuttling cockroaches. He had stopped calling then. When the sound of that voice registered in his ears, he went instantly mute. And he hadn't spoken her name aloud since, because he was afraid if he did, it would come out in that voice, the ugly, ragged voice of loss and grief.

"Lyla," Jack said.

Chapter Twenty-Five

Lyla's face formed in Jack's mind, the details as clear as a digital image on a hi-def television screen. Two-dimensional, of course. He could never summon her face into his mind as she had looked alive. It was always just an image, like a glove after the hand has been removed, with the detailed stitching on the outside plainly visible, but with no force to animate it, give it form and depth.

At first, he wouldn't allow himself the indulgence of remembering. Memories were no comfort. The mental history of their years together, days, moments, sliced him open to the bone whenever he went anywhere near it.

But when the pain was no longer eviscerating, he found he could gut it out for the muted joy of paging through the catalogue of their lives, flipping from one memory to the next, the touch of her skin, the just-washed smell of her hair, the bubbling lilt of her laughter, her grin when she'd kiss her palm and then blow it to him.

He'd been harsh. He could remember the sound of his own voice, hear it sharp and cutting. Even after all these years, the sound of it made him sick. How could he have spoken to her like that? How could that critical, unyielding tone have colored the last conversation he ever had with her?

"What. Is. This?" Jack speaks each word individually, drops them like rocks that clatter into the silence of the room. Lyla looks up from the sink where she's washing the breakfast dishes and her cheery countenance drains away.

"What?" she asks. But she knows what he's talking about it.

"Why would you do this, go here without even telling me?"

He tosses the little white card onto the counter beside the wet dishes in the drainer and water begins to soak into it, darkening the sterile, doctor's-office whiteness of it.

"I only wanted to find out, that's all, ask some questions. What's wrong with that?"

"What difference will the answers make? So some doctor says, 'Sure, we can perform a procedure,' or 'We can...' oh, I don't know, give you some exercises or a pill to take. And then you'll be able to conceive. What good is that?"

"Jack, please listen. I—"

"Or maybe you're looking for something...what do they call it...invasive. Or Star-Wars-ish where they grow a baby in a Petrie dish and implant it right before you're due to go into labor so the kid will have a 'birth' day."

"If I knew that not getting pregnant was fixable..."

"Why would that matter? What difference would it make? We're not having children. We agreed to that."

A light flares in Lyla's eyes.

"Agreed? Excuse me. We didn't agree to anything. You decreed how it was going to be, and because I didn't launch an instant land battle to get my way, you took that as agreement."

"You never said—"

"I didn't know, Jack! In the beginning, I didn't know. I didn't say anything because it didn't occur to me at the ripe old age of nineteen how much it would matter to me in a few years. How much I'd want to become a mother."

"And you think that's acceptable? To do a one-hundred-and-eighty-degree switcheroo on me. You think I shouldn't be upset. Neither of us wanted children on the day I put that ring on your finger and now—"

"Are you saying you wouldn't have put it there if you'd known then what you know now?"

"Don't put words in my mouth, Lyla."

"You wouldn't have married me if you'd known I'd want kids someday—is that it? Because if that's the way you feel about it…"

She tosses the dish cloth into the sink where it lands with a plop that splashes dish water onto the front of her bathrobe and then turns to leave. He catches her by the shoulders and holds on.

"I didn't say that. I'd have put that ring on your finger if you'd had three heads and every one of them uglier than Mrs. Pugh." That was the old lady who lived in the apartment beneath theirs, who actually had hairs growing out of her crooked nose and banged her cane on the ceiling if they made too much noise when they made love.

She doesn't look at him, but she doesn't try to wiggle out of his grasp either.

"Lyla…what's wrong with the way things are? Aren't you happy? Am I not enough?"

"You can't fill a hole in me you weren't meant to fill. Nothing can fill that emptiness except…a child. Your child. Oh, Jack, it would be so precious with your—"

"Don't start, Lyla. We've been over and over this. It's because a child would be adorable that I don't want to have one. I will not bring a child into this world. You wouldn't want to either if you'd seen what I've seen. If you'd seen crack mothers pimping their ten-year-old daughters, kids living in squalor you wouldn't let a pig—"

"And because you see ugliness every day at work, you think there's no beauty anywhere. Jack, God created a world of incredible love and beauty if you'd—"

"Don't play the God card, Lyla. You know there's not one in my deck. I've heard you. At night, I hear you whisper, ask God to 'soften my heart.' So why hasn't he?"

She looks up at him then, a look of anger and defeat on her beautiful features.

"Maybe your heart is so hard even God can't change it."

"If my heart is hard, it's only because it's jammed so full of love for you that it's like…you know, like…an impaction."

She bursts out laughing, doesn't want to, but can't help it. And as soon as she starts, he gets caught in it, too.

"An impaction? You missed your calling. You'd have made a fortune writing Valentine cards."

"It would work. You could rhyme it with attraction."

"Or putrefaction."

And they are off again, roaring until their sides hurt and tears run down their faces. Jack knows he's won, though. At least this round. He leans over and kisses the top of her head.

"You better scoot or you'll be late for work," he tells her, shoving her gently toward the bedroom door with a final pat on the butt. "I think I'll spend my day off looking up words that rhyme with…there's subtraction and…"

She has left the room. He reaches over and only

glances at the soggy card as he tears it in two and tosses it into the trash can: "Bessinger Fertility Clinic, 9 a.m., September 11, 2001.

Jack changes out of his uniform as Lyla showers, puts his gun in the bedside drawer where he always leaves it and gets ready to go to bed as the day is starting for his wife. Ahh, the joys of a split shift. But he'll be on days again next week and he's planning a surprise. He has snared tickets to that new off-Broadway show Lyla hasn't shut up about.

He is stretched out on the couch in his shorts and t-shirt, dozing, when she leans over to kiss him goodbye. Her perfume settles over him in a fragrant haze. Lyla always smells like flowers. He opens his eyes enough to see that she is wearing that red dress, his favorite, the one with the full skirt. As a joke, he bought her a bright-red, taffeta petticoat to go under it. He wonders if she's wearing it…but she is gone and he drifts back off to sleep.

The waking nightmare begins with the sounds of sirens, hundreds of sirens, wailing and warbling in a haunting symphony he would hear in his nightmares for the rest of his life.

The view out their bedroom window shows the top two or three floors of Tower One high above the distant skyline. He teases Lyla that when she waves at him from her office window there, he can see her. She says she can see him when he waves back.

The view from the window today shows no one waving. Only flames and smoke.

After that, there are only snapshots.

Speed Dial: Lyla. All lines busy.

He snaps off a button on his shirt as he tries to put it on while he's running. It arcs in slow motion up into the air and looks for a moment like a dark planet in front of the sun of the flaming buildings.

Speed Dial: Lyla. All lines busy.

Traffic is stopped, snarled, frozen and so he runs.

Speed Dial: Lyla. All lines busy.

A crazy soap box preacher proclaims the end of the world; men in business suits and Italian shoes loot a camera store where crowds desperate for a picture of "history" have broken out the window and door glass.

Speed Dial: Lyla. All lines busy.

In desperation, he grabs a bicycle from a kid and barks "police business," but the youngster doesn't even protest. He merely stands there, looking up.

Speed Dial: Lyla …

"Jack! Jack! Is that you?"

He slams on the brakes of the bicycle, loses his balance, and falls. The stampede of people running away threatens to trample him, so he rolls over into a doorway, holding the phone to his ear in fierce desperation.

"Lyla! Are you all right?"

If he can keep her on the line talking to him, the very force of their connection will keep her safe.

"There's smoke…" she coughs violently. "It's everywhere. It's burning below us. We can't get out."

"You'll be fine, Sweetheart. They'll send a helicopter, take you off the roof of the building. You need to get to the roof."

"Can't see. There's too much smoke." She is coughing out the words rather than speaking them. Then he hears a rumbling sound and she screams, "The fire broke through. It's coming!"

"Get to the roof, Honey. If you—"

"I don't want to burn to death, Jack!" She cries out the words in hysteria. "I can't…I—they got a window open!"

"Lyla. Lyla!" She doesn't answer. He can still hear noises, so the line is not dead. "Lyla, answer me!"

"I'm here." She's gasping, but not coughing.

"Honey, listen to me. You have to try to get—"

"I love you, Jack." Her voice is soft. She is crying. "I love you so much. I only wanted to have…something of you…"

"We'll have a baby! Lyla, I swear! When this is all over, we'll—"

"They're jumping."

He had seen it…something…when he was running, before he had to look down to guide the bike. Things were falling off the building. He lifts his eyes now and sees a man high up, above the rip of flames that slice through the building. The man steps out the window and…

"I don't want to burn, Jack." She's not hysterical now. "I'm sorry."

"Sorry for what?"

"That I'm going to leave you here, leave you behind."

"You're not going anywhere. You're—"

"Heaven will be beautiful…" she's coughing out words again. "I—"

The line goes dead.

"Lyla! Lyla, answer me. Lyla, I love you."

He calls her back. He has to tell her that. She has to hear him.

Speed Dial: Lyla. All lines busy.

He punches the button again and again. Looking up at the building, tears streaming down his face.

Speed Dial: Lyla. All lines busy.

Speed Dial: Lyla. All lines busy.

Then he sees the figure in red in a high window. There is no air left in the world. No breath. He stands and tries to scream. In his head, he does scream, "Lyyyyyyla." But no sound comes out his lips.

The red figure falls from the window. She is holding the hand of a man in a dark suit. The red petticoat flutters around her like the wings of a hummingbird. They fall together. Down and down and down.

Later, a long time later, he wonders who the man was, the man who died with her. Jack wishes he could have been that man.

~

Jack said nothing else. Only his wife's name. But Daniel had heard the sound of grief often enough to recognize it even in a single word. Though Daniel hadn't meant to mention Emily's affair, Jack had made a decision to tell Daniel about his wife. Daniel understood that Jack Carpenter didn't do a thing like that lightly.

"What happened to her, Jack?" he asked, and made it a point not to look at him.

"She died in Tower One on 9-11," Jack's voice was flat, toneless. He might as well have been reading the assembly instructions on a backyard swing set. "She wanted to have children and I didn't. I was a self-centered fool."

"Copy that," Daniel said, and sounded just like Jack. He'd meant to.

Jack flashed him a look, then relaxed a little. They rode together in silence. Neither felt the need to talk, but something had shifted. They both felt it. The nature of their relationship was not the same as it'd been when they got into the car in Bradford's Ridge for the drive back to Cincinnati.

Daniel could see a menacing collection of dark, bubbling clouds in the western sky. He liked bad weather. The violent crash and fury of a storm sometimes put his own problems in perspective, helped to clarify his thinking.

"I need a drink," Jack said, "a big, drown-all-your-problems drink."

"Can't drown problems like these," Daniel said. "These babies can swim."

There was a beat of silence, and when Jack spoke again his voice was unexpectedly soft and intense.

"Do you own a gun, Daniel?"

A pulse of lightning strobed the black sky.

"Are you serious? Of course, I don't own a gun!"

"You need to get one." Jack paused. "And a conceal carry permit."

Lightning tore at the sky and finally ripped open the clouds, releasing skeins of rain as fine as angel hair. Thunder rumbled and rolled around them. Neither man spoke. The only sounds were the windshield wipers and the swish of tires on wet pavement. The trees on the roadside stood shadowless in the gray light as they flew past, silent in the pregnant stillness of a coming storm.

~

Theresa looked across her wide kitchen table, watching the two men who sat sipping their after-dinner coffee. She'd fixed fried chicken and mashed potatoes, along with green beans and corn on the cob picked from Miss Minnie and Mr. Gerald's garden. She'd fried some okra, too. The boys—men, they was men—ate like they hadn't had a good meal in days—and she suspected maybe Jack hadn't.

The storm had grown in intensity all evening. Now black rain, as if from a dissolving night sky, poured down, rapped angrily at the windows and cried in sullen streams down the panes.

As they told her the tale of Michael Rutherford and the strange occurrences in Bradford's Ridge, she studied them, more interested in their faces than the story they were telling. Nothing they had to say was a surprise to Theresa. It merely confirmed what she'd already figured out her own self. A conclusion it was now time to share with Daniel and Jack.

She looked intently at one, then the other, trying to see in the men the boys they had once been. Daniel's smile had come easily and often when he was young; the earnestness and sincerity in his wide brown eyes made him irresistibly likable. He was like a Cocker Spaniel puppy, Bishop had once observed, always underfoot, but when you wanted to scold him for getting in the way, that wagging tail just melted your heart.

Some of that hadn't changed. He was still so likable folks flocked to his church because his affable presence made them feel better about the pain in their lives, and he fed them watered-down truth so's wouldn't nobody in the pews get they toes pinched by something they didn't want to hear.

Jack had changed the least, in appearance anyway. He was a bigger version of the boy he'd been. Unsmiling, serious, determined and a will as strong as a catgut rope. Though she hadn't known he was a police officer until that day he showed up in Andi's hospital room, it didn't surprise her. She might have guessed he'd go into something like law enforcement. It suited him, his sense of right, wrong, justice and taking care of those as couldn't take care of theirselves.

Theresa's eyes filled with tears as she looked at the men before her, and she felt for them the fierce love she'd had for them when they were children. These two unlikely friends had been knit to each other by the shared deprivation of orphans. Neither had functioning parents. Jack's mother was dead; Daniel's was so wrapped up in every breath his little sister took she had no attention to spare for her son. Jack's father was lost to alcoholism and Daniel's to workaholism. When Jack went home of an evening, his father'd start swinging soon as he saw him, and Daniel's father never saw him at all, looked right through him at the "hurting" person who was standing behind. The boys had bonded to each other as brothers, to Theresa and Bishop as the parents they'd lost, and to Isaac…

She couldn't go there. If she let her mind go there, she'd lose what little she had left.

Jack set his coffee mug on the table when they'd told Theresa everything they'd seen and heard, and she asked, "You want another cup?"

He nodded, then put his hand out on her arm as she began to rise.

"Sit." He stood and crossed to the counter with the coffee maker. After he poured his own cup, he held out the pot toward Daniel with a quizzical look. Daniel nodded and Jack brought the pot to the table to fill his cup.

"The coffee I had this morning in Bradford's Ridge tasted like battery acid," Jack said.

"Drink a lot of battery acid, do you?" Daniel asked.

"Tastes like that in every police department in America —required by law to keep us tough. You didn't know that did you?"

"You Cro-Magnons think you're so much smarter than the rest of us."

Theresa watched their banter. They was going back to

they old ways of relating to each other even though they didn't even remember their own friendship, their childhood feelings oozing out like water through cheesecloth.

"I'll wager nobody with taste buds ever complained about your coffee," Jack told Theresa as he sat back down again. "Or anything else you cooked. That meal was delicious. You know you didn't have to—" She waved him off and he hushed up.

He paused, looked thoughtful. "Did you used to make chocolate chip cookies with—"

"—pecans in them!" Daniel finished for him. "I have this memory of reaching into my pocket and coming out with a handful of crumbs from the cookie I'd stuck in there." He paused and his eyes widened. "And Mikey Rutherford wanted to know if I had any more cookies."

He turned to Jack. "Is that happening to you? Are you—"

"—remembering things, pieces of things? Yeah."

"Either one of you remember Bishop's library?" Their blank looks told her she would have to start at the beginning. "Come on then." She rose and lumbered toward the door leading into the parlor. "It's time for you boys to get your first look—for the second time—at what he kept in that library."

She passed through the parlor and down the hall to the house's third bedroom that had been transformed years ago into a library. She stepped inside and flipped on the lights.

It was a big room, twenty feet square. A double window opened above a love seat on the far side of the room, but other than that, the surfaces of every wall were lined with book shelves jammed with books. There was a huge oak desk in the middle of the room, piled high with papers and books that cascaded off it onto the floor. Three small tables with reading lamps were spaced around the walls, and the chairs beside them were invitations to sit awhile and get comfortable—'cause what you was about to read was going to blow your mind.

The lamps were on the central switch Theresa had flipped, as was the desk lamp on the oak desk and a lamp set on a long, narrow table behind the big desk. Above the table was a bulletin board, five feet wide, reaching all the way to the ceiling. Affixed to the cork board with stick-pins were drawings and pictures of varying shapes and sizes. Theresa watched the men's eyes swing in a survey of the room, saw them stop at the bulletin board. She waited.

Both men froze; their eyes open wide. Then, as if propelled by some unseen force, they crossed the room together to stand in front of the largest of the pictures on the bulletin board, a thirty-six by twenty-four-inch reproduction of an ancient painting, artist unknown.

Well, that there's the ballgame. If'n I needed any more proof, that's it.

She shook her head slowly. She was so tired.

Lord, I'm too old for this! I can't do it again. Shoot, I couldn't do it the first time. Couldn't you…please…?

But there was nothing for it, of course. Jesus had asked for the cup to pass from him, too. Wouldn't do her no good to plead—this was the way it had to be.

When she spoke, her voice was hushed, but she was sure Jack and Daniel heard her just fine.

"That painting, that's an efreet." She paused. "That there's the demon king we up against."

Chapter Twenty-Six

Jack stood mesmerized by the image on the wall. He'd been drawn to it from across the room, had no memory of taking steps to get there. He had seen it and the rest of the world vanished, leaving him before it, staring up in wide-eyed revulsion and horror.

Cold, greasy terror crawled relentlessly through every turning of every blood vessel in his body. He could feel Daniel beside him, knew he was staring up at the painting, too. He could feel Daniel tremble. Or maybe it was Jack who was trembling.

As if from a great distance, he heard Theresa's voice.

"That's an efreet. That's there's the demon king we up against."

Yes, it was an efreet. Jack knew that. He knew something else, too, and the knowledge stole his breath. This wasn't the first time he'd seen it.

The painting showed a man with his back turned, standing amid tendrils of smoke on the charred, desolate shore of a lake of fire. A creature engulfed in flames rose up fifty feet above him out of the fiery lake. It was obscured by the smoke that hung in a pale haze over the lake, but you could see its silhouette, a shape made of darkness, a black hole in the universe, massive, with the suggestion of wings that, when unfurled, would stretch out twenty feet in both directions.

Jack could not make out anything about the creature—and yet he could. He couldn't see it, but even in the not-seeing, images of horror in orange and red and black splashed across the transfixed retinas of his eyes. Images of a mouth with too many teeth. A head with horns. A face that defined ugliness.

What was astonishing was that the hazy dark image could convey such intense emotion. The shape, the thing hated. No, it didn't merely hate. It was hate. It wasn't filled with evil, it was made of evil. A life form devoid of all goodness and beauty, it had gathered together there in the blackness an unfathomable ugliness, the essence of cruelty and depravity. And evil. Total, all-encompassing evil. To see it clearly was to be blinded forever, to be sentenced to an eternity of darkness where no light shone, and where the darkness itself was a vicious, snarling beast hungry for your blood.

Mesmerized by the vile, otherworldliness of the creature, Jack was aware of breathing in short, panting gasps, felt his heart crash so hard against his shirt he could see the fabric move, each beat a sledge hammer blow trying to knock a hole in his chest.

Then the world went black and the image vanished.

Jack blinked, seemed almost to come back to himself from somewhere far away. He gasped, felt Daniel next to him sucking in air as well in the darkness. Theresa spoke from behind them.

"You turn around now, hear. Face me with yo backs to the wall and I'll cut the lights back on."

The men turned to face her, she flipped the switch and the lamps poured golden light back into the room. Jack started to look back over his shoulder at the picture, but decided against it. Theresa saw the move.

"You can look at it, but ain't a good idea to stand there the way you done, staring at it. That image can grab hold of you. It's so awful, the horror of it can wipe out every other thought in your head."

Jack did turn then, looked back over his shoulder at the artist's rendering of a nightmare creature. But what had grabbed hold of Jack and held him breathless was…what? A memory? Something like a memory, an image at least. An image of that creature. And the image wasn't a painting.

Jack turned back resolutely to face Theresa, who had come into the room and eased herself into one of the armchairs beside a table and lamp.

"You've figured out something here, haven't you?" He said. It wasn't a question. "Are you going to tell us what's going on?" He was surprised that his voice wasn't shaking.

"You boys pull up chairs and I'll do best as I can."

He and Daniel dragged chairs across the room and sat opposite Theresa.

"This here"—she gestured at the room—"is…was Bishop's library. He was an expert in demonology, pro'lly knew more 'bout them creatures than most anybody in the world today—though they used to be lots of people who studied demons, understood 'em. Not no more."

"That thing, that efreet…" Daniel began. But he didn't seem to have enough breath to go on so he had to inhale to continue. "What did you mean 'that's what we're up against?'"

"Meant just what I said. That's the demon that sent the

other demons out looking for you two and Becca. They was just errand boys."

"Why—?" Daniel began but Jack interrupted.

"Before we get to the why, I want to know the what." He turned and gestured at the painting. "What is that thing?"

"You don't remember, neither one of you?" she asked them, and her voice roughened, as if she was fighting tears. "You don't recall that we done had this conversation? Well, you done had this conversation, only it was with Bishop. I's just bringing in cookies and lemonade."

She paused. "I made cookies 'cause you liked them, of course, but it was more that I wanted the house to smell of them, to smell good and wholesome and…well, they's those believe chocolate chip cookies is holy and I's one of them."

It happened again, like it had before. A memory or a flashback was thrust out of the depths of Jack's mind into the spotlight and he froze, mentally gaped at it in wonder.

The room smells of chocolate chip cookies and Bishop's aftershave lotion. Jack doesn't know what the name of it is, but he's never smelled it on anybody but Bishop.

When I grow up, I'm going to smell like that.

The Three Musketeers are here, Jack and Daniel seated side by side on a lumpy couch in the small living room. Bishop sits across from them in a large chair and Becca is seated cross-legged on the floor at his feet. He leans toward them, his elbows on his knees, his huge, kind face looking intense and sincere.

"What you children needs to understand is that all them old stories—they's mostly true. Some of them creatures we laugh about now, they's real."

"Victor's demon has the ugly face of a dragon," Becca

says softly to Jack and Daniel. She looks up at Bishop. "Don't you think?"

"All they faces is so ugly, it's hard to say one's uglier than another."

Jack stares at the two of them, awestruck. They can see what nobody else can see. They can see demons, creatures from another realm, spiritual beings at war with God's angels—monsters that have turned six of their friends into savages. Ok, maybe not their friends. Cole Stuart and Jacob Dumas would never have been their friends, but they'd just have been guys. Bullies, probably, but you could stand down a bully.

"We got to look back at the stories and folklore of the past to find out about demons, because they don't come around out in the open anymore like they used to hundreds of years ago."

"Why not?" Jack asks.

"'Cause Satan done figured out that being secretive is the best way to accomplish what he wants in the world."

"And what he wants to accomplish is…?" Daniel asks.

Jack suspects Daniel already knows the answer to the question. Daniel often asks questions he already knows the answers to because he knows Jack doesn't know. Daniel's like that. He senses Jack feels "less than" sometimes, because the others are so "spiritual." Daniel also knows sometimes Jack doesn't want to let on that he doesn't understand, so Daniel pretends he doesn't understand so Jack won't feel bad.

Jack has never had a friend like Daniel Burke and he stops to wonder if he will have one—as pure and good as Daniel—ever again in his life.

Then he turns his eyes back to Bishop and Becca, and he is certain that he will never in his life know another girl as beautiful as she is. Beautiful and almost…holy.

"Satan wants chaos," Bishop responds, his voice booming in the small room. "Pain. Heartache. Misery. It's his bounden duty; his reason for existence is to thwart the purposes of God. He is pure evil, nothing good in him. He's the prince of this world and he lives to torment mankind."

Theresa appears in the doorway then with a plate of cookies. Bishop continues to talk as she sets them on the coffee table and the children gobble them up.

"Them demons that's working they mischief right now in Bradford's Ridge—six of them don't show up in one place for no reason. They ain't powerful enough to have got here by theirselves. They had to a'been sent."

Jack feels Daniel move next to him, glances over, and sees something like the same awe on his face that's likely on Jack's. It's like that all the time. He'll think something, look over, and can see Daniel's thinking the same thing.

"Sent?" Daniel echoes.

Jack thinks his voice sounds like a minister's voice, like he's standing in a pulpit preaching.

"Uh huh. Them bad boys' demons, they's only the hired help."

"Who sent them?" Jack asks.

"Ain't a who, it's a what," Bishop's voice is quiet, but seems loud in the small room. "From what I've seen and heard—only explanation that makes any sense to me is that there's an efreet hereabouts somewhere, here in our world."

Jack feels his skin go pebbly with gooseflesh at the sound of the word.

"Solomon had truck once with an efreet, least that's what it says in the Koran. You read about efreets in Middle Eastern, particularly Iranian, literature. I got lots of books talks about them."

"What's an efreet?" Daniel asks.

"It's an enormous winged creatures made of fire." Bishop gets to his feet and goes into his office in the next room. It's where he keeps his books about demons. The children don't go in there—not because Bishop won't allow it—but because the room is Bishop's and it seems like…like holy ground.

He returns with a reproduction of an ancient painting. In the painting, a pillar of darkness obscured by smoke rises out of a lake of fire. The darkness is a black hole in the world—a shape with wings.

"This here's an efreet. The Bible says that our battle is 'not against flesh and blood but against the rulers, the powers, the authorities of this dark world.' An efreet is a ruler, an authority. A powerful, powerful evil."

"This efreet…where is it?" Jack asks.

"Here in our world—somewhere close by," Bishop replies. Theresa returns with the lemonade as Bishop continues. "Only way for an efreet to enter this world is if somebody summons it." He pauses, then adds softly. "And I can't figure how anybody could have done that, 'cause what you have to use for the ceremony—the implements don't exist no more. I've read about ancient scrolls that tell how folks called forth demons from Hell, but them scrolls have been lost for centuries, and even if you could lay hands on one, they was in languages ain't nobody spoke for a thousand years."

He pauses again and sighs. "Only thing's still around is the blood."

"Blood?" Daniel asks.

"All kind of spiritual things centuries ago was related to blood sacrifices. The Jews were required once a year to bring a lamb to be sacrificed on the altar in Jerusalem."

It's Becca who speaks this time, her voice like little bells ringing. "Somebody killed a lamb to bring an efreet into the world?"

Bishop looks down on her with such care she might as well have been his own little girl.

"No, Sugar. Didn't nobody sacrifice an animal. To bring a demon like this one"—he points to the monster in the picture—"out of the spiritual realm and into the world, you got to sacrifice…a person."

Becca was pale anyway, but when he said that, all the color drained out of her face and it was as white as a clean sheet. You could see a spiderweb of blue veins on her temples.

"So if someone in Bradford's Ridge summoned an efreet," she says, her voice so soft it is barely audible, "they had to…murder somebody?"

Bishop nodded, his big face in front of Becca moving slowly up and down.

"And not just anybody. Got to be somebody who's been singled out, somebody evil has put some kind of mark on."

"How does evil put a—?" Becca began.

"I don't have no idea, Sugar. No idea whatsoever."

"The blood of a murder victim," Jack said quietly. "Someone 'marked by evil.' That's what you need to summon an efreet."

Theresa's head came up.

"You remember Bishop telling you that?"

"I did just now. A memory popped into my head. Sitting in a room with Daniel and Bishop and Becca, and Bishop was explaining to us about efreets."

"What does 'marked by evil' mean?" Daniel asked.

"Bishop said that, did he?" Theresa asked. When Jack nodded, she shook her head. "I don't remember him saying that part."

Daniel looked troubled. "I have no memory of what you're describing. But…" His face took on a look of studied concentration. "I know things about efreets, and how else would I know except from Bishop telling me?"

"What do you know?" Theresa asked.

"I know what Jack said, about the murder victim. And I know it can possess people, but only people who come in contact with it, are inside the circle."

"What circle?" Jack asked.

Jack could tell Daniel was hearing his own thoughts for the first time as he spoke them.

"A pentagram. It outlines the boundaries of where a demon can go in this world—unless it possesses a person and escapes. Bishop said it wasn't an easy thing for a demon to possess a person—that the human mind and will —and soul—fight back. It's something that doesn't happen quickly. It takes years of tempting a person away from what's good and right, years of beating a person's will into submission."

"So how did a bunch of kids—?" Jack began.

"But with simpler, less mature minds and wills—like children—a demon can shove them aside and move right in," Daniel said.

"That's what Bishop figured out," Theresa said. "It was an efreet sent demons into them boys when you was all children."

"Did the efreet itself possess any of them?" Jack asked.

"Bishop said an efreet was such a huge, powerful demon, if it was to possess a little child it…he said it'd be like putting rocket fuel in a toy truck—it'd burn up. No, somehow them children come along, and he sent smaller demons into them—"

"Why—?" Jack began, but Theresa kept talking.

"And having demons inside was how them boys could do the amazing things they done."

"That explains the desk," Jack said. Daniel looked confused. "The shooter threw a desk all the way across the room with one hand."

"So the power of the demon—?" Daniel began.

"Demons ain't got no power of they own in this world. But demons is able to call up all the power you got your own self. Like the man possessed by demons in Scripture, the one lived in the tombs. Folks told Jesus they'd tried to chain him up, but he broke the chains."

"If they control your body, they must be able to release adrenaline—so you're like that woman I read about who picked a car up off her little girl," Daniel said.

"Like a juiced-up crack head. Goody. But there are downsides to an adrenaline high." Jack didn't elaborate.

"And they don't care nothing about what happens to the body they's in, they don't feel no pain."

"It's a miracle we're still alive," Daniel said, awe in his voice.

"It ain't no miracle. If they'd wanted to kill you, they would have. Apparently, they didn't, or more likely they was ordered not to."

"Why?" Jack asked.

"Must have been a good reason, but I don't got no idea what it'd be. All's I know is that efreet got stopped twenty-six years ago, but somehow it got loose again. Soon's it did, them other demons was able to slide right back in where they was before. Must be that possession leaves you vulnerable somehow. Jesus talked about that, said if an unclean spirit went out of a person, it could go back and take seven friends. The boys them demons possessed is grown men now, but the demons had left they mark and wasn't no force of will could keep them out."

"How was the efreet stopped?" Daniel asked.

"I don't know that, neither, not for sure. I know Bishop had plans about it, but…" She paused and took a deep breath, looked deep into the faces of both men before she continued. "What me and Bishop figured musta happened was…it was you three done it. You sent it back to hell somehow."

Jack and Daniel exchanged a look of astonishment. Thunder groaned and grumbled. Rain rattled like buckshot against the windowpane.

"We did?" Jack said.

"Had to be. One day them demon-possessed boys was tormenting you, and you three was as close-knit as steel wool. The next day, the demons was gone, them boys was all tore up, and the three of you acted like strangers. Something happened and you must have been involved."

"And the efreet wiped that whole summer out of our minds so—" Daniel said.

"No, that ain't it. Wasn't the efreet." She paused. "I don't think it was. But maybe…" Theresa fell silent, then her composure broke. "If Bishop was here, wouldn't be no 'maybes!'" She looked upward. "How'm I gonna do this all by myself, Lord, 'thout Bishop?" She put her head in her hands, shook, but didn't cry.

Before Jack even had time to wonder what he ought to do, Daniel was on his feet, laying his hand tenderly on Theresa's shoulder.

"You're not all by yourself, Theresa," Daniel said. "I mean…we're worse boneheads now than we were when we were kids, but we're—Jack and I—we're…here for you. You have us."

Daniel sounded awkward, not smooth and polished, but stumbling. Not a whole lot better than Jack would have sounded if he'd tried to be comforting, and Daniel was a professional at it. Then Jack realized that was the reason Theresa was so moved. She lowered her hands from her face and looked up into Daniel's. Unshed tears made her eyes sparkle. She reached up and patted his hand on her shoulder, started to say something, then didn't. She wasn't smiling, but he thought she was beaming nonetheless.

Daniel sat back down and it was quiet. Reflections of lightning fluttered across the floor like a blue flame burning on alcohol. Theresa tried to take up where she'd left off.

"That efreet didn't make you forget. Demon can't do that, can't get inside the head of a person he don't possess and do things to his mind—and certainly not you boys and Becca. You's Christians." She paused and shook her head. "But them boys from Brewster Academy as was possessed —we heard they was a mess."

"How so?" Jack asked.

"You got to remember, this was the same time as the Twin Oaks fire and the whole town was a mess. Two of them boys had relatives died in the nursing home, and they whole families fell apart. It was all hushed up, but we heard Cole Stuart's daddy committed the boy to a mental hospital for awhile. Roger Willingham's parents sent him off to California to live with his uncle who was a monk! You got to figure—you're twelve years old and get possessed by a demon. When it's gone, how you gonna be after? I don't imagine them boys was ever quite right again."

"If the efreet didn't wipe that summer out of our minds, why'd the three of us forget it?" Daniel asked.

"If I's to guess, I'd say maybe you erased your own minds—or God did. A thing terrible as you done, I don't know what it'd do to the mind of a child. You forgetting was a blessing. You's being protected from something that would have tore you up."

Jack was reeling. He and Daniel and Becca had gotten into a fight with a monster demon when they were twelve years old. And won?

"Maybe that's what Mikey was talking about," Daniel put in. "He said we went in…somewhere…and when we came out it was like we didn't even know each other. Maybe that's when we…did whatever it was we did."

"Ok, Ok…wait a minute." Jack was reeling. "You're saying three twelve-year-olds defeated that?" He pointed over his shoulder at the picture but didn't turn to look at it. "Are you serious?"

"No," Theresa said quietly. "Not three twelve-year-olds alone. Three twelve-year-olds and an angel."

"An angel?" Jack couldn't wrap his mind around that in any way.

"That bright light you seen with Becca. It was a angel. That's how you done it."

"But if we defeated it, what's going on now?" Daniel demanded, frustration and fear coming out as anger in his voice.

Theresa shrugged, held her hands out, palms up. "It musta got loose somehow," she said.

"So we beat it…captured it, imprisoned it…took its battery out—whatever—and now it's broken out of whatever we locked it up in," Jack said, trying to work it out in his head as he spoke.

"And it's sent them other demons after you three 'cause you was the ones beat it the first time. It wants to get rid of you 'fore you have a chance to stop it, like you done before."

That was it. Overload. Jack had jammed into his mind way more than he was able to process. He stood abruptly.

"I'm sorry Theresa, but I've only got a lone synapse

still firing and if I hear one more amazing thing, it'll die and I'll be a vegetable."

"All this is a lot to get your mind around," she said, and Jack could hear the sympathy in her voice. "You need to let it all go now for awhile, both of you. Get on out of here and go home."

Theresa walked them to the door and Jack turned to her before they left.

"You do understand about the two…the ones still out there, how dangerous they are?" he asked her.

She nodded but didn't say anything.

"Keep your doors and windows locked."

She merely looked at him. They both knew locked doors and windows wouldn't even slow down what was after them.

Jack turned up his collar to the drizzle and walked away. Darkness folded around him like great black wings.

Daniel was waiting for Emily when she came downstairs in her robe after she put Andi to bed. He'd been sitting in the living room in the dark, and when she turned on the light and saw him, she jumped and let out a little squeak of fright.

"Dan, you scared me to death! I didn't even know you'd gotten home. Why are you sitting here with the lights off?"

"Emily, I need to talk to you."

He hated the way she tensed, cringed away from his words.

"We're not doing this, Dan," she said. "We are not going to go over and over—"

"That's not what I want to talk about."

"Ok, then what do you want to talk about?"

She didn't believe him. She thought he was about to launch into accusations and recriminations and…

"Demons," he said and watched an array of emotions pass over Emily's face, only one of them identifiable—fear.

She sank onto the arm of the chair just like she'd done the night he told her he knew about her and WhatHis-Name. He shoved the image out of his mind and tried to concentrate. Where could he possibly start to make her understand what was going on? The two of them had spent every day since the end of June in a choreographed minuet where they spun in circles, passed each other without speaking or touching, and each pretended nothing at all strange was going on with their daughter—who'd died! But didn't.

"Dan, I don't want to—"

"Neither do I. I don't want to talk about it. I don't want to think about it. I want to pretend everything's normal and our ten-year-old daughter can't see monsters from hell that are invisible to the rest of the world."

"We don't know that. She could have been imagining—"

"You don't believe that any more than I do. Besides, this isn't just about Andi anymore. It's about all of us."

He let out a long sigh.

"This is way more than your mind can possibly process, Emily. But what's happening is dangerous and you have to know."

She stared at him dumbstruck, didn't say a word.

He started with the school shooter, the picture and Jack. By the time he had waded through the exploits of the other team members, Emily had unconsciously begun to shake her head back and forth. Eventually, she blurted out, "Dan, stop it. You don't honestly believe—"

"I'm not telling you what I do or don't believe. I'm telling you facts. Four men who were on a Little League team with Jack and me in 1985 went inexplicably psycho in the past two weeks—fact. They either tried—or succeeded —in killing people—fact. And they were all looking for the same thing."

"Becca," she whispered. "A little girl who went to grade school with you who—"

"Who knew. Just like Andi does."

Suddenly, Emily rose to her feet, her hands balled into fists to keep them from shaking. He could tell she'd reached her limit—to pour any more in would just send her emotions sloshing up over the sides.

"I'm done. This is crazy. How can you possibly—?"

He went to her and put his hands on her shoulders, a knee-jerk reaction to her distress. He didn't realize until he was touching her that it was the first time since—

She seemed to realize it, too, because she went rigid and took a step back, away from him.

"Just understand this one thing. We don't have the luxury any more of pretending it's not real. You and Andi…could get dragged into it."

Her eyes grew wide and she searched his face, looking for—doubt, maybe; a niggling disbelief she could hook her own to and they could sail along together down the River of Denial. Whatever she was looking for, she didn't find.

"Emily, there are still two men out there somewhere— two possessed men. Eventually, one or the other of them is going to show up here in Cincinnati."

"Why? What for? What do they want?"

"They want to kill Jack. And me. "

Fear as real as a gust of wind passed between them.

~

Andi could hear their voices. Daddy had gotten home and he and Mommy were talking. She could only hear the tone of their voices, though, not the words. But they didn't sound mad at each other. They weren't yelling or anything. She'd asked Sara Henry about it, what it was like when her parents got a divorce and she said they fought all the time and it was loud and sometimes her mother threw things and her Daddy said really bad words.

Mommy and Daddy didn't do that, so most of the time Andi could convince herself that Mommy and Daddy weren't getting a divorce...that they weren't downstairs right now talking about it.

She felt a thump on the bed and heard Ossy start to purr even before she reached out to gather him close and smooth his splotchy fur.

"I could go down and listen, see what they're talking about," she said into the cat's fur, but she didn't actually want to know. She was afraid of what she'd hear if they didn't know she was listening.

When she was with them, Mommy and Daddy talked to each other just like they always had. Except it was different, all wrong—awful—and she had to pretend like she didn't even notice.

She felt her eyes well with tears. All three of them spent every day pretending, about everything! And she hated it. She was pretending she didn't know they had talked about getting a divorce. When they'd found her crying on the stairs the night Princess Buttercup came and she saw the shapes in her room, she had lied and said she was upset about a bad dream—because she couldn't tell them what she'd heard. If she said it—divorce—out loud, the word would be out there and they'd have to look at it and talk about it and maybe then it would come true.

And they were pretending everything was just fine between them, and it wasn't. Daddy never kissed Mommy anymore. He never even touched her, didn't reach out and take her hand or put his arm around her. Mommy didn't look in Daddy's eyes when she talked to him, she didn't laugh at something he said so hard she fell into his lap like she used to do. She didn't laugh at all, in fact. Neither one of them did. They didn't even smile.

God, do you do things like stop people from getting a divorce?

Andi whispered the words into the plain old darkness of her room that was different from the darkness Princess Buttercup had brought that looked like there was a light behind it.

Please don't let them go live in different places like Sara's parents. Please.

Andi had prayed her whole life, talked to God every night before she went to bed and other times, too, when she had something to tell him. But after that day at school when Uncle Jack…after that, God was…real. And some-times…sometimes she almost wished she hadn't come back when Uncle Jack had called her.

If she hadn't, she wouldn't be lying here now—scared and sad. And feeling so alone. How she wished Princess Buttercup would come! Thinking of Princess Buttercup brought to mind the vision that had been bigger than this room, bigger than this whole house, eight images tumbling over and over before her.

Splatters of colors. A square with little feet beside a telephone pole. Two silver circles, a red triangle, a bell, a cross pointed at the top and a straight brown line.

"Why did you show those to me, God? Why—?"

She heard her mother's footsteps on the stairs and quickly shooed Ossy out of the bed onto the floor. Then she closed her eyes and pretended to be asleep when her mother tiptoed into her room, took off her robe and lay down on the daybed in front of the window.

Mommy and Daddy didn't even sleep in the same bed anymore!

Andi started to cry. She couldn't help it. She cried as softly as she could, her face buried in her pillow, and her mother didn't hear her because she didn't come to ask what was wrong. In fact, it sounded like…maybe Mommy was crying, too.

~

Scott Nicholson thought it was cool the first time he ever saw it, and he still did. Every time he looked at it out the window of the Easy Stop where he worked, he smiled. On the other side of Interstate 71 sat a big white water tower with red stripes on the top that looked like a gigantic peppermint. Huge black letters on the tower proclaimed "FLORENCE Y'ALL," and that had seemed appropriate to Scott, a Michigan boy, even before he knew the legend behind it. After all, this was the Kentucky city that bordered the Ohio River, so the South met the North here, and the sign seemed justifiable southern pride.

Then he'd heard the story, one of those stories that "if it isn't true, it should be." Seems the sign, originally painted as an advertisement for the businesses surrounding it, had read: FLORENCE MALL. But apparently the taxpayers of the city of Florence didn't appreciate the use of municipal property as a billboard. Feathers flew over who should pay the expense of having the enormous water tower repainted. Might even have been a lawsuit—nobody he talked to knew for sure what did happen. All they knew was that one morning folks driving along Interstate 71 toward Cincinnati were greeted with a cheerful FLORENCE Y'ALL sign. Covering up two small lines probably hadn't even required an entire gallon of paint.

Friday rush-hour traffic had transformed southbound Interstate 71 into a parking lot, but business was light here alongside the northbound lanes. In fact, right now there were only two customers in the store and one of them stepped up to his register and slapped a package of potato chips and a soft drink on the counter.

"You got any old newspapers?" he asked, and his voice had a truly odd sound, an eerie rasp and rattle, like the brittle, whispery click of scarabs in some ancient Egyptian tomb. That's not what got Scott's attention, though. The man was what Scott's grandfather liked to call "odoriferous." He smelled ripe, like he hadn't bathed in days and his clothes looked like he'd slept in them—more than one night. The skin around the black eye patch covering a missing eye was red and inflamed, and Scott wondered if infection was contributing to the miasma around the guy. Phew.

"No sir," he said. He pointed to the racks that featured copies of the Cincinnati Inquirer, the Louisville Courier-

Journal, the Lexington Herald-Leader, and copies of Car and Truck and USA Today. "They bring us new copies every day and take back what we didn't sell the day before."

"So you wouldn't have anything that had pictures of that school shooting a couple of weeks ago?"

"Oh, that!" Scott had saved copies of the coverage in both the Inquirer and the Courier Journal. Those were pieces of history.

Scott retrieved his backpack from under the counter, pulled several newspapers from it, and spread them out for the man to see.

Another man, a fat man who smelled equally rank, joined the one-eyed man, who was searching through the newspapers as if he were looking for something in particular.

"That must be him," the one-eyed man said, pointing out to the fat man a picture of the police officer who had killed the gunman.

Then he started to tear the page with the picture out of the newspaper!

"Hey, wait a minute!" Scott said. "Those aren't for sale. They're my—"

Scott didn't even realize he'd been grabbed. One second he was standing behind the register, and the next he was inches from the face of the one-eyed man, who had snatched the front of his shirt and hauled him over the counter.

"This fella's a grade school chum and I'm taking his picture with me," he said, the stench of his breath overwhelming. "You got a problem with that, kid?"

Scott looked directly into the man's eye for the first time, and suddenly the young man felt cold all over, not from the outside in—from the inside out. A primitive, irrational terror seized him and he was so frightened he could barely speak.

"No sir. Take the page. Take the whole newspaper. You can have anything you want."

The man dropped Scott back over the counter as casually as tossing away a candy wrapper, gathered up the newspaper along with the chips and drink and walked toward the door with the fat man behind him. He hadn't paid for the chips and drink, but Scott didn't care. Scott would gladly pay for them out of his own pocket. He'd buy the guy the whole rack of chips just to get him out of the building.

The fat man stopped in the doorway and looked up at the big water tower.

"Have a nice day, ya'll," he said, and laughed. Or made a sound like laughter that had no mirth, no joy at all in it, a sound that was ugly, dark, and vulgar.

Scott's hands shook for half an hour after the two men left. He felt like he'd been in great danger, that he'd barely escaped with his life—though he'd never tell anybody that, because a simple description of what had happened sounded almost innocent. But Scott knew.

He propped the door of the store open for the rest of the day to get the stink out of the building.

Chapter Twenty-Seven

The banner stretched seventy-five feet across the floor of the Fellowship Hall, proclaiming "Dancing with the Stars" in bright red, sparkling letters. Well, they would sparkle as soon as Emily painted them with Elmer's Glue and poured glitter on them. First she had to get the helium canister to work so she could finish filling the balloons.

Every year, the church held a prom for handicapped teenagers. Emily was the chair of the committee that met on Saturdays to decorate. She loved the event, seeing the kids' reactions when the limousines dropped them off, decked out in prom dresses and tuxedos. The ones with Down's Syndrome were the best, their smiles lit their faces in something that Emily had always believed was an angelic glow.

But much as she loved the event, Emily did not want to be here working on it.

Not today. Not after the conversation she'd had Thursday night with Dan. And the text she'd gotten this morning from Jeff.

Her hand slipped on the valve of the canister and she

chipped off the end of one of her flawlessly manicured nails.

"Don't keep fussin' with that thing or you're not going to have a fingernail left," Emma Perkins said.

Emma worked on the prom every year. Emily remembered how Emma's granddaughter had looked last year, prom dress flowing out over the wheels of her wheelchair, her arms spastic from cerebral palsy, her mouth drooling the lipstick her mother had painted on her lips down off her chin. "I called Beatrice—you remember her, Beatrice Higginbotham, who lives down the street from me. Sometimes she comes to church with me on Easter Sunday. I told her, I said, 'Bea, you need to send over your handyman to help us with these decorations even if you have to go down there and drag him out of the crawl space.' She got a new furnace and has to have all the ductwork under her house changed."

"In the fix-it department, Dan says he has only two tools," Emily said. "The only two a man needs—a pen and a checkbook."

Dan—who was being hunted by a demon.

She could not, would not think about that now! She shoved the thought resolutely out of her mind as all the other women chuckled at the wit of their charming young pastor.

Jeff was different, though. Jeff could fix anything.

The text from Jeff had been only one line—two words —but they touched her heart more than an eloquent speech.

"You Ok?"

No. Emily Burke was absolutely, most positively not Ok. She'd text him back as soon as she had some time to herself.

Emily gave up on the balloons and went to work

putting glitter on the sign.

Not long afterward, the south door on the Fellowship Hall opened and a man peered in, said he was looking for Emily Burke. Emma practically squealed with delight when she saw him, rushed over and grabbed the man by the arm and dragged him to the helium canister, outlining in an unending, un-interruptible babble all the other handyman tasks they needed him to perform before he climbed back down into Beatrice's crawl space. The man looked a little surprised—probably didn't know there'd be that much to do, but he went right to work.

This late-afternoon decorating session had been a bad idea. Emily was tired—had slept hardly at all since Dan told her his bizarre story. But the rhythm of the mindless activity was soothing and Emily gradually relaxed as she slathered the red letters on the banner with glue and poured glitter on them. She remained on her knees on the floor so she wouldn't have to look into anyone's face as she worked.

Emily enjoyed where her thoughts took her. At least in the beginning she did. She recalled the glorious weekend she and Jeff had snatched together in Chicago in February. She'd told Dan she was going to the annual Christian Women's Fellowship Convention. She'd gotten a copy of the convention's agenda and called Dan every night, regaling him with stories about what this speaker or that had said. That part was easy enough. They said the same thing every year.

Other than those phone calls, Dan had never entered her mind. Jeff had filled up every moment, every thought, taking over her heart as inexorably as ink spreading out through a blotter.

She'd loved every moment she'd ever spent with Jeff. She loved his rakish tall-dark-and-handsome good looks, the cleft in his chin and his lithe, athlete's body. Jeff was into kickboxing, had won national championship competitions.

She loved his crooked smile, the sound of his voice and—

Do you love Jeff Kendrick?

Emily hadn't planned to go there! But it was too late now to back off. She'd gotten too close to the whirlpool and didn't have the strength to resist being sucked in.

Well, do you?

Simple question, yes or no?

~

Theresa was mopping her kitchen floor, or making a show of it, pushing the mop back and forth. Didn't seem like she had no energy at all anymore, hadn't had since… She used to enjoy Saturday mornings, trying to get the house all clean quick as she could so she and Bishop could do whatever it was they had planned—a walk maybe, shopping or a movie matinee.

Now, she wasn't even paying attention to mopping where the floor was sticky. At this rate, she'd still be cleaning when it was time to go to church tomorrow morning.

The sudden stench triggered a gag reflex so powerful Theresa had to clench her jaws shut tight to keep from spewing her breakfast all over the floor she'd just mopped. Then a wailing shriek drowned out all other sound. She dropped her mop and it clattered to the floor, then put her hands over her ears and shook her head slowly back and forth.

She watched her kitchen door open—Jack had told her she'd ought to lock it!—and stared in fascinated horror at what walked into the room. The man the boy Cole Stuart had grown up to be said nothing, merely looked at her—with only one eye. He had a patch over the other.

Theresa saw it then, the first time she ever had. Andi and Bishop could see demons. Becca could, too. Theresa had always been spared that part, could only hear and smell them. But when she looked up into the dead shark eye of the puppet on a string called Cole Stuart, she saw a haze around him—for a moment reminded Theresa of that Pigpen, the Charlie Brown character who walked around in a cloud of dust. This was more like a swarm of fat green flies. She could hear them buzzing, too, before the demon spoke.

"You're going to help me find Becca," the red-haired man in her kitchen said. Only, she heard the words as a rumble like gravel in a blender, mixed up with dying screams and shrieks of terror, moans of loss, cries of pain, all slathered over with pure evil. It was a sound that'd turn a body's heart to pure stone.

She needed Bishop! He'd have known what to do. But Bishop was gone. She'd have to figure it out her own self now.

"Becca who?" she asked. In her head, the words sounded strong, sarcastic and defiant. But when they left her throat, they lost all authority, come out timid and scared. She pushed on, though. "I don't know nobody named Becca. You go on, now, get on out of my kitchen. You ain't welcome here."

The man/thing laughed—a sound totally devoid of mirth or joy.

"Don't remember her, huh?" He took another step into

the room; the stench was overwhelming. "Then we'll have do something to jog your memory, won't we."

When he started toward her, Theresa was afraid her knees were going to buckle and drop her in a heap on the floor. She wanted to scream, but couldn't find the breath, or cry or run away or…

What would Bishop have done?

He wouldn't have busted out bawling or tried to run off and hide! Bishop would have stood up to the demon— did stand up to it. And it had killed him.

Well, if that was the way of it, wouldn't be long before she'd be seeing Bishop face to face.

"Ain't nothing you can do to make me remember what I don't know," she said, and was glad her voice wasn't shaking as hard as her insides was. Then she drew herself up tall as she could, forced herself to look that creature dead in its one eye. "But even if I did know, I wouldn't tell the likes of you!"

It come at her then. The thing pounced, gobbled her up and the world went black.

Jack picked up a cup of coffee that tasted like battery acid/yak pee and took a sip. Then he tried to focus on the reports in front of him, but the words ran together on the page. And he couldn't blame fatigue. When he left Theresa's house Thursday night, he didn't go home. He drove around the city aimlessly, looking at everything and nothing, trying not to think about anything at all, and after awhile the unceasing buzz in his head more resembled a dial tone than a heart monitor.

He'd eventually found himself at the river watching crowds board the Belle of Cincinnati for a starlight cruise. And the questions that he'd shoved underwater bobbed back up to the surface of his mind like submerged beach balls.

Could it possibly be true—seriously!—that there were invisible monsters among those people—that there existed a creature made out of hate more horrifying than any Hollywood-animated, computer-generated, mechanical unreality whose single-minded mission was to kill Jack, Daniel and a woman named Becca?

That was crazy! Fairy-tale-science-fiction-horror-movie-bogeyman crap!

He slumped back into the seat and closed his eyes, absolutely exhausted, pushed to the limit of who he was by the constant battle going on inside him.

Bottom line: it flat-out could not possibly be true.

But it was.

He feared the opposing forces of those mutually-exclusive realities might actually rip apart the fabric of his soul.

When he finally did go home, he lay in bed wide awake as the digital clock did its slow-mo numerical dance.

"Sleep…" he'd mumbled out loud to the universe, not a prayer, really. "Please, let me sleep."

He'd closed his eyes, and when he'd opened them again it was morning. He'd slept soundly, dreamlessly all night. After an uneventful day shift yesterday, he'd slept just as well last night. And since today was his swing to second shift—three to midnight—he'd spent a lazy Saturday morning running errands. Even got a haircut. Jack Carpenter was beginning to feel a little like a human being again.

Jack had stopped off for a bowl of Skyline Chili on his way back from a run, and with it resting warm in his belly, he dug into the pile of paperwork that Crock claimed had been sitting on his desk since shortly after the earth cooled off. But he couldn't focus. He had to come up with some sort of…plan. How do you defend yourself against—?

He was spared having to answer the question.

The hand-held radios clipped to the uniforms of the officers in the squad room all burped out a bleat of static at the same time, followed by the dispatcher's voice: "All units respond to a 10-70 at the Ichikawa Building, 392 Banks Road." Ten-seventy was the code for fire.

"Guess the chamber of commerce finally got tired of waiting and blew the place up," Peterson said as he passed Jack's desk on his way to the door.

Jack doubted that. The eminent domain court case between the city and Ichikawa, Inc. had dragged out for years, and the city fathers wouldn't likely resort to violence at this late date to remove the niggling eyesore that continued to stymie the community's efforts to revitalize the waterfront district. Actually, the eyesore was plural; there were five of them. The Ichikawa Building housed the corporate offices of Ichikawa—Japanese for "river city." It sat at the far end of a string of buildings owned by the Japanese company, which used the first two of them and leased out the rest. The buildings were arranged on the north bank of the Ohio River, west of Cincinnati, at the edge of what the Harrelton Chamber of Commerce considered prime waterfront access.

The whole Harrelton police department wouldn't ordinarily roll for a fire in an isolated office building. But next door to the Ichikawa Building was Nippon Pyrotechnics, the company's flagship manufacturing plant, where it produced world famous Ichikawa Fireworks.

Jack wasn't the first man to his cruiser this time. Paco Ramirez beat him by a step. As Ramirez pulled out in front of him onto Foster Road and flipped on his lights and siren, Jack's cell phone rang. He reached to turn it off, then saw the almost-familiar number—where'd he seen that recently?—and answered it instead.

"Sergeant Carpenter, Harrelton PD," he said.

"Bowie County Sheriff Jim Clark here. Are you the Sergeant Jack Carpenter who called here asking about Victor Alexander?"

The Texas Sheriff's words slithered into Jack's ear, an earwig carrying eggs that would hatch and eat his brain inside his skull.

"That'd be me. What's up?" he said with an indifference he definitely did not feel.

"You call asking about him last week and he escapes this week…do you know something I need to know?"

"He broke out? He's…gone?" Jack hated the little-kid whine in the questions.

"As of midnight Thursday. Why were you inquiring about him?"

"Nothing urgent. He's a…suspect…in a cold case," Jack said. He murdered a dog named McDougal, McDo, Dougal Dog, DD twenty-six years ago. "I thought you said he was locked up, that the walls were three feet thick."

"I did and they are. But that won't stop a man with a key. He had help, an accomplice on the outside." The Texarkana lawman kept talking, but the word accomplice echoed in Jack's head like a marble in a kettle drum.

"A drug-fried loser like Alexander could never have orchestrated an escape from that place all by his lonesome. Shoot, it was so slick they wouldn't have detected he was gone for hours—except the guy stopped off on his way out to murder a nurse and an orderly."

"Killed them by…?" Jack mumbled, but knew the

answer before he asked—unconsciously mouthed the words along with the sheriff.

"Broke their necks," the sheriff said. Jack could hear something like awe in the sheriff's voice as he continued. "Twisted their heads all the way around facing backward. Broke the orderly's spine, too—how'd he do that?"

Gratefully, it was a rhetorical question.

"He'll be back in custody inside forty-eight hours, though." The sheriff's tone was clipped and confident. "His blood test the last time we busted him looked like the runoff from a nuclear waste dump. That guy's ingested every chemical but Tidy Bowl. He'll be high on something before sundown, I guar-ron-tee it. We'll catch him."

"I'm sure you will."

Actually, I'm sure you won't.

Jack kept the phone to his ear for a moment after the sheriff hung up, then scanned back through his call log and found the number of Wilkerson Commercial Fisheries in Gloucester, Massachusetts. He was glad to see his hand wasn't shaking when he punched it in and that his voice was firm when he asked the office manager there if the Gypsy Baron had returned to port early. She assured him the ship was still out to sea.

"They stay out until they get their catch," the woman said. Jack had only exhaled half the breath he'd been holding when she continued. "If there's an emergency, like that sailor who got hurt, the Coast Guard sends out a Med-Evac chopper to get them."

"One of the crew of the Gypsy Baron was taken off the ship?"

"Uh huh. About a week ago. On Sunday night."

After that, Jack wasn't talking to the office manager anymore. He was merely speaking his thoughts aloud so he could hear them and believe.

"He's… back on shore…"

"Haven't heard what his condition is, though. I don't want to gross you out or anything, but that guy somehow got a fish hook in his eye! How do you do a thing like that —get a fish hook—?"

Jack disconnected and sat in a silence too deep to be real, so quiet he could have heard an egg white slip out through a crack in the shell. Both of them free, somewhere out there since…his brain finished the math.

Probably takes twelve hours to drive from Texarkana to Cincinnati.

They're here.

The cell phone still in his hand, Jack punched "favorites," then Theresa's name. As he listened to the lonely sound of the phone ringing and ringing, a lead ball formed in the pit of his stomach.

What had been surfacing with each new snippet view of his past were childhood memories of Theresa. The warmth of her tender hugs, how he often saw tears in her eyes when she tended the shiners and split lips his father'd given him.

"I'm gone call the po-lice and show them what that man done to you," she'd tell him.

"Nobody did anything to me," he'd reply. "I ran into a cabinet door."

They'd both known he was lying, but they'd also both known he'd die before he'd change his story, so it had become a sad little dance they did—Theresa begging Jack to let her report his various injuries and Jack holding tight to his "I tripped" stories. She'd hug him fiercely then, like she never wanted to let go, and croon "everything's gone be alright, Sugar. You'll see. God's got this. Ain't none of what's happenin' a surprise to the Almighty."

Now, it was Theresa who was in danger, and Jack was

all she had. If he could stop the monsters as he'd done the creature of wasps at the school—game over, everybody pick up your marbles and go home. He'd never had a chance as a child fighting the superhuman red-haired kid and his gang, but a well-placed .40 caliber hollow-point would drop Cole Stuart and Victor Alexander like it would any other scumbag.

Jack would simply have to kill them before they had a chance to kill him.

There it was then.

Between one heartbeat and the next, Harrelton, Ohio, Police Sergeant Jack Carpenter—the guy in the white hat who'd dedicated his life to protecting the innocent from lawbreakers—turned his back and walked away from the law. He would shoot Cole and Victor on sight. No preliminaries. No warnings. No "keep your hands where I can see them." As soon as he spotted either one of them, he would put a bullet in the man—two, actually. First shot to the chest; second to the head. Just like you would a mad dog.

Surprising how that resolve cleared the fog out of his brain.

The law enforcement officer within Jack surfaced then long enough to point out, oh by the way, that the use of deadly force was perfectly legal if there was a "clear and present threat that a suspect intended to kill or cause grievous bodily harm" to someone else—which pretty much defined Stuart's and Alexander's whole reason for existence.

But that part, and the fact that what he was planning would never be ruled a righteous shoot, didn't count anymore because Jack was no longer a police officer. He was a soldier and they were the enemy. He would cut them down the moment he saw them because Daniel, Emily, Andi and Theresa…and Becca would never be safe as long as Cole Stuart and Victor Alexander continued to draw breath. And there was nobody in the world to protect them but Jack.

He called Daniel. The call went immediately to voice mail, meaning Daniel's phone was turned off. After the beep, Jack spoke in a level, stern voice. "Daniel, Cole and Vic are here—right now! Get Emily and Andi and Theresa and run. Don't tell anybody where you're going. Just drive —get out of Cincinnati, go to Dayton or Indy or Louisville, find some obscure motel, check in and stay there until I tell you it's safe to come back. Now, turn your phone back off and don't turn it on again for any reason. Emily's, too. Your number's on the church website and anybody with the computer skills of a fourth-grader can track the location of a cell phone. Use the motel phone and call my cell every two hours. I won't pick up unless I have something to tell you."

Jack started to hang up, but didn't. After a pause, he said, "Dano, might be a good idea somewhere along in here to…pray."

He hung up, sat frozen for a moment, then the silence roaring around him was broken by the dispatcher's voice, rasping over his radio. "Unit four"—that was Jack—"proceed to River Road and assist in crowd control." Jack hadn't even pulled out of the station parking lot!

For years, he'd been telling police recruits that "training will take over as the default if you let it." He did. He flipped on his lights and siren and headed toward the Ohio River.

~

Emily sat still, didn't notice the slowly growing pond of white Elmer's glue that was puddling beneath the bottle hanging forgotten in her hand.

Did she love Jeff Kendrick?

How could she even think about it when a horrible darkness as black as the far side of the moon seemed to be descending all around her. Something evil was endangering everything and everybody she loved!

She…loved?

Dan.

Dan in the emergency room, holding her steady and tight, as if the force of his strength alone could protect her, shield her from their shared horror.

His words from Thursday night. Calm. Kind, even. Telling her there were monsters out there right now plotting to kill him!

What would she do if she lost him?

Lost him? Hello. Why was she worrying about losing what she wasn't even sure she wanted to keep?

What she felt with Jeff was fierce and passionate and powerful.

An atomic bomb was powerful, too, burned hot and bright…and destroyed everything it touched.

If anything happened to Dan, what would—?

"Are you Ok?"

Emily jumped at the words—Jeff's words—spoken out loud by Mary Sexton who was peering at her, or trying to as she adjusted her new bifocals to bring Emily's face into focus.

"Why, sure I'm…why do you ask?"

"You looked—I don't know—forlorn, I guess." Emily started to come up with an explanation, but there was no need. Mary's observation had been as surface as every other conversation she'd ever had with any of the women in the group. If Emily'd dared to tell them she was not Ok, they wouldn't have had a clue what to do with a revelation like that.

"You got lots on your mind, don't you, Sweetie, what with your little girl getting shot...well, let's not talk about something awful as that." She gestured around at women gathering up purses and car keys. "We're all going to go on now. I got to fix supper for Harold."

Then she smiled, displaying perfect white dentures. "There's only that one bouquet of balloons left to attach to the grape arbor." Mary nodded to where the handyman on a ladder was tying the ends of strings to the top of a trellis, then grimaced as if something smelled bad. "And we'll be back tomorrow after church to finish up. You about done?"

"Just this last S," she said, trying to smear the pond of glue out over the letter. "Actually, I'm waiting for Andi. Beth Young is dropping her off after gymnastics, so I'll work until she gets here."

The ladies filed out, their chatter like the chirping of birds in the woods. In the quiet that followed, Emily could sink back into her memories of Jeff, like settling down into the glory of a hot tub after a cold swim. She wallowed in them for a moment, the images creating a visceral reaction all over her body. Then her mind turned to Dan.

Dan, who could die any minute at the hands of a monster.

Jeff, who was the brightest light she had ever known in all her life.

Are you Ok?

She sat unmoving, so still she was aware of her own pulse, the steady whump, whump, whump sound of her heart pumping blood through her veins. Then she wiped glue off her fingers on a tissue and fished her phone out of her purse. She typed a brief message, but wasn't ready to send it. Not yet. She stared at it, the words in orderly rows on the screen.

The cell phone suddenly rang. She jumped in surprise and her finger tapped send.

"Is this Emily Burke?" a woman's voice asked. But she continued in a rush before Emily could respond. "This is Bernice Higginbotham, Emma's friend, and I wanted to call and let you know how sorry I am I couldn't do that favor she asked of me."

Emily sat back on her heels.

"What favor?"

"She wanted to borrow my handyman today, but I just couldn't give him up. He was already under the house and I was going to send him on along soon's he finished. But it got so late and he's still down there."

Emily's mind spun.

If Bernice didn't send the...

Shoes appeared in front of Emily. Work shoes. Emily hung up on Bernice Higginbotham in mid-babble and let her eyes travel up the body of the man who owned the shoes until she was staring into the face of the "handyman." He was grinning at her, his sickening body odor settling around her like a fog.

Then Andi screamed, a shriek as thin as a paper cut. Emily turned to the sound and saw the child in the doorway leading from the sanctuary into the Fellowship Hall. The little girl was staring in shock and horror at the man standing in front of Emily, her face contorted in a mask of fear and loathing.

It dawned on Emily laboriously, like lifting something heavy, that Andi was screaming at something Emily couldn't see.

Chapter Twenty-Eight

The only access to the "Five Uglies," as proponents of the waterfront project had dubbed the buildings along the Ohio River, was down River Road. It led off Conway Street across a football-field-sized area of marshes and mudflats and ended in front of the middle building at Banks Road, which branched out from there to dead ends in both directions. The center building, Ohio Agri-Business, Inc., was the largest, a warehouse full of farm equipment—tractors, hay-balers and grain combines that looked like gigantic grasshoppers pregnant with triplets.

The building east of the farm equipment warehouse was the smallest of the five. It was farther back from the road than the other four, set directly on the riverbank in a small grove of trees. Tall black letters on the side identified it as Kobayashi Paper Products, a storage facility and distribution center for paper goods manufactured by the Japanese company's three plants located upstream in Pittsburgh.

The last building in the string was unnamed and had no signage for a reason. That's because it was full of whiskey—Kentucky bourbon whiskey to be exact—thousands of barrels of it aging in racks five stories high.

Jack had worked in a bourbon warehouse one summer and marveled at the way the racks were ingeniously constructed so workers could use gravity to roll the five-hundred-pound barrels on their sides without heavy equipment. It reminded Jack of one of those contraptions where a round stone is placed in a slot at the top and then rolls to the bottom through a series of slanted tunnels.

As a barrel wagon driver, Mr. Newton's law served Jack every day. He'd park on an incline so the barrel wagon was slanted downhill, remove the gate on the back and attach guide rails. Then he'd pull out the chuck from behind the back barrel and watch the five-hundred-pound marbles roll off the back of the wagon, down the rails, and into a waiting elevator.

If the fire got out of control and spread all the way to the bourbon warehouse on the end, the whole waterfront district would be in danger. Probably twelve thousand barrels of booze—fifty gallons each. A single gallon of gasoline has the explosive power of ten sticks of dynamite—and alcohol burns hotter than gasoline.

By the time Jack arrived at the scene, officers from the sheriff's department and the Harrelton Police Department had evacuated all the buildings and were operating in crowd-control mode, fanned out to keep the rubberneckers a safe distance from the blaze. The chance to see a "fire at a fireworks factory" had drawn a crowd that quickly grew to almost unmanageable proportions, the lookie-loos enjoying themselves in something like a carnival atmosphere. Everyone had phones out, shooting pictures or videos. Kids wormed their way through the crowd to stand in front where they could get a better view, some people had even brought lawn chairs. Wouldn't have surprised Jack to see a vendor hawking popcorn and cotton candy.

The Harrelton Fire Department did everything but dump water out of the Ohio River on Nippon Pyrotechnics to keep the fire from spreading to it from the burning office building next door. But a brisk west wind was not on their side and it was soon clear their valiant efforts weren't going to prevail. It was a cloudy night, no moon or stars visible. The sky was perfectly black by the time the relentless march of flames through the Ichikawa Building ignited the dock on the west side of the factory where fireworks were loaded onto trucks for shipment. When the crates there caught fire, an explosion of light—a bottle rocket or something—shot up into the night. About a hundred feet above the building, it burst into sparkles of brilliant red light.

The crowd sucked in a communal gasp. This is what they'd come to see!

A second explosion followed almost immediately, coloring the sky bright purple. The crowd oohed and aahed. Jack grew still. There was something familiar about—

A third explosion rumbled in the flaming dock area and there was a beat of expectancy before brilliant light splattered a color into the black nothingness above the building. Green.

At the sound of the fourth explosion, Jack closed his eyes and mouthed a word he no longer had the air to say aloud.

"…blue…"

When he opened his eyes, the sky was awash with color, brilliant blue light against the velvet darkness.

That's what Andi saw.

Daniel's description of Andi's vision filled his head.

"Splashes of color—first red, then purple, then green, then blue—like paint splatters, only made out of light. And after the color came the shapes." Her vision had been about this fire, had predicted this blaze. Which meant the other elements of her vision might have something to do with it, too. But what could—?

Someone in the crowd behind Jack broke his concentration.

"Excuse me, officer," said a gravelly voice. "I need to talk to you."

Jack turned toward the speaker and saw a man about his own age, big—not as tall as Jack, but broader, thicker. He was dressed in a wrinkled and stained black body shirt that revealed the ripples of huge biceps under the clingy fabric. Steroid-juiced gym rats always wore body shirts. His hair was cropped tight, but Jack could tell that it was red.

The man's only distinguishing characteristic was the startlingly pale blue of his eye—singular. He only had one. Where the left eye should have been was a crater covered by a black patch.

This fella somehow got a fish hook in his eye! How do you do a thing like that—get a fish hook—?

Surprise nailed Jack to the spot, his mind awash with expectations retreating like a wave rushing back from the shore. It had never occurred to him that he might have to face Cole in public. He'd assumed Cole would launch a sneak attack, but this was no ambush.

Jack placed his hand on the butt of his service revolver. Was he prepared to drop Cole right now, in front of a couple hundred witnesses? Actually, he was, and that mildly surprised him. But he couldn't. He didn't have a clear shot in this crowd and there were kids running around.

Obviously, Cole had assumed Jack wouldn't recognize him, so Jack played along.

"What can I do for you, sir?" Jack said.

This brazen appearance must be part of some larger plan Cole'd mapped out. Now, it was his move.

"I sell insurance and Kobayashi Paper Products is one of my clients." He hooked a thumb toward the warehouse snuggled back in the trees. "I heard about the fire—it was all over the news. So I came down a few minutes ago to see if the building or contents had been damaged. When I got inside—"

"You've been inside that warehouse tonight? How'd you get in? How'd you get past—?"

"I have a key and I went in a side entrance—look, how I got in's not important. What matters is there are other people in there."

Jack had an idea where this was going now, so he pretended to take the bait.

"All these buildings have already been evacuated and you're telling me there are people in that warehouse right now?"

"These were homeless people and they were hiding. I just happened to come across them. They'd made a little place for themselves out of boxes. I told them they had to get out, that there was a fire. But they wouldn't budge, so I came looking for a police officer to report it."

Of course you did, good citizen that you are.

"If you'll come with me, officer, I'll show you where they are so you can get them out of the building."

Houston, we have lift-off.

There it was, the ruse to get Jack alone.

Why he'd approached Jack here, out in public like this, was still a mystery, but it was clear Cole was eager to move his encounter with Jack away from prying eyes. Jack was equally eager to spend some private time with Cole. It wouldn't take long. In fact, it occurred to Jack that if the Kobayashi Paper Products warehouse did eventually catch fire, Cole Stuart could simply vanish without a trace and nobody'd ever know what happened to him—because Jack had no intention of letting the man walk out of that building alive.

"Let's go," Jack said, and turned away from the crowd that was no longer restless and fidgety. They stood still, their rabid attention focused on the conflagration/fireworks display. No one noticed him head out across the dark parking lot with the one-eyed man, who had a serious hygiene problem. Cole smelled filthy, like he hadn't had a bath in— Was that a fish stink? Jack wrinkled his nose in disgust.

Obviously, there was a trap set for Jack somewhere up ahead. But Jack had something of a home-team advantage here. He knew the paper warehouse well.

Secluded in the trees right at the water's edge, the warehouse was filled with warm, cozy places to hole up for vagrants who ran the shore-side rail lines. Jack had been called here dozens of times to find the "squatters" and transport them to St. Bartholomew's Homeless Shelter in downtown Cincinnati. The building was stacked floor to ceiling on one whole side with boxes and packing crates of every conceivable kind of paper—typing paper/copy machine/printing paper, rolls of wrapping paper, boxes filled with toilet paper, paper towels, paper plates, and napkins. The labyrinth of aisles formed by the boxes had always reminded Jack of the warehouse where Indiana Jones and company stashed the Ark of the Covenant.

As soon as they rounded the corner of the building so it blocked the view of the crowd by the road, Jack went on hyper alert. Without appearing to, his eyes scanned his surroundings, three hundred sixty degrees, looking for anything odd or out of place, darker shade, perhaps, or a shape in a shadow. The halogen light that illuminated the fence between this building and the bourbon warehouse was out.

There were several side entrances to the warehouse, each with a small roof jutting out over the door and a light that illuminated the area under it. Cole went to the first door, where no light shone in the overhang. The glow from the light farther down lit tiny sparkles of broken light bulb glass that crunched under Jack's feet. The door swung easily inward before Jack had a chance to see the lock, but he was sure Cole had either jimmied or broken it.

When Cole pushed the door open, he said, "There's a light. I'll turn it on." Then he vanished into the gloom.

Jack waited where he was, unwilling to walk into a dark building with a man who wanted to kill him. Then Jack saw a dim glow chase long shadows into the darkness. He knew it was the light in the "office" area where the security guard kept a desk and filing cabinet tucked away between walls of boxes next to an ancient elevator, the old fashioned, metal-cage kind with exposed cables that emitted a piercing squall when it was in use.

"Over here," Cole hollered out from behind the wall of boxes.

Showtime.

Jack drew his Glock 22 service weapon, held it in both hands pointed at the floor as he edged, with his back to the boxes, toward the sound of Cole's voice.

"Yo, officer. You stop to take a leak or something?"

When he got to the corner of the wall where the light spilled out onto the floor, Jack gathered himself, prepared to spin around the corner and immediately open fire, cut Cole down where he stood.

He took a deep breath and let it out slowly, then whirled, the gun extended in front of him in both hands, a second away from pulling the trigger.

But he didn't fire.

Cole jumped, obviously surprised to see Jack with his gun drawn, but he recovered quickly.

"Unless you want to see a smile where no smile has been before, put the gun down...Jack," he said.

Cole stood behind a straight-backed, wooden chair on the far side of the small open space. Theresa was seated in the chair, affixed to it by what looked like half a roll of duct tape—her legs fastened to the two front chair legs, her arms to the wooden arms and there were long strips of tape wrapped around her chest and the back of the chair. A piece of tape covered her mouth. Cole stood behind her holding a vicious looking hunting knife at her throat.

Jack didn't move, didn't even blink, his whirring mind calculating his chances of dropping Cole before he could—

"What part of 'put the gun down' don't you understand, Carpenter?" Cole said. "On the floor, now."

Statistics were not in Jack's favor if he complied. His own voice teaching new officers ground defense, echoed in his head. "If you give up your gun, there is a ninety percent chance the suspect will pick it up and shoot you with it."

"You got one more chance...gun down or this lady joins our silent, grinning friend over there."

Obviously, Cole actually had stumbled across a homeless man in the building. He was sitting upright against the back wall, placed there for effect. The gash in his slit throat was so deep it appeared his head was only balanced on his shoulders and if he slumped over, the head would roll out onto the floor like a pumpkin.

Jack surveyed the room, tried to see where Victor Alexander might be lurking. But there was no sign of him, then he slowly lowered his weapon and placed it on the floor in front of him. His eyes were on Theresa's. He saw sorrow and regret there, sympathy, but no fear.

"The backup, too." Jack heard little-kid pride in Cole's voice that he'd known Jack would be packing a backup.

Jack did as he was instructed, took the .38 caliber Smith and Wesson strapped to his right ankle, and placed it on the floor in front of him.

"Now, step back away from them."

Jack lifted his foot as if to step away, but instead reached out with the toe of his shoe and kicked both weapons hard to the right. They slid across the floor and disappeared into the three inch space under a pallet piled high with boxes.

Cole glared at him. "Think you got away with something?" Cole's voice was colored with loathing. "If I'd needed a gun, I'd have brought one. I do better work with a knife…like to stick a man—or woman—and hear the squeal."

Once Jack was unarmed, Cole relaxed. He kept the blade of the knife so tight against Theresa's throat that a thin trickle of blood ran from it and disappeared into the considerable bosom below, but the tension went out of his body. Good. Jack was counting on that, because the instant Cole moved the knife away from Theresa's neck, Jack would jump him. Over-confidence was Jack's friend. And Cole was obviously pleased as punch with himself for getting this far.

"Chloroformed your fat friend and drove around with her in the trunk of my car for hours looking for a spot where the three of us could have ourselves a chat." He paused. "Secluded, so all the noise you two are going to make won't bother anybody. Then I heard about the fire and knew this is where you'd be—easy to find, I've got a picture. Soon as I got here, I spotted this place, big and empty and away from all the hubbub, a snug little hideaway."

When Jack said nothing, Cole continued, the self-congratulatory tone still coloring his words.

"Was planning on getting you in here by telling you Vic had a knife to your fat nigger friend's throat, that he'd kill her if you didn't come with me. Then I found my man over there"—he gestured with his chin toward the dead body—"and he made a better story."

Cole cut his eyes to where the guns lay beneath the pallet and his face hardened. "How'd you know?"

Jack didn't respond.

Cole smiled then, or what passed for a smile split open the bottom portion of his face.

"Well, as you can see, my old friend Vic's not holding a knife on this greasy black pig. He had a prior commitment —with your friend, Daniel."

Chapter Twenty-Nine

Daniel was on his way home from his Saturday evening's men's Bible study. He hadn't taught it. Clayton Abernathy, the chairman of the board of elders had, and Daniel had tried to connect to the lesson. But Abernathy, whose command of the Scripture was as legendary as his seeming inability to smile, might as well have been speaking Mandarin Chinese.

There was a strict 'no cell phones' policy in the group, and the old dudes who probably didn't even own one made sure the rule was rigorously enforced. Daniel pulled his out of his pocket and powered it up as he drove. He had six messages. He listened to Jack's first and after that, he ignored the other five. Daniel played the voice mail through twice, trying to get his mind around it.

This can't be happening, not here in the real world.

The moment the words popped into Daniel's mind a wave of déjà vu washed over him. He'd said those words, exactly those words, before.

"What's happening is the real world, Daniel," says the little girl beside him. "Just because not everybody can see it doesn't mean it's not really happening."

Her hair is the color of sunlight and her eyes the deep blue of a stormy sea. Well, Daniel has never actually seen a stormy sea, or a sea of any kind for that matter. But it sounds good in his head when he struggles for words to capture the essence of the girl whose image never leaves his mind, night or day.

"This is some kind of distraction." she continues. "You heard them. To get everybody's attention, focus it here so they can get away with doing whatever else they're planning that's even worse. We have to do something."

"Just the three of us against them all?" Daniel is grateful his voice isn't shaking on the outside because his insides are quivering.

"Don't you mean the four of us," pipes in Mikey Rutherford but they all ignore him.

"We don't have time to go find Bishop," Jack says. "Whatever they're planning, it's now. We can follow them and—" He stops as a new thought strikes him. "They might even be going…you know—there, where it is, to its lair."

"Lair?" Daniel is incredulous. "Jack, this isn't an episode of Wild Kingdom. There's a monster demon out there!" But Daniel has more than a niggling suspicion that Jack doesn't really believe that. Not deep in his bones like Daniel and Bishop and Becca do. What Jack does believe in are his feelings for Becca. And his macho attempts to impress her are going to get them all in trouble.

Jack blows by his words, intent on making his point.

"They're up to something awful." Urgency makes his already-a-man's voice gruff. "You know they are. We can't just…" his words trail off, then he continues with more strength. "Nobody will believe us! If we don't stop them, who will?"

Jack is right, of course. They can't just do nothing, not after what the Bad Kids did to the little Roberts boy.

His name was Joel or Joey, something like that, about five years old, maybe going into first grade this fall. His father drove a truck, hauled used bourbon barrels to wineries in California, so he was gone a lot. His mother worked as a waitress at Parker's Restaurant, and the grandmother who looked after him was deaf as a post and almost blind. The boy'd had to look after himself, so he was independent, no whiner.

And Daniel understands that's why Jack is so upset by what happened to him. He sees himself in the little Roberts kid.

Jack, Daniel, Becca and Mikey had been picking through the attic of the furniture store on the corner of Commerce and Baxter Streets, looking for absolutely nothing, filling up time on a lazy summer day. They had spent a few minutes earlier hanging around the white WCOH Action News First truck with the gigantic satellite dish on top that was parked in front of the courthouse. The word circulating in the crowd that had gathered around the truck was that the Cincinnati television station had sent a crew to Bradford's Ridge to do a story on all the "strange happenings"—tortured animals, vandalism, snakes in public places.

The four of them knew way more about those goings-on than anybody else in town, knew who was responsible, but nobody would ever ask them or believe them if they told.

Daniel had suggested they go explore the labyrinth of

antiques in the attic of the furniture store to get Becca's mind off how helpless they'd all felt. Old Mr. Walker owned the place. He loved kids—played Santa every year in the parade—and went to Daniel's father's church, and he'd been glad to let the kids poke around, long as they didn't break anything. Instead of unlocking the big bay doors in the back of the building where furniture could be hauled upstairs, he'd pulled down a rickety ladder that extended through a trap door like the entrance to most attics. Then he shut and latched the door behind them so they wouldn't accidentally fall through it, and told them to holler for him when they were ready to leave.

The attic ran the whole length of the building. It was dusty, laced with old spiderwebs, a museum of strange-looking lamps, hat-racks, vases, clocks and pictures of ugly, unsmiling people in big gilt frames. Little mouse pebbles crunched under their feet, courtesy of what was probably a whole city of mice that had found comfy homes in the overstuffed chairs and couches. There were huge windows on the front of the building overlooking Commerce Street, and on the back overlooking the back side of the cemetery and the Eastern Orthodox Church across the alley about half a block away. The windows didn't open, so there was no way to get even a breath of a breeze, and their movement disturbed ancient dust that hung in the air like fog.

Daniel was examining a stool, trying to figure out if it actually was an elephant's foot or was made to look like one, when he heard Becca cry out. She was standing in front of the window overlooking the church. When he and Jack rushed to her side, she could only point. When Mikey came huffing up a moment later, he let out a little squeak of alarm, too.

It was instantly clear what was happening. Five-year-old Joey was making his way along the narrow ledge that ran around the edge of the round roof of the church. Lying in the gutter twenty feet ahead of him was a soccer ball, and in the side yard of the church thirty feet below were the six Bad Kids.

Jack had raced to the trap door and began to bang on it, hollering for Mr. Walker to come and let them out. But the old man must have been in the front of the store and didn't hear Jack's cry, or was with a customer and was ignoring him. Whatever the reason, Mr. Walker didn't come to unfasten the catch on the door, so they were trapped in the attic, forced to watch helplessly as the drama unfolded, like sitting in front of a television screen with the sound turned off.

A piece of brick beneath Joey's foot suddenly crumbled away and he went down on one knee, grabbing at the tiles on the roof to keep his balance. Becca gasped. The boys watching from below laughed uproariously.

Daniel could feel his hands ball into fists, saw Jack's jaw clench in anger.

Roger Willingham picked up a rock. He threw it at Joey, but missed, and it bounced off the roof tiles three or four feet away.

Joey cried out something. He was facing the window of the furniture store, and even from where they stood, they could make out the terror on his features.

Victor Alexander picked up a rock then. His aim was better. He was the short stop on the Little League team.

The rock hit Joey in the shoulder and he cried out in pain, lurched forward, and barely maintained his balance. They could see Cole yell something at Victor, but couldn't hear what it was. Then he and the others launched a hail of stones that fell around the little boy—but didn't hit him. Joey began to cry, quickly ramping up into a piercing wail the three could hear inside the store attic even with the windows closed.

"They're trying to knock him off there," Jack whispered.

"That's why they got him to go up there in the first place," Becca said.

"I don't think so," said Mikey. "If they wanted to hit him, they could. I think they're trying to scare him so he'll cry."

"Why would they want—?" Daniel began and then Jack grabbed his arm and pointed. Though Jack, Becca and Daniel couldn't see who it was from their vantage point, it was obvious that somebody was coming down Baxter Street along the side of the furniture store toward the church because the Bad Kids suddenly dropped their rocks and ran around to the other side of the building out of sight.

Beatrice Cunningham, the pharmacist's wife, came into view moments later, about to cross the alley. She heard Joey, looked up, and her scream rattled the windows. After that, it didn't take long for a crowd to begin to gather.

Finally, the four in the attic heard the catch on the door unfasten and they scrambled down the ladder past a surprised Mr. Walker, who was sputtering "…busy so I couldn't—" and raced out the side door of the store. The Bad Kids were no longer on the far side of the church. As the wail of a distant siren grew louder, the six boys casually crossed the alley and were sauntering up it toward Jack, Daniel, Becca and Mikey. The furniture store door was sunk into an alcove between the building and the dry cleaners next door and Jack put out his hand, motioning the others to stop there, out of sight. They could hear the Bad Kids' voices as they approached, but the boys never even glanced in their direction—their eyes glued on the developing emergency on the other side of the alley.

"…should keep them busy for awhile," Cole said. "Get your bikes and meet me at Allsup's Station in five minutes."

"Is everything we need—?" said Vic or maybe Roger.

"You think he'll forget something?"

"No, I just…I—"

"It's all there and we've got a lot to do."

Then they heard an odd sound, like laughter—but with a harsh, vulgar ring, an ugly parody of amusement.

"We're gonna make 'em squeeeal," it was a voice none of them recognized. Not a human voice. The Bad Kids walked on down the alley, rounded the corner and disappeared.

Becca spoke softly after the awful sound died away. "The demons…their demons are so excited they're hopping up and down, jumping around like the monkeys in that cage at the zoo. They're planning something more horrible than anything they've ever done."

Now, Jack is determined to follow them. His question "if we don't stop them, who will?" hangs in the air.

There's a beat of silence. Daniel's mouth feels dryer than dust, than sand, than salt. He manages to form words anyway. "Don't act like you're going alone," he tells Jack.

Jack is curt, but firm. "The bike's too slow with both of us on it. We'll lose them. You and Becca and Mikey go get Bishop!"

The memory that had downloaded into his mind with the clarity of a high-def video ended there, cut off like Daniel'd flipped off the television set, leaving the warning in Jack's phone message reverberating in his ears. Jack had been curt, but firm this time, too, but Daniel could tell he was afraid—just like he'd been afraid before. He knew a lot about Jack, not facts and information, but about who he was, what kind of person. He had been absorbing more from the bursts of memory than scenes and sights. Jack was the best, the only real friend he had ever had.

Daniel felt a wave of the helplessness he'd felt all those years ago. How do you fight...?

Didn't matter. Daniel had no intention of fighting anybody or anything. All he wanted was to do as Jack had instructed: get his family and Theresa to safety. He picked up his cell phone and punched the speed dial to Emily's number.

She answered on the first ring, didn't give Daniel a chance to speak but blurted out, "Daniel, listen—"

Daniel? Emily never called him Daniel. Something was wrong. She didn't continue, though, sounded like she'd been cut off. But Daniel blew by it. He didn't have time to listen to her prattle on about her afternoon spent decorating for Dancing with the Stars.

If that was, indeed, where Emily had been.

Daniel felt a chill as deep as the one in the pit of his stomach when he'd heard Jack's words, but a different kind.

Was Emily really at the church? Or was she with... Daniel couldn't bring himself to say the man's name. He'd used it that one time when he'd confronted her and then never said it or thought it again. In Daniel's mind, his wife was having an affair with What'sHisName.

And just like that, Daniel knew he couldn't do it anymore. It felt like a tumbler had clicked into place somewhere deep in his soul. Wondering and fearing, doubt, suspicion—he'd even checked the mileage on her car!—he was done with that. He hated what this was doing to him as much as he did what was happening to their marriage.

He suddenly no longer cared about the consequences—to his life, his ministry. He would not live like this. Emily was going to have to make a choice. It was either her marriage or…Emily was going to have to chose between him and WhatsHisName. Now. Today.

~

Jack felt his throat constrict. Daniel! Victor Alexander was with Daniel? But maybe not. Maybe Daniel had gotten Jack's message in time and—

No, Jack's warning had been too late. The proof was sitting right there in front of him. Daniel wouldn't have run without Theresa.

Cole's gloating smile slowly drained off his face and his eyes went completely blank for a moment. Then he spoke, and Jack knew that every speck of Cole Stuart had left the building and some other, darker entity had wholly taken over his being.

"Where's Becca?" The voice was a deep, raspy rumble, foreign sounding, totally other. Theresa cringed. Jack wondered what she heard that he couldn't.

"How would I know where Becca Hawkins is?" Jack said. "We were friends when we were twelve years old! I haven't seen her since…I don't even remember when." He paused, then sneered. "But even if I did know, do you think I'd tell you?"

Cole's insolent voice returned. "Wrong on both counts. She said there was a strand that connects you two. So you do know and you are going to tell me."

There was a sudden boom, then a rumbling roar followed by smaller explosions and the sound of a dozen machine-guns. The fire had spread to the fireworks factory. It'd be virtually impossible to control now, and it was coming their way.

An image, a flash, an expelled memory burst into Jack's consciousness as real as Cole and Theresa and—was he imagining it—the smell of smoke. No, he wasn't imagining it. The smell was coming through his nostrils and from the scene in his mind, too.

He is in Hell. It must be, there is fire everywhere, flames all around, and he can hear the horrified, agonized screams of the damned.

There's a figure in the flames. Jack can only see him from behind, but he's familiar all the same. Someone Jack has seen before.

The flames back up from the figure, move out of his way as if shoved by an invisible hand, and he walks through them unscathed. Then the figure turns slowly to face Jack.

It was gone then, vanished as instantly as it had appeared, though the image left behind a whiff of smoke. Or was the smoke real, here?

Cole reached out with his left hand, took hold of the piece of tape over Theresa's mouth and yanked viciously. It came away with a ripping sound that left the area around her mouth raw and Theresa couldn't stifle a cry.

"Want me to slit your throat, sow?"

"You think you scare me, fool?"

Jack could tell she was scared, though, but he was proud of her determination not to show it.

"Cut my throat and you gone send me immediately and forever into the presence of Jesus."

A wave of something—revulsion, rage, hatred…fear—

washed across Cole's face and a shudder ran through his whole body. He seemed to lose his focus; his concentration faltered. Jack tensed. Another moment's inattention and—

Then Cole looked up at Jack. His lone remaining eye was nothing but a black hole in his head and Jack imagined he could see flickering there, the reflection of flames. Cole cocked his head toward the metal cage of the old elevator and Jack noticed for the first time that there was a brand new padlock on the old metal bars.

"Brought a lock and chains with me, just in case," Cole said. "But I'm not going to need chains." He gestured with his chin, his hand holding the knife to Theresa's neck unmoving. "Get in there. Sit down on the floor and stick your feet and legs out in front of you—through the bars. Unclip those handcuffs off your belt, stick your hands and arms through the bars and clip the cuffs on your wrists."

Cole was right. He didn't need chains. This was a well-thought out jail cell. Cole could use the remainder of the duct tape on the roll on the floor to tape Jack's feet together. He'd be unarmed, defenseless.

No, not defenseless. "Your most powerful weapon is your brain, soldier," Sergeant Carson used to bellow. "Use it!"

Think.

Cole was a massive powerhouse, could probably have bench pressed four hundred pounds even before the demon took control. With the monster dumping gallons of his own adrenaline into his bloodstream, the man whose muscles stretched his shirt tight was the Incredible Hulk on meth.

But hand-to-hand combat was more about leverage than strength. Jack was a trained fighter; this guy was—at best—a barroom brawler. Those muscle freaks spent all day in the gym building all their 'ceps—biceps and triceps.

They never worked on cardiovascular. Or flexibility. Jack had him there.

And there was the rage factor as well. A man jacked up on adrenaline could not think clearly, made stupid mistakes. There'd be other issues with all that adrenaline, too—if Jack could survive long enough to take advantage of them.

Which, in truth, wasn't likely. The odds were definitely stacked in Muscle Man's favor. If he got inside on Jack, started whaling on him…still, a chance at survival was better than the certain death of being locked in that cage.

"No," Jack said.

Under other circumstances, the shock on Cole's face might have been comical.

"What do you mean, no?"

"How many things can no mean?"

Cole's eyes narrowed.

"You're the same stupid jock you were twenty-six years ago, Cole. You think I'm going to waltz over there and let you lock me up?" Jack set his feet wide apart. "You want me to get in that cage…?" He crouched and continued in a parody of a little-kid dare. "…make me!"

Time stopped while Jack waited to see if Cole would take the bait.

A flush rose up Cole's neck and into his face, bright as a sunburn. Then the man literally roared, made a sound Jack couldn't believe had been produced by human vocal chords.

"I'll put you in that cage, nigger!" He tossed the knife aside contemptuously. "With my bare hands. But I won't have to lock the door. You won't be going anywhere after I break both your legs off at the knee-caps."

Cole stepped out from behind the chair and lunged at Jack.

Jack was already turning, with Theresa's long-ago words ringing in his head. "Dog'll chase you just cause you run," Theresa had told Jack and Daniel one evening as they sat on her front porch watching fireflies. "'Specially mean dogs. It's in they nature. They can't help theirselves."

Jack ran.

Cole chased him.

Chapter Thirty

The Kobayashi Paper Products warehouse wasn't completely dark. Through the ten-foot windows high up on the walls near the ceiling, the two halogen lights still burning out by the fence in back and the parking lot lights in front shown down in strips, like flaming spears stuck in the warehouse floor.

The lone bulb dangling from the ceiling that provided light in the security guard's office area had been behind Jack's head, which meant Cole's eyes would take longer to readjust to the dark than Jack's, because he'd been looking at the light and Jack hadn't.

Every little bit helped.

A conveyor belt appeared out of the darkness in front of Jack and he had no choice but to dive under it and slide on his belly to the other side. Lost a step, maybe two, but Cole would have to...

Jack heard Cole grunt, then a screeching rumbling sound, but he didn't look back. Then he heard a crash off to his left. Cole had gone neither under nor over the belt, he'd gone through it. Ripped it up off the floor and tossed it into the mountain of boxes.

Perfect. Keep it up, macho man.

Out of sight in the darkness between puddles of light, Jack leapt to the side of the main aisle he was running down, shoved himself into a tight space between a stack of boxes that opened up wider once he got past them. Then he threw his shoulder into the boxes, shoved with all his might and the pile of them began to sway, back and forth once before it toppled over into the main aisle, right in Cole's path. Jack heard Cole roar and saw boxes fly through strips of light, like they'd been made of Styrofoam instead of loaded with reams of typing paper, probably a hundred fifty pounds each.

Jack squeezed around behind the next pallet of boxes and then the next. Dumping each one in turn into the main aisle, heard Cole roaring and cursing as he picked the boxes up out of his way and hurled them in all directions. But they were slowing him down. Jack gained a few seconds on him with each load. More important, Cole was doing exactly what Jack hoped he would do, was banking on him doing. Cole was using energy.

That was the thing about adrenaline, Jack had explained to uncounted dozens of recruits over the years. When you're suddenly forced to fight for your life, your body dumps the hormone into your bloodstream. The process starts with the amygdala, the thingamajig responsible for the fight-or-flight reaction. That primitive body part has one responsibility—to keep you alive—and it will do whatever it has to do to accomplish that task. It will give you almost "superhuman powers." Equally important, it will deaden pain. Adrenaline is the most powerful anesthetic known to man. It will even slow down time, or seem to because of your faster reactions to stimuli.

But the human body paid dearly for adrenaline-induced superpowers. It was like pouring rocket fuel into the gas tank of an old Studebaker. It might go fast, but it wouldn't go far. And given enough time, the engine would blow and it wouldn't go anywhere at all.

Regardless of Hollywood hype—it was more entertaining to watch intense hand-to-hand combat go on for half the movie—real fights were over in minutes because the human body was simply not designed to hold out for long at that level. Cole had an exceptional body, but it was human. The beast possessing him would continue to dump ridiculous amounts of adrenaline into his blood to force his body to perform, no matter what the cost to Cole. Jack was counting on that. His only hope in this mouse versus elephant altercation was to continue to drive Cole until his engine blew, force the hulk to expend energy while Jack conserved his own.

The victory would go to the last man standing.

Or…to the one who vanished.

The thought crept on little cat feet into Jack's mind. He had half a minute on Cole now, enough time to simply disappear, hole up in any one of a dozen cracks and crannies. He'd be safe there. Then he could slip out…

What was the point in that? He might elude Cole this time, might even get away entirely, go for help, arrest Cole for kidnapping Theresa, put him away. But Cole would get out on bail before the trial, or overpower some officer or jailer and run. No end to what you can accomplish when you have the strength of ten men and you don't care whether you live or die. Then he'd show up again—at Theresa's or Daniel's, somewhere else, some place where Jack might be even more vulnerable.

No. One way or the other, it ended here, today. Winner takes home all the marbles.

Daniel gripped the steering wheel so hard his knuckles turned white and forced himself to focus. The important thing right now was Emily's safety, not her fidelity.

"Emily, we don't have time to talk! Just listen. The men I told you about—they're here. Jack called and told me to get you and Andi and Theresa to safety. He said the two Bad Kids are—"

"Is that it, is that what you called us—the Bad Kids?" said a male voice in his ear and Daniel almost ran the suburban off the road. "I'd tell you what we called you, but it ain't polite to curse in front of a lady."

"Who is—?" But Daniel knew who it was. "Where's Emily?" He was barely able to force the words out through a mouth so suddenly dry his tongue and palate came apart as reluctantly as two strips of Velcro.

"And that 'safety' part. You can forget about that. Your family ain't safe now, and they're going to get more 'unsafe' with every passing minute."

The voice made a sound like chuckling, but ugly and vulgar, laughter slathered with slime.

"Right now, you've got five of them—minutes, I mean —to get here, or I'm going to shoot the missus or the little girl."

Jack had miscalculated, underestimated the strength of

the possessed man scrambling behind, clawing at the air, reaching out to grab the back of his shirt. He'd thought the broken mechanical thing he'd turned over in the aisle behind him would slow Cole down more than it did. Jack had no idea what the machine was. Half taken apart, it looked like the autopsy of a robot, but the disabled mechanism was the size of a buffalo and must have weighed more than five hundred pounds. He'd never have been able to topple it if hadn't been propped up with boxes where a leg had come off. And when it fell, it wedged in between rows of butcher paper spools six feet across—stacked all the way to the wall.

Jack wasn't sure because he didn't turn around to look, but apparently Cole had merely picked it up like he'd done the boxes full of paper reams, and pitched it backward. Now he was bearing down on Jack, yelling obscenities and threats.

"...I catch you, nigger, I'm gonna bust both your knees...bend them backwards until I hear them pop."

He was panting, the words coming from only a few feet behind Jack as he raced down a narrow aisle between packing crates.

Too close!

He had no choice. He knew the layout of this side of the warehouse well. The other side was full of machinery —not the burrows of boxes that kept vagrants warm at night and hid the activities of hormone-driven teenagers. That was the distribution rather than the storage side of the warehouse. He'd only been there once, in the manager's office. The layout of the rest of that part of the building was completely unknown. But unless he took his chances with a change of direction, Cole would be on him in seconds.

Turning sharply left, Jack burst out into the open area

in the middle of the warehouse and raced toward the door leading to the offices of the small staff on the far side of the building. He could hear Cole behind him, panting, making a sound like the engine of a train.

Jack was in better shape. Thinner, a runner. Cole's massive legs were like tree trunks, but he was stunningly fast. Jack had gained a couple of steps on him when he changed direction and he saw the puddle in time to leap over it. Cole either didn't see it with his one eye, or couldn't jump it quick enough, because he hit it at a dead run. Oil, likely from a leak in a forklift engine.

He heard Cole go down hard, so close Jack heard a muffled grunt of pain and a gasp as the wind was knocked out of him.

Jack made it to the front office door before Cole even got to his feet. If the door was locked… It wasn't. He leapt inside, slammed the door behind him, and snapped the deadbolt—not that it would stop Cole. He pawed the wall for a light switch beside the door. The offices were black as a coal mine with no windows to admit the little light that filtered down from the big windows in the warehouse. He found the switch, and then squinted at the sudden illumination. A chest-high filing cabinet sat next to the door and Jack yanked its drawers open to get the weight out front, and once it was unbalanced, he shoved it from the side until it toppled over, blocking the closed door.

He turned toward the door in the back of the room he thought led to the next office, blowing the dust off the memory of the one time he'd ever been in the office complex. The picture that memory drew in his mind was of inter-connected offices, one leading into the next on the ground floor. In each was a Japanese woman whose vacant smile indicated she probably couldn't speak English. In the back of the office on the end was a staircase leading to more offices similarly configured on the second floor. He was almost certain he remembered a door on the top floor —beside the manager's office with its dignified wood paneling, big cherry desk and incongruous portrait of a totally naked Playboy Bunny occupying one whole wall.

That door had to lead back out into the warehouse, didn't it? Where else could it go? But Jack wasn't absolutely certain it was even there. If it wasn't, he was trapped. If it was, it might be locked. If it wasn't locked, Jack had no idea what lay beyond it.

~

Theresa could hear crashing sounds, like big boxes was falling down out there in the warehouse. Or more likely getting knocked down.

She spoke softly, out loud, didn't bow her head or anything like that. Wasn't nowhere in the Bible said you's supposed to bow your head when you talked to God. And she'd got used to praying out loud all those years ago when her Granny told her that Jesus was her friend and He was always right there next to her, anxious to have a conversation.

She liked to a'talked Jesus's ear off then, tellin' him how she heard things—bad, awful things—that couldn't nobody else hear. And why was that? And that sometimes she smelled things so awful it'd a made you heave up your breakfast if you's smelling them with your nose.

Jesus always listened. She knew he was listening now.

I know you got this, that ain't none of what's happnin' escaped your notice. And I know you don't hold much with a body bein' scared, because that's telling you I don't b'lieve you're big enough to handle my piddly little problems.

She made a humph sound in her throat.

And I also know it ain't news to you that whether I'm supposed to be or not, I am scared spitless right now, way deep in my soul scared!

I never did ask you why it was you made it so's I could sense what was there in the "other." But I'm askin' now. I know what Jack don't. I know what kind of thing's driving Cole, how ugly and mean and evil it is, and it's that knowin' that's so terrifying I feel all hollow and empty inside. Why'd you fix it so's I know? I don't want this, never did want this. I'd a whole lot rather be like other folks that don't see what's actually goin' on around them. Why me?

She stopped, a little smile flirted with the corners of her mouth, and she took in a deep shaky breath.

Reckon how many times a day you hear that—why me? I bet if you wasn't God, you'd be rollin' your eyes. Ain't even a proper question, is it. The real question's why NOT me?

A rumble came from the warehouse, the sound of a pile of something falling to the floor and Theresa flinched. Cole's voice was pure hate, carried to her from far down toward the other end of the warehouse.

"…I catch you, nigger, I'm gonna bust both your knees…bend 'em backwards with my bare hands…'till you hear 'em pop."

~

Jack burst out the door at the end of the upstairs hallway and slapped off the lights behind him. In the interconnected offices downstairs, he'd turned on each office's lights so he could see, locked the door behind him, then raced across the office to the next door, pulling out office chairs, turning over the water cooler—dumped an aquarium in one office—and filing cabinets into Cole's path, then turned the lights back off as he left the room.

Apparently, Cole wasn't bothering to search for the light switches—merely shattered the doors and burst through. He could hear Cole's obscenities when he ran into the debris Jack'd left in his path.

Jack had expected/hoped! this upstairs door led back out into the warehouse. It didn't. It opened onto a landing with a staircase leading down in front of it to an internal hallway below that was lit by the bilious glow from a lone florescent bulb flickering in the ceiling. Obviously, this was the storage area for the office complex. Doors opened off the hallway, three on the left side, two small ones close together, and then a set of double doors on the right. The bathrooms were here, too, side by side, the first two doors on the left.

But there was no door at the end of this hallway leading back out into the warehouse. No door at all. Dead end.

Jack could hear Cole crashing through the last of the office doors on the bottom floor, shattering one after another—hollow core office doors, true, but the crashing and ripping sounded like Cole had brought along a wood-chipper.

Knocking down half a dozen doors, one after the other, required enormous strength and endurance.

Unfortunately, that part didn't matter anymore. Jack was trapped.

When Jack heard Cole on the stairs, he didn't hesitate on the landing any longer. Cole hit the top of the stairs on the second floor as Jack leapt down the back stairs into the storage hallway where he'd make his last stand. Halfway down the stairs, his feet got tangled up. He grabbed for the rail and stopped the worst part of his fall, but he still ended up at the bottom of the stairs, upside down, with his feet sprawled out on the steps above him.

Then Cole appeared at the top of the stairs and grinned down on him. He looked like a creature out of a horror movie, his features "rearranged" when he'd face-planted on the concrete floor after he hit the sheen of motor oil. His lip was split and bleeding, two bottom teeth were missing and one top tooth was broken into a jagged shape like a vampire fang. His bloody nose was mashed over onto his left cheek, where a deep gash sliced down from the top of his ear to the corner of his mouth. His black eye-patch was gone, revealing the sunken crater of a missing eye, angry red, with infected-looking goo draining down out of it.

All those were superficial wounds, of course. The only serious injury Jack could see was Cole's right arm. It was broken in a nasty compound fracture. Blood gushed from the hole of torn flesh in his forearm, where the white stick of the radius or the ulna was protruding through the skin. His right hand and wrist dangled as useless below it as a Christmas ornament.

Cole stood with his left hand on the railing surrounding the landing catching his breath.

Then he began to laugh.

~

The sound was faint, but Theresa knew instantly what it was—laughter. Ugly, mean laughter.

As she sat helpless, she'd strained to hear what was going on, listened to more crashes and rumbles. More cursing. But then the sound of crashes had become muted, like maybe they wasn't outside in the warehouse anymore, but inside, in an office somewhere.

There'd been muffled crashes then, one after another, a whump and then a bam, like somebody was knocking down a wall. They went on and on.

Then the crashes stopped. The silence that followed rang like a Chinese gong inside Theresa's head. The quiet was far more frightening than the crashes had been. Least then she'd known Jack was still all right because he was still out there running from Cole. But what did the silence mean?

Then she heard laughter. Evil laughter.

Lord, I'm not tryin' to tell you your bidness, but you got to help Jack! He can't fight that thing all by his own self. When Cole catches up to him, he's gonna beat him to within an inch of his life, bring him back here and—

Her voice broke in a strangled sob. She caught herself. Stopped and steadied her breathing before she spoke again.

Sorry. I know what scared does. It whispers in your ear things that ain't true a'tall. Scared's a liar! So's hate. Scared lies and hate lies and evil lies. Ain't nothin' but love tells the truth of it. And you is love. You is truth, so I'm comin' to you now—not with a heart full of fear, but with a heart all full up with grateful for what it is you gone do that don't nobody expect. Some'm you've had planned out all along.

____

Chapter Thirty-One

Jack closed his eyes to blot out the sight of Cole gloating on the landing above him and when he opened them again to an upside-down hallway, he was looking right at the box and the telephone pole out of Andi's vision.

"The box and the telephone pole —the capital T's— were beside each other," he heard Daniel say in his head. "They were black and she said the box had small feet."

Jack pulled himself up on his elbows, righted his vision so he was no longer looking at the world upside down. When he looked back over his shoulder at a right-side-up world, the two black shapes he would never have noticed in the dim, flickering light had turned right side up, too. Now, he knew what they were.

Cole was drenched in sweat, panting, gasping, dragging air into his lungs in huge gulps that cut short his laughter in a strangled bark.

"Trapped," he gasped. "…rat in a trap…"

He took a step down and brandished his mangled right arm where the hand dangled at such a grotesque angle beneath it Jack felt a wave of nausea.

"…stick you now, nigger…" He heaved in another huge gulp of air. "… stick you good…"

Cole intended to use the jagged broken bone of his own arm as a dagger!

"Poke holes in you…'til you tell me where Becca is."

Jack slumped back in defeat. Held the pose for a beat, then tensed and pushed off with his feet on the stairs above him. He tucked his head, did a complete backward summersault and came up on his feet facing a surprised Cole.

Then he bolted toward the door beneath the box and the telephone pole, which, right-side-up, formed Japanese characters Jack had learned years ago trying to impress a girl. The characters spelled the word Exit.

He was out the door into the sultry night then, running. Smoke filled the air, much closer now, billowing from the roof of the warehouse to the north, the farm equipment warehouse. Though he couldn't see the fire, he could hear the roar and feel the heat. There were figures lit by a red-orange glow, people running. The fire was coming this way fast.

Theresa!

Cole was right behind, the engine on a freight train, rumbling at him, remarkably fast. But Jack was a step quicker, straining with every ounce of his own strength to reach the slice of light that cut the darkness like a knife from the propped-open door of the warehouse in front of him. Somebody on the night shift crew—probably trying to get a breath of fresh air on the sultry night—had set a brick there. Kicking it out of the way, Jack lunged inside, turned and pulled the door shut after him all in one motion. It locked automatically. This was no hollow core office door. It was metal, mounted in a steel frame in the wall. Breaking through it would be no easy task, not even for Cole.

The voice that had replaced Emily's on the phone was oily and slid greasy words into Daniel's ear.

"You and me, we're gonna have us a nice, long conversation, Dano—that's what that nigger Jack called you, didn't he—Dano?"

Daniel's hand was shaking so badly he could barely hold onto the phone.

"We're gonna keep on talking all friendly like." The ugly voice had a hollow, echoing quality that indicated the phone was on speaker. "Don't want you getting any ideas about calling the cops. Or stopping on the way, maybe. But you wouldn't do a thing like that would you, not when your family's got just..." he paused. "...four more minutes to live."

Daniel grabbed hold of his emotions and calmed his voice.

"I'm on I-71 passing the stadium," Daniel said, trying to sound as reasonable as possible. "Where are you, Victor?"

"Your church, in the...sanctuary." Victor said the word like it tasted bad in his mouth.

"The church! It's impossible to get from where I am to the church in four minutes!"

"Then you got yourself a big problem, don't you, Dano?"

"It's me you want, Victor," Daniel said. "Let my wife and daughter go..." he paused, "...and I'll tell you where Becca is."

"You'd do that, tell me upfront and easy without me

having to do any persuading at all?" Victor was mocking him.

"I'll tell you anything you want to know. Just don't hurt Emily and Andi."

"And you know where Becca is, could lead me right to her, do you?"

Daniel scrambled for something to say to make the lie more convincing.

"Of course, I know where she is. Do you think Jack and I intend to go after your 'boss' alone, only the two of us, without the 'one who comes with the light?'"

Victor made a sound unlike any sound Daniel had ever heard before, an inarticulate cry of rage and frustration and…yes, fear.

"Noooo. You won't get the chance this time."

"Are you sure of that?" Daniel was saying anything he could think of to distract Victor from his five-minute deadline.

He careened his Suburban across three lanes of traffic to the interstate off ramp, thundered down Belmont Street and screeched a right turn. The turn was wide and for a horrifying moment, he was staring into the eyes of a stunned driver coming right at him. But he pulled back into his own lane just in time and pushed his foot to the floorboard.

"I don't think you are sure," he told Victor. "I don't think your boss is sure, either. We already beat him once, you know."

"You won't live long enough to come into his presence ever again, none of you!" the voice roared, but it didn't sound like Victor's voice anymore. It was deeper, throaty and ragged, the voice of a man who has swallowed gravel. Or of a creature that wasn't a man at all.

"You might be able to stop Jack and me. You know

where we are. But you don't know where Becca is. You aren't sure she's not going to show up someday at…"

Where? Daniel had no idea where the creature was.

Then an image, a memory exploded into his consciousness, was propelled out of the shadows in his mind with such force it shook his vision. He recalled what Theresa had said.

"Maybe they's somebody wants you to remember. Somebody's stronger than what made you forget."

He is in a place that defines darkness, that produces darkness the way a lantern produces light. A dry hissing, rattling sound fills his ears and a musty, old-place smell fills his nostrils. But there's a more putrid stench beneath. He can sense it there. Like pus in a boil about to burst, the stench and foulness is only contained by a thin membrane, and to break that membrane is to be totally overwhelmed by the rotting evil it's holding back.

There is a heaviness here, as if the darkness has weight and substance. To move through it requires plowing through something almost solid. It weighs down on Daniel's shoulders so he feels he might be crushed beneath it, like he's holding up something huge and ponderous, a black thing whose size is immeasurable, its bulk unfathomable. He is a speck, a fleck of dust beneath it.

Every step forward requires way more than human strength. Not even Bishop, as strong as he is, could have passed through this corridor without Becca's light. It holds the darkness at bay. Like snarling wolves, the blackness crouches at the edges of the light, ready to pounce. But the illumination coming from the small, frail child beside him cuts the blackness, a scythe through wheat.

He knows, but does not know how he knows, that to stumble, to trip and fall outside the light is to be instantly devoured by the darkness. The darkness hates, too. He can feel the ferocity of the hatred and it almost stops his breathing. The darkness hates him, hates life of any kind, but mostly hates Becca.

The two of them are huddled close, walking down some sort of tunnel, and Daniel suspects that someone seeing the scene from outside would see nothing more sinister than two children walking together, a slender girl and a hulking boy by her side, a boy who'd come to defend her, cringing under her umbrella of protection.

Thoughts appear in his mind, put there by a Daniel he barely knows who is all things foul—cowardly and lustful and angry. He recognizes that Daniel, though he's pretended his whole life not to hear what it whispers in his ear.

"Run!" that Daniel's voice cries in his head. "Get out while you still can."

And oh, how Daniel wants to run, to race screaming back into the world where light lives, to feel the sun on his face and breathe the warm summer air.

He glances back over his shoulder, hoping to see a retreating circle of brightness behind them marking the way out. It's not there, but what is there freezes his heart. He almost stumbles from horror, but if he falls he will not be gobbled up by the darkness. He'll be devoured, eaten alive by what now fills the whole cavern they have just passed through.

Snakes.

And spiders.

Hundreds of them. Thousands of them. A solid, tangled mass of horror that blots out the floor.

The snakes slither along, so many they're twisted and snarled together, every one deadly—diamondbacks, sidewinders, timber rattlers, copperheads, cotton mouths and water moccasins. They are the source of the hiss and rattle he heard but couldn't identify. The bite of even one would mean instant death and there are untold hundreds of them. The snakes stay just beyond the light, visible only in the ambience of its glow. They form a rug knit together with clots of wriggling spiders. Brown recluse spiders, hobo spiders and—

And black widows.

The memory was suddenly gone, popped into nothingness, and Daniel was again in a world of light and a different kind of horror. But the truth the memory had spoken to him filled his whole soul. That was why. A monster from that ever-darkness had killed his baby sister. What he thought he'd imagined was real. The spider did turn and look at him before it bit her.

"…still there, Daniel? Don't you hang up on me. I'm gonna make two dead bodies if—"

"I didn't hang up!" Daniel tried to keep the desperation out of his voice but couldn't. "I didn't. I just…I'm driving so fast I needed both hands on the wheel."

"You better be driving fast. You only got a little over two minutes now."

Daniel was driving like a wild man—and not a police officer in sight! He'd heard sirens earlier, some kind of emergency. Where had they all gone?

"No, wait! I said I'd tell you where Becca is if—"

"And you're the worst liar I ever heard. I ain't gonna get it out of you that easy. But just 'cause you're being so cooperative, I'm gonna give you a choice. You get to decide who I kill."

"Kill? You said I still had—"

"I lied! Wanted to get you here quick without you getting the bright idea to stop off somewhere on the way and gather up some county mounties. Three's too many hostages to handle. Only need two. You get to pick which. Who dies—your wife or your daughter?"

~

The warehouse was empty, evacuated because of the fire. Obviously, workers had leapt up, dropped whatever they were doing and run. A forklift sat in the middle aisle with the motor idling. The door on the elevator beneath the racks of whiskey barrels thirty feet to his left sat open and the barrel wagon was backed up to it, with the back gate off and rails attached.

Another barrel wagon had been abandoned at the far end of the warehouse near the loading dock and another forklift sat driver-less there, too.

Jack stood panting for a moment. He'd done his best to conserve it, but his own strength was about spent. He didn't have a demon riding his coattail amplifying the affect, but Jack was dealing with adrenaline fatigue, too. He'd been fighting for his life and now his muscles were trembling from the effort.

Whump!

Cole was throwing himself at the metal door, apparently intent on battering it down with brute force.

Go for it, big guy!

There was another whump, and this time splinters flew away from where the bolts affixed the metal door frame in the wooden opening. Cole might not be able to shatter the metal door, but he could knock it out of the wall!

Jack looked around. He was too tired to keep running.

He needed a weapon, something to use as a club, maybe, but he saw nothing. Where could he go?

Whump!

Splinters and shards of wood came loose this time. Another couple of good hits…

Jack's scanning eyes landed on a narrow ladder that led up the side of the barrel racks to his left. Cole couldn't negotiate a ladder with only one functioning hand. Jack leapt up the old wood rungs, climbed to the second rack, about fifteen feet off the floor and edged along the railing.

The door jamb finally gave way and Cole crashed into the building with the door and frame.

The man lay on the door where it had fallen, panting, then staggered to his feet. Throwing himself at the metal door had apparently dislocated his right shoulder, so now that whole side of his body was useless, with the arm bone out of its socket and the bones below the elbow shattered. The side and front of his shirt and his pants were soaked in blood from the compound fracture.

Jack called out to him, taunting. "The stairs are that way." He pointed to the other end of the building.

By the time Cole got to the stairs and up them, Jack would be gone.

Jack clambered along the railing toward the barrel wagon that had been left there ready to be unloaded. Cole tracked with him, staying just below him. Suddenly, a piece of the railing Jack had just grasped came loose in his hand. He was off balance and so tired his reflexes weren't fast enough to catch him. He took one final, desperate grasp at the railing, and missed. Then he was falling and the world went dark.

There is a light ahead that spills around the corner of a tunnel, but it isn't a warm glow like the light that radiates around Becca. This light is harsh, bright desert sun that burns your skin and parches your throat so your tongue swells up in your mouth.

This light is the color of old blood. The darkness recedes from it, a viscous black liquid that shines dully in the harsh red glow.

Jack is so tired he would have dropped to his knees if they weren't holding him up, Cole on one side, Victor on the other. The air itself resists Jack's passage, though the others glide through it with ease.

Jack's senses are numb with a kind of terror that defies all reason. An empty, alone horror that totally isolates him. His inner being is utterly solitary, cut off from all life and light, lying naked in a dark that is more than merely the absence of light—a dark that is itself a being, a life form of pure evil.

The harsh light shoves back the gelatinous darkness in the tunnel as they approach a bend in the shaft, and Jack suddenly realizes that he must not go around that corner, that he cannot face whatever it is that's on the other side. But even if he could get out of Cole and Victor's grasp, the air is too thick for movement. He can't run through it, can only stagger forward.

When the three step as one around the corner toward the light, Jack is frozen with shock and the other boys stop when he does. What lies before them cannot be. It is too big to fit in the confines of any room, a lake that stretches out in every direction as far as they can see, receding into the distance where a pewter sky is stitched to the horizon by tendrils of smoke the color of ashes.

It is not a lake of water. It is a lake of liquid fire where flames lick up off the tips of waves like foam on surf.

Jack's legs give way. The two other boys let him collapse to the ground, drag him forward across a black line spray-painted on the smooth white stone and dump him there.

Then Jack hears is. Smells it. He cringes away even as he feels his chin begin to rise up off his chest. He makes no voluntary movement to lift it, but it rises all the same. His head is throbbing, heartbeat bursts in his temples that threaten to explode his skull.

No! He won't look.

His head lifts higher. Can't. Can't look.

But he does.

Jack's eyes popped open and he was disoriented, trapped in a horror world, a nightmare place whose images hung in his mind, refused for a few moments to be washed away by reason. When they did finally dissolve into the wisps of smoke from a dying campfire, reality was little better.

Jack was lying on his back on the floor of the bourbon warehouse in front of the barrel elevator. Hunks of wood from the broken railing, his handcuffs—which had come loose from his belt—and one of the raised barrel guide rails were gouging holes in his back and his head was throbbing in heartbeat bursts, just as before. Each burst blurred his vision, but even blurred he could see Cole Stuart standing above him, one foot on either side of Jack's chest, his grin displaying the bloody gap where his shattered front teeth had been.

Chapter Thirty-Two

Decide who dies.

Emily.

Or Andi.

Not happening, couldn't be happening.

Daniel's breath died in his chest and he had not the strength to pull more air into his lungs.

"Listen pal, I'm gonna pick for you if you don't hurry up. Who's it gonna be?

"No, please, listen. I…you can't…don't, please don't. It's me you want. Take me. Please, take me instead of them."

"You got ninety seconds. Ticking down now. I got me a real good watch. Took it off a smart-mouth orderly. He said he wanted me to have it since he didn't need it anymore. It's fine, got a sweep second hand. Coming up on a minute now."

"Don't…" But there were no words left.

Emily.

Or Andi.

Who lives?

Who dies?

He could not possibly make such a choice.

God, please…

No other words formed.

"Thirty seconds."

~

"There's no decision to be made," Emily said.

She'd been silent through the whole nightmare conversation, trying to think of some way out.

The "handyman" had dragged her and Andi into the sanctuary. Unlike the brightly-lit Fellowship Hall, the worship center had no windows. They stood now in the center aisle, down from the altar, while a demon-possessed madman discussed with her husband whether she or her daughter would die.

She'd have to jump him, of course, knock the gun away somehow, though he had twelve inches and a hundred fifty pounds on her and nothing she did was likely to cause him any damage.

She held Andi against her, turned the little girl's face away from the man and squeezed her so tight she must surely be strangling the child.

When Andi looked at the…man, what did she see?

Emily could hear Dan's desperate voice over the speaker.

"Take me," he said. "Let them go and take me."

Those words stabbed a dagger of regret into her heart. What she'd done to him—he deserved so much better than that.

When the man said "thirty seconds," she knew it was all over. She wasn't afraid, just unutterably sad about all the weeks and months and years of Andi's life she was going to miss.

All that mattered now, though, was getting this last part right.

"You will kill me and let my little girl go," she said, and was pleasantly surprised that her voice sounded firm, didn't tremble.

Then she felt rage and revulsion rise up into her chest and she let it take over. It gave her the power and strength she needed. "You will let my little girl go because I'm here to tell you—you vile beast!—that if you harm this child, if you touch her, you will have to kill me, too. You understand what I'm saying? I will rip your throat out with my fingernails. I will—"

"Ok, lady, I get it. I get it." He was amused, not afraid. "A kid's easier to control anyway. You get the short straw."

And just like that, Emily knew she was about to die.

But that was an acceptable trade-off if she could save Andi as her final act on this earth. She pointed toward a small door that opened off the back of the dais where the pulpit sat. It was fiberglass—the pulpit—because Dan hadn't wanted there to be anything between him and the congregation when he preached.

"I'm taking my daughter in there." She didn't ask, she informed. "It's the closet where the choir robes are stored. I'm going to close her up in there so she doesn't have to watch her mother…"

She let the words trail off. It seemed to take a long time to take in a breath and let it back out again so she could continue.

"You let me do that and I will…go willingly. Otherwise…" She literally bared her teeth at him. It just happened; she didn't plan it. She bared her teeth and both hands cramped into perfectly manicured claws. "This is going to be ugly."

The man actually barked out a cough of laughter.

"Whatever." He sneered. "I don't care where you stick her. But you try anything…"

"What's left to try?"

Emily grabbed Andi's hand and led her up the steps to the dais where the door opened off the back.

Tears streamed down the little girl's cheeks but she was too frightened to cry out loud. She looked up pleadingly into her mother's face.

"Mommy, no…please don't."

Dear God, she's going to remember this moment for the rest of her life. If I can give her a life.

When Emily got to the door, she knelt and the little girl launched herself at her mother, grabbed her in a choke hold and burst into hysterical tears. Emily was spared having to think of "last words." She knew exactly what she had to say.

She pulled the child's arms away from her neck and took Andi's face in her hands, kissed her forehead and whispered in her ear.

"When I close this door, you run. Up the ladder into the pageant storage room. Don't close the trap door behind you, he might hear it. And you hide. You're good at hide-and-seek. You can find some place to hide he'll never find you. Do you understand me?"

Andi merely looked at her, mute, and nodded.

Emily couldn't drag it out, had to do this quick before the idiot had the presence of mind to check for himself to make sure the room was a closet with only one door.

"I love you!" she cried fiercely. She opened the door, shoved Andi into the room and closed the door firmly behind her.

Emily stood and squared her shoulders. Now, she had to go back to the demon in front of the altar and let him kill her.

~

Daniel was shouting into the phone, yelling…he didn't even know what, incoherent words, pleading, cursing. But the hollow sound was gone, so apparently Victor had switched the phone off speaker.

Then he heard Emily's voice, breathless. Victor had handed her the phone.

"I got him to let me put Andi in the choir robe closet," she said. It registered somewhere in his brain what she was telling him, but he couldn't process it. "I closed her up in there so she won't have to…watch."

He careened around a corner onto Market Street at the end of the block leading to the church, jumped the curb, drove across two yards and blasted through the hedge on the other side. He was probably doing sixty miles an hour when he ripped out the rose garden and grape vine arbor in front of the church. Then he locked up the brakes and the Suburban fishtailed, tires screeching, slid sideways across the church lawn, all five of the drop-off lanes in front of the building and the sidewalk and came to rest only a couple of yards from the front door. As he leapt out of the car, Emily's voice sounded calm but tear-clotted in his ear, holding on, trying not to cry.

"Dan…listen to me. I love you. I really do. I mean it. And I'm sorry… I'm so, so sorry. Please forgive—"

"Emily, honey, it's Ok. The five minutes aren't up. I'm right out—"

Then he heard a single gunshot.

"Emily!" he cried into the phone. Then dropped it, burst through the front doors of the church, ran past the Welcome Center desk and into the sanctuary, calling out, "Emily, Em—"

Her body lay crumpled on the floor in the center aisle in a growing puddle of blood.

~

Theresa'd been concentrating so hard on listening—straining to hear a sound from Jack or Cole, that she didn't even notice it at first. It was only when she decided they weren't in the warehouse anymore—they'd run out into the night, that she saw it filter down out of the ceiling. Then she'd managed to kid herself for another five or six minutes after that, trick herself into believing it was mist. Or fog.

Yeah, right—fog.

That was just because Bishop wasn't here.

Wasn't nobody who knew her would tell you Theresa Washington was anything except an independent, secure, tough-as-boot-leather woman. The undisputed leader of the Christian women in her church, on the board of the library and the crisis pregnancy center, volunteered in the soup kitchen. But Bishop knew and understood. He knew her, knew she was who she needed to be to keep the wheels on life, could screw herself up to standing all tall and firm and strong. He was the only person—except her grandma…and Jesus—who knew she wasn't strong at all, that she wasn't a leader. He knew she was shy, painfully so, and introverted, that it would have been fine with her if she didn't never have to see nobody but Bishop—ever. She needed him, depended on him, was who she was in response to who he was for so many years she didn't know how to do things, how to do life without him.

And she sure as Jackson didn't know how to do dying all by herself! How do you wrap your mind around the reality that you're taped to a chair inside a building that's on fire?

A building full of paper.

The smoke had hung up there high in the ceiling at first, of course. But gradually it had started to sink. It had just about reached the top of that metal elevator cage that Cole was gonna lock Jack in when she heard the crackling sound in the ceiling.

"Bishop…you listenin' to me?

I know I ain't s'posed to talk to the dead. I know you's busy being in paradise, and don't likely have time for the goin's on in the world you done left behind.

But you need to listen to me, no matter what you're doing. You hear me?"

Sweat rolled down her forehead and into her eyes. It stung, made her squint, but she couldn't wipe it away. After the smoke started leaking in, it'd gotten hot quick. It'd already been stuffy in that closed-up warehouse but the temperature had shot up in the past few minutes quicker than her feet heated up when she stuck them in front of that little heater Bishop'd gotten her to warm her toes on cold winter nights.

"I didn't figure to die by burning to death, Bishop! Wasn't nothing I ever considered. If you's here and we could do it together…but…burning up, all by myself here in the dark. How'm I gonna do that?"

The last words were all tangled up with a sob, and crying took her for a time. Not long, though. She could see flames, now, dancing in the roof high overhead, dribbling little sparks that cascaded down like shiny red rain. The sparks had already started a fire in the boxes that Jack—

Jack! And Daniel, too. She had real bad feelings about the both of them. Maybe she was just…what was it that shrink'd said when they was in grief counseling after Isaac disappeared—how you sometimes projected whatever it was you's feeling off on other people.

She didn't think that was it, though. She had an awful feeling in her gut that told her they was in a real bad way and her gut feelings was almost always right.

And here she was whinin' about her own problems when those young men was fighting monsters right out of the pit of hell with nothing but they bare hands.

Lord, forgive me for being so selfish to think of nobody but my own self. I come to you and lift up Daniel and Jack to you and ask for your protection around them and those they love.

She let out a breath, felt a little better, 'til she drew it back in and caught a strong whiff of smoke that wasn't coming from the ceiling down. It was coming from nearby. She sniffed, followed the scent. First she saw a glow, then flames licked up out of a box of construction paper not fifty yards away. Sparks had set it on fire. It was gonna be a real bonfire in here in a couple of minutes.

She started coughing in earnest now.

Lord, don't you take me out of this world before you let me know them boys is safe!

When Daniel saw Emily's body, time unhooked from the world and left it dangling in a vast, empty void not governed by the laws of physics and reality. Daniel moved through that void, both so fast he had no memory of crossing the distance between him and the crumpled form on the floor, and so slowly he couldn't get there, was in a slow motion video where every movement seemed to take a lifetime.

There was so much blood. A pool of it, a puddle. He knelt in the blood and felt it soak through the leg of his pants. It was warm.

Emily was motionless. Her face looked like she was only asleep, and if he'd reach out gently and shake her shoulder, she'd open those big blue eyes and see him. You had to wake Emily gently, she hated being startled from sleep. When they first got married, he'd set the alarm clock in the other room and taught himself to be such a light sleeper that he'd hear it and be able to get to it and switch it off before it woke Emily. Then he'd return to the bed and look at her sleeping for awhile, watch her face, the gentle rise and fall of her chest.

Her chest didn't rise and fall now. The whole front of her shirt was soaked red, just like Andi's Minnie Mouse shirt had been. She lay as still and perfect as a porcelain doll. Like he could lean over and kiss her forehead as he did some mornings—early on, not anymore—or take her hand in his to wake her. But he knew when he did, she wouldn't move.

He reached out and picked up her limp hand anyway out of the puddle of blood and held it tenderly, aware on some level that he was sobbing. But the emotional release was only on the surface. In the depths of his heart he was inconsolable.

Then he heard an inhuman cry, a roar of rage, huge and Jurassic, and looked up to see a fat, bald man—a man with a gun!—standing in the open doorway of the choir robe room. Victor Alexander was sputtering in fury, inserting expletives every third word—between the syllables of some words.

"…tricked me! The kid's gone."

He seemed to become aware of Daniel's presence for the first time.

"Where's it go—the trapdoor in that closet—where's it lead to?"

Daniel merely looked at him, didn't move.

The door in the back right corner of the ceiling in the room lined with choir robes granted access to a gigantic storage area on the third floor of the church that was stacked from floor to ceiling with the makings of a full-sized Broadway production. It contained every element of the church's annual pageant called The Gospel Story that packed the sanctuary with almost fifty thousand people during its two-week run every year before Easter.

The disassembled set was there, props, costumes, stage lighting and makeup facilities for a cast of five hundred people—from half a dozen life-sized chariots for the Roman Centurions, to the three saddles lined with purple and gold satin that were placed on live camels for the Bethlehem scene, along with swords, water casks, spears, staffs, baskets and peasant costumes.

During the pageant, the choir robe closet was transformed into a "bird room," where the doves used in the temple sacrifice scene and the trained dove that landed on Jesus's shoulder in the John the Baptist scene were kept, along with the chickens for the cleansing of the temple scene.

The third-floor doors leading into the storage room would be locked, of course, so Andi would have no way to get out of the room. But if she hid well in there, nobody would ever find her.

"We're gonna have us a little talk, you and me, about old friends and the good ole days when we was kids," Victor said. "You're gonna tell me where Becca is—or that little girl of yours is gonna wind up as dead as her mama."

This was the man who had ended Emily's life, who had taken away from her all the days that should have been stretching out in front of her—Christmas mornings and walks on the beach and fixing Andi's hair for the prom. No, not the man, the being, the entity, the demon, the monster from hell whose presence in the world was an affront to the laws of God and nature.

Grief and despair drained out of Daniel like water out a hole in a bucket. They were replaced by a rage he didn't know he was capable of. He itched to leap on the monster and strangle the life out of him, slam his fist into his face over and over until…but there was Andi to think of. Emily had died protecting the child, had given their daughter a chance to live. He would do no less.

Daniel let go of Emily's hand and rose slowly to his feet, aware that his own hands were bloody—Emily's blood!—and he didn't wipe it off on his pants. He wanted it there, liked the warmth of it on his skin.

The slow-motion sluggishness that had weighed him down vanished; the anguish that had clouded his senses disappeared. He was hyper-alert, hyper aware. His mind raced, not with random erratic thoughts, but processing and planning, considering options with the clarity of a computer.

"I asked you a question." Victor actually snarled. "That door in the closet, where's it lead to?"

"To another closet," Daniel's voice was firm, strong. "A real big one, on the third floor. From there, you can go anywhere. Andi's gone. "

Vic cocked his head to the side and studied Daniel.

"Now why is it I don't b'lieve you?"

Daniel struggled to keep his face impassive.

"Why is it I think she's just hidin' up there somewhere?"

Daniel said nothing.

"Let's see!"

Vic motioned to Daniel in a come-here gesture. "You get in there and climb up that ladder and call her, tell her to come to Daddy."

"No," Daniel said, and watched Vic's eyes narrow in anger. "What are you going to do—shoot me?"

Victor couldn't kill Daniel and they both knew it.

Then a sly, sinister grin spread over the gunman's ugly face.

"Ok, then I'll call her. I'll tell her I'm gonna blow a hole in her daddy big as the one in her mommy if she doesn't come here right now."

Andi would come if he said that, and she'd become the sacrificial lamb. There was no limit to the horror Victor would inflict on the child to induce Daniel to provide information Daniel didn't have.

He had to keep Victor from calling out to Andi.

That was it then. That was what Daniel had to do to save his daughter. He harbored no illusions about his chances in a fight with the super-powered demon-possessed fat man, but there was hope that somebody—lots of some-bodies—must have seen his spectacular Nascar appearance at the church. Surely, one of those somebodies had called the police. Daniel had to stay out of Victor's grasp, keep him occupied and away from Andi, until help arrived.

Without a word, Daniel bolted out of the sanctuary.

"Hey! Don't you…I'll shoot…" Victor called after him.

But he didn't. After a moment's hesitation, Daniel heard the thundering footsteps of the man running across the sanctuary in pursuit.

Chapter Thirty-Three

"If I hadn't broken your fall, you'd have busted your head and spilled your brains all over the floor," Cole told Jack.

The words had the lack-of-resonance sound occasioned by Cole's inability to breathe through his nose. It lay in a swelling lump on his left cheek. Blood drained out of it over Cole's mouth and dripped on Jack's shirt off his chin. Cole didn't notice. Didn't notice the trail of blood on the warehouse floor from the ragged compound fracture of his right arm either, a trail that must connect to a similar trail of blood all the way back to the other warehouse.

How was he still standing?

"And I need all your brains to stay right where they are so you can tell me where I can find the little fair-haired girl named Becca."

The chase was over now. It had finally come to this, to beating the Incredible Hulk in hand-to-hand combat. Long odds, that. Real long odds. Still, Jack had a card or two left to play. He had a chance if he could get Cole in close where he could reach him. To do that, he had to go for motor dysfunction.

Jack curled his left hand into a fist and drove a round-house punch with all his strength into the femoral nerve in the inner thigh of Cole's right leg and Cole's knee collapsed out from under him like a tent with the center pole removed. The other knee responded in a sympathetic reflex and in seconds the man who'd been towering above Jack was now on his knees straddling Jack's waist.

Off balance and with no use of his right arm, Cole had been forced to catch himself with his left arm, and Jack now knocked that out from under him with a blow to the inside of his elbow. As it collapsed, Jack lifted with his left leg and Cole tumbled over onto his side and Jack rolled over on top of him.

In rapid succession, Jack landed two punishing blows to Cole's chest—using his right elbow, a harder, sharper weapon than a fist. He actually heard ribs snap, and slammed the elbow down again hoping to drive the jagged bones into Cole's lungs. He hammered another elbow shot into Cole's sternum and a fist into the front of his neck hoping to fracture his trachea.

Cole's punching power was limited. Lying on his back, he couldn't draw back his arm to gain momentum. So, instead, he grabbed Jack around the neck, pulled him toward his chest and delivered a devastating head butt, so hard the impact split Jack's scalp and blood poured down his forehead into his eyes, momentarily blinding him. Then Cole powered Jack off him, dumped Jack onto his back, and rose up on his knees beside him. With his only func-tioning hand, he hammered a blow into Jack's belly. As Jack gasped for breath, Cole drew back his fist and then stopped, barely holding his rage in check.

"I ought to smash your forehead back into your brain." The voice that rumbled out of Cole's throat was not his own. He was panting, spraying blood splatter with every word. "I ought to crush your teeth back into your throat, and shatter your sinuses. I ought—" He drew in a deep breath. "But then you'd be dead and I still wouldn't know where sweet Becca is."

Jack finally gasped in the breath Cole had knocked out of him, and watched an evil grin spread out over the ruin of Cole's face.

"You can't run if you can't see," Cole said. "I'm gonna make you eat your own eyeballs, nigger." He reached out toward Jack's face. "Gouging out an eye—that's reeeeal painful—I know, I've done it myself."

Jack turned his head to the side, straining away from Cole's hand. And that's when he saw it—saw them. It took him a moment to make the connection and to realize that the fat lady hadn't sung after all.

~

Theresa couldn't breathe; thick smoke strangled her. Then she remembered something she seen once on some television show. The fella had said not to stand up if you smelled smoke when's you's in bed, but to roll off onto the floor, said the air was better there.

She needed to get down on the floor, somehow tip the chair over. Rocking her body from side to side, she tried to throw the chair off balance on one side or the other. That didn't work.

Maybe she could topple it backwards. She lifted the front chair legs a couple of inches off the floor with her toes, then tried to throw her weight backward. The chair rocked back, the front legs came briefly off the floor, then it clunked down again.

The air had gotten so thick with smoke Theresa had to hold her breath, now, afraid if she drew in even one lung full she'd never stop coughing. She concentrated, put every speck of strength she had into her toes, pushed off a second time, and threw her head back to slam her weight backward in the chair. The front legs of the chair rose up off the floor higher than the first time. Then she hung there, going neither forward nor back for a time that couldn't possibly have lasted as long as it seemed to Theresa.

Then the chair tumbled backward and hit the floor and Theresa banged her head painfully on the wooden planks. Dizzy, coughing, it took her a moment to realize what else had happened during the fall. The old chair had shattered. The seat back with the arms still attached to it broke away from the seat bottom. The back legs gave way, splaying out in both directions as the front legs broke off the chair in a unit still connected to each other by the bar in the middle. The net effect of it all was that Theresa was lying on the floor on the crushed remains of the chair she'd been taped to.

She rolled over onto her side. The seat-back and chair arms she was strapped to rolled with her, no longer attached to anything else. Her legs were still taped securely to the front chair legs, but the chair legs were no longer affixed to the seat.

She lay panting, gasping in air that was, indeed, much better down here. Then she rolled onto her back again, bent her knees and began to scoot along the floor on the chair back, inching herself toward the elevator cage.

"What I must look like!" she said aloud. Maybe to Bishop. Maybe to God. Maybe to both of them. "A big fat ole black caterpillar that ain't never gone be a butterfly."

If she could get to that elevator, maybe she could send

it down to the basement with her in it. Air'd be a whole lot cleaner down there.

~

Suddenly, Andi heard a voice calling her. Not in her ears, though, in her head. It was Princess Buttercup.

She was squeezed into the big basket that sat by the doorway of a house in the woman-at-the-well scene. Andi used to play in the basket during pageant rehearsals—but she'd been a lot smaller then. Now the basket was only barely big enough for her, but that was good because from the outside it didn't look like anybody could possibly fit into it.

The huge storage room was dark. There were light switches on the far wall by the doors leading out to the third floor, but Andi didn't need any more than the dim glow shining up through the open trap door to find her way. She'd burrowed by feel to the back of the room where she knew she'd find the basket, had crawled into it and put the lid back on it. Even if that monster did figure out where she was—how could he?—he'd have to unload the whole room to get to her.

But maybe the demon could sense her somehow, or had special hearing that could pick out the rattling beat of her heart. She tried to calm her ragged breathing, but every time she thought about the demon crouched on the man's shoulders, her heart started hammering away again.

This one was even uglier than the one made of wasps that sat on the head of the man who'd shot Miss Lund and Mr. Bishop. She hadn't gotten a real good look at that one through the crack in the storage room door, but she knew it didn't have a face that looked like a lizard—with slanted eyes and no nose at all, a mouth with jagged teeth and a tongue that flitted in and out of it, forked like the tongue of a snake she saw once on the Earth Channel. It didn't stink, either, like the one on the fat man did, a horrible stench that made her heave like she was going to throw up. There was a brown stream of something oozing out beneath the demon that smelled like—worse than a baby's diaper. It ran down the fat man's back and dripped on the floor in a sticky puddle.

The demon on the fat man had those tentacle things, like the arms of an octopus, but more of them and they were stuck into the man, into his back and his cheek, one big one into his neck. They looked like the sprouts that grew out of an onion if it got knocked down behind the bin and nobody found it for a long time. This demon had red eyes, too, without any black spot in the middle of them at all. And no eyelids to hide them. He'd turned those red eyes on her when she came into the Fellowship Hall, and she'd screamed.

Maybe those red eyes could see her no matter where she hid. She held her breath and listened to the silence. It felt like the silence was listening to her, too. Maybe the demon would make the man come for her and—

She didn't let her mind finish. That man had said he would shoot her mommy. She'd heard a bang, like the sound of a gunshot in the movies. It wasn't a gunshot, though. It was something else. She didn't know what, but something else.

Andi, she heard again. Come here, Sweetheart, quick.

Andi didn't move.

Come now, Andi. I need you to come right now.

All of a sudden, light shone through the wicker all around her, light so bright it splattered the inside of the basket with shining jewels. Andi slowly lifted the lid, just enough to peek out. The brilliance was coming from a form floating above the open trap door, a brilliance that cast no shadows. It was Princess Buttercup, and yet it wasn't. It was more than Princess Buttercup, a stunningly beautiful being in the white dress Andi recognized, only it was shimmering like each thread was made out of light. Wings with sparkling feathers rose up high in the air above her and in her hand she held the most amazing thing Andi had ever seen. It was a sword with a handle of gold and a blade made out of…they had to be diamonds. Each stone reflected—no, refracted—light like the glass prism Miss Donaldson kept on her desk in science class. Alive with thousands of flickering rainbows, the blade was both beautiful and terrible, more powerful and dangerous than anything Andi'd ever seen. Yet the sword seemed somehow delicate in Princess Buttercup's hand, fragile and perfect and…holy.

"Hurry," Princess Buttercup said.

So Andi pushed the lid off the basket, crawled out and through all the other props. When she got to the trap door, the light still shone bright, but Princess Buttercup was no longer in it.

~

Daniel was about out of gas, had barely been able to keep out of Vic's grasp.

Vic had been skinny as a kid. Now he was an overweight, out-of-shape slob, but hyped up on adrenaline, he was as fast as a striking cobra. Daniel only managed to elude him because he knew the layout of the church—with its interconnected classrooms, prayer rooms, craft and activity rooms. He dashed from one to another, planning his route in his head, hearing Vic behind him, charging like a bull.

Victor almost caught Daniel in the Children's Ministry wing, roared into the activity area only a couple of seconds behind Daniel. Vic's big hand fastened on the back of Daniel's collar, but he wrenched free and dived into the opening of the Play Cave in the side wall of the room. A model cave with the lumpy walls of a real cavern, the tunnel twisted and turned, went back twenty feet under the raised floor of the room next door.

Daniel felt Vic's hand tighten around his ankle and kicked it viciously with the other foot, knocked it loose and scrambled farther in so he was too far for Victor to reach. He smelled Victor then—the reek of his unwashed body was sickening.

"Come out of there," Victor yelled. The cave was a tight fit for Daniel. It would be impossible for Victor to squeeze his fat bulk into it. He couldn't reach Daniel, couldn't shoot him. What was he going to do? If Daniel stayed in the cave, he'd be safe from the monster until help came.

But Andi wouldn't.

As if Vic had read his mind—had he?—the fat man leaned over the mouth of the cave and shouted into it.

"It's you or the kid, Dano. I'm gonna go back to that closet and call her. When she comes, I'm gonna twist her head off her shoulders like the top off a pickle jar."

Daniel crawled as fast as he could until he had completed the circuitous route the whole length of the cave tunnel and came out the opening in the room next door. He took a couple of deep gulps of air and ran out of the room and down the hallway, knowing Vic would hear his footsteps on the tile floor. As he rounded the corner in the hall, Vic burst out of the Play Cave room and raced after him.

Then Daniel did the only thing he could think to do. He was running out of options, so he turned into the hallway that led to the stairs to the belfry. It was a warm night. The neighbors might be out on their patios or back decks. He could yell for help.

It was a chance. He couldn't outrun the adrenaline-juiced Vic for much longer, couldn't get enough of a lead to find a phone and call 911. The belfry was a dead end, a last hope, but it was outside.

He took the stairs two at a time, the stitch in his side so painful it brought tears to his eyes. He was halfway up the circular staircase before Victor burst through the door below and leapt onto the bottom step. Adrenaline or not, Victor's body was so fat, he had trouble negotiating the narrow, twisting staircase. But he was coming all the same. He was coming.

Daniel blew through the doorway in the back wall of the bell tower, raced to the railing and started shouting, "Help! Call the police! Help!"

He ran around to the other side, called out with all the power of his preaching voice. "Call the police! Somebody help. He's going to kill—!"

Vic's long fingers closed around the back of Daniel's neck, pulled him away from the railing and flung him to the floor.

"No, he ain't gonna kill you," Vic said. He was breathing hard, panting in great gulps that sounded like a horse. Sweat was beaded on his face. A rancid stench pulsed off the heat of his body. "He's only gonna hurt you."

Vic kicked Daniel savagely in the side and Daniel

doubled up in pain. Vic kicked him again and Daniel cried out in agony, certain that the blow had broken a rib. But Vic cut the cry short by slamming his work boot deep into Daniel's belly.

"Hurt you bad."

All the wind whooshed out of Daniel and he couldn't seem to draw any more back in.

Daniel can't breathe. He can't draw in a breath. The air is too thick to breathe now, and as putrid as a well in the depths of which things had drowned and laid there rotting.

But that's not why he can't breathe it. He can't pull air into his lungs because what he sees has driven all breath out of him. Forever. The horror of it has driven everything out of his mind and filled it with a boiling black ugliness that burns away thought and desire, past, present and future. Burns everything out of his mind so the image is all that fills him.

A creature has risen out of the flames of a burning red sea. A creature made of fire. The fire lights the cavern and Daniel sees Jack on the blackened rocks beside the sea. He is on his knees, looking up at the monster.

There are other people here, too, he thinks. From the corner of his eye he can see figures off to the side. But he cannot move his eyes to look at them because his vision is nailed to the creature.

Then he feels fingers entwine with his, small fingers, warm, and soft. Becca has taken his hand. He tries to turn and look at her, but then the creature before him roars.

Daniel hears the sound with every molecule in his body. His ears go deaf, but he hears the sound with his bones and his tissue and his blood. The roar is more than sound, it is a single pure thing, flawless for what it is, a wine glass touched with a fork that emits a note in perfect pitch. Clear and horrible beyond description. It is the sound of absolute, consummate evil and to hear it is to die.

Vic sneered at Daniel, curled in a fetal position on the floor of the belfry.

"Won't kill you, but I'll make you wish you's dead." He lifted his foot as if to slam it down on Daniel's face and Daniel instinctively lifted a hand to ward off the blow. Vic grabbed his forearm and forced his hand backward on it. Daniel heard the pop when his wrist broke, but had no breath to scream out the agony he felt.

"I'm gonna drag you down these stairs and you're gonna call that little girl of yours. Then you're gonna watch me cut off little pieces off of her until you tell me where to find Becca."

Daniel's mind could form only one clear thought.

Andi, Baby, stay hidden somewhere so deep you can't hear his voice or mine. Don't come out for anything.

In the sanctuary below the belfry, Andi walked slowly out of the choir robe closet and started across the dais.

Chapter Thirty-Four

Theresa lay on the floor of the elevator coughing hard now, coughing with every breath.

Still, it had sure enough been worth a try.

She'd scooted herself like a worm across the floor to the elevator and managed to get inside, then struggled to get up on her creaky old knees so she could get to the button on the control panel, maybe push it with her nose.

That was the first time she'd been close enough to get a good look at the padlock Cole had hung on the elevator door. He hadn't just hung it there, he'd locked it in place, hooked it around a bar of the cage, and fastened it to a bar on the elevator door.

The door couldn't shut. And the elevator wouldn't run with the door open.

Game over.

Thick, black, deadly smoke was relentlessly sinking toward her, and she had nowhere to run.

But the effort to get to the elevator hadn't been totally wasted. Because the elevator was a cage, it didn't make a complete seal with the shaft that stretched out below it into the basement and she could smell cool, damp air in the crack between the floor and the elevator. She was grateful for it, fresh and clean, soothing her, though she understood now that she'd been given that smoke as a gift. She was gonna pass out soon from breathing it. It might even kill her, but if it didn't, she wouldn't know it when the fire did.

She couldn't pray out loud anymore because she didn't have any breath. But you didn't have to be able to speak to talk to God.

I'm coming home, Lord. Won't it be fine to see yore face, to know what you look like after I been imagining it for all these years. I'll cry when I see you, I know I will. Or sing, or dance or fall down on the floor laughing—somethin' grand.

A coughing jag interrupted her, the room was spinning, twirling around and around her, making her dizzy.

And soon's you and me've had us a nice long talk, I wanna see Bishop.

Then the image of a face, worn fuzzy around the edges with time, came to her mind and she actually smiled.

Bishop and Isaac!

Jack stared at the two silver circles for only a heartbeat, then shot a glance at the red triangle. Putting it together in his head. Working it out. Yes! He had only seconds to respond.

"No!" Jack cried. "Please, not my eyes!" He rolled himself into a protective fetal position facing away from

Cole, shaking his head violently and wailing. "I don't want to be blind."

When he rolled onto his side, Jack picked up one of the two silver circles now beneath him. He used his thumb to flip the catch, hooked the handcuff to the barrel trailer rail and snapped it shut.

"Don't hurt me anymore," he begged, his voice hysterical, as he gathered up some dust and a handful of wood chunks from the broken ladder. "Cole, please! I can't…my head…my head hurts…"

Jack suddenly went rigid for two seconds—as stiff as a plank. Then he began to jerk spastically, making a low moaning sound deep in his throat, his legs flailing.

"Hey!" Cole said. "Don't you have a stroke on me!" Cole reached out his only good hand and rolled Jack over on his back.

Jack threw the dust and splinters into Cole's face, right into his lone eye. When Cole instinctively reached up to wipe his eye. Jack grabbed his injured right hand, dangling beneath the broken arm, and snapped the other handcuff shut around the wrist.

In one motion, Jack rolled to the side and leapt into the small empty space between the barrel rails and the wall. He reached out then and took hold of the red triangle— the chock holding the barrels in place on the sloped bed of the barrel wagon.

Cole could see well enough to understand what was happening. He sneered at Jack and yanked on the handcuff to break it away from the rail.

Nothing happened. He grabbed his injured hand with his good hand and yanked again. It didn't come free.

He'd used it up. All the strength he had was finally gone. Cole's engine had blown.

A look of horror and fear, rage and hatred washed over

his shattered face. Then there was something else. In his eye, a flash, like Jack had seen that day years ago. The man whose body and life had been hijacked by a demon looked out at Jack through the one clear blue eye. For an instant, their eyes held and locked, and in that moment Jack understood. The real Cole Stuart who was about to die was grateful.

Jack yanked out the chock.

The first barrel crashed to the ground in front of Cole, knocked him backward, and rolled over his leg. Cole shrieked and reached up to keep the barrel from rolling any farther. Then the second barrel hit the ground behind the first and crashed into it. There was a moment's hesitation, then a grunt and the first barrel rolled down the length of Cole's body. Followed by the second. And the third.

Jack stood and watched all eight of them, one after another, smash Cole's body. When the last barrel had dropped off the wagon and rolled over Cole and into the elevator, Jack stood for a moment longer. Until that instant, that flash of humanity, Jack had not stopped to consider what it must be like to be possessed by a demon. He shuddered, then turned his back on the form lying crushed on the ground between the rails. It looked like road kill.

Jack started slowly up the incline—and smelled smoke. He looked up and saw it boiling down out of the roof on the far end of the warehouse. It'd be on fire in…

If this warehouse was catching fire, that meant the fire had spread from the fireworks factory through the other warehouses to ignite it.

Theresa!

~

Andi walked in something like a trance across the dais from the choir robe closet to the spot on the floor where her mother lay in a pool of blood.

He did it. He did shoot her.

"Mommy?" she said, maybe out loud or maybe not. She knew her mommy couldn't hear her no matter how she said it. Mommy was dead.

She knelt in the puddle of blood beside her mother and a big hole opened up in Andi where her belly should have been. The emptiness grew and grew until it was so big nothing in the world would ever be able to fill it up again.

She felt fat, hot tears slide down her face but she didn't think she was crying. Crying came from that place in her belly. That's where she felt sad and hurt and afraid, and that place was gone now. She couldn't cry, though her throat hurt and tears dripped off her chin into the pool of her mother's still warm blood.

Then she heard Princess Buttercup's voice, not in her ear, in her head.

Andi, ring the bell!

Andi looked around, uncomprehending. Why would Princess Buttercup…?

Ring the bell! Hurry. Princess Buttercup paused, then added, Andi, do it for Daddy.

Andi leapt to her feet and ran the full length of the sanctuary and out into the vestibule. She took the steps to the bell-cord room two at a time, threw open the door and flipped on the light switch.

The cord hung there in the middle of the room. And the sight of it slipped neatly into its shape that'd been seared into her mind.

Andi raced across the room to the wooden chairs

pushed against the wall. She shoved the nearest one out into the room. Not right beneath the rope, off to the side.

She grabbed the rope, pulled once on it like Daddy always did to unfasten it from the clip high above. Then she climbed up onto the chair, took a deep breath and leapt. She got a good grip on the rope and her weight pulled it down so far she had to lift her feet to keep them from touching the floor. She hadn't been this tall the last time she and Daddy played the game.

She heard the dong of the bell high above her and rode the bell rope back up into the air.

~

"…little pieces off her until you tell me what I want to know," Vic snarled at Daniel. "Where's Becca?"

Vic reached out, grabbed a fistful of the front of Daniel's shirt, and hauled him to his feet as easily as lifting a rag doll. He held Daniel upright with only one hand.

"Stand up!" he ordered, and Daniel set his feet under himself, certain that he would not be able to hold up his own weight when Vic let go. "You don't want me to have to carry you out of here. If you don't have to be in one piece so you can walk, maybe I'll snap your back like I done this."

He grabbed Daniel's hand below the broken wrist, and twisted it. Daniel's scream sounded mewling and pathetic even to his own ears, and the world started to go black around him. He fought to stay conscious and somehow managed to remain standing, swaying. Vic shoved him down the catwalk around the side of the big bell toward the belfry door.

Time slowed down then. Daniel seemed to take a long time to make the few steps around the bell and he couldn't drag his eyes off the rope. There was something odd…familiar…

Then he saw the rope tighten, slip out of the clip to form a straight brown line. That was it! He collapsed to the floor of the belfry, rolled over and lifted up his hand.

"Help me up," he said. Vic leaned over to take his hand and Daniel kicked out as hard as he had strength to kick, caught Vic in the knee and threw him backward, off balance.

The bell hit Victor squarely in the side then, an outward and upward blow that literally lifted him off his feet and threw him over the belfry railing. He cried out as he fell. Daniel could hear it until the clapper hit the side of the bell and he could hear nothing at all but the gong, gong, gong sound.

The bell seemed to ring for a long time, but Daniel didn't know that for sure. When it stopped, he hauled himself to his feet and looked over the railing. A crowd of people had gathered by that time, doing nothing, only staring. Victor hadn't hit the ground. He hung face up, looking at Daniel in a death stare, with the cross pointed at the top that decorated the wrought-iron gate of the children's play area sticking out of his chest.

~

Jack ran back across the barrel warehouse to the hole where the metal door had been. Or tried to run. The pain from his broken ribs stabbed a dagger into his side with every step. He reached up and wiped sweat off his forehead but his hand came away red. Blood, but from what wound he couldn't remember.

As soon as he got close enough to see out the doorway hole, his heart sank. This building was only just beginning to catch fire at this end, but the one next to it, the one Theresa was in, was burning. Smoke leaked out through the sideboards of the building and flames leapt up off the roof. The paper inside had ignited and paper burns fast.

He burst out the opening to a flurry of activity. New fire trucks were pulling up, called in from Cincinnati and from Florence and Newport, Kentucky, across the river. By the time Jack rounded the corner of the burning paper warehouse to the front side, firemen were already directing streams of water to the roof of the barrel warehouse as well as fighting the active fire in the paper warehouse.

Jack blocked out the pain in his side and ran to a knot of firemen who were positioning hoses to send streams of water at the paper warehouse.

He stopped the first fireman he came to.

"There's somebody in there," Jack said, then realized the fireman was Charlie Avery, who'd been on the Harrelton Fire Department since before Jack became a police officer there. He knew Jack well—which was probably why he stared at Jack in astonishment. Jack couldn't begin to imagine what he must look like.

"There can't be anybody inside," Charlie said. "We evacuated these buildings hours ago."

"There's a woman in there," Jack snapped. "Give me your respirator."

"You can't go in—"

Charlie's was a simple face-mask air-purifying respirator. Jack needed a more sophisticated air-supplied respirator, but he didn't have time to wait for one. Before Charlie could respond, Jack snatched the respirator out of his hands and started toward the building. "Right there," he called over his shoulder, pointing. "Focus a hose on that wall."

He put the face mask on as he ran.

When he pushed open the door to the warehouse, smoke boiled out at him and flames danced just inside the doorway, blocking his path. The smoke was much too thick for his respirator, too thick to see anything at all.

Then he saw the glow. It wasn't the angry red of the fire. It was a soft, golden glow about twenty feet ahead and off to the right, a gentle light that didn't so much shine through the smoke and flames as…it seemed that the glow pushed the smoke and fire away, created a path for Jack. He was sure he'd seen a light like that before.

Jack staggered toward the glow.

Flames curled and danced all around him, but the fire receded, pulled back away from the lighted path he followed. There was no source for the glow, and it didn't appear to move. Jack never seemed to draw any nearer to it as he ran than he'd been when he was standing in the doorway. Then the security guard's office appeared, and the glow grew brighter there, illuminating every object in the room. Jack noticed that the light left no shadows.

Theresa lay in the elevator, still bound by tape to the back, arms and front legs of a broken chair. She was on her side, unconscious, with her face pressed up against the side of the elevator where it met the floor. He knelt beside her, rolled her over on her back, took the respirator off and began to fit it to her face. When he did, he noticed the fresh air. All around her was fresh air, coming through the crack between the elevator and the floor. The air was cool, chilled, smelled…sweet, and it swirled around and around her, blowing the smoke away. Jack could breathe.

He fastened the respirator on Theresa's face, but there

was no way to pick her up, not taped to pieces of the chair like that. But even if she hadn't been, Theresa Washington was a big woman and Jack was…so tired, utterly exhausted.

Instead of trying to lift her, Jack grabbed hold of the chair back like a handle, took a deep breath of the clean air, and began to drag Theresa across the floor.

She was heavy and he struggled slowly forward, one lurching step after another, and it was immediately apparent he couldn't possibly drag Theresa's body all the way out of the building in the minute or two he could hold his breath. And once he breathed in that smoke…

He staggered on, and as the seconds ticked away, he should have felt the urgent, holding-your-breath need to gasp building in his chest. He didn't. The air he'd filled his lungs with had been so fresh and pure. And with every step forward, his weariness seemed to drain away. He felt strength surge through him, like he was a kid again.

The glow moved ahead of Jack, illuminating the way, moving aside the smoke and flames until the doorway emerged from the swirl of smoke in front of him. Then the glow vanished.

Jack staggered out the door of the warehouse, dragging Theresa behind him, and collapsed in a heap. The breath he'd been holding for—how long? At least five minutes. Probably closer to ten—exploded out of him and he dragged in a smoky breath that made him cough. The surge of strength he'd felt—it was his last. He had no reserves. He was totally spent, unable even to walk.

Firemen swarmed around them. Two lifted Jack off the ground, drew one of his arms around each of their shoulders and dragged him away. Back behind the fire line, they set him down and suddenly paramedics were everywhere, shoving an oxygen mask on his face and speaking to him.

But their voices were the hum of a beehive, and he couldn't make out individual words.

Then Theresa was beside him on the ground, an oxygen mask matching Jack's covering her face. He saw a quick, confused look pass between the paramedics before they snatched out the scissors they used to cut surgical tape and freed her from the duct tape on the seat back and chair legs. Then they lifted her onto a collapsed gurney, snapped off the catch, pulled it up waist high and began pushing it toward an ambulance.

Paramedics soon had him tethered to a gurney like Theresa's. Then the red glow of the fire reflecting off the clouds overhead was replaced by Crock's face. He looked a thousand questions at Jack, but knew he wouldn't get answers to any of them right now. Jack shoved the oxygen mask off his face, grabbed the front of Crock's shirt and pulled him down so he could whisper into his ear. He didn't have enough air to speak out loud.

"Daniel Burke…" Jack was surprised to discover that even his whispered voice was hoarse. "…Reverend Burke. Send a car—"

"That man's church is swarming with law enforcement," Crock said.

"He's alright isn't he? Not—?"

Jack found he couldn't put words onto the end of the sentence.

"Reverend Burke is alive and on his way to the hospital." Before Jack could ask, he continued. "Far as I know his injuries aren't life-threatening."

Jack relaxed back on the gurney, and the paramedic slipped the oxygen mask back over his face.

"What you were doing in that warehouse with Theresa Washington, her all trussed up in more duct tape than a hillbilly's pickup truck, has something to do with what went on at Burke's church tonight."

It wasn't a question, but Jack wouldn't have been able to answer it even if it had been.

Crock knew that. He looked at Jack sympathetically and Jack thought again to wonder what a sight he must be —what injuries he had sustained that would make their presence vividly known as soon as the anesthetic effect of adrenaline wore off. Then Crock patted his arm and the paramedics lifted the gurney up into the ambulance beside the one holding Theresa.

The ambulance bumped across the ground toward the road, dropped over the curb and turned toward town, lights flashing and siren wailing. Theresa seemed to be breathing well. Jack looked questioningly at the paramedic, pleaded with his eyes.

The young man hesitated. "I'm no doctor," he said. "But I think she's going to be fine."

Jack relaxed back on the gurney. It wasn't until then that he realized Crock hadn't said anything about Emily and Andi. Where were they?

Too much. He couldn't think about that right now. He closed his eyes and pondered the wonders and mysteries of the last few minutes.

The air. The fresh basement air around Theresa. Warm air rises, cool air sinks. Basic physics. Cool air wouldn't have…couldn't have…

Then he let it go.

Chapter Thirty-Five

When Crock appeared at Jack's hospital room door, Jack tried not to let it show on his face how badly he did not want to talk to the man.

Oh, he could have pleaded that he was badly injured and not up to answering questions right now. That's what the doctors had been saying about him every time Crock showed up for thirty-six hours now.

He could put it off. Then Bishop's words swirled up out of his memory.

Son, if'n you got to eat a frog, don't look at it too long. And if'n you got to eat two frogs—

Bishop. That's where he'd gotten that phrase! Jack smiled at the memory and Crock took the smile as an indication that Jack was glad to see him, and eager—well, at least willing—to talk to him.

Jack relaxed back on the pillow and prepared to eat a frog. The big one.

"You look like death on a cracker," Crock said as he crossed the room to Jack's bedside in his swaying, sailor-on-the-deck-of-a-ship-at-sea gait. His legs were so bowed that Jack once pointed out if he danced with a knock-kneed girl they'd look like an egg beater. Crock sat heavily in the chair beside Jack's bed.

Jack knew he looked a mess, probably worse now than when he got here, since bruises got uglier and more colorful with the passage of time. Being black helped. They were harder to see.

But his right eye was swollen shut, his lip had required two stitches to close the split in it, his scalp had required six to close the gash, and his nose was flat, though it had been moved off his cheek and returned to more or less its original position above his mouth. Doctors said it would have to be "re-shaped" eventually. Jack was looking forward to that.

Add to that two cracked ribs, a concussion, badly bruised kidneys, a shattered sinus, a dislocated thumb. And two broken fingers.

Not as bad as Daniel's broken wrist, which he might never have full use of again.

Daniel wasn't thinking about the future right now, though. His world in the present had come crashing down around him and he couldn't see anything but the debris.

They'd made Jack promise he wouldn't get out of the wheelchair if they took him to see Daniel, because they knew if they refused to wheel him there, he'd get up out of the bed and walk to Daniel's room under his own steam.

When the door closed softly behind the nurse, there had been only silence. Jack had no idea what to say. And Daniel knew that—knew how uncomfortable this made Jack.

Feelings as tangled as last year's Christmas lights clogged Jack's throat so he couldn't have spoken even if he'd known what to say. Daniel knew that, too, spoke into the awkwardness, eased it away.

"You got Cole." It wasn't a question. Daniel knew if Jack hadn't killed the man, Jack wouldn't be here.

"Yeah, I got him." The how didn't matter—though when Daniel got around to asking, he'd tell him. Jack knew the basics of what had happened between Daniel and Victor, how he'd somehow managed to throw the man off the bell tower of the church. He didn't ask for more information, but Daniel gave it.

"I didn't get Vic, Andi did. She pulled the bell rope—the straight brown line—and the bell knocked Victor over the railing. She said an angel told her to do it while she was kneeling beside her mother."

There it was. Emily.

"Daniel, I'm so—"

"If Andi hadn't rung the bell at that precise moment…"

"Andi saved my life, too," Jack said. "Her vision did." He'd tell Daniel about that, too. But not now. "I'm…sorry about Emily."

"She told me she loved me. On the phone, she said she was…sorry." Then Daniel started to cry. And Jack broke his promise about staying in the wheelchair.

Jack had remained in Daniel's room for hours, wouldn't leave even when the nurses ordered him to, silenced their threats with, "You need to do whatever it is you people do when you don't get your way because I am not leaving this room. We clear on that?"

When he and Daniel finally got around to that part, they had agreed they'd tell the authorities the truth—up to a point. They'd say they had no idea what had "possessed" these two men to try to kill them. Theresa had been put on the cardiac ward because of a heart condition she hadn't bothered to tell them about, and Jack couldn't bully his way in to see her—so there was no telling what she might say. But she had, after all, lived her whole life a witness to things other people couldn't see. She'd obviously figured out some way to deflect questions about it.

Jack was about to develop his own skill at that right now. He looked at Crock and genuinely didn't want to mislead him. But there flat out wasn't any way to tell him the whole story.

"You ready now to explain why you and Reverend Burke got the crap stomped out of you and the reverend's wife…" Crock stopped, looked down. "We got several calls from neighbors who lived near his church." He shook his head. When Crock spoke again Daniel knew the words were an effort to convince himself. "Fighting a five-alarm fire, it's hard not to back-burner a complaint that somebody's pastor just ran over a rose bush."

"Tell me what you already know," Jack said.

"So you can figure out how much information you can withhold and I won't figure it out?"

Jack took a deep breath and unloaded the whole story on Crock—except the parts he wouldn't believe, the parts that would earn Jack a room in a padded cell in St. Somebody's Home for the Bewildered.

Crock let him give his whole spiel without interruption. When Jack was finished, Crock reached up and took the hearing aid out of his right ear. The major had a strange kind of hearing loss, only certain frequencies, couldn't hear specific music notes and speech sounds. But when he was wearing his hearing aids—which he called Sonny and Cher—he could actually hear a dog whistle.

"I was just checking," Crock said. "Figured Cher must

have died on me, because you couldn't possibly have said what I think you did. That story's got more holes in it than a wino's raincoat."

Jack said nothing.

"You're not going to tell me why two guys who, as far as we can determine, haven't seen each other since high school got together and decided to kill two other people they hadn't seen since they played baseball together when they were twelve. What'd you and Burke do, give them wedgies in the locker room?"

"Everything I've told you is the God's own truth, Crock. I swear it is."

"Oh, I don't have any doubt about that. I just want to know the part you haven't told me."

Again, Jack said nothing.

Crock studied him, then stood and stepped nearer the bed. He put his hand on Jack's arm and said in an earnest voice.

"I'm only trying to help, Jack."

"There's nothing I need help with."

"How about what's going on in Bradford's Ridge, Kentucky? You need help with that?"

"How do you—?"

"When Sheriff Lincoln heard what happened to you and the reverend, he gave me a call and the two of us had a nice long talk." Crock stopped, seemed to be considering what to say next. "Shoot Jack, I know there's something going on here that isn't…something that's outside what you can set down in neat rows on a police report."

He stopped again, then continued in a soft voice.

"Something not governed by the law…not the laws of man, anyway. Jack, you've been up against something that's…other."

He drew another breath.

"I was raised Catholic, quit going to church when I was a teenager, then went back to take my kids when they were growing up. Haven't been in a church since…But I believe it. I believe in…supernatural good and supernatural evil. I believe they're real."

"I know they're real," Jack said. But that was all, and after awhile Crock gave up asking and headed for the door.

He stopped before opening it, though, and turned back to Jack.

"According to Sheriff Lincoln, there's more fish to fry back there in that hometown of yours."

Jack said nothing.

"And if I know Jack Carpenter, you're going to be right there in the middle of it." He stopped, seemed to be considering what to say or how to say it. "If you ever need a friend, a friend who'll believe whatever you tell him no matter how bizarre it sounds—you've got me on speed dial."

~

The new normal of Daniel's life was entwined with Jack's and Theresa's lives as naturally and effortlessly as their lives had been entwined twenty-six years ago. It wasn't just that together they harbored a horrible secret. It was because with the lifting of some of the fog from their minds, Jack and Daniel had recovered more than just memories of past events. They'd reclaimed the emotional connections that went along with them.

It was nice to have a brother again. And Theresa was

so good with Andi, who desperately needed a mother figure in her life right now.

Emily.

Everything always came back to Emily. Daniel had learned a valuable lesson, one every minister needed to know. He'd learned that the axiom, "Time Heals All Wounds," was a pile of the warm, sticky substance you found on the south side of a horse going north. Time didn't heal, it only blunted. After awhile, the loss didn't slice you open with a switchblade, it hacked at you with a rusty Boy Scout hatchet.

He missed her with every breath, with every memory, and the desire just to hold her, talk to her, was so powerful sometimes he'd get in the car and drive around with the windows rolled up, yelling and crying until he was hoarse and exhausted.

Andi kept him sane, centered and focused. Emily had brought her into the world at great risk and then given her life to save the child. He would do everything he could to love the little girl enough for both of them.

The doorbell rang, and when he heard Andi squeal, "Miss Theresa!" he smiled.

Daniel had been teaching himself how to prepare meals that required more skill than popping a Healthy Home dinner into the microwave. Despite the awkwardness of maneuvering his still-casted wrist, he'd discovered he actually enjoyed cooking. For this get-together, he'd selected steak—which Jack ate so close to raw it was downright disgusting. Theresa'd stopped by Miss Minnie and Mr. Gerald's on her way, and arrived bearing a cache of homemade jellies, jams and Miss Minnie's famous tomato preserves.

There was laughter now among them, gentle and soft

as confetti. It struck Daniel that each had suffered such great loss that the blessing of laughter was a grace as unexpected as it was joyful.

They'd been in a war, were still in a war.

In war, there were casualties; innocents died.

In war, everything good and pure was damaged; lives were changed irrevocably.

In war, you learned to treasure what you had left with a fierce, determined delight. Because in war, it could all be taken away from you in a heartbeat.

As Daniel served after-dinner coffee in the living room, Jack turned on the television set to see if the Indianapolis Colts were playing. They were—behind twenty-one to nothing—so he hit the mute button. That way he could glance at it now and then but not have to endure the play-by-play agony of yet another loss.

"Bishop was a Steelers fan," Theresa said, "and they's my team, too."

"A pox on you," Daniel said.

"I liked you a whole lot better before you told me that," Jack said.

"I'm gonna make brownies," Andi said, both cheeks dented with deep-dish dimples. "Well, heat them up in the microwave so they smell like I just made them." She headed off to the kitchen with Ossy following, his tail stuck as straight in the air as a flagpole.

In the brief beat after her departure, Jack dropped words nobody wanted to hear, into the room.

"Sheriff Lincoln called yesterday," he said. "He's got a little boy up before the juvie judge this week for—caught red-handed trying to set fire to a cat and—"

"We can't wait no longer," Theresa said. "Them young-uns is only doin' little-kid harm now, but just 'cause they's too young to do something awful don't mean we can let them stay like they is, suffering inside like that."

~

Jack remembered the flashes he'd seen of Cole Stuart's tortured soul and shuddered. Still, he hadn't wanted to bring it up, didn't want even to think about it. But there was no way around it. Poor Daniel was only beginning to lose that desolate, haggard look, just beginning to get some bounce back into his step.

And Theresa had aged. Jack might not be remembering properly, but he could have sworn her hair had had only a few streaks of gray around the temples when he saw her that day in Andi's hospital room. Now, the gray was rushing out over her whole head in streaks. It was almost pure white around her face.

And Andi...she'd have to be a part of this. His whole mind and heart backed up from that.

It had started the day Daniel went in for the second out-patient surgery on his wrist. Uncle Jack sneaked off with Andi and taught her how to shoot pool. To her father's great distress, Jack had later reported solemnly that the child was destined to become a shark someday. Jack taught her how to roller skate, too, at an old rink a friend opened on Saturday mornings just for the two of them. He'd taken to renting movies every so often and they'd all curl up with a big bowl of popcorn—Daniel, Theresa, Andi, Jack and Ossy—and enjoy Andi's favorites, putting Jack on a first-name basis with beings he'd never dreamed existed—Woody and Buzz, Sully and Mike Wazowski, Nemo and Dorie and Wall-E and a rat chef in Paris. Jack was already planning what he was going to get Andi for her eleventh birthday and it was still months away.

To drag that little girl into a battle with a monster demon…Jack could still feel her limp body in his arms, her warm blood soaking into his shirt.

I don't ever have to be afraid, Uncle Jack, because you'll always keep me safe.

He'd lay his life down for that child, but that would be small protection, a fragile, pallid shield against the dark monster rising out of the lake of fire.

"Seems like the first thing we need to do is understand a lot more about what we're up against," Daniel said. "It's all there in Bishop's study…somewhere. We—"

He stopped. The Colts game had given way to a news short and apparently Bradford's Ridge's famous native son was the subject of the story.

Daniel picked up the remote and flipped on the sound as Jack grumbled under his breath.

"The president issued a statement earlier today and I am humbled by his faith in me," Chapman Whitworth said. "This position is not one I have sought out or desired but I am compelled by a responsibility to serve my country—"

"Oh, please." Jack rolled his eyes.

"—and I have therefore accepted the president's nomination to the vacant seat on the Supreme Court of the United States of America."

"Goody," Jack groaned. "Chappy's gotten more mileage out of one simple sentence than Lincoln got out of the whole Gettysburg Address."

Chapman Whitworth stepped back from the podium to thunderous applause and cheers. He smiled, raised both hands in victory and waved.

"You'll have to go through—" Jack began, mocking

Whitworth's pompous tones. Then he froze, stopped breathing. Whitworth had touched the fingertips of his left hand to his forehead and snapped them upward in a strange salute to the crowd.

Flames all around him. Harsh heat and red light. Screams of agony.

Chapman Whitworth stands next to a hospital bed in a burning room where a skinny old man in wet pajamas is feebly trying to push him away. Whitworth turns to a table —his eyes never leaving Jack's face—and picks up a vase that flaming silk flowers have turned into a torch. That's when he does it. He touches the fingertips of his left hand to his forehead and snaps them upward in a strange salute to Jack. Then he drops the flaming flowers on the old man. The man is an instant fireball from head to foot. His pajamas—that was gasoline! Whitworth watches him burning and screaming, writhing, twisting for a few moments, then drops a blanket on him to smother most of the flames and—

A shriek like the sound of ripping cloth came from the doorway into the kitchen. Jack turned as Andi let the plate of micro-wave-warmed brownies slip out of her fingers and shatter on the floor at her feet. Then she backed away, shaking her head, her eyes fixed on the television screen in the corner.

Daniel ran to the child, grabbed her into his arms and asked her what was wrong.

"That man..." she couldn't go on.

"Is there a demon—?" Daniel began.

"No!" She shook her head violently. "Not a demon. It's...there's red light coming from him, all around him, he glows red and there's a face in the light." Jack could see she wanted to look away but couldn't. "The face…" She shook her head, couldn't describe it. "He's so angry, so full of hate. His teeth are like—"

"They look like knives, three rows of them." The voice came from behind them. It was Theresa. She wasn't looking at Whitworth, though. She was looking at Andi. "And he's got red eyes with a black center that's slit up and down like a cat."

Andi nodded, her eyes fixed in horror and revulsion on the screen until the image suddenly blinked out. Daniel had picked up the remote and turned the television off.

Andi fell against her father's chest as if released from some unseen force. Theresa slumped back on the couch and put her hands over her face.

"Perfect possession," she said, her voice so low it was barely audible. She lowered her hands and looked from Jack to Daniel. "That's not like when a demon possesses a person, forces his way in, shoves the person aside. It's called perfect possession when a person invites a demon in. Asks for possession. Joins with the demon. Only a powerful demon, one with the authority to—"

"The efreet." Jack heard the word come out of his mouth before he thought it. "Chappy invited it. Wanted it. Shoot, maybe even summoned it—that'd make sense, with his father, the sticky-fingered anthropologist, going to all those ancient digs."

Jack struggled for words to continue. "I just…saw something. One of those expelled memories."

Suddenly, he understood. "The Twin Oaks fire—I was there! I saw Whitworth, and he—"

"—done all those amazing, heroic things he done because he was in league with the Devil," Theresa said.

Jack took in a great gulp of air that smelled like brownies. "And now that demon prince—"

Daniel's voice was almost too soft to hear as he finished Jack's thought.

"—has just been nominated to the United States Supreme Court."

The End

A Note from the Author

Thank you for reading *The Knowing*.

If you enjoyed this book, please consider writing a review of it on your favorite bookseller site so other readers might enjoy it too? Just a couple of sentences would mean a lot to me.

Thank you!

Ninie Hammon

About the Author

Ninie Hammon (rhymes with shiny, not skinny) grew up in Muleshoe, Texas, got a BA in English and theatre from Texas Tech University and snagged a job as a newspaper reporter. She didn't know a thing about journalism, but her editor said if she could write he could teach her the rest of it and if she couldn't write the rest of it didn't matter. She hung in there for a 25-year career as a journalist. As soon as she figured out that making up the facts was a whole lot more fun than reporting them, she turned to fiction and never looked back.

Ninie now writes suspense--every flavor except pistachio: psychological suspense, inspirational suspense, suspense thrillers, paranormal suspense, suspense mysteries.

In every book she keeps this promise to her Loyal Reader: "I will tell you a story in a distinctive voice you'll always recognize, about people as ordinary as you are--people who have been slammed by something they didn't sign on for, and now they must fight for their lives. Then smack in the middle of their everyday worlds, those people encounter the unexplainable--and it's always the game-changer."

Also By Ninie Hammon

Cornbread Mafia

Fire In The Hole

Blown' Up A Storm

Ridin' For A Fall

Nowhere, USA

The Jabberwock

Mad Dog

Trapped

The Hanging Judge

The Witch of Gideon

Blown Away

Nowhere People

Through The Canvas Series

Black Water

Red Web

Gold Promise

Blue Tears

The Taken Saga

The Taken

The Changed

The Hidden

The Saved

The Unexplainable Collection

Five Days in May

Black Sunshine

The Based on True Stories Collection

Home Grown

Sudan

When Butterflies Cry

The Knowing Series

The Knowing

The Deceiving

The Reckoning

The Fault

Stand-alone Psychological Thrillers

The Memory Closet

The Last Safe Place